THE
BODY
SCOUT

THE BODY SCOUT

A NOVEL

LINCOLN MICHEL

orbitbooks.net

Orbit
Hachette Book Group
1290 Avenue of the Americas
New York, NY 10104
orbitbooks.net

First Edition: September 2021

Orbit is an imprint of Hachette Book Group.
The Orbit name and logo are trademarks of Little, Brown Book Group Limited.

The publisher is not responsible for websites (or their content) that are not owned by the publisher.

The Hachette Speakers Bureau provides a wide range of authors for speaking events. To find out more, go to www.hachettespeakersbureau.com or call (866) 376-6591.

Library of Congress Cataloging-in-Publication Data
Names: Michel, Lincoln, author.
Title: The body scout : a novel / Lincoln Michel.
Description: First Edition. | New York, NY : Orbit, 2021.
Identifiers: LCCN 2021003803 | ISBN 9780316628723 (hardcover) | ISBN 9780316628716 (ebook) | ISBN 9780316628693
Subjects: GSAFD: Mystery fiction.
Classification: LCC PS3613.I34515 B63 2021 | DDC 813/.6—dc23
LC record available at https://lccn.loc.gov/2021003803

ISBNs: 9780316628723 (hardcover), 9780316628716 (ebook)

Printed in the United States of America

LSC-C

Printing 1, 2021

For my father, who gave me my first science fiction books.

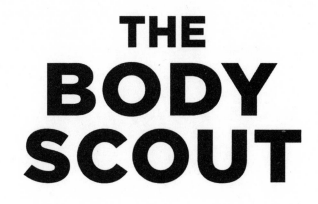

THE
BODY
SCOUT

Perhaps there is no such thing as a cruel future. The future, properly speaking, is already cruel by virtue of being the future.

—Kōbō Abe, *Inter Ice Age 4*

The future ain't what it used to be.

—Yogi Berra

1

THE DARK HOURS

When I couldn't fall asleep, I counted the parts of the body. I used the outdated numbers. What they'd taught me back in school when only the ultrarich upgraded. Two hundred and six bones. Seventy-eight organs. The separate pieces floated through the fog of my mind, one by one, like strange birds. If I was still awake by the end, I'd think about everything connecting. Miles of nerves and veins snaking through the pile, tying tibia to fibula, connecting heart to lung. Muscles, blood, hair, skin. Everything joining together into a person, into me.

Then I swapped in new parts. A second cybernetic arm or a fresh lung lining for the smog. Cutting-edge implants. This season's latest organs. I mixed and matched, tweaked and twisted.

I didn't know if I was really getting myself to sleep. I might have been keeping myself swimming in that liminal ooze between waking problems and troubled dreams. It was a state that reminded me of the anesthetic haze of the surgery table. Like my mattress was a slick metal slab and the passing headlights were the eyelamps of surgery drones. Outside, the world went by. Construction cranes hoisted buildings tall enough to stab the clouds. Cars cluttered the skies. But inside, my senses dulled, the world was gone. I was alone and waiting to wake up as something different, better, and new.

I'd been piecing myself together for years. With surgeries and grafts, with shots and pills. I kept lists of possible procedures. Files of future upgrades that would lead me to an updated life. My brother, JJ Zunz, always laughed about it. "One day I'm going to wake up, and none of you will be left," he'd say. That would have been fine with me.

We're all born with one body, and there's no possibility of a refund. No way to test-drive a different form. So how could anyone not be willing to pay an arm and a leg for a better arm and a better leg?

Sure, we're each greater than the sum of our parts. But surely greater parts couldn't hurt.

Each time I upgraded it was wonderful, for a time. I had new sensations, new possibilities. I was getting closer to what I thought I was supposed to be. Then each time seemed to require another time. Another surgery and another loan to pay for it. Two decades of improvements and I still wanted more, but now I had six figures in medical debt crushing me like a beetle under a brick.

That night, as I was Frankensteining a new body for myself in my head, my brother called. The sound jostled me. My imaginary form collapsed, the parts scattering across the dim emptiness of my mind. I opened my eyes. Yawned. Slapped the receiver.

A massive Zunz appeared before me, legs sunk through the carpet to the knees, face severed at the ceiling. He was so large he could have swallowed my head as easily as a hard-boiled egg.

"Kang," he said. He paused, then repeated the name with a question mark. "Jung Kang?"

I shrank his hologram to the proper size. He glowed at the end of my bed. For some reason, he was wearing his batting helmet. It was 3:00 a.m.

"Um, no. It's me. Kobo. You dial the wrong address?"

Outside, the bright lights of the city illuminated the nighttime smog. A billboard floated past my window, flashing a Growth Cola ad. *The Climate Has Changed, Your Body Should Too.*

"Yes. Kobo." He shook his head. "My brother. How are you?" Zunz spoke haltingly, as if he either had a lot on his mind or nothing at all. He looked healthy at least. A lot of players in the league wanted the retro bodybuilder style, muscles stacked like bricks, but Zunz made sure the trainers kept him lean and taut. When he swung a baseball bat, his arms snapped like gigantic rubber bands.

"Shit, JJ. You sound like you got beaned in the head with a bowling ball. What do the Mets have you on?"

"Lots of things," he said, looking around at something or someone I couldn't see. He had several wires running from his limbs to something off feed. "Always lots of things."

Zunz was a star slugger for the Monsanto Mets and my adopted brother. After the apartment cave-in killed my parents and mushed my right arm, his family took me in. Gave me a home. Technically, I was a few days older than him, but I never stopped thinking of him as my big brother.

"Kobo, I feel weird. Like my body isn't mine. Like they put me in the wrong one."

"They? You gotta sleep it off. Hydrate. Inject some vitamins." I unplugged my bionic right arm, got out of bed. Tried to stretch myself awake. "Here, show me your form."

Zunz didn't have a bat on him, but he clicked into a batting stance.

"Fastball right down the middle."

He swung his empty hands. Stared into the imaginary stands.

"Fourth floor. Home run," I said. Although his movement was off. The swing sloppy and the follow-through cut short.

Zunz flashed me his lopsided smile. His dimples were the size of dugouts. He got back into his stance. "Another."

When Zunz had first been called up to the Big Leagues, he used to phone me before every game to get my notes. I never had much to say. Zunz had always been a natural. But I was a scout and it was my job to evaluate players. Zunz needed my reassurance. Or maybe he just wanted to make me feel needed. As his career took off, he started calling me less and less. Once a series. Once a month. Once a season. These days, we barely talked. Still, I watched every game and cheered.

"Sinker," I said. My arm creaked as I threw the pretend pitch.

I watched his holographic form swing at the empty air. It was strange how many ways I'd seen Zunz over the years. In person and in holograms, on screens and posters and blimps. I knew every curve of his bones, every freckle on his face. And I knew his body. Its shape and power. At the Monsanto Mets compound, he had all the best trainers and serums on the house. I'd never get molded like that, not on my income. But watching Zunz play made me want to construct the best version of myself that I could.

"You look good to me. ChicagoBio White Mice won't know what hit them."

Zunz pumped his fist. Smiled wide. He may have been in his thirties but he still grinned like a kid getting an extra scoop of ice cream. Except now he frowned and shook his head. "I feel stiff. Plastic. Unused. Do you know what I mean?"

I held up my cybernetic arm. "Hell, I'm practically half plastic already. But you look like a million bucks. Which is probably the cost of the drugs they've got pumping through you."

I lit an eraser cigarette and sucked in the anesthetic smoke. After a few puffs, I felt as good and numb as I did before an operation.

Thanks to Zunz, the Mets had built a commanding lead in the Homeland League East and cruised through the division series against the California Human Potential Growth Corp Dodgers. As long as they could get past the ChicagoBio White Mice, the Mets were favored to win the whole thing.

"Give the White Mice hell," I said, blowing out a dark cloud. "Show them a kid from the burrows can take the Mets all the way."

"Will do, Kang," Zunz said.

"Kobo," I said.

"Kobo." He cocked his head. I heard muffled yelling on his end of the line. I couldn't see what was around him. Zunz's hologram turned. He started to speak to the invisible figure.

He shrank to a white dot the size of an eyeball. The dot blinked. Disappeared.

The call had cut out.

I finished my eraser cigarette and went back to sleep. Didn't think about the call too much. The biopharms always pumped players with new combinations of drugs in preparation for the playoffs. Hoping to get the chemical edge that would hand their team the title, which would lead to more retail sales that could purchase more scientists to concoct new upgrades and keep the whole operation going. Zunz was a high-priced investment. Monsanto would keep him together.

And I had my own problems to worry about. Sunny Day Healthcare Loans was threatening to send collection agents after me again, and I had to skip town for a few days. I took the bullet train down to North Virginia, the latest break-off state, to scout a kid whose fastball was so accurate he could smack a mosquito out of the air. It was true. He showed me the blood splat on the ball.

The Yankees had authorized an offer. The number on the contract made the parents' eyes pop like fly balls. But when I gave the kid a full workup, I realized they'd been juicing him with smuggled farm supplements. The kind they pump into headless cattle to get the limbs to swell. The kid's elbow would blow out in a year. Maybe two.

The parents cried a lot. Denied. Begged for a second opinion. I gave them the same one a second time.

I was one of the few biopharm scouts left who specialized in players. Other scouts plugged the numbers into evaluation software and parroted the projections, but I'd spent my whole life desiring the parts of those around me. People like Zunz, who seemed to have success written into their genetic code. I watched them. Studied them. Imagined myself inside them, wearing their skin like a costume, while I sprinted after the ball or slid into third.

I still liked to think baseball was a game of technique and talent, not chemistry and cash. I guess I was a romantic. Now it was the minds that fetched the real money. That's what most FLB scouts focused on. Scientists working on the latest designer drugs. Genetic surgeons with cutting-edge molecular scalpels. For biopharm teams, players were the blocks of marble. The drugs sculped them into stars.

By the time I got back to New York, the playoffs were in full swing. I got a rush assignment from the Yankees with a new target. I'd planned to go to the game, watch Zunz and the Mets play the White Mice from the front row with a beer in my hand and a basket of beef reeds in my lap. But the Yankees job was quick work and easy money. Which meant I could quickly use that money on another upgrade.

The prospect was a young nervous-system expert named Julia Arocha. Currently under contract at Columbia University. She was working on a stabilization treatment for zootech critters. Her charts were meaningless scribbles to me, but I was impressed with the surveillance footage. Arocha was a true natural. She glided around centrifuges as easily as an ice skater in the rink, holding vials and pipettes as if they were extensions of her limbs.

The next night, I grabbed a cab uptown to the pickup spot. The playoffs were on in the backseat.

"What the hell?" the driver shouted as a Pyramid Pharmaceuticals

Sphinxes fielding error gave the BodyMore Inc. Orioles a runner on third. The man flung his arms wide. They shook like he was getting ready to give someone the world's angriest hug. "You believe that shit?"

"Bad bounce," I offered.

"Bad bounce? My ass. Hoffmann is a bum. We'd be better off with some Edenist who'd never been upgraded playing right field instead of that loser. Don't you think?"

"If you say so. I'm a Mets fan."

He scowled. "Mets," he said, gagging on the word.

The taxi flew over the East River. Great gray barges cut blue paths through the filter algae below.

"Mets," he said again. "Well, the customer is always right. Zunz is a good one, I have to admit. They don't make many players like him anymore."

"They're trying. You see the homer he smacked on Friday?"

"Right off the Dove Hospital sign. The arms on that guy. Wish we had him on the Sphinxes."

"He's going to take us all the way," I said.

We flew toward the giant towers of Manhattan with their countless squares of light pushing back the dark, both of us thinking about JJ Zunz. Imagining my brother's hands gripping the bat, his legs rounding bases in our minds. His body perfect, solid, and, at that point, still alive.

2

THE NEW PROSPECT

The handoff was going down at an uptown sushi joint named Kamome. Their gimmick was having the sashimi delivered by seagulls. The gulls were only drones, but they squawked like the real thing.

I was in the back corner of the rooftop, spinning a glass of luke-warm shochu in my cold metal hand. My stomach felt sour and my nerves were tingling. After all these years, I still felt nervous on the job. I pulled out an eraser cigarette and sucked it down as quickly as I could. Let the anesthetic smoke numb me.

Julia Arocha was across the roof, dunking gyoza with Columbia deans in spiderwool suits. The deans had struck a trade deal with the Yankees in exchange for a sizable donation to the School of Business Ethics. I guess they wanted to give Arocha a final meal before they explained they'd sold her rights behind her back.

Between us were the usual assortment of customers rich enough to spend a month's rent on chunks of petri dish tuna. You could tell how wealthy they were by looking at them. Idle rich venturing out from their cloud condos to show off their latest enhancements. Investment bankers built like linebackers. A pair of socialites clinking martini glasses, one elongated with curved bones like giant noodles and the other spilling over the seat with reinforced curves.

The only ones who looked out of place were a wide and knobby pair at the far table beside the seagull docking station. The woman was squat and muscular, stuffed into a crocodile skirt suit. She had thick arms and a brow you could have balanced a champagne glass on. The man was taller, wider, and paler. His suit was dark and sharp while his features were all smoothed out. You could have mistaken him for a human-sized bar of soap that had been used a few too many times.

Trogstoys, people called them. Neanderthals cloned and grown to work the Siberian mushroom farms. Rare in the Remaining States, where cloning sentient beings was illegal. I'd never seen one in person. The woman seemed to be looking at me, but it was hard to make out her eyes under that brow.

We were all on the 201st floor, which was a good thing because the lower part of the city was marinating in smog. It was the big cloud, the gunk that coalesced around the One China factories, thickened above the Pacific oil fires, and then floated across America like a dirty tongue licking the land.

But up here, the air was cool and crisp. Ion vacuums in the shape of lollipops ringed the building below us. The oxygen being pumped in felt like it was blowing straight from the last chunks of the Arctic. I took a sip of shochu, closed my eyes, and breathed in deep.

I liked being up high. Zunz and I had grown up in the burrows of SoCroHi, South Crown Heights, back when those underground apartments were touted as the solution to the housing crisis. Some Silicon Valley architecture firm pitched them as the way to provide low-income apartments without affecting the skyline. They were dirty, dark spaces with air so full of mold we might as well have been chewing on it. Ever since I'd escaped, I'd never been able to go underground without panicking.

A gull flew by me with a tray of shrimp tempura rolls in its beak. A red light beamed like a third eye in the center of the gull's head. Congress had recently passed a law requiring warning lights since animal forms were the latest drone craze and most were covered in plastiflesh to seal the smog out of the circuitry. People didn't like being tricked into thinking something fake was real.

I checked my screen. In the Patriot League, the Orioles and Sphinxes had gone to extra innings. I switched over to the Mets game. It was the middle of the fourth, still scoreless. Game four of the Homeland League Championship Series, Monsanto Mets looking for a sweep of the ChicagoBio White Mice. The fielders trotted to their positions.

The center of my plate erupted in static. The AI waiter appeared with a digital grin. "Have you decided on any sustenance this evening, sir?"

"I'm fine with the shochu."

"May I suggest our dragon roll? It's the chef's latest specialty. The synthetic Komodo has ninety-nine point three percent accurate musculature."

"Okay, sure. One dragon roll."

"May I also suggest—"

"Nope." I doused the plate with soy sauce until the waiter disappeared beneath the dark pond.

A gull dropped an orange glob of fluorescent uni on Arocha's plate. She placed it on her tongue and smiled as it dissolved. As she talked to the three deans, she stabbed the air with her chopsticks. She was describing some big plans, about changing the world or some other beautiful horseshit dream. I wondered how many years it would be before the biopharms figured out how to slice off a prospect's head and preserve it in a jar. Cut out the middleman, call it efficiency.

Baseball was a nasty business. I told myself all the usual things. How it would be some other asshole doing the job if it wasn't me. How this was just how the modern world worked. It didn't help. But dreaming of what the money could buy me did. A down payment on the shoulder tune-up, I thought, or maybe a new module for my eye. At least if I could buy some time from Sunny Day Healthcare Loans.

Bottom of the fourth, Lex Dash at the plate doing a curtsy after dodging a curveball that cut behind her knees. Dash was the Mets' leadoff hitter and was built like a kangaroo. The Mets lab team had her on a strict lower-leg regimen that had her halfway to first base the moment her bat cracked the ball.

The ChicagoBio pitcher wound up. Flung. The pitch dropped low, bounced off the dirt. The floating strike zone flashed red. Fourth ball. A walk. Dash pranced mockingly to first and the pitcher threw his glove at the ground. The White Mice were one of the only all-male teams left, and still hadn't gotten used to women in the league, much less other genders, and a switcher like Dash was good at getting under their skin.

"Line them up," I mumbled. Walking batters was never a smart idea with Zunz in wait.

My sushi came, and I threw a piece into my mouth, almost choking. Over a decade having a bionic arm and I still hadn't mastered chopsticks. As I chewed, I thought I noticed the Neanderthal woman watching me. She had an odd smile on her face. The kind that wanted to creep up behind you in the dark. I shifted my chair around to obstruct her view.

Sam Tzu struck out without much of a fight. Henry "Hologram" Graham was on deck and Zunz was waiting in the hole. I could see the brown smudge at the corner of Zunz's smile, a small birthmark he'd declined to laser off because he thought it was shaped like a baseball glove. "The game is etched in my skin," he liked to say.

Out of the corner of my eye, I saw the woman in the crocodile suit stroll toward me. She walked with an odd mix of power and grace. Her legs put tree trunks to shame.

"Mr. Kobo, I'm afraid I have bad news." Her voice was higher pitched than I'd expected. A little nasal on the vowels. She had freckles as faint as ghosts on her skin and a nose the shape of a baby's fist.

"Oh yeah?" I pulled out an eraser, offered her one from the pack.

"I only smoke naturals," she said.

"Wouldn't have guessed there was anything natural about you."

Her lips made a crevice of a smile. "If you're referring to my laboratory origins, I'll remind you we Neanderthals evolved before you sapiens. Perhaps that makes us the truly natural ones. The archaeological evidence suggests we were quite happy before your ancestors murdered us all. May I sit?"

"Sure, and my apologies," I said. I figured she was a Sunny Day officer here to haggle over money I didn't have. There was no point in pissing her off with a debate about prehistory. "I'm glad we brought you back."

"It was the least your kind could have done." She tossed one leg on top of the other. Her eyes were large and green. "You can call me Natasha, Mr. Kobo. I know you sapiens prefer to be on a first-name basis. It establishes a sense of friendship, a closeness. Yes?"

I glanced at the screen. Graham had two strikes. Zunz was taking practice swings.

"I don't get close with loan sharks. But you can tell Sunny Day they don't have to worry. I'm on a job tonight and will have a nice payout when I deliver."

"See, that's the bad news I was referring to." Her long lips frowned affably. "I'm not a loan officer. I'm here representing the interests of Dereck T. Mouth. Owner, CEO, and president of the Monsanto Mets."

"You're a scout? I haven't seen you at the conferences."

"Let's call me an executive assistant. I'm afraid Julia Arocha is no longer on the market. My employer heard the Yankees wanted her and so he decided he wanted her more. You know how these owners get."

My breath came out hot and slow. If I didn't bring Arocha in, I didn't get paid. And then Sunny Day didn't get paid and someone a lot less friendly than this Neanderthal paid me a visit.

"The deal is already worked out," I said, standing up a little too quickly. "There's a contract."

Natasha laid an upturned hand on the table next to the wad of wasabi. "Oh, everyone has contracts. But only one can have possession. At least until we get the kinks of duplication cloning worked out."

I saw her mean-looking friend amble toward the Columbia table.

I needed to get there first, talk to the deans, figure out what rotten stunt they were pulling. Or simply nab Arocha and get her in the van, haggle over the details from the sealed Yankees compound. Possession was nine-tenths of the law in contract negotiations.

"Please, Mr. Kobo," Natasha said. She placed her warm hand on top of mine. "I'm telling you as a professional courtesy."

I called my backup, told him to fly the van over for a quick evacuation job. But my legs got wobbly. Like someone had swapped out my bones for rubber tubes. I fell down beside a pair of slender, engineered legs attached to one of the socialites. "Ew," the owner said. Pushed me away with one of her elongated heels.

Natasha strolled over and grabbed the metal of my forearm, pulled me up as easily as a bag of feathers, and flopped me back into my chair. She waved over a seagull and ordered an espresso and a glass of water.

"You Americans have always been unsuspicious of your restaurant food," Natasha said. "Dereck Mouth owns this restaurant, among many other fine establishments in the city. Although I'm not sure how I feel about it myself. Raw flesh? Even synthetic, I don't understand the appeal. When my people discovered fire, we never looked back."

Natasha put two white pills beside my soy sauce dish. They looked like two moons about to be sucked into a black hole. "When you're able to move again, take these. They'll help with the headache. You'll want help."

"Fuck you," I tried to say, but it came out half a syllable. I wanted to grab her throat and squeeze. My arm only twitched.

"You have what they call *heart*, Mr. Kobo. Perhaps we can work together at a future juncture."

I watched Natasha walk away, turning as blurry as a bigfoot photo. I blinked. Looked to where the Columbia table had been. A big, wide figure was lifting an unformed shape.

My head throbbed. The restaurant seemed to be dissolving into thick mist. The waiter reappeared in my plate, his face faint beneath the puddle. I couldn't hear what he said. Something about dessert options. I couldn't move, yet I felt at peace. As if I was evolving, or devolving, into a human jellyfish. A clear hunk of skin drifting in vast waters without struggle.

The figures left. The other customers seemed disturbingly unperturbed. They'd stopped looking at me, began looking at their screens.

I could only move my eyes. I looked down at the screen where the game was still playing. I thought I was starting to hallucinate. Zunz was at the plate, but he wasn't swinging. Not exactly. His body was shaking, glitching almost. His skin seemed to be turning blue.

A drop of blood dripped out of his ear. Another from his nose. Then red strings were streaming down his face.

I closed my eyes. Opened them.

I saw Zunz drop his bat, collapse. My best friend, my idol, my brother. Knees and face in the dirt.

"He's dying," someone said.

Zunz looked up. His eyes and mouth were wide open. Three big circles.

I tried to move.

The sound was off, but a man at the table next to me screamed "No." I couldn't make out any of the other words. Only "No." Then again, and louder. "No. No. No!"

3

THE DIFFERENT DEATHS

It wasn't a hallucination and it wasn't only Zunz's face. Whatever poison they'd slipped inside him traveled through his system, turning the skin strange colors. Blues and greens blotched with red. Chunks of liquifying matter had dripped out of his nostrils alongside the blood. Splattered on the plate.

His teammates ran toward him, then stopped. Backed away. Zunz was on the ground, a red puddle expanding under his face.

I learned all this from the replays when I got home. I was shaking all over. I dropped Natasha's painkillers on the kitchen counter and forced myself to see what happened to Zunz with undrugged eyes.

On the news a woman in a white blazer stood outside of the golden Mets stadium, dazed fans stumbling around behind her. "Police say it is too early to call this an act of terrorism although Monsanto insists the death could only have been caused by a new bioterrorism agent or advanced nanobot attack. Monsanto CEO Dereck Mouth, known affectionately as 'the Mouth,' accused the Mets playoff opponents of foul play." The footage switched to the

Mouth, his golden face grinning with a surgically elongated smile, waving off reporters as he strolled into his segmented limo. "Mets manager Gil Stengel hasn't commented on how this will affect the starting lineup when the game resumes tomorrow night. No matter what we learn, this is a sad day for baseball and a tragic loss for the Monsanto Mets."

My mind tried to swat the words away. It refused to believe. But my body understood. My hands shook. My stomach turned into a hunk of iron, twisted around, tangling up my insides. I knocked an eraser out of the pack, lit it. Puffed it down in thirty seconds.

The news was now talking about Zunz's charity work. Young children waved foam fingers and wept outside of a run-down school. "The Mets star, who grew up in the Ebbets Field subsidized subterranean apartments, was known for his work with the No Body Left Behind fund. NBLB works with international philanthropists to provide physical and cerebral upgrades to low-income NYC schoolchildren."

I switched channels and there was a report on the new GenSlice B3-Bees. "These will be the only agricultural zootech genetically tailored to pollinate. Is that right?" the host said. The GenSlice scientist nodded, turned on a hologram of tiny bioengineered legs scraping across a flower. "With the collapse of ninety-eight percent of native pollinating moths and other insects, farmers and—if I can be frank—world governments will need to purchase our B3-Bees to sustain current mass agriculture production."

"Now we go to the tragedy shaking the sports world and the entire nation."

Zunz was at the plate. He had that gap-toothed grin I'd known since childhood. Yet something was off. His eyes looked vacant, painted on.

"The first signs of trouble started in the fourth inning, when Zunz slipped at the plate." I watched him swing, lose control of his balance, and take a knee to the ground. "Zunz recovered and knocked a single to right field. But by the eighth inning, Zunz was visibly ill." You could see pustules emerging along the limbs. Behind him, a robot ump stared silently.

My brother died again. Horrifically, painfully, and absurdly. I rewound it and watched it a second time. A third. I felt dead and drained.

I switched to the hologram feed to see everything in the worst details. Took control of the image, moved it up to JJ's face as the pitch came in. His pupils were so dilated they were practically black holes. A drop of blood appeared at the corner of one eye, like a red tear. I zoomed back. Zunz's mouth was open now, but you couldn't hear him scream.

"No," I said quietly, to no one at all.

Even with the eraser smoke in my lungs, I could feel my insides being torn apart. Static flowed through my veins in place of blood. I vomited, finally.

Zunz had been the only steady thing in my life. The one rock I could cling to when the world was a storm. I couldn't help thinking that if I hadn't taken the Arocha assignment, I'd have been in the stadium and done something. What, I didn't know. But something that wasn't doing nothing at all.

I turned off the hologram feed. Turned off my screen. Turned off everything until I was alone in the dark.

In my dingy Brooklyn apartment, I felt small and alone. I desperately wanted to pick up the phone and call Zunz. Have him calm me down. Have him say something about how "we'll get through it, man," or "you can only look down so far until you swing around and start looking up." He'd always been an optimist. And things had kept working out for him in the end, until the end.

I walked over to the window. Pressed my face into the glass. The air was murky and filled with indiscernible objects. In my tiny window of my tiny apartment, I might as well have been a lost microbe in a foreign, hostile host.

I stayed at the window for some time.

4

THE OLD DAYS

Before he was my brother, Zunz was the best friend I'd ever had. I'd been an only child, and for many years that simply meant I was alone. My father was out the door each morning before I woke up. He was a parts gardener, tending lips and ears growing in lab dishes. My father made sure these future features of the wealthy got the proper nutrient inputs, the necessary bacteria scrubbings. It didn't pay as well as you'd think.

When I was eight, my parents got evicted from their Bed-Stuy stack apartment to pave way for a new fifty-story condo complex. We were relocated to a burrow in SoCroHi. The subseventh floor.

The subway train rattled past our walls every ten minutes or so. Black mold lined the hallways, thick as paint. My father grew angrier. My mother spent more and more time in her augmented-reality romances, helmet obscuring her face. I didn't have any brothers or sisters. No real dogs or cats, and no money for robotic ones. I was short, sad, and alone. Until I met JJ Zunz. Julio Julio, "So nice you have to say it twice."

When I was chasing a ball through the underground hallway, a gangly kid with a goofy smile and a birthmark shaped like a tiny glove on his cheek picked it up. "You like baseball?" he said. He spoke fast, with exclamation points. "Do you collect sims? I've got twelve! Including my favorite, Derek Jeter. He was a player from my grandpa's day. He was super good! Have you heard of him? Do you want to trade?"

"Sure," I said, despite never having watched a single game.

I went to his place and he showed me his cards and virtual sims. His family's apartment was smaller than ours but cozier. Brightly patterned blankets hung from the water line running through the living room. Dozens of candles burned with natural fire. Back then, it felt like the most comfortable place in the world, even with the rats.

Pretty soon, I was going to Zunz's a couple times a month. Then a few times a week. Then every day.

We'd watch dating shows with his abuela on her ancient flatscreen, or help his father cook dinner while his mother worked. Every morning at 6:00 a.m., Mrs. Z commuted to a warehouse in Queens where she was hooked into a remote suit and spent thirteen hours controlling distant orange-picking machines in the offshore groves. A way to get around regulations. You couldn't unionize a robotic arm.

At school, we became so close the kids called us ZuBo. As if we were one person. I think the name was supposed to be an insult, but it made me smile.

My homelife was unremarkable. Then nonexistent.

When I was twelve, I woke up gasping under a pile of dirt and rubble. A wall had collapsed in the burrow. Subway line maintenance in a tunnel nearby, or so the city later said when they denied the insurance claim.

I was trapped under the jagged mound for hours. It felt like years.

I couldn't see anything. Could barely breathe. And I couldn't get out. My arm was pinned down by steel and concrete in the dark. My own body keeping me trapped. When I screamed, dirt rained down my throat.

I cried out for my parents. They weren't around to cry back. Their bedroom had completely caved in. Everything inside, everyone, crushed. Eaten by the dirt.

All I could think about was trying to escape my own body. How my own flesh was killing me, pinning me there. How I'd never let myself be that helpless again.

Eventually rescue workers dug me out, but my right arm was mangled. Deep scars snaked around my arm, trenches through the muscle down to the bone. The surgeons snapped off three of the fingers as easily as dead twigs on a broken branch. They left the rest of the limb in place. Not that there was much I could do with it anymore.

The city tried to find a relative for me to live with. There weren't any around. When they threated to put me in the Rikers group home, Zunz's family took me in. Gave me a bunk in JJ's room, said I could stay there until I graduated high school.

I was angry and depressed for a long time. Could barely sleep. But Zunz kept me sane. He distracted me with video games and shows. This was when he really got me into baseball. We used disposable phones to trade the latest Topps player sims, trying to build the full rosters of our favorite teams. We'd project them on the table and battle each other for imaginary pennants.

I had a hard time being underground, so when we got older Zunz and I would go lounge around Reunion Square with the skate rats or sneak into bars to watch the games on holofeeds.

Whenever the air quality was good enough, we'd run to the park with our gloves, bats, and balls. I couldn't do much with my injured arm. But I was desperate to get out of the ground and into the open park where my claustrophobia would fade into the fields. I loved running through the wet grass to catch that arcing white ball. Loved drinking sodas on the damp benches and yelling at the tourists. Days passed that way. Summers. Years.

There was a whole group of us who played together out there. Friends of Zunz's who became friends of mine. Big Clarice, Jamal, the Boyle brothers, Hot Pete, Ugly Pete, Aizat, Barack, Yamamoto the Motor, Bug Eye, and Okafor.

It's a cliché to say the New York you grew up in is the last real New York. People have been saying the city's dying for two hundred years. Still, I think we really did live in the last New York. At least the last where all kinds of people mingled together, breathing the same air without filter masks or lung grafts.

Prospect Park is now a theme park, and the burrows have all been repurposed for the rich, rebranded as meditation caves and upscale nostalgia hotels. All the green of the city has wilted in the yellow smog. The island shrank as the waters rose. But back then, we could smell the grass, hide from the police in the trees, and whack leather balls until the sun dipped behind the scrapers and the whole sky shone red as blood.

5

THE HARD MORNING

All these years later, and I'd still wake up in the middle of the night at the sound of any rumble—washing machine, a neighbor moving furniture, the muffled rattle of a supraway line—panicked the ground was tumbling down on me. That there had been an earthquake or a targeted nuke and I'd been buried alive. Again. I still couldn't sleep with any blankets on me, not even a sheet. I needed to wake up without the feeling of weight on my skin.

The day after Zunz died, I woke to that sensation. Trapped. Hidden under miles of dirt, rocks, and detritus. I opened my eyes, gasping, unable to move. There was a sound boring down on me. Drilling right toward my skull.

I looked around, realized where I was. My apartment. Tenth floor. My screen was ringing.

"Hello?" I said.

"Kobo, can you tell me the number one quality we look for in a Future League Baseball scout?"

I yawned. Offered, "Knowledge of the game?"

"Very funny. You hear me laughing. Ha ha." Steinbrenner paused. "I'm not laughing. That was an imitation laugh. Mockery. An insult."

"I understood, sir."

"Discretion, Kobo. Discretion is the number one trait we look for. Prudence. Discipline." Steinbrenner had a repetitive way of talking. Like he couldn't remember what he'd said one second before.

"That was my next guess."

"We've been very fair to you. We've kept you on although you haven't brought us a top prospect in years. The last in the pipeline is Maxine Frisch. She's still in a Double-A lab doing centrifuge work. A scrub. Bench player. Mickey Mouse shit."

"Frisch has drive. Give her a chance."

"Then you lose Julia Arocha. To our historic rival no less. Our enemy. Our crosstown competitor."

"I'll get Arocha back." Steinbrenner's words had slapped me awake. I needed my job badly enough that, for a moment, I forgot my brother had just been murdered. "Hook me up with an extraction team. Two or three scouts with field experience. We'll fix this."

"No, you won't. Your badge has been deactivated. You're done. Kaput."

I looked at the palm of my left hand. The badge was a silicon chip the size of a grain of rice somewhere in my thumb pad. Was I supposed to dig it out? Or did it float uselessly in the muscle for the rest of my life?

"Can you deposit my last check today at least? I need the money."

"A last check. Now that's funny. A joke. Humorous. That we can laugh to. Haha. Hahaha. Ha. Goodbye."

I sat up, rubbed my temples. I felt like I'd been drained of muscle and bones, my skin stuffed instead with cotton. My brain couldn't quite process the information much less its implications. I knew it was bad news, but it was a mere drop in the bucket that was overflowing with Zunz's blood.

In the kitchen, I got a glass of water. Poured some in the aquarium for the shock slugs. They were the latest zootech. Genetically manipulated gastropods that could short-circuit security systems. I tapped on the tank a couple times. The gray slugs didn't respond.

After a couple weeks, most zootech died. Dissolved into yellow gunk. It was programmed into their DNA. Planned obsolesce to send you back to the store. As a Yanks freelancer, I'd been able to get the zootech at wholesale. That was over now. Which meant these gray lumps were my last five.

I needed to take my mind off things, but no matter how fast I clicked through the channels I kept catching flashes of Zunz. His body glitching. "A tragedy." His mouth screaming. "A dark time for the sport." His face disappearing in a mask of red. "A sad, sad day for the country."

So I decided I needed to put my mind back on things.

The news wasn't any use. The talking heads were tossing out every possible scenario. A terrorist attack by the SoCal separatists. An act of war from Russia or One China maybe. Or an unhinged zealot from the Edenists or Anti-Maxxer cults that considered upgrading oneself a mortal sin. They issued death threats to star players all the time. Yet there was no evidence, just speculation. So far, video analysis couldn't detect any projectile. Everyone agreed that whatever it was had been slipped inside him or his clothes, then activated as the game began.

I knew one person who might have an actual clue. Sergeant Silvia Emmanuel Okafor. Back in the day, they were the closest friend Zunz and I had at school. Now, Sil was my best contact at the police. Or the only one who'd still return my calls.

On-screen, Okafor appeared in their office, arms crossed against the bulky out-of-the-box regulation frame. The police force was one of the only industries that encouraged cybernetic applicants. Easier to get insurance on metal than flesh.

"You ass leech," they said. "I've called you five times. Where the hell have you been? What the hell is wrong with this world? And how are you?"

"Not taking it well, Sil."

I'd never planned on getting cybernetics, not until I realized the Cyber League was my only chance to play professional ball. But Sil had wanted them. They'd never been that comfortable in the limited options of flesh. Always said they wanted to remake themselves from scratch. I remembered when they were a tall dark kid with gangly grace holding down third base. Okafor was the first person I'd ever kissed, the first who took off my clothes and slid onto me, our parts locking into position with an awkward thrill. But that was years ago. Decades. After skin grafts, replacement parts, and plain old aging, nothing of our teenage bodies remained.

"No shit, not taking it well. I can't imagine how you're feeling, Kobo. You should do what you need to do. Get drunk. Take a vacation. Beat up a boxing bot at the gym. Just don't do anything stupid."

"What does that mean, Sil?"

"Don't get involved. I know he was basically your brother. But let the police handle it. We've got a whole team on it. When we find the fucker who fucking did this, I'll yank out his guts for you and choke him with them. I don't care who is listening. Hear that, B.O.B.?"

"Who's Bob?"

"A monitoring program. Cop stuff. Don't worry. I'm joking, B.O.B. Erase last eight seconds. Code T-S68."

"You've got a bot listening?"

"Not for you. Backup recording for lawsuits. The kind we

accidentally erase on purpose if we get sued. Erase those last five seconds too, B.O.B. The point is the police will get the person."

My stomach was grumbling like I hadn't eaten in two days. And maybe I hadn't. I poured whatever packs I had in the cabinet into my meal printer.

"What makes you think it was a person?"

Okafor sighed. Tapped their fingers on the desk. "I can't talk to you about the case. Still. Explain?"

"The other teams in the playoffs stand to gain the most."

"Murder is a pretty risky way to win a pennant."

"The pennant is just a flag. The big prize is customers, sales. Fans buying upgrades with the winning team's logo. Plus, President Newman gives the World Series champ first bid on government contracts."

"Well, it's a theory," they said. Okafor chewed it over for a minute while I chewed on my printed spinach nodes with beef dust.

"What leads do you have? Suspects?"

"Look. You know how these corporations are. It occurred on Monsanto property. We don't have jurisdiction. We can't even examine the corpse. And you don't have access either, so don't get involved."

"I won't," I said, thinking about how the police might not be able to get inside a biopharm compound. But a scout could.

"I'm serious, Kobo. I know you're hurting. I am too. I knew him even longer than you. Did you know our mothers were pregnant at the same time? They used to share prenatal injections to save money. That's why you should listen to me when I say leave this to the professionals."

I sat in my living room, where Zunz was looking down on me. A massive video poster of him hitting the walk-off home run in last year's opening game. He grins as he swings, then flips his bat in his signature home run move. Even in poster form, Zunz was the big brother watching over me. Next to his was a smaller static poster of my rookie year in the now defunct Cyber League. They'd pasted me over an abstract pattern of wires and lights. I'm holding the glowing red baseball and smiling stupidly.

Then I remembered the late-night call. How Zunz had been not just preoccupied but dislocated. Strange. There had been something wrong then, days before he died. I was furious at myself for not calling back and grilling him, getting him to spill all his secrets while they were still inside of him.

But I did remember he called me someone's else name. Kang. Jung Kang. At the time I'd figured he'd just dialed the wrong number, but why had he been dialing this Kang in the middle of the night? And right before a playoff game when he should have been resting? And why, when I looked Kang up, was he a player for a rival team?

6

THE SEEDY BAR

I walked through the Midtown fog, purifier kissing my lips. Nothing in this part of town matched anything else. Prewar buildings sat beside post-crises skystabbers on streets patched up like a kindergartner's art project. I ran my out-of-date bionic hand through my graying hair. I was a collage myself, flesh and machine, parts stuck together without any coherence. Maybe that's why I still loved this city despite everything.

The creepeasy rolled toward me. Its headlights were the eyes of a sea monster in the watery smog.

Zunz and I had first sneaked into a creepeasy our senior year of high school. We saved up enough money to purchase fake ID chips and played hooky during the homecoming game. The drinks were strong, made our heads feel filled with light. "God, this is the best feeling ever," Zunz had said before vomiting across the counter. We got booted, laughing, near Duracell Park.

They were novelties back then. Now with the traffic mostly in the air the streets were free for these roving water holes. They were also about the only safe place for a scout to drink anymore, thanks to their comm blockers. And there was a specific scout I needed to see. My old teammate and ex-lover, Dolores Otero Zamora. She was a scout for the Pyramid Pharmaceuticals Sphinxes now. Jung Kang's team.

This one had a neon sign that glowed the words *Pharaoh's Dive*. A mummy blinked a beer to its lipless mouth. The creepeasy slowed to a stop by the booth, and the doors opened with an old-fashioned mechanical wheeze.

A robot dressed in the style of a 1920s flapper greeted me. "Don't take any wooden nickels with a screen, dewdropper. This joint's got an anti-comm field." I made a show of turning off my screen. Handing it over.

The robot gave me an anachronistic thumbs-up. "Swanky and swell. Go have a snort."

The interior of the bar was dimly lit with hologram torches. The bartender was modeled after Anubis with a layer of furry plastiflesh over the metal. The lab-grown fur looked wrong. Mangy. They got the smell right though. The jackal head woofed in pleasure as I flicked him a two-dollar tip and took my whiskey to the back.

The bar was filled with the usual sorts lying low from prying eyes. Young lovers, old adulterers, crooks, thugs, and my fellow scouts. Some of us worked for the sports teams, others for cosmetic manufacturers or military contractors. Everyone was shrouded in their own private cloud of eraser smoke.

This was a Sphinxes bar. Filled with loudmouth Jersey fans, tube and tunnel types. The booths ringed the edge of the bar and in the middle sat a large holopad illuminated with the playoffs.

The Sphinxes were up three games to two on the BodyMore Inc. Orioles, looking to nab the Patriot League pennant. Everyone had been expecting the winner to face the Mets in the World Series, before Zunz was killed.

A reporter was interviewing the Sphinxes' starting pitcher, "Throwback" Bobak Nazari. A lean, tall pitcher with a braided beard that reached halfway down his sternum. He spat golden globs of eraser juice and waved to his mom at home with a left arm notably larger than his right. "What happened to Zunz was a tragedy," he said. He pointed at the black ribbon on his hat. "We all mourn him. But today the Pharm Fam is focused on taking down the Orioles."

The opening ceremony proceeded with painful normalcy. Drone mascots danced around the sidelines. The crowd stuffed their faces with overpriced burgers and beer. No one was acting as if anything was wrong. Not as if a star player had died on-screen a couple days before.

Money talks, but it silences a whole lot more.

"Hey. Aren't you Kobo the Killer?"

An old man with a metal mask hanging from his neck swiveled around on his barstool. He had a can of preserver on his back, tube hooked to the mask. He wore a blue and yellow Sphinxes jersey.

I nodded.

"Thought I recognized you. Saw you pitch a shutout against the Cathode Rays. You had a hell of an arm," he said. He took a sip of beer, then lifted the mask to his lips and huffed.

"That was a long time ago."

The old man let the mask drop again. He reached out and touched my right arm. Squeezed the metal through the sleeve.

"Do you mind?" he said, lip curled. He looked disgusted, like he'd slid his fingers into the belly of a rotting fish. "How much did that robot arm cost you, huh?"

"Too much," I said. Although technically the arm had been free.

The Cyber League had started when Major League attendance was plummeting and tech tycoons set out to disrupt the sport. Other sports had banned all upgrades, then got bogged down in trying to enforce hormone levels and genetic codes. The tycoons knew cybernetics, genomods, and steroids weren't going away. They created a spin-off league. Needed players fast and they had the VC cash to build them. Schmucks like me were the perfect candidates. Turning poor burrow kids into stars was good marketing. I was drafted by the Boston Red Sockets with my cybernetic arm as the signing bonus.

It's hard to describe what it's like to upgrade the first time. To really upgrade. Not to tweak yourself or take a course of steroids over months. Not to diet or exercise. But to change yourself in a day. To suck in the anesthesia and wake up a new person. You don't simply have a new limb or implant. You have new senses. New vibrations. I woke up that day on the surgical table, a gleaming new arm sutured to my shoulder, and I was expanded.

Other people didn't necessarily see it that way though, like this old man in the bar. They wanted players they could imagine themselves as while they watched from the couch. Pretend it could have been them on the field if they hadn't had that knee injury in high school or hadn't knocked up their college sweetheart. Even if they'd never have the money to upgrade like Zunz, it was an easier delusion than imagining themselves with cybernetic parts. So when the biopharms started the Future League, all cybernetics were banned.

The FLB and CLB duked it out a bit, but the FLB was destined to win. After all, the biopharm vaccines had brought sports back after the Apex Zika pandemic. And then again with wolf flu and the green sweats and a dozen other diseases until people rooted for Pfizer or GenSlice as passionately as any sports team. So when the companies started a professional league, the public was already primed to follow, cheer, and buy.

In the bar, the old man pushed my arm away and spat a glob on the floor.

"I could have played if I'd been rich enough to buy a pitching arm."

"If you say so."

"You think you're shit? You had to buy that talent. Goddamn machines. I'm all man."

He pounded his chest with a dull thunk. I smiled at him and moved on.

"Go, Sphinxes!" he screamed after me. "Glad they kicked you oilers out of the game. They should kick you out of the country."

I walked to the back, looking for Dolores. The game was about to start, and the players were settling into their positions. The bright holofeed filled the center of the bar. I didn't see Jung Kang on the field. That was suspicious.

But, in the back booths, right above left field, I saw who'd I'd come for. "Deadeye" Dolores Zamora, sitting alone with a black martini and her reinforced eyes glued to the game.

7

THE FORMER FLAME

If it isn't Kobo," Dolores said. She was wearing a dark jumpsuit with chameleon fabric that had browned to the leather of
the booth. Her black hair was buzzed on one side and flopped over
the other in a crashing wave. Her enhanced goggles were a glittering
jade.

She signed something I couldn't decipher. I tried to spell out *hello*.
I'd forgotten most of my sign language lessons after we broke up.

"You know, some old asshole recognized me from the Cyber
League," I said out loud, letting her goggles transcribe my words.

"Good to know we still have fans."

"Something like that. Seemed like he would have been more of a
fan of seeing me socked in the jaw."

She touched a button on the jade goggles, and the metal legs
tapped and twirled the aperture. Dolores was deaf. She was born hard
of hearing and was happy to keep it that way. Opted to enhance her
other senses instead. Got the inside of her nostrils replaced with sensor cilia and a full retina replacement job. When we'd dated, I always

wondered how awful I'd smelled to her. Only time in my life I took four showers a day.

"The fans never loved us, Kobo. Not really."

"They bought tickets," I said.

"To watch us like creatures in a zoo. With fascination, not love." Dolores gave me a good once-over, then went over me a second time. "Anyway, you look like shit."

"You need enhanced vision to see that?"

"It's still nice to see you," she said, lips curving in a smile. Then her smile went straight. Inverted. "I'm so, so sorry about Zunz. I know how close you were."

Hearing his name out loud made me tense up. I mumbled something and we clinked drinks.

President Newman was on the mound, ready to throw the opening pitch. His aides removed his trademark lab coat he wore over his suits. Newman was the first test-tube president, his genes cut-and-pasted in embryo with enzyme scissors to possess "all the traits of the Founding Fathers." At least that's what the rebranded Grand New Party claimed. That was nonsense, but he was designed all right. And connected to all types of gene separatist groups, racists who tried to genetically edit themselves until they were whiter than lab mice.

"This fastball is for the Chinese. Either swing at our arms treaty or we'll strike you out." He tossed a low one that sent the catcher scrambling. The crowd cheered anyway.

Nazari shook Newman's hand, then took the mound. Sigrid Ortiz stepped up to the plate for the Orioles.

"This is the strangest part of the season," Dolores said. "When the playoffs start, my job is on hold. I've got nothing to do except be bored."

"The Yanks have a different philosophy. Tried to make me bring in a prospect named Julia Arocha last week."

"Really?" Dolores said. "We had an Arocha on our target list for next season."

"Well, the Yanks lost her. By which I mean I lost her."

"How's life at the Evil Empire anyway?"

The name was used mockingly now. The Yanks weren't an empire anymore, but they had been the only MLB team who'd had the brains and resources to transition into a full-fledged biopharm corp. They used their cash reserves to buy Bleedr, a start-up machine that let people oxygenate and "youthify" their blood at home. There was a big scandal and a class action lawsuit after it was discovered a bunch of hedge fund managers were draining their maids and butlers. The Yanks survived though while the rest of the MLB teams faded into irrelevance or sold their trademarks to biopharm corps.

"They fired me."

"Over the Arocha thing. They must have had big plans for her. That's a bad break."

"You heard about that?"

Dolores shrugged. Although her cybernetic goggles transcribed conversations around her, she was studying my lips. Seeing how much they trembled, I guess. "I'd heard they cut you over a botched pickup. You know how scouts talk."

"They talk about how Zunz was murdered?" It came out nastier than I'd intended.

Dolores reached across the table and rested her flesh hand on my metal one. "He was a good guy. I can't even imagine. I remember when he threw you a surprise birthday party. He had us all wait in dazzle suits for you, turning them on right when you came in."

I laughed. "I was blinded for a full five minutes! God, that was a long time ago."

"He cared about you. I'm so sorry."

"Sorry like you're sorry a stranger died of cancer, or sorry because you know something?"

Dolores sat back, gave me a sad sneer. "Is that why you asked to meet up? To accuse me of assassination?"

The bar erupted in cheers as Nazari struck out an Orioles batter to end the top of the first. The birds went three up three down. Not a great start. Some baboon in the back screamed, "Hell yeah! He melted at the plate quicker than JJ Zunz."

A glistening scarab drone the size of a baby floated around the booths. The waiter in this joint. I signaled the beetle for another drink. It clicked a confirmation and putted off.

"I'm sorry, Dolores." I tapped the side of my glass. "I know you play it clean. But you still work for Pyramid. The same biopharm who paid half a billion in damages to the families in Detroit who'd been mutated by lab runoff. You're telling me you all aren't capable of killing a rival player?"

Dolores shrugged and sipped her martini in a single movement. "Every team is capable of that. Whether they'd do it is another question. Zunz's death was being streamed to the entire country. That's a risky venture."

Another wave of claps went through the bar as the right fielder Alvaro "the Sandman" Sanchez hit a homer over left field. From the bar's central holopad, the ball soared toward me and disappeared a few inches from my face.

Dolores cheered too. "Damn, I miss playing. Don't you? Being out there under the bright lights instead of hiding in the shadows."

"Yeah, I miss it," I admitted. "I don't care if the fans were gawking. People have been staring at me my whole life. I liked being looked at with admiration instead of disdain."

I still dreamed of those days. Standing on the mound, ball in my hand, batter at the plate, and all around me thousands and thousands of fans. With the floating stadium lights, I could barely make them out. But I could hear them cheer. I'd been looking for that feeling ever since.

"It kills me they banned cybernetics. The stuff they pump into these guys is at least as powerful as our bionic parts. I bet I could still throw a breaking ball that would break their minds." She stared at the game, her head shaking back and forth.

It was nice shooting the shit with Dolores. She'd been the only partner I'd ever had who I could discuss anything with. We'd spend hours in bed, talking nonsense and making plans until it was so late we'd have to run to practice. Coach would yell at us for drinking before a workout, never realizing we hadn't sipped a thing.

But when the Cyber League fell apart, I didn't take it well. I couldn't handle my body backsliding without team-subsidized operations. I took out loans. Bought off-brand upgrades. Worked odd jobs for dwindling pay. Ended up with a mountain of debt crushing me and I hadn't wanted another person to be buried in the rubble. At least that's what I'd told her at the time. And myself.

"I don't see your outfielder today. Jung Kang."

"What about him?"

"That's what I'm hoping you'll tell me."

She took another sip of her martini. "And here I was hoping this conversation was more social. Like the old days."

She still had her hand on mine. Tapped her fingers around my knuckles. I didn't move.

"Okay. Have it your way. Kang. Recent acquisition, thrown in with the big bullpen trade. Point seven two three OPS. I heard he caught that new skin fever that's been flying around. He got demoted out of the lineup recently. Honestly, a pretty unremarkable player."

"That's all you know?"

"What else is there?"

I looked at the holofeed as Nazari checked the runner on first before he could steal.

"Listen, I'm lost here, Dolores. You know I scout players. That's my specialty. I've never been good on the laboratory side. I never understood the chemistry like you did."

"What do you want to know?"

"Let's say, hypothetically, you were going to kill a rival player like that. How?"

Dolores leaned back into the booth cushions. Her face went blank, which it always did when she was thinking. "There's a lot of ways to destroy a person. Gas, zootech, toxins. We develop a new way to destroy each other every year. Then someone else comes along with a new upgrade to make people think they're safe. Sell one guy the sword, the other guy the shield. This is the business we're in."

"Zunz was a star. He had enough money to buy safety."

"Maybe. All I know is his death was quick and seemed to affect his whole body. That suggests destabilization at the cellular level. Radiation would be my guess, but that would hit a lot more than just Zunz. Whole lot of people would have gotten sick. It's like dropping ink into a glass of water. That crap gets everywhere."

"Doesn't ChicagoBio do RadGen?"

"Sure, so does half the league. The machine is gigantic and nowhere near the field."

Dolores was right, I was reaching. Whoever killed Zunz did it with some weapon the public didn't know about yet. And it didn't matter what killed him as much as who and why.

"Why were you asking about Kang?"

"Zunz mentioned him to me a couple weeks ago. It was one of the last things he mentioned to me." My voice trailed off. I looked at the holopad, then back at Dolores. "Could you get me inside the compound? To talk to Kang? Just talk. For old times' sake?"

Dolores sat back, shaking her head. I thought I saw her roll her eyes beneath the goggles. "Come on, Kobo. You know I love you, but I love my job too. And that love pays the bills."

"Yeah. I know. Had to ask."

Suddenly a great tiredness came over me. Despite the erasers, I could feel the weariness in my bones. I wasn't ready to deal with a world without Zunz. I wanted to go home, sleep, and hope I woke up in a new reality.

I tipped back my glass, finished it. "Well, keep an ear out, will you? Figuratively speaking." I slid her my encrypted address, told her to send me any info she might uncover.

"Of course." Her goggles looked me up and down, then back up again. "You know, you look like you could use a break from work. How about another drink, without the splash of business?"

I couldn't find a reason to disagree and sat back down.

8

THE MORNING LIGHT

Since Zunz's death, I'd become paranoid my own body was falling apart. That at any moment my fingers would snap off, or my toes would end up clogging the shower drain. Or my eyeballs would melt and dribble down my cheeks. The molecules that made me would forget what they were doing. Protons, neutrons, and electrons wandering apart like lost children. If it could happen to Zunz, it could happen to me.

But when I woke up, I felt peaceful for the first time since his death. The apartment was filled with light. Outside, the cars of the city sputtered by and pigeons cooed to each other through the smog. Dolores had her arm draped across my chest, her breath hitting my neck in warm little puffs. My muscles ached and my hip hurt, but I felt good.

I imagined myself living there. Getting up to make coffee in the morning as Dolores slept in. Checking the news while eating breakfast on the enclosed balcony. It was the life I could have had, maybe, if I'd been interested in building a life instead of buying new parts.

Dolores started to stir. I closed my eyes. Pretended to be asleep. She slid her arm off my chest, slipped out of the bed. I opened them to watch her disappear into the bathroom. On the nightstand beside me was a small human figure displaying data across the corresponding parts. Heart rate, blood sugar, bladder level. I saw the teeth on the figure light up as Dolores started brushing.

I let myself relax. Tried to fall back to sleep. But with my eyes closed, the images of Zunz filled my mind. I heard the screams. Saw the panic in his face.

I checked my bionic eye. The scan of Dolores's iris looked complete. My ticket inside the Pyramid compound where I could pay Jung Kang a visit. I felt bad stealing a person's eye pattern while we were making love, but happy the old software still worked. Plus, Dolores was alive and Zunz was dead. I had to give my loyalty to the person who needed revenge.

I told the wall screen to turn on. The local channel projected a hastily made biopic on the life of JJ Zunz, "an American icon cut down in his prime." A bad actor was sitting in what was supposed to be a tiny apartment, but was three times the size of the hole we grew up in. His haircut was a style that wasn't popular when we were kids.

"Will I ever make it to the Big Leagues, Mama? Can a poor boy like me catch a fly ball break in the outfield of life?"

The Mrs. Z actor knocked her stirring spoon against the pot. "Anyone can make it in America, son. As long as they know how to dream." The screen had noticed Dolores's goggles were disconnected, and an androgynous holographic figure appeared beside it to sign a real-time transcription.

I skipped to the next channel.

It was the game show *Hands on Your New Body*. A group of people huddled over a cadaver made of replacement parts, some metal, others pulsing flesh. Each contestant was touching a different piece—a leg, a lung, a set of teeth—that they could win. The people looked sick, and almost certainly were. A woman gripping the wet-frame lung kept coughing blood into her other hand.

"This one is going to be a squeaker, folks," the host said. She was a tall, pale woman with freckles engineered into swirling patterns on her arms and legs. "Who do you want to see win a new organ? Send in your vote."

I scrolled through my messages. It was mostly condolences from old friends I hadn't seen in years, mixed with a few threatening messages about my late medical-loan payments. The Yankees had cut off their support. I'd probably get a visit from Sunny Day Healthcare Loans soon.

Dolores was in the shower and I got up, looked through her drawers. I didn't find much. But her bytewallet wasn't encrypted and I flicked a little bit of her cash to mine. Not much. Just enough to get me through a few days. I told myself the old lie about paying her back when the case was closed.

"Switch to the news," I said.

President Newman was giving a press conference about One China's testing of nerve mosquitos on protesting Tibetan monks. Hundreds had been paralyzed. Newman was saying zootech "should only be used for peacekeeping, never as weapons of war." Not that he honored this rule himself. On the side scroll, the feed said *Mets Honor Zunz and Zoom to Win*. Monsanto had finished off ChicagoBio by two runs to one. The Mets would face the Sphinxes in the World Series after all.

Dolores's shower ended. I told the wall to turn off, then started to get dressed. My body wanted nothing more than to crawl back into those sheets and have Dolores wrap her warm limbs around me. Relive old times. But my mind was focused on JJ.

I needed an excuse to leave. Get to the Sphinxes stadium before Dolores realized I'd stolen her iris access. I thought of telling her I had to go to Zunz's funeral, but she'd know that the Mets were holding on to the corpse until after the World Series. He was corporate property, even when dead.

The bathroom door slid open and Dolores emerged fully dressed, wrapped up in a red jumper with crimson goggles to match. Her neck was decorated with pomegranate pearls.

"Do you want children?"

I froze, hunched over with my pants halfway up my legs. "What?"

Dolores laughed. "I wanted to see your face. Anyway, this was fun, Kobo. You want to spitball the case, or spitball something else, give me a call."

"I'll do that," I said.

Dolores held up two earring options, one a set of fashion succulents and the other tiny holoprojectors of her own face in Cleopatra garb right below the lobe.

"For a Pyramid board meeting."

"The latter," I said.

"Thanks." She put them on. "Well, I have work to do. Preliminary scouting on a bone lab in Baltimore. Sorry to fuck and run on you."

"Oh," I said. "I mean, sure. Me too. I was going to say the same thing."

At the door, she looked back at me. "Listen, I really am sorry about Zunz. He was a good man. I know he cared about you. I'm here to help if I can."

"I'm not good on a team."

Dolores shook her head, sending her holographic heads spinning. "You like to screw yourself over by not taking help when it's offered."

"Old habits and all that," I said.

Dolores scratched her neck and looked at me for a long second. "I know what you mean." She blew me a kiss. Walked to the door. "Good luck. The door locks itself."

9

THE LOAN SHARKS

I swung by my apartment to clean up and grab supplies for the Pyramid compound, including one of my remaining shock slugs in case Kang wasn't home and I needed to break in. I put on my nicest suit, which was my only suit without decorative moth holes. Midnight-blue spiderwool lined with silver threads for the shine. It was a decade out of fashion, from back when they used CRISPR to splice silk producing genes into sheep embryos. The resulting wool was so sticky the sheep would get stuck to anything they walked by, so they had to be raised in nonstick cages and fed grass through tubes. Nowadays they had eight-legged ewes that secreted threads right out of the udders and the fabric was half as thick. Still, I was holding on to mine in case it came back into style.

Locking my door, I felt a metal hand grab my right elbow, and then another clamp on my left.

"Have you been on vacation, Mr. Kobo? We haven't heard from you in a while." The woman's voice was as low and dull as a thudding fan.

"Yeah, Kobo. You on vacation?" the other one said.

The two women pushed into me, lifted me up.

"I was working," I grunted as I was carried back into my apartment. "Can we do this another time? I've had a long week."

"I'm afraid it's about to get longer," the first woman said.

"Haha. Gonna get longer," the other said.

My legs were smacked into the table, then the chair as the women twirled me around trying to find a place to deposit me. Eventually they settled on the couch and heaved me into the cushions.

I got myself sitting straight. Flipped one leg over the other and tried to look comfortable. I slid an eraser out of the pack and slipped it between my lips.

"Hello, Wanda. Hello, Brenda."

Wanda and Brenda Sassafras worked as medical muscle. Upgrade loan sharks for Sunny Day Healthcare Loans, the country's biggest medical-loan outfit. The company's slogan, stitched above the sisters' half-human hearts, was *It's Always a Sunny Day When You Have Your Health.*

"You ever clean this place? It's a pigsty," Wanda said.

"Yeah, it's a pigsty!" Brenda guffawed. She slapped her metal hand against Wanda's back with a sharp clack. Then she tugged on her ear. "Hey, Wanda, what's a sty?"

"Shut up, Brenda."

"What?"

"I'm not your personal dictionary."

Brenda's face deflated. She hung her head. Her hair flopped over her eyes. "Don't tell me to shut up. I don't like it," she said to the floor.

I lit my eraser and got a good look at my visitors. The Sassafras sisters were big ones, the size and shape of cryotanks and just as cold. Both were oilers like me. The right side of Wanda was bionic. As for Brenda, it was her left side made of whirring dark machinery. They wore two-toned jumpsuits, black on the metal halves and pastel blue on the flesh. Standing next to each other, they looked like one person separated by a black hole.

Brenda and Wanda went everywhere together. They were former conjoined twins. Hadn't been separated until they were teenagers and their parents could afford to have their missing halves replaced with metal and wetframe. Wanda had enough live wires to be called the brains of the operation. How Brenda could have identical genes yet be five times as dull was one of those genetic mysteries science still hadn't solved.

"We're working, Brenda. Be quiet."

"I'm just saying it's not nice."

"Okay, Brenda. Noted. Your complaint has officially been lodged."

"It's not sisterly," she whispered.

Wanda shook her head and rolled her eyes, the red iris following the hazel one with a fraction of a second delay. "So, long week means you're working? That's good. Working means money. Money means you pay us back. Paying us back means we don't break things."

"Shucks," Brenda said.

"Well, not as many things."

I'd taken out my first medical loans in my third and final Cyber League season, right when revenues dipped and the teams pressured the players to get increasingly flashy upgrades. "What about a new eye?" Coach Brumder had asked me after a five-run loss to the Toronto Blue Jets. "Something that glows bright enough to see from the stands? It'll pay off in the long run."

At the time it seemed sensible. More upgrades meant better stats, which meant bigger contracts. Hell, with an entire league getting new parts each season, if you didn't upgrade, you'd be left behind. Then the league folded, and I was even more worried about being left behind. I kept taking out loans and upgrading as my income slowed, then trickled, then evaporated.

"My brother just died. Isn't there bereavement wiggle room?"

"You had a brother?"

"Adopted. I grew up with JJ Zunz. The baseball star." I nodded toward the poster on the wall of Zunz sliding home. He grinned behind the cloud of dust.

"Wanda, isn't that the guy from the news? The one who went all drippy?"

"We're a SouthernChem household," Wanda said. "Their Apex Zika cure saved our grandmother's life. We buy from and root for the Rebels. Still, I'm sorry. That looked like a bad way to go." I thought I saw a bit of human emotion leak into Wanda's face. She frowned, looked away from me. Then she rattled her head. The sympathy drained away like sludge through a sewage grate. "How come you can't pay us with all these fancy brothers? That makes me angry, Kobo."

"I live a lavish lifestyle," I said, waving my hand around the dinky, cluttered apartment.

"You bought new parts. You pay for them. Or your lifestyle will be moaning in a hospital bed."

"Yeah, we'll send you to the hospital."

"Shut up, Brenda. I already said that."

"I know you said it. I'm just saying."

"Give Mr. Kobo his present already."

Brenda's grin curved exponentially toward her ears. "I like presents." She dropped a green bag on the floor, squatted to unzip. Stood back up with a long metal spike, about the size and shape of a pool cue. Spindles of electricity crackled at the tip.

My heart was pounding so hard I thought it might stab itself on a rib. I tried to get up. "Look, I'm on a case. Big case. The money will come rolling in soon. Let's take a rain check, and I'll throw in a bonus for both of you."

Wanda shook her head robotically. "Stop making us come back here. It smells, and the commute is an hour. Have a bytewallet ready next time, or we'll slice out all the parts that Sunny Day paid for."

"I'll have it. There's no need for any threats."

"Sorry. Company policy. We need to send in photos of at least one injury or our boss will dock our pay. We're trying to save up for a down payment on an East River floater home."

"No, listen. One minute."

I turned to Brenda, thinking maybe she'd be a better bet for mercy. She wasn't looking at me. She glared at her electric pole with a strange grin.

I kept protesting, yet there was no point arguing with lugs like the Sassafras sisters. And part of me was ready to accept what was coming. With Zunz dead, and my lungs filled with eraser smoke, I was numb to everything. Or so I thought.

Wanda held me down, stretched my bionic arm across the couch. Brenda lifted the buzzing rod. "Look, we got other clients to visit. This job ain't all fun and games. We got our own quotas to fill. Please be quiet."

I was never good at following instructions. Wanda wanted me to shush, but as the spike went through my hand all I could do was scream.

10

THE ELEVATED PARK

My hand was twitching so badly that on my way to the Pyramid compound I had to get out at Reunion Square and run to the nearest kiosk. Brenda's spike had popped the nerve module like a pimple. I'd hidden the injury inside a black glove. It was already filled with thick blue discharge, which began leaking down my wrist.

With the module broken, my nerves didn't understand what they were attached to. My brain didn't know what to feel. I could sense my childhood arm, the one that had been injured in the apartment cave-in, floating in the broken metal case. The phantom hand was trying to grip, trying to hold on to something. Cyber surgeons never tell you about that. How the flesh misses what's been cut away. How your body wants to be whole. Only the right electrical pulses keep that need at bay.

"You look awful, pal," the kiosk worker said, without taking off his video game visor. "How about some dope chews? They'll put a smile on your face."

I showed him a pained snarl. "Pack of erasers. Mets."

"Yanks okay?"

"Is that all you have?"

The guy paused his game and frowned. His arms were all curves, muscles so engorged they were striped with stretch marks. He'd clearly been sampling his wares. "Look, bud, this is a Yankees kiosk. We don't sell Monsanto. Smoke Yank or go home."

I bought the pack anyway, plus a tube of sealant. I stumbled through the elevated park, chain-smoking the erasers.

We were twenty floors above the old Union Square, which had been sold off to developers when I was a teen. Reunion Square might be higher up, but it hadn't changed. The park was filled with over-dressed tourists, underdressed goths, hover skaters, and chanting activists. Genohippies sold organic pearl necklaces they'd secreted from oyster glands spliced into their necks, and head hackers hustled games of 4D chess, black beanies hiding their implants from the rubes.

The supraway entrance had a row of medical beggars, each holding a sign that listed the operation they needed and the code for their bank account. One of them had a screen that said *Mextexan Vet with Lichen Lung Pls Help* and a video of the disease. I watched the bio-engineered spores travel down a cutaway of a human form, black patches spreading across the walls of the lungs.

I didn't give him any money. But I did consider plopping down next to him, seeing if I could trade my pity for enough change to patch up my injured hand.

Someone next to me spat on the ground. Elbowed me. "Mooch-ers. Get a job and pay your bills like the rest of us, right?" He handed me a flyer that said *Keep America for Americans* above a description of President Newman's second-term plan to boost fertility rates while locking out climate refugees. *The American dream is for American genes.*

"Can we count on your vote?"

The man was white as a lab rat, all the pink bleached out with epidermis upgrades. He had a Rebel Reborn tattoo on his neck. A bald eagle clutching a pair of nukes. It looked like it had been burned into the skin.

"Not much of an America left to keep these days," I said, flexing my hand and grimacing.

His pale lips looked like dead earthworms as he scowled. "You don't like it you should go the fuck back to—" He looked me over trying to decide what ethnic slur to hurl, then gave up and settled on my cybernetics. "The fucking trash heap!"

I crumpled the flyer up as he walked away. As I tossed it, I saw a hulking man in a trench coat and a Jupiter hat pulled low on his face. His chin was overgrown with black scruff, and beneath I could just make out the blotch of a glove-shaped birthmark.

It was Zunz. Back from the dead.

"Hey!" I shouted.

I pushed through the crowd, knocking people away with my arm, too excited to wince. He kept disappearing before me.

Reunion Square was one of Zunz's and my old haunts. We'd spent countless teenage nights fighting with kids from other schools or spitting on the rich dorks playing augmented reality games from the benches.

"JJ?" I said, grabbing his shoulder.

The man didn't turn around. "Back off, weirdo." The stranger disappeared into the crowd.

The pain in my arm was making me delirious. I was hallucinating. I stumbled. Wiped a slick of sweat off my brow. I needed a doctor. A legit one I could afford. Which is to say, I wasn't going to a doctor.

I walked by a bone band plucking strings between the frets and bridges implanted on their forearms. Their skin vibrated with each pluck. The arm violinist was crooning about lost love. "I'd sever my limbs / to touch you again. / I'd burn off my skin / to kiss you again."

Then I saw Zunz towering above me, immobile as stone. He was green and grinning.

I stopped. Stared.

It was a busker dressed as JJ Zunz, a human statue on an injection pad. His sign scrolled *R.I.P. to a New York Hero. Ya Gotta Bereave!* The busker was posed with the bat out, having finished an imaginary home run.

Across the path was a Sphinxes busker dressed as a pharaoh with a baseball glove. Every time he moved, he sang, "Beat the Mets! Beat the Mets!" and passersby cheered or booed. America had always been like that. Coke or Pepsi. Republican or Democrat. Monsanto or Pyramid. You were expected to pick a side and then scream like hell.

A thin, sickly girl stood next to me in front of the Zunz busker. She had that frail bone structure that you see in old movies and history exhibits. A twig. There was a sticky sheen to her skin that I guessed was sunscreen. She wore a gray-and-blue tunic. Probably a No Grow or an Edenist, one of the sects that claimed that living without upgrades was what god had intended for humanity. As if god intended anything about the way things had gone.

"He was a good guy," I said.

The twig heard me, twisted her head with a blank expression. "I heard he was a piece of shit."

I ignored the comment. The human statue looked down at us with begging eyes. They were the only part of him that could move while the chemical was circulating. White balls rolling in the green field of his painted skin. "If you flick him a dollar, he gets an injection that lets him change poses."

The girl scrunched her face. "Thanks, Mr. Creepy Stranger. I'm twelve, not four. I know how muscle concreter works."

I looked away. I'd forgotten how nature had genetically modified preteens to be assholes.

"Zunz isn't dead! It's a hoax!" someone yelled. "They can even fake holorecordings now. You can't believe anything you see with your own eyes."

The human statue didn't flinch. I flicked the man a few dollars, and the pad whirred. I thought I saw him grimace as the needle stuck into his ankle. A tremor moved through him, relaxing each part.

I got dizzy. Stepped back. Grabbed the railing. He was collapsing again. Just like he did at bat.

But the busker didn't collapse. Instead, he spoke, voice cracking as the larynx softened. "Go Mets! Win the World Series for JJ Zunz. M-E-T-S Mets!" He tapped the platform three times with his bat, then crouched into a batting stance. A needle went into his other ankle and slowly his flesh froze again.

A few people cheered.

"Look! Abomination transformed into idolatry." I turned to see an old man shouting, wrinkled hands sticking out of a gray tunic. It looked like his thin flesh was barely hanging on to his skeleton. His two-foot beard dangled down to his belly button. "Zunz died for his sin of self-pollution. He rotted himself from the inside. So will you, unless you repent."

He pointed his wrinkled finger at different people in the crowd. There were boos and hisses in response.

My blood was gurgling, working its way to my flushing face. I grabbed him with my broken hand. Winced as it clamped.

"What do you know about Zunz?" I said. I pushed him into a nearby fence. Anger flowed through me like electricity through a filament.

"God's genes! Let go of me, you filthy oiler." The old man spat out the last word, glaring at my cybernetic eye. The crowd grew bigger.

I saw several people livestreaming. They shouted different things. "Shut that twig up!" "Be peaceful!" "Fight!" "Love!"

I let go. My hand was killing me. I didn't have time for this. Fighting with religious nuts wasn't going to solve Zunz's death.

"See the violence that electric defilement leads to?" the old man shouted after me as I stumbled away. "Drain yourself or be damned."

I stumbled to the tube station. When I looked back, I could see the young girl staring at me with half of a smile on her face.

11

THE RIVAL PLAYER

The sealant had closed the hole in my hand, and the pain was subsiding. Still, I smoked another numbing eraser on the ride across the Hudson to the Pyramid Pharmaceuticals compound.

Pyramid was the third FLB team in New York's six boroughs. Greater Newark may have incorporated into New York ten years ago, but it still smelled like Jersey to me. The compound was impressive though. A walled-off corporate headquarters on a ten-foot bed of concrete to fight against the rising waters. In the middle was the Pyramid stadium itself. Bright red and constructed from sound-absorbing bricks. The top layers were glass and at the apex a golden sphinx sat with a baseball in its mouth. The ball was swapped out when the Pyramid hosted other events. A basketball when the Jackals played, soccer ball for Pyramid FC, and a tennis ball when the US Mech Open was in town.

As I walked to the employee entrance, I noticed shining silver nests inside the bushes. Heard the warning buzz of security zootech. If Dolores's eyeball scan didn't work, I'd be twitching on the ground in seconds. But it did. My bionic eye re-created her brown iris, and the door slid open. The modified wasps stayed sleeping in their mechanical homes.

Inside, the compound was hectic enough for me to pass around unnoticed. People ran around setting up stands as delivery drones restocked supplies. Everything was humming and alive. The World Series started in two days.

Kang's house was in the back of the compound, small and unadorned. Only a tiny American flag hanging in one window and a sprinkler drone dog that barked *woof woof* as it sprayed the yard with insecticides.

I tried to clean myself up as much as I could. Wiped the grimace of pain off my face. Straightened my spiderwool lapels.

Jung Kang answered the door sucking on two smoothies. One bright blue and the other a pale yellow. Sphinxes team colors. He wore shorts, moss shoes with bioengineered soles, and a sweat-absorbing shirt. The shirt wasn't working. Drenched oblong patches flowed like oil spills from his neck and armpits.

"Time for the tests already?" he said, letting the straws drop from his mouth. He was jogging in place. "Great, I'm almost finished."

He nodded for me to follow him inside. Jogged ahead of me into the living room.

His place was sparsely furnished. There was a couch. A large wall screen with different video game modules. I could see the top of a pop-up fridge beside the couch. Otherwise, the room was filled with workout equipment. Free weights next to a muscle-stim bed and an AR rock-climbing rig on the wall. Only a few photos on the walls and no other artwork or plants. It was the kind of place where you felt like the person living there had never lived in it at all.

"No offense, brother, but you look pretty pale. Do you need an energy shot? Immune boost? Activation chew?"

"I'm okay," I lied. I kept my injured hand in my jacket pocket.

"If you change your mind, I got it all." Kang sucked furiously on the blue smoothie and then the yellow. His face turned red as the glasses drained. He slammed them on the table while continuing to jog in place. "I've been following the instructions. Every morning. Protein and swellers in one, vitamins and stabilizers in the other. No fat, dairy, or sugar. See, I'm committed?"

"Committed?"

"To getting off the bench," he said. He flexed for me while he continued to jog. His arms were slathered with something that shined under the fluorescent lights. "I've got the whole routine down. Activate my organs the moment I wake up with charcoal-infused amino water. Half cup of nut sand, half cup of fiber nobs, and a half cup of detoxed yogurt. Half hour weights, half hour resting muscle-stim, half hour overclocked cardio, and two hours hand-eye training in the SluggerSim. One, two, three, four, repeat. Been trying that Neanderthal fitness craze at night with the free weights. It works. My bones are like steel. I bet I could punch a woolly mammoth in the trunk right now."

"That's good," I said, sitting down in the room's only chair. He had a handful of photos on the wall. A couple video and a couple still. Official team photos. One of a young girl with angry eyes that reminded me of the Edenist I'd just seen at Reunion Square. Two of Kang and a woman smiling by beaches. One where the same woman was in a hospital bed. A framed copy of his Pyramid Pharmaceuticals contract. Nothing else.

"It feels good, it feels good. Yeah, good as hell." He whooped. Bent down and touched the ground. Then did a set of suicide sprints across his living room. I watched him go back and forth a few times. "Do you have your test kit? I'm ready to go."

"I'm not here to test you. They'll be doing that later." I'd need to be quick. Whoever he thought I was might be on their way. I looked out the window to see if any medical teams were walking up the street. "I'm just going to ask you some questions. It won't take long."

Kang came to a stop. His smile collapsed. "Fucking hell." He fell hard into the couch. Threw his inflated arms across the back and spread his legs wide. "Do you know how hard it is to get yourself all ready?" He gazed over his arms and legs as if he was selecting cuts at the butcher and the meat was himself. He shook his head again. "I'm humming on way more than the recommended doses here. I feel like I'm vibrating so hard I might come apart at the seams. I need to get into the playoff lineup. If I don't, I'm cut in the off-season for sure. What the hell am I supposed to do then?"

"You're looking good. I should know, I'm a scout." I figured some false encouragement might loosen his tongue.

"Thanks, brother!" His smile was toothy and his eyes were bright.

I pulled out an eraser cigarette. Began to light.

"Wow, please. Not in the house."

I put it out on my metal arm and slid the cigarette back in the pack.

"I'm here about JJ Zunz."

I expected Kang to freeze up, show me a sign that I knew about something I wasn't supposed to know about. But instead he bolted up like he'd just had a stimulant injected in his rear. "Do you have the money? Is it on you? I knew you didn't look like a doctor." He slapped his hands, then looked worried. "Shouldn't we be doing this at the club?"

"Which club?" I said.

"We only went to one club." Now Kang started moving slowly. He leaned back in a businesslike fashion. Flattened his voice. "The late Mr. Zunz owes me some money, that's all. I thought maybe you were delivering. God rest his soul."

"Money for what?"

Kang squinted one eye almost shut, looked at me with the other. His voice had a whine in it now. "Sorry, that's private. Let's just say he owed me some money and now that he's dead, I'm screwed. As usual."

"What was he buying from you? Headquarters isn't mad. We just need to know. We're trying to figure out how he died. Was it micronetics? Biometal pills?"

Kang looked at me like I'd dropped a centipede in his smoothie. He stood. "What the hell are you talking about? You think I'm selling illegal upgrades? I'm not risking my career. You know, I've never seen you before. I don't think you work at Pyramid at all!" Kang pulled out his screen. With his other hand, he flapped his fingers. "Hand over your credentials and I'll just give them a little check."

"Calm down. Wait a second." I was rusty with my interrogation techniques.

"Calm!" Kang threw his arms in the air. "Calm! Dude, you interrupted my routine before a playoff game. You don't have any money for me. Guess what? You better get me money. Now. Or we'll see how security makes you pay."

I debated whether I should try more drastic tactics. Kang might have been strong, but he didn't look like the type who would take kindly to even the softest roughing up. Not with the way he was obsessing over his physique.

Kang was still waving me at me to hand over whatever I had in my pockets. I made a fist of my broken hand. Figured I could get at least five punches in before something else in my hand broke.

Then the doorbell rang and the whole scene froze.

It rang a second time.

I looked at Kang warily and he looked back with exasperation. He put his screen next to the smoothie glasses. Walked over to the peep feed and sighed. "Jesus Christ. I'm never going to get my work-out finished."

Dolores walked in with her badge out, security code blinking. She looked at me, lifted one finger, and wagged it back and forth.

"Are *you* doing the exam? I need a couple minutes to get ready," Kang said, already forgetting about me. He began jogging in place again.

"I'm here for this one," she said, walking over and grabbing my collar. "Smith, I told you not to bother the players." She shook her head for Kang, gave him the what-can-you-do-about-underlings face. "A new hire. Overeager. I told him the players were off-limits in the playoffs, but he's a huge fan."

"Of me?" Kang said.

"He's got all your cards. Posters. Even owns your VR simulator."

"Really?"

Dolores stared at me with eyes grinning behind the goggles.

"Yeah," I said. I tried to nod enthusiastically. "I'm a big fan."

"And now he must go. We've got that presentation in twenty minutes, remember? I'm sorry he distracted you before the game. I'll put a good word in your file." She took my hand, yanked me up. Mouthed "you fucking asshole." Hurried me out the door.

"Hold up!" Kang yelled. "One second here."

I looked back to see him jogging in the doorway. He pointed at me.

"Don't you want an autograph?"

12

THE HUMAN PHONE

As Dolores flew us out of the Pyramid compound, she shook her head back and forth.

"Grief is no excuse for being stupid. Did you think Pyramid wouldn't notice two people using the same eye access? And did you think I wouldn't notice you gazing at me like a malfunctioning robot while we were fucking?"

"I'm sorry, Dolores. Stealing your iris was a dirty trick."

"You've been naughty. And not in the ways I enjoy. I should have let the Sphinxes' interrogation teams pull you apart."

I felt jittery and sick. I wasn't sure if it was because of the injury, the medicine, or the fact that I'd failed my brother again.

I took out another eraser, let the smoke dull me.

"How many of those poison sticks have you smoked today?" Dolores said. She rolled down a window and I blew into the sky.

"Not enough," I muttered. "I can still feel the tips of some of my fingers and a few of my toes."

Dolores reached over and grabbed my hand. Pulled off the glove.

Blue fluid had coagulated into plastic globs around the edges of the hole the Sassafras sisters had rammed through my palm.

"Jesus. Kobo. You need to see a doctor."

"Doctors are expensive."

We were approaching Manhattan now. I could see the storm wall snaking around the island. There were scattered buildings on the other side of the wall, like a child had colored carelessly outside the lines. Buildings sacrificed to the surging waters. The waves lapped at their foundation.

"Kang said Zunz owed him money. He's a clue. I need to go back."

"Are you going to steal my other eye?" Dolores said. I started to apologize again, and Dolores cut me off. "Oh, zip it, Kobo. You're going to make it up to me."

"With what?"

"With information. You've got information on the Yanks plans, information I can use to get a leg up on the competition. And maybe a bonus. I'm a little tight on money myself right now. My parents' medical bills eat up half my salary."

I said I was happy to tell her what I knew, but that it wasn't much. I was just a freelancer at the Yanks. I never sat in on the big meetings.

"Start with Arocha."

"Arocha?"

Around us, taxis honked and a couple blimp buses puttered by on a school trip to study clouds or something.

"You think the Yanks and the Mets were the only ones eyeing her? I was planning to scout her after the season."

I told her everything I'd found out about Arocha, and how I'd lost her to the Neanderthals. Although I skipped over the most embarrassing details. "She was working on zootech, close to a serum to stabilize them," I said. "Get around the genetically wired obsolescence."

"So she's an idealist. I wonder what on earth the Mets wanted her for," Dolores said, looking out toward the glittering city. She seemed to be calculating something. "Well, that's a start. We'll talk more later. Think of it as getting back at the Yanks as much as helping me out. And, hey, lucky you."

"Lucky?"

"You get a partner."

"You don't want to get mixed up in this."

"You should have thought of that before you crawled into my bed and scanned my eye to sneak into my employer's compound."

It was a fair point. I didn't argue.

"All right, drop me home and I'll send you what files I have." I looked out the window as we flew over white construction cranes that stood around Manhattan like the skeletons of enormous birds. It was a bright day with thinning smog. I was feeling hopeful and numbed.

Dolores laughed, flipped up the lenses of her goggles to stare me square in the face. "Kobo, I said I'd help you. Not be your chauffeur."

Dolores offered to drop me off outside of the Penn Station Hub. "Be a little more careful next time," she said as we landed.

"I'll try."

"Okay, now I'm going to go get screamed at about how I let someone steal my access. I'll just turn off my transcription and nod my head appropriately."

I watched her fly away.

The Penn Station Hub towered over me. It was composed of gigantic steel-and-glass arches and a central hub of tubes that spilled out in different directions. I could see them above me, snaking out toward the rest of the city, like the station was the dark heart of the city pumping blood to every distant limb.

Outside was a buzz of activity too. I pushed past a group of protestors projecting slogans in the air. Some about this war or that one, others about the last election or the next one. A group of Nu-Buddhists chanted by a levitating taco truck while a line of people waited to drop their blood into the TempVendor stations to see if they qualified for any job openings.

A thin man walked by with a placard flashing info on an Ill Uprising protest happening later that day. He caught my eye and raised his fist, saying it was time to "start the revolution."

"Isn't it always time?" I said.

"But this time it's really the time, comrade."

I bought two lab-grown tongue tacos and a double-hydration water. Ate on a bench while staring at a wall of screens cycling through the channels. The baseball news was just about the opening game of the World Series. What lineups were projected, who was injured, what the odds were at the bookies, and more accurately, what the odds were at the stock market. Investors were betting on the Sphinxes, and Monsanto's stock had tanked 4.3 percent since Zunz was killed.

Otherwise, the world had moved on. In the NNBA, the Plethora Suns had just acquired Maximus Diggs for a half-dozen lab prospects. In entertainment, the lead story was Stanton Dune severing both of his legs for his latest movie role. The limbs were being put in cryopots, and the talking heads were assuring fans they could be reattached when shooting finished. Dune was a Hollywood star known for extreme body modification. Taking intravenous lard to beef up for a sumo biopic, then working with a team of genochemists to shrink his bones down to fifteenth-century levels for a three-part historical epic on the War of the Roses. "I act with every part of my DNA," Dune told the reporter.

Overhead, a Plethora Emporium blimp floated like a gigantic airborne grub. I checked my bytewallet. Tried to calculate how many days I could last on the number it displayed. I was constantly checking numbers. Reopening my accounts and spreadsheets, hoping some magic of math had changed them. Now, like always, I was exactly as broke as I knew I'd be.

I did have enough to buy a cyber patch kit and another pack of erasers. A few seconds later a drone shaped like a pelican fell out of the sky, my purchases in its pouch. The drone was covered in plasti-flesh and feathers, but it was designed with Disney in mind. Gigantic eyes and a smile carved into the bright yellow beak. It was caught in some grotesque tug-of-war between machine, flesh, and cartoon.

I figured the animal-shape trend was nostalgia, a pining for the biodiversity we'd lost. A lot of the national parks had even purchased animal drones to roam around the hills and geysers, letting tourists pretend the wilderness was still wild. Personally, I disliked the pretense. I hoped the chrome robot style would make a comeback soon.

I slipped into the dank stench of the public restroom. Held my breath while I fixed my hand up as well I could. Which wasn't very well. At least the patch closed the gash and still let me bend all the fingers. But the damage had worked its way into my brain, made me start feeling a third arm. A crooked, injured thing flexing with pain. My original arm. The one that had been crushed in the cave-in, and then sawn off when I joined the Cyber League. The phantom limb was occupying the same space as my broken plastic and steel arm. A ghost trapped inside of another ghost.

Outside, I sat down, inspecting my hand and debating what to do next.

"You're looking rough, pal." The man sitting beside me wore tattered clothing, odd fungal growths erupting through the holes. He was so dirty he blended into the bench. When he smiled, I could see yellow gunk along his gums.

"Just having a bad day," I said. "Couple of days," I corrected.

"Bad life more like, am I right, pal? I can relate." He guffawed. A sweat smell, like fresh blood, followed his laugh. He reached into his pocket and held out some black pills in his trembling hand. "You want to buy some nuroids? Off the back of the blimp, if you know what I mean."

"I'm okay."

The pills smelled of burning oil. The casings were half dissolved. The man chuckled, then groaned. He grabbed his side and leaned forward. He'd pumped himself up with rancid upgrades like these. Black market stuff stretched with microplastics and laboratory run-off. There were people like him all over the country. Poisoning themselves with medicine. Infected from the inside out.

The tremor passed. He leaned back and made a gurgling sound. "Hey, you got any change you can spare, bud? I'm an oiler too. We gotta stick together. Screw the norm bods, right?" He lifted his many shirts to show me a kidney pump sutured into his side. Little dials spun and blinked. Home surgery. The skin was purple where the flesh met metal, poisoned red veins spidering off along his yellow stomach.

I told him I was broke and offered him an eraser "for the pain."

He looked confused, then angry. He snapped the eraser in half. Threw it at me. "I don't smoke that shit." He slapped his chest, sending the growths dancing. "This is all me. Pure reality! I'm not hiding from it."

"It helps with the pain. I smoke them all the time."

"Fuck you, asshole. It's my pain."

I nodded and walked off. Looked around for another bench, one that was empty.

When Zunz and I were kids, we used to have a couple guys like that sleeping in the park across the street from our burrow. If we failed a test or came home late for dinner, his mom would drag us upstairs to the ground floor, pull us to the park by the ear. "You fail at school, you end up the same as those bums."

Now, I was another run-in with the Sassafras sisters away from being like him. If I didn't find a way to pay off Sunny Day soon, they'd find a way to take back what they'd paid for. Reverse surgery. The only kind they didn't charge you for.

As I was looking up information about Kang on my screen, trying to find any info on his connection to Zunz, I noticed a man with an orange ball cap staring at me. He was trembling, barely able to stand upright. But somehow he managed to put one leg in front of the other until he was at my bench.

"Stay sitting, I've got a message for you." He spoke oddly, like he was surprised at each successive word.

"And you are?"

"This is Dereck T. Mouth the Second speaking. President, board chairman, and CEO of Monsanto Agriculture, Biotechnology, and Baseball Concerns."

I laughed. The Mouth was an older, balder man with gold skin and a bevy of bodyguards. This guy could have been a void-juice junkie begging for change.

"You look different on TV."

The man didn't respond. He stared at me, mouth half open and eyes dull as dishwater. "You're a funny guy, Kobo. This is the Mouth *speaking*. You're looking at my human telephone."

The man's hands twitched. He reached up and scratched under his hat, and I could see a dark metal tumor bulging under the brim.

"It's new tech. Beta testing on this beta nobody." The man's cadence was off. He'd speak slowly then quickly like he was playing catch-up. "Neural mesh melded onto his gray goop and receivers rammed into the temples. Repeats whatever I say." He paused for a second. Cocked his head. "Make a fortune. Next time a new disease pops up, hire a temporary body and do your errands without ever leaving home. Want to go on a vacation without dealing with the airport? Hire someone to see the globe through their eyes from your couch."

"Wouldn't it be easier to call me?"

"Easier but riskier. I'm an important man, Kobo. A rich man. I can't have anyone intercepting my communiqués. There's no better encryption than gray matter." The human telephone spasmed, started to fall, and I jumped up to grab him. His skin was so slippery with sweat I could barely hold him. He trembled in my arms. The Mouth went on talking through him. "Still some kinks to work out. But see how easy it was for my human telephone to get a fix on your real one? We're calling it Astral, as in Astral projection. I suggested Slaver but our publicists said that's a no-no. Now let's talk business."

I moved away from the man. He seemed to be standing up okay now. I could see there was a camera clipped onto his right ear. I thought about what Natasha and her thuggish friend had done to me back at the sushi restaurant. How the Mets hadn't protected my brother from dying at the plate. But maybe he had information I needed. So I squeezed a little honey into my voice.

"Hi, Mr. Mouth. I'm a lifelong Mets fan. To what do I owe the pleasure of your...do I call it a call?"

"The pleasure. Haha. You're like an old movie character. And don't call me Mr. Mouth. That's my father's name. Just the Mouth will do."

"Okay. The Mouth."

"You learn quick. Not as quick as I learn, or else you'd be the boss. Right? I need you to come to my office for a little face-to-face with my actual face. I plan to hire you."

"That's funny, your girl Natasha is the reason I'm unemployed."

"Natasha's not a girl. She's not even a woman. She's a Neanderthal. Tough as a triceratops skull and nearly as sharp." When he laughed, the man in front of me relayed the sound without even a smile. "But she likes you. She's actually the one who recommended you."

"For what job?"

"Finding the person who killed my beautiful slugger. Julio Julio Zunz."

"That's a coincidence, I'm already working on that on my own."

"No, no," he said. I could almost hear his finger wagging even though the human telephone's hand stayed at his side. "You're working for me."

Before I could think of protesting, the Mouth had hung up. The pupils of the man in front of me were dilated. He bent over. Retched a yellow puddle on the cement. He wiped his lips with his sleeve.

"I feel like a hand reached into my skull and used my brain for a stress toy," he said. He wiped his mouth again and then tried to smile at me. He held out a hand. "Hey, how about a tip?"

"Here," I said, passing him an eraser. "Smoke it till you can't feel a thing."

13

THE GOLDEN SMILE

The butler at Mouth Tower gave me the once-over two or three times. He was old, but his skin was taut around the skull. His face had been stretched and re-stretched so many times it was as thin as wax paper. You could see all the blue veins underneath.

I'd come straight from Penn Station and was in rough shape. There was dried fluid on my suit and my right arm shook involuntarily. A few sparks shot out now and then.

"*You're* meeting with the Mouth?" The words wheezed out of a narrow gap between his unmoving lips like steam escaping through a manhole cover. He was wearing a long blue coat interwoven with gold threads buttoned up to the neck with buttons that seemed to emit light. He bobbed back and forth behind the desk. "Dressed that way?"

"I'm not thrilled about it either."

"I'll have to check." The man ran a finger down his screen. "Double-check even. You are Mister…" He spun his gloved hand around in a circle.

"Tell him it's Kobo."

I lit an eraser, sent the anesthetic smoke out toward the butler in a little cloud. The man's lips curled back, like slugs shriveling under salt. He showed me his lengthy teeth.

"It can take a while," the butler said. "He's a very busy and *important* man."

I went to look at the directory by the mag lift. It listed everyone who lived here, but not their names. Only jobs. The Sushi Chef. The Barista. The Massage Therapist. The AI-puncturist. The Accountant. The Fitness Trainer. There were dozens of these people, the Mouth's own private economy of workers.

Still, they were the lucky ones. Much of the economy had been replaced by drones, algorithms, and zootech pack animals. The mega-rich considered employing humans to be a sort of charity. Or maybe it was simply more satisfying to order around people than robots.

"Oh, Mr. Kobo, Mr. Kobo," the man rasped. He bowed as if he'd been socked in the gut. He stayed in that perpendicular position and looked up with his blue-veined face. "The Mouth will see you now."

Riding up the marble mag lift, I started to worry I was walking into a trap. The Mets had the most access to Zunz. Control over his diet and upgrades. But even if you wanted to kill one of your own players, why do so in public with the cameras rolling? It would have been easy enough for Monsanto to kill him in secret in the compound.

The Mouth was sitting in an enormous wing chair at the back of a massive room. The walls were lined with nude golden statues. Living tissue. Flesh sculpted in re-creations of Renaissance paintings. Madonna and child. Venus trembling on a gigantic marble clam.

The sculptures moved, slightly and erratically. They were just flesh, no brains or nerves. Tubes on their backside pumped in nutrients and electrical currents. The biosculpting was equal parts impressive and disturbing. The fingernails needed trimming and a layer of dust was drying out the skin. They hadn't been cleaned in a while. When I looked closely, I thought I saw smudged handprints along the rumps.

"You like them?" the Mouth said, leaning back behind his gold-encrusted desk. "Imported from Milan. Cost a fortune, believe me."

The Mouth was gold too. Or at least a dull yellow. He had a napkin tucked into the unbuttoned collar of his French-cuff shirt. The napkin was a good idea. A little archipelago of ketchup stains had formed on the silk.

I sat down across from him, tried to look relaxed. Pretended sitting in a room where even the chairs were worth more than my entire life was no big deal.

Behind the Mouth, two people sat sporting blank expressions. The Neanderthals from the sushi restaurant. Natasha wearing a doctor's coat over her leopard-print suit, and then a big squat man built like a refrigerator in a black tailored suit. He had the same Neanderthal features as Natasha, except they were all smoothed out as if his genes hadn't bothered with the details.

The Mouth waved a hand without turning around. "You've met Natasha, my executive assistant. The gentleman in the corner, don't even worry about him. Coppelius is our liaison to the Department of Human Limits. Government stuff. Nothing concerning you."

Neither of the Neanderthals spoke, although Natasha gave me a little wave with her big hand.

The Mouth spoke though, nearly tripping over his words. "This is a mess. Very bad, I don't like it. I don't mean the burger. The burger is fantastic, beautiful. Have you had one? They call it the Mouth Burger. We'll be serving them in the stadium. The chefs who cooked this up are scientists! Literally. You've never tasted a burger until you've tasted mammoth. You'll feel like a caveman chomping on one of these. Give me a spear right now, I'd stab a dinosaur right through the lizard's skull! Ha ha."

He had a greasy, wet laugh. It sounded like it was dribbling down his chin.

"Never had mammoth, sir."

"We've got 'em all. Mammoth burgers, teriyaki tyrannosaur wings, saber-toothed gyro platters. Those cocksuckers thought they could avoid being eaten by going extinct. Bunch of buffoons. Didn't count on human ingenuity. We can eat anything these days. Eat the past, present, or future."

"It's a wonderful time to be alive," I said, tucking my injured hand in my pocket to hide the sparks.

"You know what I love about the caveman times? Everything was giant back then. Massive animals, huge trees. A time for heroes and ogres. Now dinosaurs have been shrunk to little lizards. Cold-blooded dorks. Pathetic."

"I thought they evolved into birds."

"Birds, lizards, whatever. Dinky pieces of shit either way. My point is they used to mean something. They used to inspire terror. You ever pee your pants at a sparrow? Of course not. We're bringing the scary ones back though. In burger form."

He took another bite and groaned with pleasure. "That's the stuff." A rivulet of grease dripped down his yellow cheek. His mouth was huge and wide. I'd heard it had been surgically extended about half an inch on each side. When he smiled I could see all the way to his molars. "The burger I like. This thing with Zunz I don't like. Hate it. He was a heck of an investment. I like juice squirting out of my burgers, not my players. You understand?"

I pulled back my lips into a straight line, pretended it was a smile. "Yeah, I understand."

There was a freagle in a cage next to him, beak pecking on the wire. It hopped like a frog, but when the Mouth put a bit of meat through the slot the squawk was all eagle. Monsanto had created the freagles on a government contract for Newman's midterm election campaign. Newman had warned that changing climate was killing off the patriotic species and it was time for new splices that would "eat up the foreign fauna spreading through the homeland." Now the government was selling them in collectable editions to help pay off the Franco-German debt hounds.

"Look at this, a creature that didn't exist until last year eating a creature that went extinct millions of years ago." He spread his hands, smiled with his extra-wide lips. "The future. We're growing the future in the Monsanto labs. Where were we?"

"You were going to tell me why you wanted to see me."

"This is a man who gets to the point," the Mouth said to the freagle. He rubbed the feathered head, pressing down so it couldn't hop away. It croaked a small squawk. "You know that they killed my star player? My JJ Zunz?"

"Zunz was my brother. Yeah, I've heard."

The Mouth looked confused. His face wrinkled up like a rotting squash. He turned around to Natasha while pointing back at me.

"Did we know Kobo here was Zunz's brother?"

Natasha walked behind the Mouth's chair. Ran her thick fingers across his wrinkled bald head. "Yes. Adopted. He's got a personal interest in this matter. That's why I suggested him for this assignment."

She looked at me and scrunched up one eye. A wink, I guessed.

The Neanderthal man stayed sitting, regarding everything with large bored eyes beneath his brow. Every now and then he adjusted his tie.

The Mouth nodded. He looked at me and started speaking as if the thoughts had just come into his mind. "Your personal interest in this matter is why I wanted to give you this assignment. Plus, I hear you're a wonderful scout. I gobble up all the winning scouts I can. I eat you guys up and take your power. Shit out a winning baseball team."

"What's the job exactly?"

"Solving Zunz's murder." He raised a golden finger for emphasis. "And letting the press and police know that Monsanto isn't responsible. That's important too."

"Surely there are enough cops and reporters on the Monsanto payroll for that."

The Mouth laughed. Little chunks of mammoth were stuck to his chapped golden lips. "Bluntness. I like it, but don't do it again. I'm the blunt one. Don't worry about the police and reporters. We've got that covered. I need someone who knows baseball, ugly underbelly and all. Because someone in baseball killed Zunz. Some jealous bastard working for the White Mice or Novos or the Sphinxes. That bastard Tuscan tried to trade for Zunz last year. Could be him. Who knows? Well, you're going to know, right?"

It wasn't that I didn't want the job. I needed it, desperately. But I wanted to know why.

"What about these two?" I said, gesturing toward the two Neanderthals. "They seem like they know how to get their hands dirty while keeping yours clean."

The Mouth shrugged and placed his hands on his desk. "They have their big hands full with other matters. Remember, I've got a whole empire to run. Zunz was a top player, but he's only a player. Baseball is baseball, sure, but it's also only baseball. Upgrades are business. We have dozens of divisions, scores of sectors."

"Zunz's killer is a top priority," Natasha said.

"Sure, sure. Listen to Natasha. She's your contact."

"We heard you were snooping around the Sphinxes compound

today." She smiled at my change of expression. "We have our spies like everyone else. Don't worry. We think that shows initiative. Did you learn anything?"

I figured if they knew I broke in, they probably knew who I'd visited. So there was no point in lying. "I went to see a player named Jung Kang. Zunz had mentioned him to me before…well. Before. I thought he might be a thread to pull on but didn't get much of a chance to tug."

I saw the government liaison, Coppelius, type something into his screen.

"Good. We have reason to believe that the Sphinxes were involved in the unfortunate matter," Natasha said. "Keep tugging. See what it unravels."

"What reasons?" I said.

"We're hoping you'll find them out," Natasha said.

The Mouth was looking down at his hands. They were pale, wrinkled things. The withered fingers looked like the hot dogs Zunz and I would buy from Prospect Park carts after practice. Waterlogged and the color of sand. "I'm losing my color. Natasha! Give me another shot."

The Neanderthal opened the white coat, revealing a lineup of syringes. She took one out and inserted it into the Mouth's neck. Smiled a little as she plunged.

The Mouth gurgled in either pain or pleasure. His head flipped back and his mouth hung open. I could see his tongue squirming behind the teeth. His skin started to grow brighter, a metallic sparkle in the epidermis. He shook his head around, ran his hand over his smooth lemon dome. Grabbed a mirror from the desk. "Gorgeous," he said.

Natasha flashed the syringes for me, offering me a shot of canary juice or whatever the hell it was. I shook my head.

"The World Series is about to start," the Mouth said. "This is a big marketing opportunity for us. We've got a lot of new products to roll out. We can't have the Zunz business dragging us down. You solve this murder before the World Series is over, and Monsanto will pay off your medical debt. How much was it, Natasha?"

She said the number, my number. She had it down to the decimal point.

Suddenly, I felt like my bones were filling up with bubbles. I was almost floating. I couldn't remember living without massive medical debt pinning me down. Couldn't remember what it was like to wake up and not immediately think of the gigantic number crushing me. If I had my debt cleared, I'd be free of the Sassafras sisters. Free of spending hours looking at spreadsheets, trying to figure out how to escape the numbers in the cells. And I'd be free to buy new upgrades. Good ones. The ones I'd been dreaming about for years.

Then I dropped back to earth. The Mets were without their star player. They didn't have anyone who could be plugged into the hole Zunz's corpse left in the lineup. And even if they could make it a series, somehow, I'd only have about a week to solve the case.

"That's not a lot of time. I'm a scout, sir. Not a detective."

"The Mouth."

"What?"

"You said 'sir.' It's the Mouth. Just the Mouth. And I hear you're more than just a scout, I hear you're a great scout. Or a pretty good one at least. Is that right, Natasha? I assume you're good or we wouldn't hire you. Look, when I was a kid, a scout drove around like a dummy to different high school games. He ate hot dogs with the parents in the shitty aluminum stands and looked at the bodies of young boys. Disgusting." The Mouth spat a little on his desk. The frightened freagle hopped away from the glob. "We don't do that anymore. You scouts do real covert operations. My own personal army of ninjas. I send you to grab the scientists I need. Not watch little boys play T-ball like a pervert. That's what I like about the modern game. It's more civilized. We've got plenty of cops we can rely on, but I want someone who's a little, how do you say, above the law too. Natasha." He snapped his greased fingers at her name.

Natasha walked over with a small blue device in her hands. She asked for my palm. "The flesh one, please."

I held it out and she stroked it with her large fingers, tickling my lifeline. She touched the device to my thumb pad. Clicked. A needle went in.

"Ouch."

She gave me a small stone-age smile. "The thumb chip will open all the doors you need opened in Monsanto Meadows. You're officially a Mets employee."

I wondered how many ID chips I had in my hand. Every job I'd ever worked had injected me with one, but none of them paid to take them out. Just deactivated them and shoved you out the door.

"I could use some of the money up-front," I said. "For expenses."

The Mouth guffawed. "That's a good one. I didn't get rich paying for jobs people haven't done."

"We can give you a modest per-day stipend," Natasha said. "But I assure you, we'll be good for the total amount. If you solve the case."

"Guess I've got no choice."

Natasha guided me to the door. Shook my newly chipped hand. "Welcome to the team."

14

THE RETIREMENT HOME

While I mulled over my agreement with the Mouth, trying to force myself to like the taste, I got a call. It was the nursing home Zunz had stashed Mrs. Z, my adopted mom, inside after her mind had faded away. Early-onset Alzheimer's fast-forwarded by decades strapping her brain into a remote-control helmet at work.

The retirement home director, Dr. Finnegan, said he needed to talk to me about "future payment arrangements" given Zunz's untimely death.

"Is now the time to be talking to me about that?"

Finnegan's voice was high and pleased with itself. "We here at Second Youth Assisted Condos merely want to ensure a continuation of care for our thriving residents. You wouldn't pull up a flower right when it's blooming, would you?"

I thought I'd tear up the whole garden bed if it wiped the smug grin off the man's hologram face, but I said I'd come. I felt like a bad enough son already. I hadn't been to visit in months and I was dreading it. She'd surely been informed of JJ's death, but with her leaky memory I'd have to be the one to break it to her again.

I took the supraway uptown and arrived at a tall brick building with rows of hedges enclosed in glass around the front. There were sealed-off balconies on every floor, each with a couple people sipping tea and glaring down at me. As I walked inside between the polished marble columns and rows of exotic flowers edited to survive indoors, I realized I'd made a mistake. Even seeing the bill on this place was likely to give me a heart attack.

Second Youth cost a lot and the money went right into the residents' veins. They were getting the best treatments. The latest surgeries. Hell, looking at them jog by I wouldn't have been surprised if they were getting daily sponge baths of biopharm preservatives.

Dr. Finnegan greeted me at the front desk. He wore an emerald-green suit and had a thick grin. His dimples were perfect divots in his cheeks. He led me past a glass room where octogenarians were lifting weights and contorting themselves into yoga poses.

"At Second Youth, you really do get a second youth," Finnegan said. He gestured toward a bowl of green and pink virility pills by the wine dispenser. Winked and leaned over to whisper. "Don't worry, all residents get disease screenings."

"It's pretty wonderful," I said, plastering on a smile. "Mind if I visit my mother before we get into finances?"

"Certainly. Of course. You'll find her in the game room, I believe. Just signal an orderly if you need any help." Finnegan patted one of the robot orderlies on the shoulder. It was shaped like a svelte panda and had a beaming red light on its forehead. "You know this is real fur? Grows from a wetframe right under the casing. The residents just love petting our orderlies. I think you'll find you get your money's worth here. Here, give it a hug."

Finnegan flashed me his million-dollar grin. His title said doctor, but he was a salesman through and through.

"I'll pass on the hug."

"Suit yourself."

I strolled toward the game room sniffing the sanitized air. Small cleansing drones with microbe catchers were floating around the ceiling. The residents ambled around looking confused. They might have been preserved on the outside, but their brains were a different matter. The human mind was the one thing the biopharms hadn't cracked. Fingers, bones, and hearts were easy. Gray matter was another matter entirely. Money could buy you a few more years of clarity and short-term boosts, but eventually your mind would turn into the same mush as everyone else's.

Past a long aquarium of fluorescent lobsters and a media room where red-faced pundits screamed about illegal immigrants with genetically enhanced lungs, I found the games tables. It was quieter than the other rooms. Residents punched the interfaces at random, eyes vacant. I found Mrs. Z by the chessboard. She was studying a rook in her hand. She placed it across the board in front of her opponent's queen. The board buzzed. *Illegal move.*

"Hush," she murmured.

The man on the other side of the board was asleep. Drool dangled from his chin like a man on a bridge working up the courage to leap.

I stood there, watching her. She looked beautiful still. Barely aged a day in fifteen years. I was half expecting her to jump up and offer me a tray of pastelitos, saying "Julio's waiting for you in the bedroom with a new action figure." Or to tell me to keep my coat on because she was going shopping and she needed "a big strong man" to carry the groceries.

Watching her, my gut felt like it was being wadded up and tossed away. Mrs. Z had taken me when no one else would, and I'd forgotten her here. Told myself she was getting the high-end treatment thanks to Zunz's money with no financial help from me, so what right did I have to visit?

Then the board buzzed again as she grabbed one of his knights. She turned to look at me. "Shut up this machine."

"Hi, Mrs. Z," I said.

She smiled politely. Crow's feet fluttered around her eyes, but her hair only had a scattering of gray among the black. She pointed at the board with the rook in her hand.

"It's me."

She ran her hand through her hair. "Sí. Sí. Of course." She looked away, then back. Then her smile widened as the recognition stirred in her mind. "Bobo? My Bobo."

"Aww. You know I hate that nickname, Ma."

She reached out for my elbow. "My little darling. What happened to your arm?"

"They cut it off and gave me this metal one. Don't you remember?"

She let my hand go. Shook her head. "You always were clumsy."

Behind her the window was a drop screen that displayed trees blowing in a summer breeze. A robin flew toward us, chirped, and sped off into the digital distance.

I pulled up a chair. The snoring man across the board didn't mind. His drool had made the leap and landed on his chest.

I took her hands in mine, making sure not to squeeze too hard.

"How are you doing? Are they treating you well?"

She nodded, looking over my shoulder. I glanced back and saw one of the panda robots standing there, staring at us.

"It's good to see you." She smiled, her eyes crinkling in that magic way I remembered from childhood. But then she frowned. Pointed toward the drop screen of a fake outdoors. "They won't let me go outside. They say the air is poison."

"Yeah, smog is thick as phlegm today."

"Well, I like to walk," she said. "I've always liked to walk."

"I'll talk to Finnegan. Maybe they can get you a filter helmet," I said. I started to choke up. "Ma. Listen. Did they tell you about JJ?"

"Julio." She waved her hand. "He doesn't visit me. Nobody comes here."

I could feel the hot tears inching toward the corners of my eyes.

"Julio passed away. Someone killed him."

This dislodged something in her mind. Tears welled up, spilled out. She squeezed my hand.

I squeezed back.

"I'm trying to find out who. No, I'm *going* to find out."

The moment passed and her expression was wiped clean. She smiled and asked me if I wanted to play a game of chess.

"Did he ever mention a man named Kang? Jung Kang. It's important."

She waved a hand in front of her face. "Kang was a girl. Kenneth, I'm hungry."

"What? What do you mean?"

"Never liked her. Too preachy."

"What are you talking about? Jung Kang?"

I wondered if Kang had transitioned. It wasn't unheard of in the league. But I didn't think so. The way he'd gawked at my cybernetic arm, I doubted he'd ever risked changing himself beyond what a team doctor demanded.

"You tell Julio to find someone—" she started to say, but then she stopped and leaned forward. She was close enough I could smell her lilac perfume. Same one she'd used for decades. I could see she was looking past me. I looked over my shoulder and the panda orderly seemed to still be staring at us. "I don't like the nasty man with the red hair," she whispered.

"What man?"

She tapped the back of her neck, right where the spine was

showing beneath her hair. There was a small, puffy scar. "He keeps poking me with needles."

"They probably just need to test you. They're doctors."

She shook her head back and forth, lip jutted. "He has an ugly face. And the needles go so deep."

I started to ask her if she knew what specific tests they were doing, but then I felt a hand alight on my shoulder. I looked up and Finnegan had appeared, grinning.

"We do need to have that talk. Plus, it's lunchtime. Isn't that right, Mrs. Zunz? Chicken and dumplings today!"

She nodded, face blank. Then she reached for her queen, and the board buzzed again. She grunted. Looked at Finnegan. "Can you fix the board?"

"I'll have a technician take a look pronto." He turned to me. "Shall we?"

I said my goodbyes and told her, "I'll visit again soon." I started to say, "I promise," but stopped myself.

Finnegan guided me to the office, while offering his condolences about my "recent bereavement" through his grin. I wondered if he'd fixed his mouth that way permanently to please the residents.

"I'm more of a basketball fan myself. Go Glaxo Celtics! But I'm told the late Mr. Zunz was one heck of a slugger."

The office was old-fashioned with wood furniture and a set of busts on each side of the desk. The busts were pale and freckled, with a tinge of green to the skin. Retro biosculptures, a thin layer of chlorophyll-encoded flesh stretched over the marble. Finnegan wiped the busts with his handkerchief. "Condensation is a real pain. A lot of yeast and bacterial infections with these. This is Paul Beaumont Finnegan Senior and my grandfather, Silas Beaumont Finnegan the Second. The previous directors. This is a family institution, where we respect our elders. Which brings me to Mrs. Alejandra Zunz."

"You don't look all that related," I said. Ignoring the green tinge, the statues were white as milk while this Finnegan was at least three shades darker.

"Well, my family has a few roots in the subcontinent. But they didn't have racial-adjustment surgery back then."

I started to pull out an eraser. Finnegan frowned.

"Not around the sculptures, please."

"Speaking of my mom, she isn't happy with one of the doctors. The one with red hair."

Finnegan steepled his fingers and drummed on his lips. "No one with red hair here. Happy to show you the staff directory, but she must be mistaken. I'm afraid her memory is, well, spotty to say the least. We have some exciting new therapies we're planning to try soon. Assuming her continued stay in our care."

"So what happens if someone can't pay?" I said, sliding the pack back into my jacket. "You chop them up and sell their organs on the exchange?"

Finnegan's smile stayed glued on. "Please, nothing like that. Although we do have a legal right to recoup expenses."

"Listen, I'm not sure what you think I earn, but—"

The man laughed. "Oh, please. Mr. Kobo. Don't worry. We're not asking *you* to pay. Our facility has a strong relation with Sunny Day Healthcare Loans and we're aware of your financial obligations. You came right up on the warning list." He laughed affably. "No, no. We just need your authorization."

"Authorization?"

The man was riffling through a file of screens. He pulled one out and slid it across the desk. "Mr. Zunz had several tracts of real estate around the city on file as guarantees. You were listed as the executor in case anything unfortunate happened. I assume the estate has been in touch with you?"

I shook my head.

"Ah, well, corporate approval can take a while. Once they do, you can authorize a sale to cover her fees. There are some fetching assets here. Mr. Zunz was a very thoughtful son."

There were several properties on the screen. His cloud condo in Midtown, part ownership of a ridiculous restaurant called Balls, where the plates were shaped like baseball gloves and every dish was molded into a sphere, and a couple sky parking lots downtown. I was familiar with all those, had even eaten at Balls with Zunz and a couple of his Mets business partners. The meatballs weren't bad, but the croquettes were soggy. There was another property I'd never seen before. A tiny two-story house on Governors Island. I'd never heard Zunz mention it. It made sense that he'd have a place to hide away from the paparazzi and the fans and everyone else who bothered him, but I'd never thought I'd be on that list.

"I'm sure you'll want to consult with some brokers. However, I might suggest the Midtown condo should prove more than adequate."

"Yeah, I'll need to talk to some people." I stood up. "Probably a lot of people. Want to check all my boxes. Can you send me a copy of these files?"

Finnegan was still grinning. "Just don't check them too long. Our grace period is, well, not the most graceful."

I returned his smile. "That seems to be the way these days."

15

THE SECRET HOUSE

I turned off game one of the World Series after the Mets pitcher gave up two runs in the third inning on a wild pitch. They were already down 1–0 after Sanchez had homered on the first at bat and it was depressing me to watch. The team was playing confused, awkward. Like Zunz had been their compass as much as he'd been mine.

The ferries to Governors Island shut down at night, so I spent the rest of the evening following clues that didn't lead anywhere. Remembering fragments Zunz had said and cold-calling friends to see if they could fill in the blanks. Zunz's high school coaches, old neighbors from the burrow, ex-teammates. They all told me the same thing. That they were sorry. That they couldn't believe this had happened. And that they didn't know a single useful thing.

In the morning, I grabbed a pair of shock slugs. The one I'd been carrying around had died, dissolving into yellow mush. I headed downtown and took a seat in the back of the earliest ferry sub. Held up my screen, pretended to watch the news. The scroll said *Sphinxes Turn No-Zunz Mets into No-Hit Mets, Win Game One 4–0.*

As we sank, the water through the porthole was the greenish-brown of muck at the bottom of a garbage can. From the seafloor, broken structures jutted up—the skyscrapers at the edge of Manhattan that had toppled before the engineers built the storm wall. The wall couldn't hold the seas down, but it could protect real estate investments during the hurricane season.

A school sub loaded with high schoolers went by, yellow lights pulsing in the murk. The kids were looking down at their screens, eyes glazed over.

Governors Island had been a dinky clump of land for hundreds of years. As the sea levels rose and washed away Manhattan real estate, the city scrambled for new places to build. They were purchasing giant tankers of sand from the expanding Mextexan desert to shore up the underdeveloped island. Create a new floating tax base that wouldn't need a storm wall. At least not for a few decades.

When the submarine ferry emerged, I could see the large floating ships spewing fountains of sand into the harbor. Huge tan arcs from every direction. They looked like a flock of robotic penguins vomiting up breakfast for their young.

Construction of the new condos was only partially complete, and the existing houses were all below three stories. It was a little time capsule with an old army fort in the center surrounded by vacant fields of grass. Lawns, I guess you'd call them. The roads were tiny paths that couldn't even fit a creepeasy. A few oak trees lived, barely, their bark coated in gray slime.

The house that matched the address was all wood, with pale blue paint molting off the facade. It had white columns that had been stained brown over the years. I could smell mold in the boards. I didn't even need to pull out one of my shock slugs to short-circuit the door. I knocked it open with a few swift kicks.

I pulled out my gun and went inside.

The interior was a museum. Wooden chairs, an antique Ikea couch, and a large LCD TV. I walked slowly into the living room. The walls were covered with posters of old New York baseball stars: Derek Jeter, Mike Piazza, Aaron Judge, Barack O'Neil, Colton Diaz, and Matt Haddock. Heroes from back when the game was pure.

A bookshelf filled with knickknacks lined one wall. I realized I knew all these items. They were Zunz's and mine, the toys and posters we'd had as kids. Framed photos I'd thought had been lost by movers and action figures I'd assumed had been thrown away decades ago.

For a couple minutes, I sat on the couch and absorbed it all. My childhood laid out in objects. I could picture myself and Zunz on the scratchy blue carpet of our burrow, playing with those toys. I sucked in all the memories like my mind was a giant vacuum. I'd never realized Zunz cared about those days as much as I did.

Then I got angry.

Zunz had taken our things and set up his own little oasis away from the world. It didn't surprise me that Zunz had a secret home. Most star athletes did. I could understand that he needed a place to hide from the paparazzi, but did it have to be a place he also hid from me?

I picked up a plastic Mr. Met figurine, a rotund and beaming baseball head on a human body. When Monsanto bought the Mets, they kept the name and colors but ditched the mascot. The new one was a floating metal hexagon that fired lasers into the air between innings. I dropped the anthropomorphic ball. Decided to finish my snooping and then get the hell out of there.

When I went into the kitchen, I was surprised to find a jug of unspoiled milk and an open box of cereal. The sheets in the bedroom were ruffled. There was a headset plugged into the wall. I wondered if a squatter had broken in after Zunz died.

In the back of the closet, beneath a rack of vintage MLB uniforms, there was a black security box. I could hear the electric current humming through it. I didn't see the key anywhere, so pulled out one of the two shock slugs I'd brought with me. It slithered into the lock. The box sparked and the poor creature melted with a hiss that sounded like a cry. The room filled with a rank smell.

The box popped open.

Inside there was something black and metal in a velvet-lined case. I unfolded it. Held it up. It was a black, fleshy mask with small nodes dappling where the skull would go. There was a thick red tube around the base of the mask. The preservation system, I assumed. On the back, near the base of the neck, was a circular black device that looked like a robot's mouth. When I clicked it on, a metal spike of a tongue shot out and nicked my finger.

It was strange and also somewhat familiar. The nodes around the skull looked similar to the bands Mrs. Z had worn to sync up with the orange-picking machines when Zunz and I were kids, except the tech here was much newer. The only other thing inside the box was a small chipcard stamped *The Janus Club: An Out-of-Body Experience That's Out of This World*. There was a Midtown address underneath.

Was this the club Kang had mentioned? It certainly looked like the kind of place that would be discreet enough for dirty deals. I folded up the mask and put it and the card in my pocket, then went to look around more.

These old buildings weren't wired for modern machines, so I turned on the old LCD wall mount. I scrolled through the recently watched videos. Most of them were what I was expecting. Short clips of cute new zootech creatures crawling their first crawls, news highlights, war updates, and reruns of pre-Dissolution era baseball games. But in the middle of these were videos from a channel called the Diseased Eden with titles like *Pick Your Side in the Coming Flesh War* and *Juice and Oil: Corporate Corporeal Control*. Edenist propaganda,

I assumed. Not the kind of thing you'd expect a Future League player to watch.

I played the first video and a fat man with a beard as scraggly as a tumbleweed stood in the middle of a flowering field. On his right, there was a meal printer. On his left, a bloated feathered creature that I realized was a headless chicken. The neck ended with an inflamed nub topped with a metal ring for the feeding tube. I'd been eating headless meat for years along with everyone else, but I'd never bothered to look at one up close.

"The Buddhists believe the body is the vessel of the soul," the fat man said. "What happens to our soul when it resides in a mixture of circuits and poisons? Does not the vessel sink the soul? The corporations call them upgrades, but they are downgrading our spirits. Reducing us. Christians taste the body of their lord, drink the blood of his blood and eat the flesh of his flesh. Society offers us only the poisons of its labs, the wires of its factories."

I sat back, tossing an old leather baseball between my hands. I'd never heard Zunz express any sympathies toward groups like the Edenists. At most he'd smile, shrug, and say, "Hey, some of them buy jerseys too." The Edenists didn't just dislike people who ate modified meat. They hated anyone who upgraded at all. What could a biopharm baseball player like Zunz have to do with them? Zunz was tuned up with as many upgrades as anyone else in the Future League. Next to an Edenist, he'd been so modified he might as well be a different species.

Had Zunz himself started having doubts about what he'd been swallowing and injecting all these years? Did he come to this house, surrounded by antiques, wishing he could rewind his body to a previous form?

A young girl came on the screen. She looked so reedy I thought the wind would snap her in half. She held a knife as big as her forearm.

"Flesh above machine," she said. She stabbed the knife through the top of the meal printer. It shattered. "Blood above poison," she said and sliced into the chicken. It shook noiselessly, struggling to get away as she sawed. The chicken split apart. Two headless halves inflating and deflating, blood seeping out onto the ground.

Yes, it was the girl. The one I'd seen by the human Zunz statue in Reunion Square. The one I was almost sure had been in the photo in Kang's house. And, yes, I was shocked to see her materialize on-screen.

I was even more shocked when I turned around and saw her face pressed against the windowpane.

16

THE ISLAND CHASE

It doesn't matter how upgraded you get. How many steroids or growth hormones or tendon stabilizers you swallow. If you don't use your body, it starts to decay. Science hasn't been able to change that. The physical doesn't want to remain. It wants to destroy itself, to dissolve. Finish its decades-long race into the dirt.

I was reminded of this as I ran after the girl, huffing and wheezing.

She had a good lead on me. My lungs inflated rapidly and sadly, like a fish tossed on land. The girl, though, could run. She had the natural adrenaline of youth. By the time I was out the door, she was already far down the path, weaving between the trees. Her little legs were a blur.

"Wait," I shouted.

She didn't.

We ran out of one row of houses and into another. She was several hundred yards ahead of me, then stopped in front of the old military fort. Knelt. Coughed up something wet and red. Looked back at me, ran again.

I followed her into a cobblestoned courtyard inside the abandoned military fort. Old houses ringed the yard. Soldier barracks, I guessed, from some ancient war.

I spun around, looking for the girl. Saw her spindly legs slide through a broken window.

I balked at the front of the house. The windows were caked over with black gunk. Layers and layers of it in thick and gloopy coatings like a child's painting. A sticky film stretched off the window when I touched it. I knew that substance. Void spit.

I jerked the doorknob, wasn't surprised when it didn't turn. I smacked it a few times with my shoulder, then cracked the door open with a kick. It took a while to push it inward.

The smell rolled out in a fetid cloud. The stench was followed by moans.

Three dozen people were inside. Maybe more. Mainly adults, but some had toddlers tucked into their armpits. Their clothes were tattered, bodies dressed in dried fluids. Blood. Shit. Drool. Void juice. The same substances shellacked the floor. Broken steel dispensers were scattered around the room. The people barely moved and when they did the dried void spit screeched.

I pinched my nose to block the smell. The people let out weak moans. They weren't capable of noticing me. They'd been transported away from everything. Lost in their own bodiless worlds.

A vanishing house. Where the dull jobs came to disappear. Eraser cigarettes weren't enough for them. They shot a pure form of the substance directly into their decaying veins. An eraser helped dull your senses. Let you unwind after work or calmed you before an important meeting. It was a kind of inhalable anesthesia, got you nice and numb. But an eraser was diluted, a drop per cigarette. I'm not saying it was a healthy habit, but it was a habit. The pure stuff was a disease.

Originally, void juice was sold by doctors after you upgraded. A way to ease your body into accepting new organs and alterations. It was too powerful to stay legal. If you injected yourself with a thimbleful of void juice, you didn't just forget your pain. You forgot pain existed. The black liquid went through your veins, dulling each part one by one. Your senses were cut off. Bones and muscles and organs were a distant dream.

At least from the dull job's point of view. The rest of us could smell their bodily functions continuing without their knowledge.

It was the type of sight that made you think maybe the Edenists had a point.

I stepped carefully around the bodies, my shoes squishing on the soggy floorboards. I listened for the girl.

The stairs creaked.

I followed.

When I emerged onto the roof, she was gone. I looked around every antenna and filter box big enough to hide a child. The girl had given me the slip.

I sat on the edge of the roof. Tried to catch my breath.

Down below, all I could see were the tiny houses of the island and, in the distance, the gigantic silver buildings of Manhattan rising out of the sea like the silver fingers of some bathing robot god. They soared up out of the murky smog of the city floor into the sky where, beneath the sagging white bellies of clouds, clusters of glittering cloud condos nested. Elsewhere, black ocean liners skimmed the green water around Manhattan. Yellow cranes dropped floors on top of each other, stacking new buildings up to the sky. If the city was a living thing, it was a mutating, cyborgian one. Constantly growing, expanding, and shooting out new bizarre limbs. A collaged monster changing and expanding itself each day.

The ferry sub honked in the distance, getting ready to make its next departure.

Only a few people walked around the island. Tourists mostly. A class of history students studying the preserved houses. Plus a whole crowd down by the ferry stop, waiting to board. None of them looked like Edenists, much less like the girl.

My bionic eye stored a few hours of footage, and I rewound the feed. Past the vanishing house, past the trees and buildings, all the way back to that face in the window. I'd barely had time to start recording before she sprinted away. Her face was gaunt but somehow familiar. Like someone I used to know decades ago. Light brown skin, with a slight gap between the front teeth. I captured a still. A small dimpled girl with fierce eyes and brown hair.

I called Sergeant Okafor. Started to explain what happened as soon as they appeared on my screen.

"Kobo, slow down. Are you staying out of trouble?"

"I don't have time for a lecture, Sil. Get to this location." I shared my coordinates. "It's a vanishing house. About thirty bodies, and at least twenty of them still alive."

"That's a job for vice management."

"Then tell vice. They need help, and the building needs fumigation. Call them, and then look up this girl," I said, sending a still from my eye.

"Who the hell is this?"

"A girl. An Edenist, I think."

Okafor tapped their fingers against their coffee mug. "Maybe this doesn't mean shit to you, but I'm in homicide. I investigate murders, likes Zunz's. Not drug users or fanatics."

"It's about Zunz. I'm at his house."

Okafor tossed their hands in the air, gave me that look they used to give when Zunz and I were planning a prank and didn't invite them. "Kobo, fucking hell. I told you not to get involved."

"He was my brother, Sil."

"And I've known him since I was a baby. It kills me too."

The ferry horn honked in the distance like a dying prehistoric bird. I tried to pitch my own voice for pity.

"Can you do me this one favor? Find this girl for me and let me talk to her. Just for a couple minutes, face-to-face. That's all I'm asking."

"Christ, Kobo."

"Sil, you've known both of us for decades. I need this one thing. Someone killed Zunz. Maybe one of her Edenist friends. I'll never be able to live with myself if I don't talk to her."

"Fine. If I can even find her, I'll let you talk to her. We'll call you a CI. Then you're giving me a statement with everything you know and backing off."

"Thanks, Sil. I'll owe you one. Or two. Or twenty."

"Kobo. Hold on. Kobo, do not—" I clicked off the call as I saw the girl speed down the road on a hover bike. Heading down the hill toward the docks. The ferry sub sat waiting, bobbing in the dark green waters.

I took the fire escape down, leaping as fast as I could. The structure was old and rusted, barely clinging to the wall. It almost cracked off the bricks and ended my case right there. But I made it down, dangled from the last floor. Dropped.

The girl ditched her bike right at the edge of the crowd and squeezed herself on board.

My lungs were rebelling. Trying to convince me they'd pop inside my chest if I didn't stop running. I didn't listen to them.

The horn honked.

There wouldn't be another sub ferry to Manhattan for half an hour. Only the surface ferries to Brooklyn would be left.

I got up to the throng of people, panting. "Hey," I shouted. I could see her tunic weaving between the tourists. I pushed closer. Reached out. She was in front of me, maybe a foot beyond my fingertips.

"Hey," I said. "One second!"

Then I ran into a twin wall of muscle and steel. Next thing I knew, I wasn't looking at the backs of heads but the bottoms of clouds. I could taste a little blood in my mouth.

"Kobo, we thought we'd find you here."

"We found you. We did!"

The Sassafras sisters stood over me like two large axes ready to chop apart a log.

Wanda knelt on my chest and grabbed my cybernetic arm, pinned it to the pavement. "You went on this lovely trip and couldn't pick up the phone to invite us?"

"He can't use a phone? Really?"

"Clam it, Brenda."

The ferry sub operator was scanning around for stragglers. I saw the girl look back at me, smile, and shake her head. She waved, then went beneath.

Brenda kicked me when I started to shout.

"You ladies could ask me on a date. You don't have to follow me around."

"You used your account to buy a ferry ticket, dum-dum," Wanda said. "Sunny Day monitors anyone late on payment."

I tried a new tactic. "Listen, Brenda Sassafras. Wanda Sassafras. Did I ever tell you Sassafras is a beautiful word? Rolls around the tongue like a breath mint. Let me be straight with you. I need to get on that ferry. I'm chasing someone who will help me get a real check. One to pay you off for good."

"No ferry, Kobo. That's not an original trick."

"It's not a trick. And you already broke my hand."

"You have another hand," Wanda offered.

"Let's use the hammer, Wanda. Come on. The hammer!"

"Okay." She patted her sister on the shoulder. "You can use the hammer."

Brenda pulled open a control panel on her forearm, typed in a code. Her fingers began cracking, rotating 90 degrees in the wrong direction. Her cybernetic arm clicked and buzzed.

While Brenda's arm finished transforming, I maneuvered my left hand in my coat pocket. "Look, I'm begging you," I said, gripping Brenda's cyber ankle with my right hand. Wanda was still holding the upper part of my arm. All three of us were connected by our metal parts.

I found what I was looking for. The other shock slug I'd brought. I tried to relax my muscles.

"Hammer time," Brenda said.

I tossed the shock slug into my mouth. Prayed I didn't bite off my tongue.

At first, it didn't taste good. Then it tasted like nothing but pain. My whole body trembled. The sky seemed to turn black. I must have screamed.

All three of us were on the pavement, convulsing.

I rolled on my stomach. I wasn't sure how much time had passed. Angry flashes of light danced around my vision. Aftershocks pulsed from my throat to my toes. I rolled to my side, spat up the slug along with a good amount of blood. The spent creature squirmed in the red puddle. Began to dissolve.

"Gwaaarg," Wanda said, grunting low and slow. "What? Urgh?"

I got on my knees. Stood up. Fell again. I couldn't stop my right hand from twitching. I had to force my eyes open. I vomited more.

"Wanda. Wanda, where are you?"

"Brenda," Wanda moaned. "Brenda." Her arms were flailing around on the ground.

"Wanda, I can't feel you. I can't touch you."

I staggered to my feet. My whole body felt dried out, scorched to a crisp.

I left the sisters rolling on the ground, groping for each other. Ran as fast as I could. It wasn't very fast. I felt like I was moving through a pool filled with molasses. I could barely move myself down the hill.

The ferry sub was closing its hatch. Then it was sinking. Then it was gone. All that was left was a circle of dark blue water inside the layer of green filter algae on the surface.

Either Wanda or Brenda was shouting. "Please, touch me. Sister, touch me!"

I stood on the edge of the water, looking at the ferry sub carrying my clue into the murk.

There was a bobbing two-story boat on the other dock. The floater ferry. It was heading to Brooklyn instead of Duracell Park, but at least it was heading away from the Sassafras sisters. I got on board. Leaned against the railing. Retched a little more into the surf.

The electric shock was still thrumming inside me, but growing fainter.

From the top deck, I watched the sisters struggle up, groping for each other. They were reaching out blindly. Their arms barely missing one another. Wailing. They crawled across the pavement. Found each other. Grabbed hold to make sure the other was real, pulled their bodies close together, and wept.

17

THE UNEXPECTED VISIT

While I was looking for a way to break open the case, the Mets caught a lucky break. The Sphinxes started game two with a bang. Two-run dinger from shortstop A. G. C. Thompson right over the left wall. Smacked a jellyfish vending drone on the third level. Beer rained on a row of fans. But the Mets pitcher, "Mad" Marsel Schultz, settled down after the second inning, switched from her fastball to cutters and sliders. Kept the batters walking right back to the dugout.

The Sphinxes had Capablanca on the mound. A smart young kid whom my pal MacGill had found smashing beer bottles on the streets of Havana with a perfect four-seamer. But he was young. Only his second year in the league and no playoff experience. The Mets started to wear him down. By the sixth inning, Capablanca's arm couldn't have stirred a pot of soup. The Mets loaded up the bases before the Sphinxes pulled him. It was too late. A double from Van Young and a single from "Triple M" Morgan and the Mets were up 4–3. The score stayed that way to the end.

I felt bad for Capablanca. That kind of loss stayed in your head. But I didn't feel that bad. It was a little bit of vengeance for Zunz, plus an extension for me. I had at least another day to dig and maybe get my medical debt cleared.

I could still feel ripples of electricity flowing through me from the shock slug. I fell asleep on the couch without undressing.

I slept fitfully, dreaming that I was an ever-expanding mound of flesh. My cyborg parts were gone. Most of my human ones too. I didn't have features, not even a mouth. I was a sphere of skin. My flesh absorbed everything around me, the objects osmosing through my skin. I ballooned like a gargantuan baseball until I covered the city, then the planet, and then I was alone, floating in the cold dark ether of space.

When I woke up, I had several missed calls. Four were from the Sassafras sisters, two from Dolores, and one from Natasha. None of them, luckily, were from the super whom I paid some of my last cash to warn me if any cyborg sisters, especially pissed-off ones with matching outfits, came calling.

The shock slug had fried all my systems, both flesh and machine. The painkillers had worn off, and I pulled my outdated form out of bed. In the bathroom mirror, I could see my torso was covered with bruises. Some fresh and dark purple, others faded to pale green or sickly yellow. My skin was a bouquet of the world's ugliest flowers.

I went through my morning routine. Brushed teeth, lubed bionic joints, shaved facial hair back down to the skin. Scraped under my fingernails and inside my data ports. Went through the entire list. I wondered how many hours I'd spent maintaining my self instead of living my life.

Shaved and washed, my face in the mirror was uncanny. Not the same as the face that floated in my mind when I imagined myself. The eyes were tired and bagged. The flesh between my chin and neck sagging. The hair populated with strands of gray.

I was getting old.

The only thing that still looked relatively new was my bionic arm. Apart from the hole the Sassafras sisters had jammed through the palm, it was smooth and gleaming. A metal sculpture. I realized that my arm would forever look new, no matter how much my flesh decayed. The rest of me would wither, but my arm would remain. I'd waste away to a stooped skeleton of a man with white hair and blotches all over my baggy skin. Yet my frail, dying figure would still be dragging around a large shiny arm.

When Zunz and I were freshmen, they defrosted the first cryocase. Some tech baron named Peter Coin from Silicon Valley, way back when it was a valley and not a manmade libertarian island in tax-free international waters powered by floating mini nuke plants. Coin had been an eclectic billionaire who'd used government subsidies to buy up NASA and turn it into a commercial space cruise line. *It's one giant leap for tourism* went the ad.

Coin had advertised the service in space itself, suspending reflective sails in orbit. You needed a telescope to see it, but the solar-powered pixels spelled *NASA Cruises* right next to the moon.

Before his hypercancer spread, Coin had frozen himself with a plan to turn up the heat when a cure was discovered. Coin's thawing fifteen years later when RadGen therapy was developed was a huge event. Every channel was begging him for interviews.

"What are you going to do, Mr. Coin?"

"I'm going to see the future."

"This is the future," the reporter said, laughing. "You're here."

"I was born eighty years ago, but my body is only sixty-five. With the current medical tech, I can make it look at least forty. It's a start."

"Are you planning to get back to work? To develop new technologies to help our present? Your future?"

"No," he said, grinning. "I'm going to the *next* future." His plan was to keep freezing himself, waking up every twenty-five years to get the latest youth treatments. "I'll grow younger and younger as the future rushes past. In one hundred years, medicine will make me as young as a teenager. In three hundred, they'll be able to shrink me to a baby so I can start life all over again. They say you only live once. Well, I like to think outside the box. I'm going to disrupt mortality."

Zunz and I were enamored with the idea. We watched all his interviews from the rug in front of his parents' flat-screen.

"When I get rich, I'm buying us cryolockers, Kobo," Zunz had said. "We'll wake up and play for the Mets again and again. Never aging."

"The time-traveling baseball brothers," I said.

"Exactly. Space-time sluggers."

"I'm in, JJ. I'm in."

We sliced our pinkie fingers with an exposed nail on the banister, rubbed the blood together as a pact.

It was a childish dream. And anyway Peter Coin's second cryo-tank was blown up by Mextexan rebels in the Dissolution years. The corpse was never recovered. He's disrupting in heaven now, if you believe in that kind of thing.

After showering, I threw on my old houndstooth robe and printed some breakfast. Before I could play my messages, there was a dull knock on the door.

Anyone could have been after Zunz, and by the transitive prop-erties of sticking your nose where it doesn't belong anyone could be after me. I popped the floor box, grabbed my dual-shock revolver. The gun sent out a small EMP with the bullet. Made sure you immo-bilized a human or robot with equal force.

When I looked through the peep feed, I could see another eye. One a lot larger than I was used to and partially obscured by straw-berry blonde hair. "Mr. Kobo, I know you're there."

I tucked the gun into the pocket of the robe, cinched it shut, and opened the door. "Come on in," I said as Natasha strolled past me.

"You look to be in bad shape," she said. She placed her hand on my shoulder, right above the metal. Her hand was heavy and warm, and the feeling made me shiver. She was wearing a green jumpsuit that seemed to be made from some hybrid moss fabric. "I'm going to touch you. My people like to touch when we say serious things. We believe the truth can be felt. A superstition perhaps."

"Okay," I said. Slid my hand toward the pocket with the gun.

"I wanted to apologize to you in person about the whole Arocha situation at the sushi restaurant. I hope you know that it was, as your kind like to say, just business."

"A nasty business. But isn't all business nasty?"

"Exactly. It will not, I hope, affect our current professional relationship. Solving the murder of Julio Julio Zunz is in both of our interests."

There was nothing sexual in her touch, but somehow that made me more uncomfortable. I stepped back. Let her hand slide off my shoulder.

"Don't worry," I said. "If I kept hard feelings about everything in this biz, I'd be weighed down so much I couldn't walk."

"Good. I knew you were a sensible sapien." Natasha walked over to my couch, dropped into the blue cushions like a bag of bricks.

"What about your big friend? Am I supposed to be square with him too?"

"My friend?"

"The big guy in the black suit. The thug with the unfinished face?"

She curled her lips down in thought. "Ah, Coppelius. He was there that night at the sushi bar, wasn't he? That's not nice to say about his face. Not all clones turn out as smoothly as me."

"I wouldn't know."

"No, you wouldn't. Anyway, I've come here for two reasons."

"Maybe I should get dressed before hearing the first," I said. I was still in my ratty bathrobe.

Natasha shrugged. The suggestion seemed irrelevant to her. I might as well have said I should go hop around the kitchen and ribbit. "Both will be quick. The first is to ask you if you saw the game."

"Game two? Yeah, I saw. Congrats."

"It's good news for you. The series will go at least five games. More games, more time to investigate. I wish I could give you many weeks. But the Mouth will move on to other things when the World Series is over, I'm afraid. As will the public."

"Guess I'm rooting for the series to stretch to seven."

"How's the case going? Do you have anything to report?"

"I normally report when I'm paid," I said. I shrugged myself. "As we say, that's just business."

Natasha seemed to like that comment. Her laugh was sharp and to the point. "Then I should have led with the second reason. I've scrounged up that petty cash for you, for expenses." She handed over a bytewallet with a number that didn't make my heart sing, but would get me through the next few days. If I didn't run into the Sassafras sisters at least. "It'll refresh each day while you're on the case."

So I gave her a report. What I was willing to share at least, which wasn't much. I didn't know if the Mets had me tailed, so I told her I'd been to Governors Island to see Zunz's secret pad. Described the old toys and posters. Didn't say anything about the Edenist girl, much less the Janus Club mask I'd found in Zunz's island home.

"And what about Jung Kang?" she said, leaning forward with her elbows on her knees.

I shrugged. "I haven't been able to get back inside the Pyramid compound. I'm trying though."

Natasha nodded. "I'd try again. I was digging through Mr. Zunz's finances, and there's a steady and mysterious withdrawal every month. And soon after, he'd place a call to the Sphinxes compound."

Kang had mentioned Zunz owed him money, but I didn't know it had been a recurring fee.

"Any idea what for?"

She cracked her big knuckles one by one. "Aren't we paying you to find that out? My gut instinct, to use a strange sapien idiom, is that question holds the key to the murder. Maybe Kang has accomplices that are outside the compound. Relatives perhaps? Let me know if you find one." Natasha stood and straightened her clothes. "I'll be in touch after game three. Let's hope our team's luck continues."

She held out her hand to shake. Grabbed my right hand before I offered it. Pulled off the glove, inspecting the broken chrome. "Hmm." She jabbed one of her thick fingers right into the hole. The pain shot through me with an electric volt.

"What the hell?"

"This is not good, Mr. Kobo."

"It sure doesn't feel good."

"I'm going to insist that you visit one of our doctors." She wiped off the goo from my palm on a handkerchief, then she reached into her pocket and pulled out a business chipcard. "I've taken the liberty of providing him with your gene profile and cybernetic specs. He'll have the equipment ready. The expenses are on us."

"That's generous," I said.

"We want all our Mets employees in tip-top shape." She placed the card on the counter and then walked to the door. "The last thing we want is another Zunz on our hands."

I couldn't help but smile as I showed Natasha out. "The expenses are on us." The world's most beautiful phrase. Maybe I could convince the doctor to sneak me a few serums on the side. Put it on Natasha's tab while he injected the upgrades into my veins.

I went online, started looking at the latest boosts and treatments. I already had files of ones I wanted, but it was thrilling to see what was new. The sun was dripping out of the sky and I wouldn't have time to visit any doctor that day. So I thought it was time to check up on the one clue I had: the Janus Club.

I pulled out the card I'd taken from Zunz's house. *An Out-of-Body Experience That's Out of This World.* It was a vague slogan, but then I supposed secret groups liked to keep things that way. The address was on the west side, in what was left of Chelsea after the storm wall went up.

I had a hard time imagining Zunz at something as stuffy as a secret club. To me, he was still the happy-go-lucky teenager who wanted to play baseball all day and watch what he called "tough-guy movies" at night. The only club we were ever in was the Mets Teen Aces Fan Club, which we'd saved up to join by selling handmade anti-surveillance ski masks outside of school. They were balaclavas decorated with reflective sequins that probably didn't do shit against the cameras, but they looked cool enough. All we got from the Mets club were two decoder rings and a link to a coupon for a cell phone app.

But wealth changed people. Fame didn't help either. The more Zunz got of both, the less I saw of him and the less I recognized when I did. More than any upgrades, money warped you all the way down to the DNA.

I put on my spiderwool suit, grabbed the fleshy mask, sucked down an eraser, and headed out.

18

THE JANUS CLUB

In the supraway to Chelsea, I squished between the bodies of other passengers. The air conditioner was broken and no amount of filtering could suck away the rank smell of dozens of people inside a hot metal car. Most of the passengers had micromesh masks on, hoping to strain out any new diseases floating in the air. I strapped one on myself when the old lady next to me started coughing.

In the middle of the car, there were a couple break-break dancers doing old-school hip-hop moves with limbs that had been upgraded with extra joints. "Showtime," one of them yelled, and began spinning his arms at the second elbows like windmills while another flipped a Merk Knicks hat back and forth between his prosthetic feet.

When the song ended, I sent their account a couple bucks, then stepped out into the Highline Tube. There was so much smog that night I had to use my screen light to guide me down to the street. I held my filter in my right hand and a lit eraser in my left, pressing one or the other to my lips as I walked.

The Janus Club door was hidden behind rows of black ivy so thick

I could barely make out the brick beneath. There was only a small opening between the leaves. It was marked with a brass engraving of a double-faced man. A pale blue light shone next to the slot.

"Hey, man, wanna buy some jizz jazzers?" someone behind me said between coughs. "Make you come rainbows, I swear."

"Why would I need that?"

"Aren't you going to the club? Make it an experience." He dug around in his coat and then showed me a variety of colored pills. "You want more stamina? Quicker reload? I got anything you need."

"Got a pill that makes strangers mind their own business?"

The man looked at the pills in his hands, then back up at me. "Yeah, well fuck you, limp dick."

Once the man had wandered off, still cursing me, I slid in Zunz's card.

The door creaked open and a small drone ushered me inside. It was amorphous and fleshy, with glowing protrusions dappling the body. The pink skin covering glistened in the dim light. It looked like some kind of erotic germ.

"Delightful to have you back with us, Mr. Zunz," the drone said. Luckily for me, the drone hadn't been keeping up with the news and didn't realize Zunz was dead. "No companions this evening?"

"Just me," I said.

It bobbed there, waiting.

"Your face, sir."

"What's wrong with it?" I said.

The drone throbbed with soft pink light. Its imitation of a laugh. "You forgot to put it on."

"Oh, right."

I pulled out the mask I'd found at Zunz's house and stretched it over my face. I could see dimly out of it but wasn't sure how to turn the whole thing on. The mask had been molded to Zunz's features and fit awkwardly on my face. Still, I felt close to him with my skin rubbing where his once had rubbed.

"Allow me," the drone said. Despite its strange shape, it had been programmed to speak like a butler in a British whodunit.

It floated around behind me and turned the mask on. The tube around my neck started to warm up and I heard a wet click as the mouth device at the back powered on. The tongue needle shot into my neck, tapping into the spine.

"The usual nondisclosure agreement is still in place," the drone said. "As is the anti-comm field. No photos, videos, holos, or recordings of any kind are allowed. Please enjoy your experience with maximum discretion."

The pink drone floated back into a slot in the wall and I was left alone in the long, dark hallway.

The metal tongue was secreting something into me. I felt hot and strange.

I walked.

The hallway twisted and turned, seeming to snap back around itself at sharp angles, bringing us deeper into some unknown lair. The dark path was illuminated only by purple phosphorescent mushrooms shaped like different sex organs. They sprouted in the corners, indicating where to turn. Violins played faintly in the background. Mist creeped along the floor. If I was being led to my death, at least the killers had a flair for atmosphere.

Instead, I emerged into a large room trapped halfway between a brothel and a hunting lodge. Great wooden walls, elegant silk couches, and the heads of extinct and newly engineered animals mounted on the walls. Polar bears, gray rhinos, green rhinos, mammoths, and even a large lioniger rimmed with a mane of black-and-orange fur. Most of them were illegal to own in the States, let alone hunt. But there were sporting cruise ships that stayed in international waters where the rich could take shots at predators between bites of brunch.

Robots in antiquated outfits rolled around, offering drinks in ram-horn goblets. I grabbed one. The room had about a few dozen guests inside, mostly international biopharm executives and tech barons flying in from Silicon Island from the look of their attire. Everyone's face was hidden beneath the black, fleshy masks. A few men were stooped over, heads ducking beneath the undulating chandeliers. Basketball players I assumed.

I grabbed one of the android butler's arms as it passed. "Hey, where does a fellow get the real action?"

The butler scanned my equipment. "You're a Code Gold guest. You may enter the VIP room at any time," it said, pointing toward a curtain on the left wall.

"You ever get any FLB players in here?"

"The Janus Club takes all types, in its exclusive way."

"Are there any here tonight? A Jung Kang maybe?"

The robot's face was welded on, unmoving. Still, I thought I could sense a frown.

"The Janus Club is exclusive and secretive. While here, you can remain anonymous, like everyone else." It rolled back to the bar.

I sipped my red drink through the slit in the mask. It tasted like cinnamon mixed with cough syrup.

Two men walked through the curtains, woozy and talking excitedly to each other. They high-fived.

"Next time, pick the same guy and I'll go downstairs and watch."

"You're a freak. I love it!"

I was feeling alive, like I was a balloon inflating with hot blood. I wasn't sure if it was the drink or the neck needle or both. I took another sip before heading in.

19

THE SKIN COSTUMES

As soon as I stepped through the curtains, I realized I hadn't had enough drinks. Inside were dozens of people floating in tanks of pink water. They looked like sensory deprivation tanks, but the people were sensing all right. They moaned, groaned, and grunted, splashing the water up the sides.

The people seemed nude, except for the masks. The nodes glowed and lit the room with a multitude of faint blue lights, like eyes of bizarre fish encountered on a deep-sea dive.

There was another drone in here, in the same amorphous yet vaguely sensual shape. It took my arm and I could feel the warmth of its plastiflesh. It guided me to a free tank and instructed me to undress. It asked me to put on a thin and clear plastic suit that was lined with yellow nodes. I did so. The warm waters reached above my ankles.

"Lie down, please."

The bot connected a red, fleshy tube to the back of the mask, on

the other side of the mouth device. The screens over the eyes turned
on and my sight lit up with options. *Solo, Couple,* or *Group.* I could
feel the nodes humming around my head and a strange sensation in
the spine like it was being licked. I said "solo" and it was selected.
Then my screen lit up with people. Lots of people. A treadmill of bodies went by all in different shapes and sizes. Big, tall, wide, or skinny.
Skin of various shades and genitals in every known configuration.
All of them had devices embedded on their temples. Ones that looked
like the devices on the human telegram the Mouth had used to call
me outside of Penn Station.

I selected one more or less at random. A skinny male body with
stimulator rings embedded along his shaft. *Costume is currently worn
by another member. Please select again.*

I picked the next one, a sleek androgynous body with genitals that
had been edited smooth all over. *Dressing,* the screen said. The humming around my head turned into a roar. My vision flashed white
and black. Then I was gone.

And then I was somewhere else.

I was with the person I'd selected. Or rather inside them, looking out from their eyes. They were looking down at their skin and
when I wondered how it felt, the right hand ran along the body and
I felt what their fingertips felt. The skin was so different than mine.
Smoother, softer. And yet I could also, in some part of my brain, feel
my own body sitting in the tank.

"What do I do here?" I said. But when I said it, they said it.

"What do I do here?"

They were in a small bedroom with no one else around. Beside
the bed was a table with an array of plugs, rings, squealers, and other
sensation devices. I thought about sitting down on the bed and, with
about a two-second lag, they moved to the mattress.

I was controlling them. It wasn't just like the device the Mouth had used to speak with me on the street. It was the exact device. I realized why Zunz was a member of this club. It was a Monsanto club. A test ground, perhaps, for new devices they hadn't yet brought to market. Suddenly, I felt angry and afraid. I wanted to get out of them. The person was screaming, because I was screaming. We fell backward off the bed and hit our head.

Then I was back in the tank. Another amorphous shape floating above me, this one pale blue and covered in wiggling protrusions. It lit up as I sat up. It held a needle with green liquid in an extending claw. "Sir, would you like a shot to calm yourself? Stress can disrupt the connection."

"I'm good," I said. "Just getting used to it."

"Very well. I am required to remind you that any damage to the Astral will be deducted from your account."

I took a minute to calm myself. Then I went back in.

I was at the start screen again and this time picked "group" and a costume that seemed to be a stout, hirsute man. *Please wait a moment while we transport the costume.*

When the nodes hummed and I was transported into the man, I realized I'd made a mistake. My senses were overloaded by the moans, touches, and licks of a dozen bodies. I was in a pile of people inside a hot, small chamber. You could have called it an orgy, except the controls weren't precise enough. Everyone moved as awkwardly as glitching robots. When I tried to stand up, the man moved to his knees, then fell back down. We steadied ourselves on someone's behind. Our feet slid on the sticky floors.

There were several of the amorphous drones floating around the orgy like bizarre clouds. They were all different colors. Violet, orange, crimson, sage, umber. They had long arms extended, and they were hoisting up the people. Helping them stroke, grab, spread, and thrust.

I had to keep adjusting my movements to fit this different form. Shorter arms, wider girth. The simplest thing, like snapping a finger, felt uncanny in this shape. I could feel everything though. The sensations were perfectly passed directly to my body, the one sloshing in the tank. Too perfectly. The parts rubbing over his parts, which felt like my parts. It all crashed over me like a tidal wave.

In the tank, I sat up and ripped the cord out of the back of my neck. Some hot fluid dripped on my back. I felt both ashamed and angry. I wasn't sure at who. Zunz for coming to this fucked-up place. The Mouth for making it. Or me, for enjoying it. Because I did enjoy it. Less the sex than the skin. The ability to move myself into another body like I'd always wanted.

It wasn't perfect tech, that was for sure. There was a lag between thought and movement, between neurons and nerves. And there was resistance throbbing in the space between that pushed back on me. I guessed that was what philosophers called *will*. Still, I couldn't deny I felt alive.

I got out of the tank and ripped off the plastic suit. The smell of human fluids of all different kinds filled the air of the dim room. One of the drones floated by, and I reached out to squeeze one of its protrusions. It was warm and wet.

"Where was that?"

"Where was where, sir?"

"The people I went into. Where were they?"

The slick red drone hummed in the air. It tilted downward. "Why, right below you, sir."

I looked down and realized all the sounds and smells weren't from the people in the tanks, they were from the people down below. The costumes, the system had called them. Through the opaque-glass floor tiles, I could see them rutting, moaning, and rolling around in a large glass structure with the assisting drones floating between them. And I could make out other people, the ones watching and cheering.

Back in the jazzy room, I found myself desperately thirsty. I chugged a glass of water from a droid's tray, then two more. I could still feel the outlines of the bodies I'd been in. Like they were following me around in vengeance. But the effect wore off after a couple minutes and I found myself back in the dull reality of a sleazy club filled with obnoxious people laughing loudly and bragging about their exploits.

"I can't wait until this gets on the market," I heard a woman say. "Imagine showing someone precisely how you want your kitchen cleaned."

"That's grotesque, Cynthia," her friend said. "You want to be *inside* the help?"

"Oh, it was just a joke. Lighten up."

I looked around for a while, on the off chance I might see a physique that resembled Kang's. But I couldn't make out who anyone was with the masks. I headed outside, pulling off the flesh hood, and telling myself that what I'd done didn't count if I left quickly after.

Outside, I saw two people in black coats alternating between smoking and breathing through filters. One pale and androgynous, the other a short woman. The first's brown eyes and short fingers looked familiar to me. Then I realized why. I'd been inside them.

They looked at me and then looked away. I didn't see any recognition in their expression. So I pulled out an eraser and joined them.

The woman noticed me gawking at the nodes on her temple. She flared her nostrils. "They come out, if you're wondering."

"Although not the neural mesh they injected," the smooth-bodied one said. "Gives me weird dreams at night."

"Do you mind telling me? What it's like, I mean." I smiled in what I hoped was a friendly way. "I'm a prospective member."

They sighed and then exhaled a cloud of smoke. "I do mind. First off, I'm not allowed to talk about it. The contract is pretty explicit. Secondly, we're on break just trying to relax, okay."

I nodded. Looked away.

"Oh, it's fine. Could be worse," the woman said. She took another drag. "I don't have to worry about the clients' diseases or freak-outs. We only touch other workers, and I can count on them to be professional, at least."

"It's steady employment. Not a lot of that going around," the other said.

"I can relate."

"Somehow I doubt that." They pointed at the mask I had in my hands. Then tapped one of their nodes. "You know, you people linger up here. A little bit of you remains. Like an infection. So I know exactly what you're like."

A little line of blood was dripping out of the woman's nose. She cursed and wiped it with her coat. She turned to her friend. "We should be going back. Tick tock."

The two workers finished their cigarettes and flicked them on the ground. They slid back in the employee entrance without saying another word.

I thought about shouting that I wasn't like that. That I was a working stiff too. But instead I sat there against the wall, smoking my eraser, wondering what else I didn't know about my brother's life. What other secrets had he been hiding?

I was feeling pitiful enough that I wanted someone to cheer me up. Someone to touch my actual skin. I thought maybe Dolores would be up for the task. I called her, pretending it was about the case.

"Jesus, Kobo, where have you been? I called you twice."

I couldn't see where Dolores was, but there were lights flashing behind her.

"Couldn't check my phone. I think I found out where Kang and Zunz were meeting up," I said. "I was just there. You aren't going to believe it."

"It's Kang I'm calling about." Her voice shook and her skin looked pale. "He's dead."

20

THE SURVEILLANCE FOOTAGE

I got home late, drained and still partly drugged from the Janus Club mask. I scratched the back of my neck where the metal tongue had gone in and lapped my nerves. It was inflamed but didn't hurt.

If there was one immutable fact of life, it was that you got one body and that was that. You could shape it. Upgrade it. Pray it didn't get injured. But there was just one vessel for your consciousness. You didn't get a do-over. It was the one thing that put everyone on the same level. And now someone had invented a loophole. A device that could pour your mind into a different vessel. Sure, the connection was wonky. It was like driving a car with a broken axle and two tires missing. You could move it, but not the way you wanted. Still. It was thrilling.

Before I could worry more about the ethical implications, there was a knock on my door.

"I'm starved," Dolores said, walking right by me and into the living room. "Let's order pizza."

She was wearing a black jumper made of light-absorbing fabric that made her appear as a flat silhouette. Her hands and face seemed to float in the air, attached to a two-dimensional form. It was more than enough to see though.

"Do you know how long I got chewed out about letting you slip into the Pyramid compound?" she said. She was wearing sleek black goggles, like twin black holes. "You could at least offer me a drink."

"Right, right," I said and headed to the fridge. There wasn't much inside, just a couple beers and energy waters. I cracked two of the beers and handed her one. She drank half of it on the spot.

I looked around my messy apartment. There were clothes tossed around in piles and a big stain on the couch from where the Sassafras sisters had stabbed through my hand. But it was too late to clean, so I sat down across from Dolores and asked her if she saw the game.

"I did. Those bastard Mets got lucky in the seventh. Casares almost never misses that throw."

"O'Gorman was a beast on the mound though. His sinker was dropping on a dime. Best of our bullpen."

The Mets had evened things up 1–1, and it looked like they'd make it a real series. That meant I had some time to solve the case and get my medical debt erased.

Dolores stretched her arms and sighed. "Don't you remember what it felt like to have all those gigantic lights shining on you as you stepped up to the plate?"

As she said it, I could see those lights, floating like angels above me.

"It was better times. For me at least."

"For us too. We were good together, back then."

"Yeah," I said. My voice sounded very far away.

Getting nostalgic with Dolores made me feel sad. Regretful.

Which was something I couldn't afford to feel any more of right then. I switched the topic to something less painful.

"Tell me about Kang. You said he died?" I felt suddenly cold. I leaned against the counter. "Was it like Zunz?"

Dolores shook her head, waving her hand in front of her face. "No, he had what looked like a heart attack. But wasn't."

Dolores explained that the Pyramid doctors had ruled it a cardiac arrest, but it was too much of a coincidence for her tastes. She'd dug through the security feed. "The footage had been scrambled somehow, but I was able to decode it enough to see. Well. Let me show you."

Dolores reached into one of the pockets of her jumper and pulled out a small pill-shaped object.

"You seen these deodrives? Use DNA strands to store data. This baby could fit the entire Library of Congress server inside. And since it's genetic, hard to scan or track."

I held up the drive between my fingers. A viscous white fluid sloshed inside the little capsule.

She slid it into an adapter and connected it to her screen. Brought up the security footage. "I was able to descramble a segment." A large figure sneaked into Kang's house, but they looked strange on camera. I asked Dolores to zoom in to the face and when she did I saw the issue. It wasn't just the layer of static over the footage. The person's skin was changing. It shifted colors and configurations every few seconds. The lips would expand or shrink, cheeks grow scruff and then turn into a smooth ruddy red. I could barely discern the outline of the face underneath.

"It's kaleidoscopic skin," she explained. "Advanced espionage biotech. A living membrane that transforms color and shape. Uses modified cephalopod chromatophores controlled by a signal pack. Emits a frequency that adds sheets of noise to most cameras."

"Shit. Anti-surveillance tech has come a long way since we were teens painting reflective triangles on our faces to shoplift at the mall."

The morphing figure talked to Kang for a while, with Kang backed against the couch, arms out. At some point, Kang hung his head. Seemed to weep. The figure pulled out a needle and slid a shot into his neck.

I asked Dolores to play it a few times. The intruder's skin was a kaleidoscope, but I could still make out his size. Bulky and mean. Chest like a barrel. I couldn't say for sure, but I thought it was Coppelius. If he worked with the Department of Human Limits, he'd have access to the latest tech.

"Shit," I said. I pulled out an eraser, lit it with shaking hands. I'd barely spoken to Kang for ten minutes. Yet I might have led to his death.

"Can I get one of those?" Dolores asked.

I lit a second eraser off mine, the tips sizzling red as they met.

Dolores blew the smoke out in a little ring. "These things do numb you, don't they? I can see why you enjoy them."

After we'd numbed ourselves, Dolores asked me if it would be useful to spitball the case. "I know you like to talk things through."

I gave her the rundown from Zunz's pre-death call to the Janus Club visit. Both the sex and the tech. Dolores seemed particularly interested in the latter. She asked me to see the mask and I pulled it out.

"Might be a bit sweaty inside," I said.

She ran her fingers over it with awe, muttering terminology I barely recognized.

"You know, Pyramid has been working on something like this, but using optogenetics and a neural lace. It's been a bust. Genetically editing neurons to respond to light is tricky business, and the subjects kept having aneurysms." She put the mask down gently on the table. She sipped a little more beer. "Okay. So where does this leave Zunz?"

I shook my head. "I've got a lot of pieces, but no idea how they fit together. And half the pieces are gone. The girl escaped and Kang was a dead end."

"That's a macabre pun."

"Sorry, not intentional."

"Well, I can tell you one more thing. While you were busy not returning my calls, I did a little research. Did you know Kang had a sister? Hana. And she went to high school with you and Zunz."

"Never heard of her. It was a big school though."

"Zunz did. Knew her quite well, if you know what I mean."

I realized that's why Mrs. Z thought Kang was a woman. She was. Just a different Kang. Dolores had some photos of her on file. I didn't recognize her. Then again, dating in high school was one of those areas where I was watching Zunz from the sidelines with awe and jealousy.

"That's interesting smoke," I said, "but I'm not sure what direction it blows. A jealous ex killed Zunz, then a Neanderthal murdered her brother?"

"I don't know. But I'd bet that's his connection to Jung Kang."

I tried to imagine Kang, the eager player who was ecstatic to sign an autograph for me, killing anyone. The picture didn't make any sense in my mind. He seemed like the type who would squirm if he had to smash a fly.

"Kang seemed pretty depressed that Zunz was gone. Well, that his money was at least." I picked at the seal over my cybernetic hand's wound. The sealant had dried around the hole like a large, purple scar. "Anyway, I owe you, Dolores."

She smiled oddly. "I have an idea of how you could repay me actually."

"Oh yeah?"

She picked up the Janus Club mask again. Held it open across from her face and admired. "Let me borrow this. Just for a couple days. I'd like to run it by a few of our guys. Maybe it'll give them ideas."

That seemed to be a fair deal after what I'd put her through.

"Be my guest."

Dolores said she was going to call her team about it. She knocked my chin lightly with her fist as she stepped by me and into the hallway. I scratched the back of my head, tried to knock something loose in my mind. Why would Natasha have asked me about Kang right around when her friend was killing him? Either she didn't know or didn't think I would find out about his death anytime soon.

I decided to let that settle while I checked in with Okafor.

"I got other cases, you know, Kobo." Okafor was frowning and in their squad car. I could see the skystabbers flying past them. "I'm off to check out a potential double homicide. Twin brothers with mob ties who were hit with genetically tailored toxin. We don't even know which one had been targeted."

"I know, I know," I said. "I really owe you."

"Look, I've set an alert in case her face scans on our cameras. We haven't hit anything yet. I'll let you know."

"Oh, another thing. Do you remember someone from our school, Hana Kang?"

Okafor thought a bit. "Yeah, quiet girl. Back-of-the-classroom type. Had those weird religious parents, right? Wouldn't let her eat any of the cafeteria food."

"Do you know where she is?"

Okafor hummed while doing a search. "Shit. She died of lichen lung years ago. Painful way to go."

"Okay, thanks, Sil."

So that ruled out another suspect. I did some more thinking, but then thought I wasn't going to solve anything tonight. I drank a little more and smoked a lot more until my body felt as strange to me as the Janus Club costumes had. I kept remembering flashes from the club. Sensations.

When Dolores came back inside, I stood up. Then I sat back down.

"Do you need to go?" I said. My mind was racing with images now. I needed to get out of it. "Or could I bounce a few more things off you?"

"Depends on the things," Dolores said.

We talked awhile longer. Then we moved to fooling around. It was just like the old days, when we were together. Our bodies remembered exactly how the other liked things. Between the erasers and Dolores's touch, I was feeling nothing and everything at the same time.

"That was fun," Dolores said, as we lay naked on the bed. "But I was thinking about before. When we were dating. You used to have all those options…"

"Yeah?"

Back when I'd been playing in the Cyber League, the money had seemed endless. Contracts, licensing deals, advertisements. They were being showered on us. At least at first. I'd gone wild. Gotten a whole set of bionic eyes, different detachable fingers for my hand, and a half-dozen sensation machines that could be swapped out. Of course, as the debt collectors came knocking, I'd pawned most of the parts. And I'd traded some of the nether-regions modules to the identity-confirmation nonprofits for tax rebates. But I'd kept a few. I guess I'd grown sentimental about them.

"Not that what you have right now isn't functional, mind you."

"That's good to know," I said.

"I'm someone who likes choices."

"Now that you mention it, I haven't swapped out my unmentionables in some time."

I told Dolores to give me a few minutes, went into the other room. I wasn't sure if the other ones would still work. They were old models. Antiques at this point. But right then it felt like a fantastic idea. My blood, both real and artificial, was racing through my veins.

I pressed the release on my thigh, and my crotch popped out a half an inch. I grabbed the edges as gently as I could, turned it 90 degrees. I let the gravity slide the module out. I left my penis on the coffee table. It wobbled over, the tip plopping onto a coaster. The cool air flowed in my empty groin. An odd sensation. The absence of your own organ.

Dolores's jaw dropped a couple of centimeters, like someone was passing a magnet beneath her smile. But it was a smile.

21

THE SHATTERED HAND

I went into my shower feeling like an electric eel had slithered across my skin. Alive, I guess you could say. Alive and on a mission. I felt like I could pull through, find the killer, avenge Zunz, pay off my debt, and settle down with Dolores in a little cabin in an eco-preserve with a white electric fence and a weathervane on top to spin in the natural winds. Sometimes it's nice to dream.

Dolores was in the bedroom and I went into the kitchen, started a pot of coffee. I pulled out an eraser, then thought better of it. Pressed it back into the pack.

My arm still ached, and even that problem could be solved. I had a free upgrade waiting from Natasha's friend. I picked up the chip-card she'd left. *Dr. Earnest Ignatius Setek, MD, PhD, ED, CMD: Flesh, metal, or hybrid.*

Setek. The name hit me as hard as a brick to the face.

I'd met the doctor before. He'd done a little bit of surgery on me. A weird guy with unkempt hair and a predilection for robotic legs. It was only one time, but that one time was with Zunz.

A few months before Zunz died at home plate, he'd shown up at my door. It was one of the last times I saw him alive in person. He'd seemed healthy and happy then. He'd smiled in my doorway. "You got an upgrade you want, dude? My treat."

I had many I wanted and several I desperately needed. But Zunz was my brother, not the director of a charity for out-of-date oilers. I told him no, and to come on inside. "I feel like we haven't hung out in a while."

Zunz had a black coat draped over one arm. He looked around in amazement at my dinky Brooklyn apartment. It was barely bigger than a dugout, but Zunz was smiling. "This is it. Right here. This is all you need, right?"

I didn't tell bother to tell him that in the daytime the view from my window was a rusty ion fan. Or how roaches had started nesting in my air filter and when I turned it on little brown wings fluttered around the living room.

"I'd take the stadiums and the money and the fans," I said. "You know, if you want to trade."

Zunz laughed, his smile creeping into the little birthmark on his cheek. "I'm trying to say that you've done well. I'm proud of you."

"Is this the first time you've come to the new place?"

I'd moved into this apartment about two years earlier. It was on the tenth floor, which was higher than my income could afford if it hadn't been shade subsidized. The building rotated slowly through-out the day that so the expensive apartments constantly faced the sun. I'd been claustrophobic ever since the building collapsed on me as a child, so staying high up was more important than natural light. All my plants were plastic anyway.

"Sorry, it's been a super busy season." He smiled. "Well, couple of seasons. Shit, I forgot a housewarming present. Next time!"

Zunz hardly looked any different than he had in high school. The

Mets were pumping him with enough preservatives he was practically embalmed. Then Zunz slid the coat off his arm. I gasped. His hand was encased in a glass bowl, his fingers the filament in a dead bulb. A reconstruction glove. Inside the glass, thin yellow worms swam around his hand, seeming to nibble at the joints.

"Jesus. Is that from the broken bat?"

A few months before, a Leones de AstraZeneca second basemen had snapped his bat smacking a fastball, and the jagged tip crashed into Zunz's hand. I'd wanted to go to that game, but couldn't afford the plane, boat, and entrance tickets it cost to get to the floating barge stadium off the coast of Havana. But I heard the crunch on TV as the broken bat hit Zunz. It had cracked the bones and sliced a variety of veins. He was on the injured list for several months.

"Yep. That Leones asshole smashed it up good. The Mets can't get it to heal right. Not even with these new surgical worms. You know how tiny the bones are in a hand?"

"The news said you were recovering fine. You should have told me."

"Mets don't want any bad press heading into the final stretch of the season. That's where you come in. I need a second opinion from someone who's outside of the Monsanto payroll. Dr. Earnest Setek."

"Never heard of him."

"He's mostly a military contractor. Works on traumatic tissue regeneration. If he can patch up bullet-ridden soldiers, I'm hoping he can fix a stupid baseball injury. You know, you might remember him."

I was holding Zunz's glass-encased hand in mine, looking at the mangled skin inside. It reminded me of my own arm, the flesh one I'd had snipped off and replaced. I looked up. "Remember him?"

"Yeah, Setek was part of the whole astroclone disaster."

"The *Colossus* shuttle crash?"

"That's the one."

When Zunz and I were teens, then President Vega had started a program to clone the smartest minds in the nation to keep pace with One China and the Franco-German Union. The test case was a pair of astronauts who'd just returned from a mission to Mars. The only thing more arduous than the trip was the training, so cloning was the perfect solution. The project involved several biopharms and took years, but eventually they figured out how to use a combination of bioprinting on wetwire scaffolding and growth hormones to make it work. It took over a year to gestate them.

I could still remember the day of the launch. Mrs. Z gave us extra bags of snacks, and after the final bell rang we ran with Okafor to Prospect Park where a gigantic holopad had been set up for the event. "Look at the size of that thing," Zunz had said, elbowing me, as the *Colossus* shuttle appeared. The park was filled to the brim with people. We cheered as "the Amazin' Astroclones," as the media had dubbed them, were loaded into the shuttle door. But we'd gotten bored and started tossing around a baseball up the hill.

I was running after a ground ball when I heard Okafor shout, "Oh my god!" When I looked back, the shuttle was falling back to earth. It hit the ground. The explosion filled the holopad in the middle of the park like a massive bonfire.

It wasn't an accident. The clones had overridden the system and crashed the ship. Suicide. The issue was upstairs. You could grow gray matter in a lab, but that didn't mean it would work right. The clones had been unstable the whole time. Nightmares, seizures, aphasia, loss of motor and cognitive function. The government had been covering it up, hoping that once the astroclones got in space the computer controls could handle the mission.

There were hearings and trials. Mostly they didn't go anywhere. But it was the *Colossus* crash that made Congress completely outlaw the cloning of sentient beings with the Rank Act. Nothing with a functioning brain. Only zootech creatures with preprogrammed life spans.

In my apartment, I let go of his injured hand.

"Why go to a doctor who was involved in the biggest biopharm disaster of our lifetime?"

Zunz gave me his grin. "Hey, everyone deserves a second chance, right? Remember it was their minds that went haywire. I'm just trying to get a hand fixed."

"Well sure. I'll come."

I remembered Zunz clapping me on the shoulder, thanking me. "The ZuBo team, back together. Keep an eye open when we're there. Be my backup while I get a second opinion."

And I remembered hopping in his car and flying out like partners in a buddy cop show. Zunz and me, windows down, and the cool air caressing us while we laughed about the old days. He turned up the music and drummed the steering wheel. New York rolled along below us. I could have leaned out the windows and spat on the whole city.

Nothing about the doctor's office seemed notable. Except the doctor. When Zunz said his name to the desk drone, the office door had swung open to let a billow of red detoxin mist spill across the floor as the doctor scuttled out. *Scuttled* was the right word. Dr. Setek's upper half was attached to a set of robotic crab legs. A metal girdle clasped his torso in place of a belt.

"The Z man! Let me get a look at you." Zunz let the doctor grab his shoulder and look him up and down. They knew each other. If this was a second opinion, it was the doctor's fifth or sixth one. "You are a work of art. They should put you in a museum. The *Mona Zunza*."

Setek carefully picked up the injured hand. Ran his fingers over the glass. Murmured. "Even works of art need touch-ups now and then."

The two of them disappeared for a long time. I looked around. Checked for tails. Scanned for bugs. Photographed the equipment. Nothing was out of place.

Eventually Zunz came out looking excited and whistling, although his hand was still in the reconstruction glove. I told him it all seemed okay to me. He threw his arm around my shoulder. "It's good to have someone watching your back. Listen, I have a Mets meeting. Can't stick around. You understand, right? Training. But Setek will put your tune-up on my bill." He shouted and pointed at me. "You hear that, doc? On my tab."

Zunz left, and the doctor waved me into his office. Ran a finger up and down my bionic arm. "Haven't seen this model in some time."

"Guess I'm a little out of date."

The doctor clapped his blue-gloved hands together, laughed. Rapped his knuckles on his spider legs. His voice had a hint of helium in it. "Aren't we both? Still, it's a fine time to be alive. Can you imagine living in olden times, when you couldn't do anything about it? You'd get older and more broken each year. No medicine or upgrades to halt the decline. You couldn't do a damn thing. Only sit back and watch as your teeth fell out, your skin wrinkled, and you broke apart piece by piece."

"I guess that still happens to us, just takes a little longer."

"I don't accept it." He stuck a needle in my arm, drew blood, and squirted it into an analyzer. "You know, we oilers might get our true flesh back one day with a little luck."

"I can barely remember what they lopped off," I lied.

"Keep faith!" The doctor rubbed his chin while looking at my readout. "Well, I can tell that you smoke and drink. Too much on both counts. You need a fresh lung lining, the left one is burned-out. Could develop lichen lung if you're not careful. Wouldn't hurt to get a new liver either."

"Bullshit," I said. "I paid fifty thousand for a new liver four years ago. Surgeon said it would last a decade."

The doctor laughed. "It should have. But that's the rub of modern life. We build better livers, and someone concocts stronger booze. We get sun treatments, then our chemicals burn up the ozone even more. Cure one disease, and another pops up. The pitcher juices up his throw, and the batter juices up his swing. On and on it goes."

"I guess you get paid either way."

"Quite!" Setek said. "It's all about picking the right team to play for."

I looked through his catalog of modifications. I wanted everything, but I couldn't make Zunz pay for it all. I'd rather go around half finished than have him feel like I broke his trust. The doctor and I settled on a lung lining. A simple expanding one, excreted from a scope right into the bronchi.

"You need a new shoulder fitting on the cybernetic arm," the doctor said. "Your current one is degraded and the skin is inflamed. I'll throw that in for free."

Setek hooked me up to a canister of gas and twisted the valve with one sharp creak.

On the surgical table, waiting for the gas to put me to sleep, I had assumed that Zunz had been doing me a favor. That he hadn't needed me as backup but felt bad that my career had stalled while he'd become a superstar. He was back on the team a few months later, both hands working just fine. He never mentioned Setek again.

But now, standing in my apartment and holding Setek's card, my brain was spinning in a different direction. I was thinking that Setek might know not only know how people got patched up. He might know how they got broken down.

22

THE STRANGE SURGEON

Dolores walked out of the bedroom, stretching. "Don't tell me you're already hoping for another inning?"

"Actually, I wanted to ask you for a favor."

"Sounds like I need to get dressed."

I explained the details, asked if she'd be willing to come with me to Dr. Setek's office and snoop around while I got my arm fixed. To be my backup as I'd been Zunz's.

"Backup?" she said.

"Okay, okay. Partner."

I didn't know if Setek was involved in killing Zunz or if he was the one who could tell me what substance had done it. But he was a clue. There weren't many of those left with Kang dead and the girl missing. Plus, my arm had started spazzing uncontrollably, trying to tear itself off from the shoulder. If I didn't fix it soon, I'd have to rip it off myself and throw it in the trash.

Setek had moved offices. When Zunz had taken me there, it had been downtown. A big, open office overlooking the storm wall. Now, his card said he was in Midtown. Mouth Tower.

"Maybe the Mets purchased him?" I said.

"I can check."

Dolores made a call to another scout at Pyramid to see if they had any opposition info on Setek while I made breakfast. I cracked a half dozen eggs into a pan, scrambled them with a lot of butter and a little hot sauce. The way Mrs. Z used to. Tossed them on a bed of fried rice with a pile of onions and handful of synthetic cilantro. Filled the coffee machine with triple-caffeinated beans.

"We don't have anything recent on Setek," Dolores said. "Nada. If he was purchased by Monsanto, it wasn't public. But after the *Colossus* disaster, he's been radioactive. I guess if I was hiring him I'd do it off the books too."

We ate, dressed, and then took a taxi uptown, weaving through the skystabbers and dodging the retail blimps. The smog was thin that day and we could see the golden mouth sign glowing from blocks away. It enlarged, the twinkling lips growing until it swallowed us. We landed on the red-carpeted tongue.

"Being rich doesn't buy you any taste, does it?" Dolores said, looking at the ornate golden bats and baseballs on the wall of the marble lift.

The doctor's office was about fifty floors below the Mouth's penthouse. I hoped he wasn't monitoring the security feeds. I didn't want to be called in for an impromptu case update.

Dolores and I sat in the waiting room looking like an actual couple, like we could be going home that night, meal printing a few bento boxes, and watching holographic soap operas for hours until we started drooling and snoring on each other.

"Do you think this Setek works personally for the Mouth? Or he's on the Monsanto payroll?" Dolores asked.

"Either way, Natasha said the Mets were covering the bill."

"Are you sure this woman's a real Neanderthal? We'd heard rumors at Pyramid, but I assumed it was slander."

"She's Neanderthal all right," I said. "Or at least heavily upgraded to look like one."

"I'd love to get a look at that DNA."

"I'll try to suck a little blood out next time I see her."

"If you're serious, I'll get you a syringe."

I laughed, a bit too loudly. Someone shushed us. There were only a few other people in the waiting room. Elderly people in fancy suits, skin starting to wrinkle despite the upgrades. They glared at us over their screens.

"You hear rumors about the Mets. That Monsanto has unreported government contracts, and the upgrades they're working on are being pumped right into the troops. Lot of the Sphinxes' scientists think their ballplayers are using nanobots in the bloodstream and zootech parasites that secrete steroids as they feed. Stuff that should be illegal if President Newman wasn't making the Department of Human Limits turn a blind eye."

"At the Yankees, we heard the same rumors. Of course, we heard them about the Sphinxes too."

Dolores was laughing when the doors swung open and Dr. Setek slithered out. His upper half was screwed into a cybernetic tail somewhere between a snake's tail and a gigantic tongue. He bobbed up and down, moving toward us. His red hair erupted from his skull like a forest fire. His long green tie swayed back and forth as he licked his way across the plastic floor.

Dolores looked between the doctor and me. Leaned over. Whispered, "You let this guy operate on you?"

"He used to walk differently," I said.

As he got closer, I could see the tail was sealed with porous skin that leaked a trail of mucus on the floor.

"Kobo, my boy, Natasha said you'd be coming."

I stood up and Setek went up on the tip of his tail to meet me eye to eye.

"Surprised you remember me."

"Oh, I remember every patient." He tapped the side of his head. "Sometimes gray matter is more powerful than a CPU."

He ushered us into the examination room. We followed, walking a bit to the side to avoid his lower half's secretions.

"Do you remember the man I visited with last time? Julio Julio Zunz?" I said, a little too sharply.

"Certainly. One of my favorite patients. Such a tragedy."

"You remember anything about his charts that could explain what happened at the plate?"

The doctor had been examining my arm, and dropped it. Looked at me seriously. "Zunz was a beautiful man. The most gorgeous genes I've ever analyzed. Very unique. His cells could absorb more upgrades than almost any other player. We used to call him the Henrietta Lacks of home runs!" He swiveled at the hip to face Dolores. Looked her over with a zigzag scan. "And who is this tantalizing specimen?"

"Dolores Zamora," she said, keeping her hand unextended. "Just here for moral support."

"Brilliant. We all need all the support we can get in this cruel, crazy world. Give me a second while I switch legs."

The doctor slid to the corner on his bionic tail. He undid the clamping, freed his torso. Pushed himself up with his hands, and hand-walked across the table toward a set of motorized wheels. "God, it feels nice to get a good breeze down there."

He lowered his trunk into the new lower half. Screwed himself onto the base, swiveling around in a way that made me dizzy.

"Lost the legs in the third Iraq war," he said to Dolores. "Acid mites. Sneaky bastards had the whole area littered with pits of them. Must have bought them off the Russians. Lots of blood, lots of screaming. They had to amputate me right there on the dune. All better now though." He rapped a little rhythm on the metal base. "I bring it up only because it puts some people on edge."

"Not a fan of normal bionic legs?" Dolores asked.

The doc spun on the wheels to face me. "Nope nope nope. At least until I can put my brain in a fresh body, I'm going to embrace variety." He took hold of my arm, tapped it gently up and down with one knuckle. "Haven't you ever wanted a bear claw, a pincer, or, hell, a tentacle? No need to be stuck with the human shape you were born with."

"I get called enough names with this arm," I said.

"Your limb, your call. That's my motto. Although that arm is so out of date it's practically Paleolithic, in cybernetic terms."

"Are you offering a free replacement?"

The doctor chuckled. "I'm afraid Natasha isn't covering that. Although if you want to work out a layaway plan..." He nodded toward a display of limbs on the walls. Arms and legs of different shapes and materials ringed the room. Some were bionic, others faux flesh still attached to the feeding troughs. They were adorned with different protrusions. Talons, fingers, and claws. Others were original creations, utilizing bizarre geometry and strange joints. "Variety is the spice of life."

"Sorry, doc. I've got a case to solve."

"Okay, okay. I can take a hint."

"Speaking of that case," Dolores said, interrupting. She was leaning against a blood filterer by the cabinets. "Do you have any theories on what could do that to Zunz?"

"It's surprising how fragile we are, isn't it?" Setek said. "All our science and technology can't stop that fundamental truth."

"Still. Any ideas?"

Setek thought about it. He spoke a little slower than normal. "I'm more of a fix-'em-upper than a break-'em-downer. But I'd say that from how rapidly the symptoms spread, it was something slipped into his skin or his helmet that activated that day."

"Is there anything that stood out to you?" I said. "Anything that might help. He was my brother."

The doctor's eyes widened at this, although he mumbled a perfunctory condolence. "Brother, I had no idea. I'd love to get a look at your DNA and compare. Let me get a sample."

He reached for the row of syringes on the wall.

"I was adopted."

"Ah." He put the needle back and ran his stethoscope along the curve of his chin. "Are you in contact with any living blood relatives? If we could compare a sample of a relative's DNA to his, we might get an idea what happened."

Something clicked in my mind. I looked at his red hair. Squinted. "Have you visited our mother?"

"Oh yes, yes," Setek said. "Mrs. Zunz was quite forthcoming."

"I'd appreciate it if you'd lay off. She's been through a lot."

"Not to worry. All finished. We did take a sample to analyze, but unfortunately it didn't tell us as much as we'd hoped. She was missing a few of the key mutations. If only his father was still alive." He sighed. Then went to a drawer and pulled out a pair of instruments. "Now, let's take a look at this hand."

Setek poked and prodded. Ran a scanner over my arm, then my other parts. He took a large blood sample and a sample of the fluid in my hand. Pulled out the swaps, ran the currents, knocked on different bones. The whole time he muttered, "Well, well, well."

I looked over at Dolores, whose face couldn't decide if it wanted to giggle or peel back in disgust.

"Well, this is doable, although I'd recommend you buy a new arm within the next two years," he said. "I'll have to rewire the palm. Add a new stabilizer and nerve module. But it's doable. Take the next few days off for rest."

"Not an option."

"Well, don't listen to me, I'm only the doctor." He looked at Dolores. "What about those ears? I can see you're using transcribers. I could rejigger your ear canal in an afternoon. You wouldn't feel a thing."

"I'm happy with the senses I have."

Dr. Setek clapped. "There's sense in that! There's sense in that, I say again. Sense in the senses. Yes, ma'am."

"Glad you understand."

He held up his hands, a couple syringes in one, a bottle of red oval pills in the other. "So, gas, shot, pills, or shock?"

I opted for the gas, and he slipped on the mask. I let my mind sail off into the black.

While Setek worked on my arm, I couldn't feel anything. Couldn't think of anything either. Nothing except that I couldn't think. No dreams or visions. When I was a child, my sleep was always fitful. My dreams filled with crumbling walls and screams. In the blackness, if I cried out, Zunz would reach over and hold my hand. But here, I couldn't feel Setek touching me. The drugs carried me beautifully.

Sometime later, I woke up on the warm metal table. The air was calm and quiet. My senses tiptoed back to me.

"Hello, darling," Dolores said. She helped me off the table. "You know you snore when you're drugged?"

The doctor was gone. I looked at my arm. It seemed healthy and strong, no holes that weren't supposed to be there. I flexed. Tapped. Twisted. It was all in working order. Now I needed to make sure the Sassafras sisters didn't try another gut renovation.

"He went over you pretty good," Dolores said. She nodded toward the monitor drone, which was an owl with comically large eyes. Dolores put a finger to her lip. "A thorough doctor. Let's get out of here and get you something to eat."

We headed down to the street level. Walked a block or two before the air started making us cough.

"No one else came in. Just the doctor mumbling to himself and me twiddling my thumbs in the corner."

"Good."

"But he did make a call while you were under. Walked into another room like he was worried I was recording. Rightly." Dolores laughed. "My goggles could pick up some of the words. I didn't get a full transcription. He definitely mentioned 'unviable donor' and Zunz."

"We should try to tail him," I said.

"From Mouth Tower? That might be hard," Dolores said. "And I have other work to do. Paying work. But I do have an employee plus-one for the home games. We could go to game three tomorrow. Watch the teams hit some balls with a few dogs and beers. Plus, you'll get a chance to snoop around."

"Last time I went to the Pyramid a player died."

"I could use a date. Shouldn't you actually get in the field, dig your hands in the muck?"

"I just got this hand cleaned."

"You talk smart, Kobo," Dolores said, shaking her head. "You should work on thinking smart. Going to the stadium will be the best shot for you to sneak into Kang's house. Head out in the fourth inning. The guards will be watching the game. I can give you the security code. Maybe there's something the police missed."

I smiled, suddenly and stupidly. "I hadn't thought of that."

Right then I was feeling tired, still woozy from the surgery table. I told Dolores I'd think about the game and went home. Spent a while scouring the various internets for information on Edenists and their beliefs. They were a strange group, half in bed with the Grand New Party's immigration crackdown and half with pious monks doing charity work between anti-upgrade sermons. I tried to search for the Janus Club, but the web was scrubbed of references.

Then I spent the rest of the evening looking at my tuned-up arm. Testing it. Admiring its gleam. Checking the data that was stored up on my screen and spreading salve where the flesh met metal.

I fell asleep thinking not of the case but of what I'd buy when I solved it. I was at a banquet table filled with parts of every type— petri dish organs, shining bionics, slick new wettech—and piled my plate all the way to the ceiling. Setek was there too, serving me new parts every time I chomped.

I woke up, smiling, to a call. It was Okafor.

"Morning, Sil."

"Kobo, that girl you were chasing? The little twig that was at Zunz's house?"

I sat up, cracked my neck.

"Did you identify her?"

"No," Okafor said. "We arrested her."

23

THE CAGED GIRL

My arm felt fresh off the assembly line. The rest of me was in a state of ache and decay. Doctors never fixed everything at once. You could have an old, dull skull with state-of-the-art eyeballs, or a rotting gut housed in a new chrome stomach. Anyone could be made new, sure, but only one piece and one payment at a time. I suppose this made me feel a little sympathy for the Edenist girl. Maybe she'd seen what a racket upgrading a body could be and figured she'd roll the dice on mother nature. A gamble too, but cheaper.

"You look chipper," Okafor said, greeting me at the front desk. The station was large and surprisingly quiet. Most of the cops were lounging around sipping coffee or else strapped into holofeeds, reexamining evidence recordings. I'd always been nervous around cops. Zunz and I had spent half our childhood hiding from them. But Okafor was more friend than police to me. I smiled and looked them over. They seemed bulkier than I remembered. Sharp angles under the uniform.

"New torso?"

"New everything. Mandatory upgrades for the whole division." They grabbed me, clapped me to their steel chest. "Shit, Kobo. Can you believe that jerk went and died on us without even asking permission?"

"He never did like to give you a heads-up."

They laughed, still hugging me. "God, right? You'd get a text saying, 'pickup game in the park, ten minutes' and have to sprint right out the door. Fucker never was good at time management."

Okafor had known Zunz even longer than me. The Okafors had run daycare out of their home for neighbors like Mrs. Z who spent most of the day and some of the night plugged into remote gear. I'd always been jealous that Okafor had known Zunz since before he could walk.

I let the hug last a few seconds, then pulled back. "Have you learned anything?"

Okafor got back into a cop position, thumbs tucked into the belt near the guns. They shook their head. "Let's not talk out here."

They led me to the break room—"the only place we don't bug"—and poured us both cups of coffee in mugs that said *To Protect (Our Asses) and Serve (Your Asses)*. "A security drone found the girl loitering around a Monsanto zootech depot. She's a feisty one. Tried to bite my guy's hand when he took her in. She was carrying this."

They held up a cage with a bright red newt inside. When I touched the glass, it leapt at my finger. Its skin was coated in a sticky yellow film.

"A pet?"

"A weapon. The saliva produces enough neurotoxin to leave an elephant brain-dead." Okafor saw my face and quickly added, "No, it's not what killed Zunz. It wouldn't cause bleeding like that."

"Why would an Edenist go near a zootech depot?"

"We've been building a dossier on an Edenist splinter cell calling themselves the Diseased Eden. They're less religion, more terrorist organization. Had a big split with the main branch over their 'collaboration' with politicians. You know how these extremists get. The Diseased Eden steal zootech. Liberate them, I guess they'd say. Remember last year when a cloud of nausea gnats was released in Old Times Square?"

Old Times Square was a place I avoided. Historical preservation laws kept all the buildings in the area under fifty stories and hologram billboards were banned. It was all neon and LCD screens. A quaint tourist trap for nostalgia addicts. Still, that didn't mean I approved of infecting masses of out-of-towners with weaponized flies.

"The city was hosing it down for weeks. That was these Diseased Edenists?"

"We think so. No one was ever prosecuted."

"And this girl is one of them?"

"Who knows? Maybe she just likes red lizards."

Okafor couldn't tell me much more about the girl. Her DNA didn't register in the system. She wouldn't give a name. No identity implants. Would only give her address as an Edenist center in Queens.

"Listen. I said I'd do you this favor. Out of respect for Zunz. But you won't have long. The Edenists are already sending lawyers down here with threats and briefcases. And she's underage. We'll have to set her free soon, and I need you gone before they get here."

"You're going to release her when she's carrying illegal zootech?"

"It oughta be illegal, but these biopharm corps pump out new species a lot faster than the government can catalog them."

I tapped the side of the glass and watched the bright red creature scurry around. The right designer zootech could have killed Zunz. Smart to have a weapon that can crawl away.

"Did the girl say anything about him?"

Okafor shook their head as we walked to the interrogation chamber. "Maybe you'll have better luck than me. I'll wait outside. Like I said, ten minutes."

The interrogation room was a small concrete box with a table in the middle. The table's top had screens displaying the captive's heartbeat, vocal pitch, and other data. I walked by it, went up to the wall. Pulled out an eraser. "Send her around," I said. The giant gears of the station's holding cell system groaned. The cells spun until the girl was in front of me.

The kid in the cell was a scrawny thing. A stick figure in a tunic. She was leaning against the back wall of the glass cell, twirling a lock of black hair around her forefinger. The tray of food on the floor was untouched.

"Not hungry?"

"I'm a picky eater."

"You look like you're hungry all the time," I said. "You look like someone who's never been full in their entire life."

She picked up a slice of pale meat from the tray with the farthest tips of her fingers. A flat, off-white oval. Held it toward me with a stiff arm. "You see how white this is? It's the color of a sheet of paper. What's it supposed to be? Tuna? Pork? Chicken? No animal is this white." She sniffed the circle. "Real meat doesn't smell like soap either."

She flung it against the wall, where it stuck in front of my face on the glass. A gigantic pupil-less eye. It slid down, leaving a pale trail down to the floor.

I let a puff of eraser smoke bounce off the wall. It rippled out along the glass, then faded away. "You like baseball?"

"Sure. But I don't like talking to cops."

"I'm not a cop."

"You look like a cop."

"And you look like a guilty little girl." I sat down at the interrogation table and watched as her data streamed in. Her heartbeat and vocal pitch were steady. She was apparently used enough to interrogations to not be intimidated. "What's your name?"

"My friends call me Nails."

"Are we friends?"

"Nope. That's why I'm not giving you my real name."

Despite my better instinct, I was starting to like her. Twelve years old and already good with the sneer.

"All right, Nails. Since I'm not a cop, I can give it to you straight. A star baseball player has been killed. Julio Julio Zunz." She flinched a little at the mention. "The cops, the media, and Monsanto are going to throw all their weight at anyone they can pin it on. And there's evidence tying your Edenist friends to the murder."

She showed me her sneer again. "Unless you're planning to frame me, I'm not worried."

"FLB players have been getting lots of death threats from your little group. What were you doing in JJ Zunz's house?"

Her eyes narrowed. "Don't know him. I'm sorry he died. People shouldn't die like that."

"You live in his house yet you've never met him?"

The girl sat down on the floor, began tracing inscrutable shapes on the dusty floor. "If you aren't a cop, what are you?"

"Right now, I'm a guy trying to solve a murder. I used to be a scout."

"A cyborg scout? Aren't you banned from the league?"

"Only from playing." The FLB had banned all cybernetics after the failure of the Cyber League, but only on the field. They still let cyborgs like me work off camera.

"That doesn't bother you?"

"My landlord isn't picky about where the cash comes from."

The girl hugged herself, staring at the floor. She seemed to be having trouble breathing. "That's how the whole country ended up this way. No one cares about anything except money."

"You say that like it's a new thought. They've been singing that one since cavemen crawled out of caves."

"Look at your arm, your eye. Even your body parts are another thing they buy and sell."

She was right but also young. You could afford to be right when you didn't have bills to pay and loan sharks to avoid.

Suddenly she bent over, began coughing wetly. When she wiped her mouth, I saw blood on the back of her hand. A red smear from the knuckle to the wrist.

"Are you okay? Do you need water?"

"What do you care, pig?" she said, still coughing a little.

"I keep telling you, I'm not a cop."

She finished wiping her mouth on the back of her sleeve.

I sat down on the floor on the other side of the glass. Tried to look her straight in the face. "You seem like a good kid. Let me tell you something. Whoever killed Zunz didn't just kill a baseball star. Didn't just murder a symbol of corporate human manipulation, or whatever you believe. They killed an actual human. And a good one. You know how few of those are left?"

She was shaking her head, looking back at the floor. She said something that sounded like "a piece of shit."

"I thought you didn't know him?"

"I said I hadn't met him. Why do you care about him anyway?"

"He was my brother. Maybe you've never lost someone important to you, but I need to know what happened." She hadn't looked up for a bit but did when I said *brother*. "If you can tell me anything, I'll do what I can to help you."

She laughed sadly at the line. "Old men are always saying they can help me. I'm sorry about your brother dying. It wasn't me who killed him though. Go bug someone else."

"Maybe not. But I know you're connected somehow."

Her head shook back and forth.

"Don't deny it," I said. I was getting angry again. My blood was speeding through my veins. I stood up and walked around.

The girl looked at me, shaking a little. Her face scrunched up. Something was building up inside her. I couldn't tell if she was going to laugh or scream.

"I know you were at Zunz's house," I continued. "I saw you staring at his statue in the park. I want to know how you're connected."

Then it came. It was laughter.

And it was a laughter I recognized. As soon as I heard it, I could see it all. Those dimples the size of dugouts in her cheeks, just like his. The curve of his eyes and that strong jut of jawbone.

"You're his..." I started. "Jesus, you're his daughter?"

She was still laughing. "Wow. You really are a bad detective, Uncle."

24

THE ENGINEERED GARDENS

I'd always thought no matter how our lives diverged, and no matter how we drifted apart after my baseball career collapsed and Zunz's took off, that Zunz trusted me. That I was someone he could lean on. Confide in. The one true friend among the yes-men and fair-weather fans who flutter to a star player like moths to a streetlamp. But Zunz had never told me about a daughter. Much less a daughter he'd paid to have hidden away.

The girl was standing up now, leaning against the cell wall with her arms crossed. She regarded me with an amused pity.

"JJ was your father?" My mind tossed back and forth between betrayal and confusion.

"Technically. And only technically. I got his genes and nothing else, not even a birthday card."

I tried to picture Zunz and her together. Him hoisting her on his shoulders at the beach. Or giving her an ice-cream cone as they strolled through the park, a little robopup tugging at the leash. The images didn't make sense. They formed and dissolved. I guessed they didn't make sense to Zunz either.

I thought back to Kang's house. The pictures on his wall. "Your mother. She was Hana Kang?"

She nodded while looking away.

"Is that how you became an Edenist?"

"My grandparents were Edenists but my mother didn't really believe. She drifted away from the church for a long time. Guess that's when she met my dad." She tried to sneer again but it came out more of a frown. "It was him and my uncle who sent her back to the church. Seeing what they did to their bodies. Uncle Jung was good to me. Helped me out when he could, but I know my mom thought he was juicing his body to oblivion trying to chase fame. Anyway, I'm glad she raised me with principles. Those are hard to come by these days."

"And Zunz? Your father, I mean."

"The only thing I have from him is a spare key to his hideaway house. Uncle Jung gave it to me when he died, said he figured my father owed me that much."

I was still trying to imagine this other Zunz, the father he'd decided not to be. The Zunz who existed in an alternate universe where he hosted playdates and swung by concert recitals instead of away games. For some reason, I felt angry. "Why didn't JJ take you?"

She might have been the twig, but her look almost snapped me in two. "Why did my father abandon me? Geez, I dunno. Great question."

I heard someone knocking on the door behind me. Five loud thunks. It was Okafor, telling me my time was up by waving their hand across their neck. But I needed to figure this out. To understand. Or maybe to explain.

"Zunz wasn't that way when I knew him. He liked taking care of things. Had lots of pets."

"Pets." Her face was as sharp as a needle.

"I just mean. I don't know. I just meant that's not how I knew him."

"Well hooray for you," she said.

"We'd had it hard, back then. He and I. We grew up pretty poor."

"Save it," she said. "I'm twelve. Both of my parents are dead. My uncle too. It's all crappy water under the crappy bridge of my life."

The door opened behind me. I could hear several people shouting. Okafor grabbed my shoulder, forcefully turned me around. Their voice was hot in my ear. "You have to leave now. The lawyers are here."

I looked back as Okafor pulled me out of the room. The girl gave a sad laugh. "Bye-bye, Uncle."

Okafor kept pulling me, down a side hall, past the training rooms, and out onto the street. They pushed me into the wall. People on the streets started filming.

"You said you'd go when I needed you to go, Kobo. Damn it. I knew it was a mistake to help you."

Okafor stared at me hard. But I must have been staring off somewhere else. They relaxed and let me off the wall. Stepped back.

"What the hell is wrong with you?"

I shook my head. Tried to get the pieces of my mind to click back together. "Never mind," I said. "Thanks, Sil. I owe you. I won't bother you again."

"What did she say? Did she know who killed JJ?"

"No," I said. "She didn't have anything to do with it. Nothing to do with it at all."

I stayed against the wall thinking, or trying to, after Okafor went back inside. At first my mind simply denied. Said it couldn't be true, that it was an elaborate joke, or else some conspiracy I didn't understand.

I went across the street and around the corner to see the station entrance. A group of Edenists in gray-and-blue tunics came out with the girl in the middle. They all got inside a large black van and levitated away.

I had to follow them, force them to let me talk to her again. But as I was getting in a cab, I saw a man sitting on a bench in the terrarium park across the street. A tiny triangle of land with a glass bubble to block out the smog. The man was bulky with big, knobby hands. Most of his face was hidden behind a screen, but I could see his thick brow. Coppelius.

"Just take me around the block," I told the driver.

We flew off down the street, away from the Edenist van.

When we circled back, Coppelius was gone. Which meant he was following me. I could see a cab behind us, bobbing low in the smog.

I called Dolores. Didn't tell her all the details. That a Neanderthal spy was following me or I apparently had a quasi niece. I only asked her if I could still take her up on her partner offer.

"What do you need, Kobo?"

"I want you to tail a little girl," I said.

Coppelius's taxi followed me as we zigged through the city's skystabbers. I told the cabbie to tag behind a Plethora Emporium blimp. I watched the pelican drones drop out one by one, packages in their pouches. But Coppelius didn't get bored. So I decided to get dropped off at Monsanto Meadows. Figured that was a place where I couldn't lead the Neanderthal to any more clues. Plus, maybe I could uncover a few more if I talked to some of Zunz's teammates.

"It's closed for the playoffs."

"I'm part of the team."

The driver's cam in the backseat looked me up and down. "Think they only take full human types there."

I could hear the distaste on his tongue. This guy was the same species of asshole who made jokes about my childhood arm on the playground. Then they mocked the replacement I'd gotten. I didn't let it faze me. I knew he was as antiquated as me. A human taxi driver in a self-driving car. The industry had paid off enough senators to pass a law requiring a human in any flying vehicle. A live body if the algorithms failed. But everyone knew the law would be changed soon, and they'd be shoved out the door without a safety net.

"I'm a scout. Got the chip in my palm and everything."

The man squinted. "They used to have rules back in my day."

"What day was that?"

"The good old days." He spat out the words like they'd been phlegm in his throat.

I was confused and bitter by the time I landed. Yet, the Monsanto compound still took my breath away. Since the FLB was run by international biopharms, they'd been able to expand the league to other countries and international waters. There were stunning parks all over. But Monsanto Meadows might have been the most beautiful. Better than even the snowcap stadium of GenSlice Future up north or the silver ziggurat of Los Tigres de Plata del Bayer de México. It was called the Meadows, but we scouts called it the hanging gardens. Babylon.

The Meadows took up the entirety of what used to be Central Park. Monsanto had bought up the park after the city went bankrupt trying to kill the rat population with zootech sewer snakes. It worked, but then they had to purchase a designer virus to kill the snakes flowing out of the subway tracks and snacking on tourist toes.

The park was ringed with a high wall, dotted with massive filter fans to keep out the smog, spies, and external fauna. The stadium itself was at the north end. The research laboratories, staff quarters, and corporate communications offices were scattered between gardens and lakes. The waters were filled with fluorescent fish, swimming in dreamlike patterns in water the color of candy. Small gardens of flowers floated around on levitating plots. Flightless birds hopped between the floating plots as they passed. Green parrots, pink flamingos, spotted pigeons. Everything was moving and alive.

The public could stroll through part of the grounds for a fee, and I saw couples walking around, holding hands and gawking at the zootech. Convenience store blimps floated between the trees, selling the latest Mets-branded products.

Dolores called me as I was approaching the stadium. "I'm following this girl, but the van dropped her off at a supraway station. She was gone by the time I got to the platform."

"Maybe she's going back to Zunz's island house. Can you check that out? I'll owe you."

"That Neanderthal blood sample?" Dolores laughed. "No, sorry, K. I've got a presentation on the best transgenic splicer prospects in the university circuit."

I figured the girl would avoid the house, since I'd found her there. My best bet was the Edenist center in Queens that had sent out the lawyers. But while I was here, I figured I might as well talk to a few of Zunz's old teammates.

The golden Monsanto Meadows stadium was up ahead. I strolled toward it through the hanging gardens.

25

THE FORMER TEAM

I found Lex Dash on the edge of the field, soaking in a stim tank. Thin needles were nestled into each of her muscles, stimulating them with little electric shocks, while tiny beetle-sized drones rolled over her body and massaged as the muscles were flexed. She opened her eyes when I rapped on the tank.

"Yes?" She looked me over, realized I wasn't a coach. "Oh. I know you. Zunz's brother, right?"

I gave her a surprised-you-remembered-me smile. I'd only met Dash a few times when Zunz let me tag along to Mets events.

"Right. Kobo. I'm working for the Mouth on a special case. JJ Zunz's case, actually. I was hoping you had a couple minutes to chat."

"I've been trying not to think about him."

Few players in the FLB were truly close. The players' lives were managed down to the minute when they were playing or training, and then they went home to their separate cloud condos to recuperate alone. But Dash and Zunz had been close to something like friends. They were known to frequent the downtown clubs and uptown galas, buying rounds of champagne wherever they went. They'd been the fun, public faces of the Mets franchise. There were even rumors they were lovers, which Zunz denied. Still, whatever was between them might make her sentimental enough to talk. Indeed, Dash's eyes looked a little watery when I said his name.

"Okay, maybe I can find five minutes."

Dash yelled over to her coach who told her she had a couple minutes till they rebalanced her hormones.

"I'm transitioning after the playoffs. Takes about six months to complete so we're getting it started now."

"You'll be starting next season as a man?"

Dash smirked as she picked up a duffle bag. "We'll see how the HL East pitchers deal with me bulked up and batting third. We need slugging with Zunz...well. You know. Anyway, you're going to have to let me swing while we talk."

"Sure thing."

We walked over to the first base foul line and Dash opened the bag. Inside was a bat and a red, fleshy drone in the shape of a gigantic mouth. The drone flew out a couple dozen feet, spun, and spat a ball in her direction. Dash popped it high and the drone flew up to scoop it out of the sky.

"Was Zunz acting strange before—" I hesitated a second. "Before the incident."

Dash bent her knees and spun the bat's tip in little circles over her shoulder. "He seemed a little out of it. You know, forgetting big things like what position to play. Then suddenly remembering extremely specific things. Like, he kept asking me about my dog, Oats, who I'd had to put down the year before. Fuck, curveball."

She swung awkwardly but tipped the ball, which bounced beneath the pitching drone's lips and hit the safety net. The drone floated over and unrolled a red tongue to slurp up the ball.

"The Mouth makes us use these mouth pitching drones," Dash said over her shoulder, a tinge of disgust in her voice. "I miss when we had metal ones. I don't need my drones to look like orifices."

"Do you know what JJ was on? Were they giving him new drugs?"

Dash turned around, frowning. "Surely you know the players' regimens are private. All I can tell you is mine hasn't changed." She shrugged. "Although, you know something did happen with Zunz about a couple weeks before he died. He'd been a bit out of it all day and then collapsed out in the field. I remember when the medics carried him past me, he had blood leaking out of his ears."

"What? When was this?" I'd watched all of Zunz's games that season and hadn't seen any injuries except the shattered hand from the broken bat.

"It was at practice. Soon after he'd come back from that nasty hand injury. The docs told us it was just an issue with blood thinners and the high altitude from our game against GenSlice up in their mountain stadium. Anyway, he was back to normal a few days later."

If my timeline was right, that game would have been about a week before they hired Arocha. That timing didn't feel like a coincidence. Maybe they'd realized the problem then, but hadn't stopped it in time. I needed to find her next, see if there was a connection.

"What about Jung Kang? Did he ever mention him to you?"

Dash got back into position. Tapped the imaginary home plate three times with the bat. "The Pyramid benchwarmer? Can't help you there. He wasn't even in the lineup last game."

"He's dead."

Dash looked back at me as the pitch spat out of the mouth drone. It flew past us and rolled into one of the recuperation tanks with a dull thud.

"Christ. It's not safe being an FLB player anymore, is it?"

The stray pitch had caught the attention of the coaches. One trotted our way, waving their arms, and I figured it was time to head out. I asked her if there was anything else she could tell me, but she said no and anyway she'd been grilled a dozen times already. "I'm sure my interviews are all on file."

Walking back across the field, past all the players stretching, tossing, and swinging, I felt a great longing for when I'd been one of those players. When my arm was new, oiled up, and ready to pitch. Then I got angry. Angry thinking of how easily the game had spit me out. And angry thinking what the Mets might have done to Zunz.

As I was heading back to the tunnel, Gail O'Shea, the second base coach, stepped in front of me. "I don't think you're part of the staff. How'd you get in here?"

"Ask Natasha," I said, pushing past.

"I will!" she shouted after me.

I had one more person to see. Someone the Mets had needed so desperately they kidnapped her in the middle of the playoffs.

I found Julia Arocha in one of the practice labs, cursing. She was standing before a transparent plastic tube that was connected by spokes to a clump of folded gray matter covered in red veins. Inside the tube was a curved spine. Blue fluid ran through the tube and spokes. The whole thing was connected to an oxygenator.

Arocha had a blue visor on and was dabbing the mushy hunk with a beeping tool. It sizzled with each poke. She still had the touch, I could tell. My scouting hadn't been wrong.

The fist-shaped clump of brain wasn't taking it well. The surface was turning black, cracking as it charred. Arocha cursed again, loud and long.

I knocked on the doorframe.

Arocha turned around, startled. She flipped up the visor.

"Tell him I need more samples. Another half dozen at least."

"More samples of what?"

Arocha stopped. Collected herself. Then she asked me who I was.

I told her the truth. About Zunz and my relation to him. While I spoke, she tugged on the metal security collar around her neck.

"Do you know anything about what happened to him?"

She looked past me while shaking her head. "I was brought in here after he died. Traded if you want to call it that."

"Did you analyze the remains?"

Her mouth stretched into a taut line. "I'm afraid I can't help you with that or anything else. I'm really pretty busy here." She gestured toward the door.

"Have you heard anything? Any of the other coats talk at the mess hall?"

"I don't get to talk to too many other people. And believe it or not, baseball players aren't what we spend our free time discussing. Goodbye."

As I left, I saw her pull out her screen to make a call.

26

THE PRACTICE SWINGS

I walked around the Monsanto grounds for a while, watching the strange zootech and disguised drones. It was getting harder and harder to tell the difference between the living creatures and the machines. Although only the drones were carrying ads for Mets products. A parrot-shaped drone with a red light in its forehead flew up to me and squawked. "Dash like Lex Dash with Monsanto Dash Dots. They make your hemoglobin hemo-go-go-go!"

Seeing Dash bat around had gotten me hungry for some swings myself, and I remembered the batting cages in the subbasement that the players didn't use anymore. "They got those old-timey robot pitchers you can program to mimic players," Zunz had told me. "The exact same models they had when we were in school." He took me there a few times in the off-season, and we batted around balls for hours. Maybe it was time to test my new metal arm on some old leather balls.

I found a free cage. The pitching machine was slumped over, head scraping the floor. When I tapped the plate three times, the machine sprang to life. Unfolded into a blue robot whose parts were dotted with squishy orange protrusions. They hadn't bothered to make the robot look overly human, but it did have a smiling face painted on the front and a red baseball cap on top.

"Lefty, righty, ambi, or player simulation?" the pitching machine asked.

"Player sim. Jaiden Schwipper," I said, naming the White Mice pitcher who'd been facing Zunz when he died. In the replays, Schwipper starts out seeming annoyed when Zunz gets sick. Like he thought Zunz was icing his throw. Then as Zunz bleeds, Schwipper steps backward. He walks off the mound and keeps moving back, shaking his head in denial of his eyes.

I got into a batting stance. Pretended to be Zunz. It wasn't hard since I'd been doing it my whole life. I imagined my cyborg parts were pure muscle and the rustle of the ventilation system was the roar of a distant crowd.

"Batter up," the machine said. A blue strike zone box lit up in front of me. Then the robot reshaped itself into the approximate height and size of Schwipper. Tucked the hat low over its imitation eyes. Lifted its right leg. Pulled back. Flung.

I missed by a mile. In fact, it took me five swings to even foul a pitch.

"Dial down to seventy percent velocity," I said. The robot threw a nice slow one over the plate. I smashed it dead center. Smiled at the clink against the mesh wall.

I kept smashing the balls without thinking about anything else. Putting metal to leather, feeling the reverberations down my arms when I fouled a ball and the beautiful crack when I hit it dead-on.

Then I was smashing them and thinking about Zunz. What must have been going through his head when he faced down the real Schwipper as he was starting to die. How scared he must have been. All alone with a million eyes on him.

And then I thought of the girl. His apparent daughter. My alleged niece. Living life in hiding with unupgraded fanatics. Abandoned by my brother.

I let a curveball swerve past me. Sat on the bench. Checked the time.

As I was heading toward the mag lift, someone whistled at me. A tall woman peeking out of a dark room. It was Julia Arocha.

"In here," she said.

I joined her, and she locked the door. It was a storage closet filled with replacement parts for the pitching machines. Arms, legs, torsos, and heads. They were piled up in different mesh crates. In the one closest to me, fifty chrome faces smiled in different directions.

"I couldn't talk in the lab. You know they record everything, right?" She'd disabled the camera above the door; it hung unblinking from its stand. She kept looking around at the walls and corners as if there might be others.

Arocha leaned against a crate of chrome legs. She relaxed a little. "You're Zunz's brother, right? I looked into you. If you find out what happened to Zunz, will you get the word out? To the press?"

"I'd do anything to find the killer."

"What if there was no killer?" she said.

"Is this a riddle?"

"Monsanto had been making overtures to me about a week before Zunz died. Said they were having a nervous system issue they thought I could fix. I rebuffed them. Not that it changed things. Anyway, I'm not the only one they brought in. Monsanto has been buying up experts left and right. Nerve systems, tissue stabilization, cell growth. Two others were brought in this week. And from the drugged look of their eyes, I don't think it was voluntarily. My comms to my family are heavily monitored. They don't want me to leak any info."

"You think there's a leak I can spring?"

"I hope so. Monsanto has big things in the works. Things bankrolled by Newman's government. There are Department of Human Limits agents all over our labs."

I was feeling uncomfortable with the way the conversation was heading. That is, directly into my line of work. In the tiny storage room, I felt claustrophobic. There was a reason I never talked to prospects after the teams signed them. I didn't want to know how much I'd fucked up their lives.

"What are you saying? Monsanto's drugs killed Zunz?"

"I'm only telling you what I know. They were putting more growth hormones and brain stimulators into him than a human body can stand. You need to look into why."

"Why are you telling me this?"

"So you'll do something. Get some revenge for me. The assholes here forced me into this contract and I don't get out for five years. Can you believe that's legal?"

"I can't," I said, lying. I knew who wrote the laws.

It wouldn't surprise me if Monsanto had killed him by accident. But why hire his brother to investigate if you did? I dug out my Mets eraser pack. Inhaled some numbing smoke.

I offered one to Arocha.

"Those things take years off your life."

"I hear they can add those back on these days."

She shook her head, waved away the smoke when I exhaled. "The human body is meant to feel itself. It needs to respond to pain. Send white blood cells, grow new skin, regulate functions. It needs to feel to do its job. You dull it with smoke and it doesn't know what to do. Just shuts down."

I didn't tell her a shutdown is what I was hoping for.

"Listen, I can't do anything with vague rumors from one

disgruntled employee." I finished the eraser, lit another. We were crammed in so tight among the robot parts, she could have leaned over and kissed me. "Do you have anything else I can go on?"

She frowned, checked her watch. "I have to go. But I can tell you they're promising us new stem cells to work with. From some child."

That woke me up. "A girl? What kind of child?"

"I don't know."

"An Edenist?"

"Could be. We were told the samples would be pure. Most of the players have been so juiced, tweaked, and edited that the strands are frayed."

Whether Coppelius was still on my tail or not, I needed to pay this Edenist center a visit.

I wondered if Arocha had a little girl of her own out there. I must have read her personal history when I scouted her, but I couldn't remember the person. Only the stats.

"If you weren't here, what would you be doing?" I asked.

"I wanted to work on zootech," she said, smiling sadly. "You know how most zootech die in a few weeks? We create these creatures, these living creatures, and we treat them like trash. Program cell death right into their genes. We have animal rights laws for 'organic' animals, but no laws protecting our own creations. They're just products. Same as sneakers or protein powder."

"You wanted to save them?"

"I wanted to help them live actual lives. Created or not, they're still living creatures."

For some reason, that dark room seemed to be shrinking. The walls looked like they could topple on me at any moment. I wasn't sure if it was claustrophobia or guilt.

"Listen, I have to tell you something. I know who you are. Julia Arocha. Formerly at Columbia. Twenty-eight years old. Undergrad work on cephalopod nervous systems." I looked away. "Before the Mets scooped you up, I'd been scouting you for the Yankees."

"Yes," she said, speaking slowly and looking me dead in the eye. There was something hard in her pupils. "Like I said, I looked you up."

"If I'd gotten my way, you'd be in the same situation. Just in another borough."

She shrugged, strapped her visor back on her head. Powered it back on. "You make allies wherever you can find them. Believe me, I've made some strange ones."

She asked me to wait fifteen minutes before leaving. She closed the door and clicked off the light.

I sat in the darkness for ten, tapping my fingers on a robot's pitching hand. Thinking. Then I headed out to find the girl before someone else did.

27

THE GOLDEN FROWN

W hat are you, a garbage rat? This place is garbage! You live here like a disgusting rat."

"Yeah, you live in garbage. Ha ha."

Wanda and Brenda Sassafras were in my apartment, livestreaming its destruction to my screen. I was in the mag lift of the Mets stadium, moving up to the ground floor.

Wanda Sassafras dropped my meal printer onto the living room table. Brenda had a baseball bat, one signed by Zunz, and was whacking dents in the walls. They must have been at it for a while. Everything in my apartment looked smashed, crushed, shattered, or burnt.

"Are you watching this, Kobo?"

"Look," Brenda said, pointing the bat. "Those snail things. The ones he tricked us with."

Wanda walked over to my aquarium of shock slugs. She pressed her face into the glass, gazing at the two remaining slugs. She leaned her head back. Screamed. Threw the tank against the wall. It shattered. The creatures fell on the ground with little sparks. They tried to squirm away, but Wanda and Brenda stomped around the ground in a brutal ballet.

Wanda came up close to the camera, her broad half-silver face filling the frame. "Should we call the trashman to throw this whole apartment in the garbage or will you give us the money?"

"Wanda." Brenda was squatting, urinating on my kitchen tiles. She stood up.

"Should we ring him up, you deadbeat? Get him to toss your whole life away?"

"But Wanda."

Wanda snapped her head back. "What?"

"Can a trashman lift up an apartment?"

"Huh?"

"How can a trashman lift a room? Isn't it connected to other rooms and the whole building?"

"Shut the fuck up, Brenda! I'm making a point! This isn't about realism!"

I slid the screen into my pocket as I reached the ground floor. Just because my life was being crushed piece by piece didn't mean I had to watch it happen. I wondered if Okafor would let me crash at their place. I started to message them as the lift opened. When I looked up, I froze. Natasha was waiting for me, thick arms crossed and smile wide.

The shock must have shown on my face, because she frowned. "Mr. Kobo, are you unwell?"

"Just got off an unpleasant call."

Natasha was wearing a blue dress woven with magnetic threads. When she put her screen away, it stuck directly to her side. She ambled toward me.

"I heard you were enjoying our facilities."

The words made my guts twist into knots. If Natasha had seen me talking to Arocha, then either she or I or both of us were about to have a very bad day.

"I was cracking the old bat, trying to get my head in the game."

"You seem a bit perplexed. I hope that is the right emotion. We Neanderthals use slightly different facial expressions than you sapiens. Something about your tiny eyebrows changes everything. You wouldn't think such a small variation in bone structure could change so much. But it does."

"I'm sorry," I said, trying to straighten my face. My screen was still on in my pocket, and I could hear the miniature screams of the Sassafras sisters. I reached in and clicked it off.

"One of our coaches mentioned you were, well, I won't say interrogating. Speaking with some of the players. So I thought I'd come find you. The Mouth would like a word."

"I don't have anything to report yet," I said.

"All the same, the Mouth will see you. He wants to know if there's anything he can throw in Elmer Tuscan's face before game three."

Tuscan was the CEO of Pyramid Pharmaceuticals. A playboy executive who spent more time hosting orgies on low-orbit space flights than running the company. Or at least that's what the tabloids said.

"Maybe you'll think of something on the way." Natasha smiled and slipped her arm into mine, led us toward the door. She guided me down the hall with quick tugs to the joint. "How are you finding our facilities?"

We were walking down a large hallway lined with gold columns carved to look like Mets stars of decades past. Aquariums of blue and orange fish were built into the walls, and a large hologram of the Mouth waved at passersby when motion was detected.

"It's quite something. Let's say elegant."

"The Mouth's taste is garish. But we don't work for who we work for because of their interior decorating skills, do we, Mr. Kobo?"

"Why do you work for him?"

"We aren't close enough friends for that conversation. Not yet."

The stadium sloped upward like an enormous coiled snake. The white marble floors looped around, with rows of flowering plants sandwiched between the tiers. A throwback style. At the top of the stadium, the golden dome glowed in the sky. When you were sitting down inside, looking up, the dome appeared as a gigantic grinning mouth.

"Do you still enjoy the game?" she asked me.

"It's the great American pastime."

"I must admit that, myself, I'm tired of people with bats and balls. It's a bit unsophisticated."

"I didn't realize trogstoys had such refined tastes."

The slur didn't halt her stride. "I would think an *oiler* such as yourself would know how unfair prejudices can be. Did you know we Neanderthals have larger brains than our sapien cousins? We made tools and formed societies in Eurasia before your ancestors arrived. We were more advanced, in many important ways. And yet we disappeared. Why?"

"I wouldn't want to speculate."

"My belief is that we were killed because we weren't sufficiently murderous. We weren't as bloodthirsty as the sapiens spilling into the continent. Brutality beats brains, quite literally. Fossil records are filled with the cracked skulls of my ancestors. Then you got to write the history books."

"You Neanderthals seem capable of brutality," I said. "At least according to the news."

Last month there had been a Neanderthal uprising in Russia. Footage of tanks exploding in front of the subterranean mushroom farms was all over the news. The streams had the beefy workers impaling guards on spike rigs, cheering. President Petrov was promising the hard slap of the motherland's hand.

She smiled curtly. "We all learn to adapt to our environments."

The Mouth's stadium office was about a third the size of the one in Mouth Tower, but exactly as golden. The back wall was decorated in robotic mouths. Entirely. They were stacked on top of each other from the floor to the ceiling. Hundreds of them, all with gold plated teeth and gold lips. No tongues. Only silent moving lips and the babbling of a thousand little drool waterfalls.

I let the mouths talk silently behind my back. Looked at the Mouth, who was showing me his own back. He stood at the window looking out at the sprawling park. His pet freagle was on his shoulder. A dark stain expanded where the freagle sat. The Mouth didn't seem to notice.

"Can you believe I bought all this, Kobo?" He was pointing out the window.

"Sure."

The Mouth frowned. His face twinkled like cheap nail polish. "No, I don't think you can believe it. I own it. I *own* Central Park. I own two of the six faces of Mount Rushmore. The good ones. I'm not talking the dorks like Jefferson or Washington. I've got Rockefeller Megacenter. A fourth of the solar farms of Nebraska. A fleet of floating nuke plants. I've got some of the most elegant properties in the entire world. Next, I'll get them on Mars after we terraform that red hunk of crap. I own the Monsanto name. Brilliant high-value brand that Bayer had shut down because a bunch of babies whined about designer seeds. Bought it back for a song and slapped it on a Future League Baseball team."

"It's hard to remember it all," Natasha said.

"Did you know my grandfather was a politician? He didn't have his name attached to anything except a few silly laws. Not much money in that either, legally at least. Now look at the Mouth name."

"It's famous," I said.

Then I realized he was nodding toward a glowing sign above the

park that read *Mouth*. Silver birds floated around the sign. The ones
that landed began to glow.

"We had to genetically engineer those falcons to conduct electricity. The old feathered ones kept trying to fuck the signs and dying.
Can you believe that? Nature is dumb. It doesn't work, not by itself.
That's why all the animals are dying out. Climate change? Invasive
species? Please. Nature always has some excuse. We humans are still
here because we're smart. We innovate. We disrupt the planet quicker
than it can disrupt us."

Given the constant water wars, sinking cities, and millions of climate refugees, I wasn't sure that was a safe bet. But I kept my own
mouth shut. The Mouth was still pointing out the window. Then he
swung his finger to a small wooden chair in front of his desk. He sat
in the large leather one on the other side. Natasha walked up behind
him, began rubbing the rind of his bald head.

"You know what the best part of Zunz dying is?"

"There's a *best* part?"

The Mouth frowned. With the surgical extensions, the lips
seemed to curl back around on themselves. "Yes, no, no. Of course
not. I didn't say that. We're all sad. Human life is precious, okay.
It's a tragedy. I said it. You heard me. But I'm talking business, and
nothing drives business like martyrdom. Our sales are through the
roof. People are rallying around the Mets. Buying hats, steroids, and
upgrades by the bucketload. Can't you smell it?"

I couldn't smell anything except the faint odor of freagle piss.
"Smell what?"

"The success! The smell of success. I could sniff it all night, like
mana from the tit of god."

He shouted "success" again and the little freagle on his shoulder squawked something that sounded like the word. I wondered if
they'd added a pinch of parrot genes in the mix.

"It's going to get even better when we let everyone know the Sphinxes did it. Where are we on that? It would be good for us to leak the news. Is the investigation soaring like a rocket yet?"

"Still on the launchpad," I said, settling into the uncomfortable chair. "I looked into Jung Kang, but I don't think he was the killer. Anyway, someone killed him before I could learn more."

I watched them, but neither gave a sign they knew Coppelius had been the one.

The Mouth shook his head. "That's too bad, too bad. You're telling me you can't prove it was the Sphinxes? Not yet?"

"I don't think it was."

"Don't think. Still could be." He smirked like a child smuggling cookies from the kitchen at midnight. He spread his faded gold palms. Shrugged. "Thinking isn't knowing. It's only our job to make people think. It could be them, just like you said. No one could disagree with *could*. It wouldn't hurt to let the press know we think it might have been them."

"Of course, sir. I did an hour ago," Natasha said.

The three of us were silent for a moment. The Mouth looked at me, his smile lessening centimeter by centimeter. It grew straight, began to frown. His eyes seemed to stop noticing me. He looked out the window again. I got the impression I was meant to go.

Instead, I talked. "While I'm here, could you two tell me what Zunz was taking?"

The Mouth swiveled his gold face to me, fingers tapping against his dry yellow lips. "Taking?"

"His drugs, upgrades. His medical routine."

"Who cares what he was taking?"

"Maybe I could talk to the team doctors. Get a list. His regimen."

Natasha put her hand on my shoulder. "Our upgrades are proprietary. Trade secrets."

"What he was *taking*?" The Mouth stood up, slammed his knuckles on the desk. The freagle jumped off his shoulder in surprise, squawking as it hit the wood. "He was taking the best goddamn drugs in the world. Mets drugs. Do you know how much we pay to make those drugs? We didn't bring you on for medical advice. Are you a doctor? You want to massage my prostate? Whack my kneecap? No! We brought you on to find evidence the Sphinxes killed Zunz."

"If they did."

"If, if, if, if." The Mouth smacked his desk with each iteration. The freagle hopped away from the blows. Cowered behind the gold phone, its feathered head bobbing behind the ringer. "I'm not looking for ifs. I am sure as hell not paying for *ifs*."

I was ready to protest, tell them I was only concerned with the truth. But the truth was I needed the Mouth's money. Perhaps now more than ever. The numbers of my medical debt flashed before me again.

"Okay," I said. "Got it. You're right, I apologize."

I stood up, leaned over, and rubbed a finger along the freagle's feathered head. It snapped at my pinkie.

"She's a beauty."

"She's a he. I don't want frog eggs, or eagle eggs, or any kind of egg on my desk," the Mouth said, his own mouth opened in an expression halfway between disgust and pride. "Limited edition, with the bullfrog genes. Not those discount toads the government sells to the public. Only two of these in existence. I gave the other to Newman personally."

"Well, I've got leads to check out. Some of them lead to the Edenists. Heard of them?"

The Mouth began to smile again. "They protest at our stores and stadium all the time. Send our players death threats. I hate those treesuckers. You can point a finger at them? Brilliant. Would prefer to take out a rival team, but get me dirt on the Edenists and we'll consider it a fair wage."

"They're good leads. Though it would help if I could get an extra advance on my payment. My expenses have been getting expensive."

The Mouth laughed and sat back down. Spoke to Natasha while pointing at me. "This guy's a bastard. I like bastards. Give him some digits for cab fare." He waved a finger at me. "But remember, you aren't getting your medical debt erased unless you give us something a lot better than that. And quickly. No one's going to care about Zunz in the off-season."

Natasha handed me the money, but as she did, she held my hand. Inspected it.

"I see you visited Dr. Setek. Good. Now that you're in good health, how about you join us in the Mouth's luxury box for one of the games."

"I've actually got a date to game three."

"Bring your date. Watch the game in style," the Mouth said. But Natasha whispered in his ear. He frowned.

"Game four would be better for us," she said to me.

"Yes, yes. You and your date are coming to game four. My box. You'll want to be there. I insist."

I started to argue, but the Mouth had already swiveled back to survey his domain.

28

THE TRUE BELIEVERS

After messaging Dolores the bad news about game four, I powered down my eye and pulled my hat as low as it would go. Slid my metal hand into my pocket. Tried to look as little like an oiler as possible as I approached the Untainted Gardens Edenist Center.

The center was out at the edge of the city, nestled up against the storm wall. The whole block smelled of stagnant water. The rooftop of the building was covered in dark moss while green ivy swarmed up the sides. Guards with shock rifles and blue cotton robes manned the walls. The one at the gate looked at my cybernetic eye and frowned.

"Can I help you?"

"I've got a delivery," I said. "For the old man."

"Which old man?" she said.

"The one with the long beard. Likes to shout about defilement and holiness. Tell him it's from Jung Kang."

The woman glared at me, but sent the message. She told me to put my arms out and step forward into the scanner. I'd left my gun at home, and when the scan pinged clean, the guard cracked the gate enough for me to squeeze through.

It might be a religious cult, but inside no one was praying. They were training. The courtyard was filled with sweaty Edenists doing martial arts, old men shouting at them in their ordered rows. Others climbed ropes or lifted free weights.

The old man I'd seen at Reunion Square ambled toward me, stooped in the shape of a question mark. His long scraggly beard was almost licking the dirt.

"You said a Mr. Kang sent you? My you're a big fellow," he said. There was meanness between the wheezes. "We don't get a lot of big fellows around here."

"I'm not a twig, if that's what you mean."

The old man wrinkled up his already wrinkled face. He leaned on his wooden cane. "We don't use that term here. *Twigs?* No, no. Twigs snap easily. We don't." He nodded toward the acolytes lifting weights and boxing with drones.

"I thought you types weren't big fans of machines."

"We don't live in caves and fear fire. We simply believe men are supposed to live in the vessel they are born into. We were not made in the divine image to pollute ourselves with the chemicals and corporate replacement parts."

"Good story. Here's mine. I'm here about a little girl. Maybe twelve. Goes by the name of Nails."

He leaned on his cane. Sucked in his wrinkled lips. "She's generating a lot of interest lately."

"Someone got here first?"

The old man studied my face. Seemed to find my concern authentic. "A big man came by. Bigger than you and with an even nastier way of talking. Tried to rough up a few of our guards. Succeeded, to be honest with you. Said he'd be back with backup."

"Did he talk to the girl?"

"No. And we didn't tell him anything. We don't give out information to self-polluters. That includes you, I'm afraid. If you have nothing from Mr. Kang, then goodbye."

He grimaced and began to turn around.

I moved in close, grabbed his thin, bony hand with my metal one. Whispered angrily in his ear. "Pollution comes in handy, like how my fingertip can inject nerve poison that would kill you before you can even scream."

It wasn't true, but I figured he was the paranoid type.

"You'd kill an old man?" He almost choked on the words.

I squeezed his hand until I heard a crunching sound. Then another. I figured one more squeeze and I'd hear a snap. The old man made a yelping sound like steam escaping a broken pipe.

"God's genes. I knew it." There were tears in the wrinkles of his eyes.

"Knew what?"

"That you oilers have no respect for your elders. You think we're out of date, because you fear you yourself are out of date. You can't possibly keep up with the future you have thoughtlessly unleashed."

"I'm trying to help the girl. I'm not here to hurt anyone."

"My hand!"

"Your hand isn't broken. Yet."

The guards were starting to look our way. One raised his gun. I squeezed a bit more and the old man waved them off. "Okay. We'll talk inside."

He groaned as I dragged him toward the warehouse. I kept my grip on his hand. The Edenists in the courtyard stopped their training. Started to form a circle around us, but the old man held up his other arm. They looked like scarecrows in their cloth outfits. Beside the large barn doors, someone had scrawled *Bring the Diseased Eden* in glowing spray paint.

Their Eden already seemed diseased to me. There was a foul smell, a rank musky stench that reminded me of our high school locker room after a game. In the next room, I realized why. The warehouse was filled with animals locked in small cages with barely any room to move. Rows of them stacked atop rows. The waste dripping down from one tier to the next, then collecting around clogged drains on the floor. Wings, snouts, tails, and hooves pressed into their glass enclosures. A whole menagerie in misery.

And all with heads. Wild-eyed and squawking or grunting heads. I'd never realized how black and large the eyes of animals could be. Tubes were attached to their mouths, muffling their cries. Other tubes were fastened to their udders and backsides. Edenists in white smocks ran around, collecting jars of yellowish milk and scooping up eggs.

"What the hell is this?"

"It's food. Real human food."

"It's illegal is what it is. They can barely move. And they have heads! They're screaming in pain."

He could barely shuffle with his hunched-over back. Still, he looked at me indignantly. "Humans, real humans, have eaten real animals for thousands of years. Living animals, not flesh cells grown in petri dishes. Not mutated monstrosities that couldn't survive outside of a lab. Real animals. Why do you think you are better than your ancestors?"

"I'm cleaner at least," I said, looking at the rivulets of piss and shit draining through slots in the floor. I'd heard that Edenists sold illegal meat, but had no idea it was at this scale.

"Who are you? A health inspector? We already paid the city off last month."

I shook my head. "I don't care about your farm scam with the city. I care about the girl."

When we got to the offices in the back, the man opened the door marked Oldblood Jonas. It was a dim, perfumed room, decorated with rugs and pillows. Incense was burning, and self-blowing wind chimes added music to the room.

"Okay, you brute, let me go."

I did so. He held his hand up. It was red and curled in a claw. He was even more stooped over now, perpendicular to the floor. "You could have broken it." He flexed the hand, and then walked over to pick up the exobrace he kept hidden behind the door. He strapped it on and powered it up. Grunted as it tightened. Soon he was sitting up straight and smoking a pipe. A sweet smoke filled the air.

"Didn't figure you for an eraser man."

Smoke leaked out of his nostrils in thin strands. "This is tobacco. Regular tobacco, not some transgenic hybrid concoction. No infused vitamins or caffeine. Just smoke. You've probably never even tasted it."

"I don't smoke for the taste. I smoke for the medicine."

He shook his head slowly, swirling the gray cloud around him. "So. What do you want with Lila?"

Lila. I filed away the name. "Are you a baseball fan?"

"The modern league is an abomination of mutants that would make our ancestors spin in their graves," he said between puffs. "But, yes, I watch. I grew up in New England back when it was separate states, so I root for the National Genetics Red Pills. Death to the Yankees and all that. Why?"

"Then you know about what happened to JJ Zunz."

"Yes, the news does manage to reach Queens."

"The people who did that to Zunz are after Lila."

The old man shook his head, unbelieving. "That's absurd. We've raised Lila for years. She gets into trouble, sure. Runs away sometimes. Has gotten involved with some of our, well, lost brethren. Never been fully one of us, I guess you could say. But I can't imagine anyone would want to kill her."

"What do you mean she's not one of you?"

"We raised Lila as, well, let's say as a favor."

"Did the favor come with a fee?"

The old man smiled, yellow teeth peeking from beneath his gray beard. "We accept donations."

"Let me guess, a guy named Jung Kang delivered it."

"That was the name on the receipts, yes. Obviously you know that or you wouldn't have dragged me in here." The old man kept glancing at the screen embedded in his desk. He seemed to be getting agitated by whatever it showed him. "I guess we can't expect any donation this month, then?"

"You can expect all you want. Kang's dead."

I showed him Kang's corpse on my screen for emphasis. A still from Dolores's security feed.

"My god," the old man said. His eyes flicked back and forth between me and his screen. "No matter how much poison you pump into yourself, you still end up a brittle, broken thing in the end, don't you?"

"The man who did this is hunting Lila. And they won't be keeping her on any Edenist diet if they catch her."

I could hear a commotion in the halls of the building. People running outside. Shouts. They didn't seem to be running this way though.

"And what will you do if you catch her? Buy her a ponycycle? We protect our own here. Including wayward souls."

The door slid open and an Edenist rushed in holding a screen in his hand. He was tall for an Edenist and wore a green coverall uniform instead of a tunic. "Oldblood Jonas, we've got a problem." He noticed me and stopped himself. "Can you come outside?"

"One second, Youngblood Meers. This gentleman was about to leave."

"Was I?"

"I certainly hope so. Meers, help him out?"

Meers put his hand on my shoulder. I put my elbow into his stomach instead. He grunted and doubled over. I grabbed the gun he had tucked into his back pocket. Meers dropped his screen on the ground. It displayed different security camera feeds.

The old man reached across the table to try and yank the gun from my own hand. I put the steel barrel into Meers's soft stomach and grabbed the old man's hand with my free one. I was tired of talking, and of his refusing to talk. I put my thumb and forefinger around the old man's pinkie, a few centimeters apart. Squeezed. The pinkie snapped like a piece of pink celery. It had the same wet crunch.

The old man kept moaning.

"Take me to Lila," I said to Meers. "Now."

Meers just stared at me, eyes filled with hate. The old man laughed. His hand was turning purple, but he laughed. "You fool, I've already sent her an alert. She's long gone."

I looked down where the screen had fallen. In the bottom left feed, I saw a young girl running into the courtyard.

29

THE ESCAPE ROUTE

When I caught up to Lila, she'd already stopped running. We were in the middle of the courtyard. Everyone around us was moving. There were shouts. Orders and exclamations. The Edenists scurried like ants in a freshly stomped colony. Then I realized why.

Hovering above the walls, a fleet of police cruisers sat flashing lights and blaring sirens.

"We have an executable search warrant for forbidden livestock. We've broadcast it to your screens. You have five minutes to read it and comply."

The squadron hovered in the smog.

The sight of cops made my heart stumble a few beats. They were like the world's worst houseguests, never helping and always showing up when you could least afford to deal with them. I wondered if Okafor was in one of those cars. If they'd switched from warning me off the case to using me as bait. They wouldn't ever betray me on purpose, I didn't think, but they were the type to follow orders no matter what. Which was to say, Okafor was a cop.

Through the gates, I could see a large, smooth man whispering in the ear of a police sergeant. Coppelius. The two of them laughed.

"Listen," I said to the girl. "We need to get out of here. And fast. And now."

Lila looked at me, wrinkled her face up a bit. "If it isn't my uncle the cop."

"I'm not a cop. And these ones definitely aren't with me."

"Piss off," she said and sprinted in the other direction, toward the storm wall.

I followed her.

We ran. We ran through the courtyard, weaving between the scattering Edenists. Ran down the side of the warehouse, hopping over streams of animal waste running toward the curb. Ran out of the compound, feet slapping in the wet pavement, across the street through the traffic of creepeasies and street cleaners, over the bridge, and down the sidewalk into a hazy park. We disappeared into the smog like two nails dropped into a vat of oil.

Back when I was a ballplayer, I kept in shape. I worked out each muscle group every other day, a small black drone beeping encouragement in my ear with each pump. I drank protein smoothies, took steroid injections, and slept in a muscle massager. Back then, I knew my body's limits down to the inch. Knew exactly what each limb could lift, how much water or carbs or protein I needed to digest each meal. Back then, I could run for days.

Now my lungs were more used to eraser smoke than filtered oxygen. I was wheezing as badly as the old man by the time we entered the park.

Despite being a twig, the girl was holding up better than me, just like on Governor's Island. She was into the cloudy park before I was across the road. But then she stopped, coughing and clutching a fence by the baseball field. I caught up with her. The field was ringed with a rusted chain fence, and the electronic scoreboard blinked an unchanging 0-0. A few smog lights partially illuminated the field. The benches were home to pale fungi feeding off the wet air.

Still, a group of kids were playing ball with filters strapped to their faces. Same way Zunz, Okafor, and I had done back in the day. The girl at bat fouled the ball high, and it clanged against the overhanging fence.

Lila stopped coughing. Cupped her hands around her mouth. "Hey, Pigface."

The masked boy in left field waved. He trotted over. "Hey, Nails. You want to play? We need a center fielder."

"I gotta hide. People are chasing me. Ping me if the cops or anyone else follows me, okay?"

"Like that guy?"

She looked back at me panting. "Like that guy, yeah, but anyone else. Any other guys like that guy."

"Sure thing, Nails." He pulled his blue baseball cap low on his head, then ran back to the left field.

Lila and I ducked behind a self-cleaning outhouse that had stopped cleaning itself. Sat down. We caught our breath in the thick smell of piss and shit. Human this time, which was even worse than the warehouse animals.

Other than the kids, the park was mostly empty. Fat gray rats scurried between bushes. A bodega drone floated around the path, shouting at no one in particular. "Hot dogs! Pretzels! Getcha hot dogs and pretzels! Credit and bytewallet accepted!"

A group of pigeons pecked the ground by an overflowing trash can, hammering their beaks into weird rocks I realized were food. Fossilized pizza crusts, petrified bagels. An archaeological dig of leftovers.

I pulled out my filter mask. Started breathing a little easier. Lila didn't seem to be though.

"Do you have a mask?"

Lila had her head between her knees. She shook it. She wasn't looking at me, and I was worried she'd sprint away again, leaving me without any answers and Coppelius on my tail.

But she was bent over. Her breath was heavy and wet. She seemed like she might vomit.

"Take mine," I said, holding it out for her.

She waved it away.

"I just need to rest here a second."

She coughed again and I thought I saw blood on her lips.

"You're bleeding."

"I'm used to it."

I peeked around the outhouse. Didn't see any flashing lights in the smog. Didn't see anyone who could see us. We were hidden in the haze.

Game three would have started. I stole a quick look at the score on my screen. Bottom of the second, game still tied at zero. Mike Truk was on the mound for the Mets, working a full count against Marius Lupu. Truk threw a two-seamer that sank on command. Yet Lupu got a tip on it. The ball bounced over shortstop Van Young's glove, and Lupu made it safe to first.

Lila was looking back now too. Her body shook.

"I'm trying to help you," I said, offering her the mask again.

"I don't need help. Just tell me who that giant at the gates was. The big guy with the prehistoric features. I've been dodging him for a while."

"His name's Coppelius. Or that's his code name at least," I said. I was happy to change the topic. "Lab-grown spy. I've had several unpleasant run-ins with him myself. And no pleasant ones. I think he's taking orders from Monsanto."

"I thought you worked for Monsanto."

I shrugged. "Yes, but on more of a freelance basis."

Her laughter transformed into hacking. She leaned over, nose to the grass. Her little body heaved, spat. Then she was still.

I looked out at the smoggy park. The handful of living trees were coated with gleaming slime, either accumulated pollution or else genetically engineered bark that kept the pollution at bay. It was hard to tell the difference between the problem and the cure these days.

"So, not like I really care, but who did it?"

"What?"

"Killed my father. You said you were investigating it."

"I don't know yet. It might have been an accident. Bad batch of Monsanto drugs. I'm not sure."

Her face was a cocktail of disgust and frustration. She stood up, paced around a bit, looked down at me. "Swell. Well, what a pleasure to meet you. Glad you tracked me down to tell me nothing at all."

"You should come with me," I said, forcing my aching body up. "It's not safe with the Edenists."

"Yeah, sorry, my father told me to never go home with strangers. I mean, I assume he would have said that if he'd been a father."

Her screen pinged with one word: *RUN*. She looked around the outhouse, then back at me. Coppelius, flanked by cops, had his hand around Pigface's throat. He lifted the boy into the air. His legs kicked pointlessly, stirring the smog.

"Okay, never mind. Let's go. No more dumb questions though."

30

THE DROWNED TUNNEL

Lila led us to an abandoned building with a faded painting of a beach on the facade. Palm trees, leaping dolphins, and a red sun beaming for miles across the ocean. An antique tanning salon, from before they developed sun cream that would tan without baking cancer into your skin.

The storm wall towered behind the building. Few people lived on this side of the wall, and only the exiled—climate refugees unable to get citizenship—lived on the other. The salon's lock had been broken long ago. We maneuvered through tables of creams and ointments. Plastic streamers in different colors dangled from the ceiling. Weird sponges and rusty tools. Bundles of dried plants. It was like being in the hut of some medieval witch.

"Downstairs," Lila said.

Everything from my knees to the floor was stained, rotting. Dried-up seaweed and bits of sand were scattered around. Lila moved toward the back stairwell.

I stopped. "Stairs?" I wasn't a fan of crawling downstairs in dark buildings. I could feel a panic attack coming on. A burning seed in my gut beginning to sprout.

"Let's hide up here," I offered. I gestured at the rows of tanning booths that lined the floor like robotic caskets.

"Yeah, that doesn't seem like a good idea."

In the distance, I could see the lights of police cars faintly blinking.

"I know a secret way out. Come on."

I didn't move.

"Okay," Lila said, waving her hand in exaggerated arcs. "Goodbye, Uncle. Goodbye yet again."

Lila disappeared into the dark throat of the stairwell.

The sirens grew louder. Fragments of light sliced across the antique walls.

I looked at the stairwell. Listened to the sounds of Lila disappearing. I couldn't help but think of the cave-in that had crushed my arm. The hours I spent trapped under rubble while my family died.

I lit an eraser. Smoked it as quickly as I could to tamp the claustrophobia. Tossed it on the floor and followed her into the damp gloom.

Several flights down, I lost all reception on my screen and cybernetics. The seed of panic was blooming inside me, angry red petals spreading through my gut. Still, we kept going. Down and down.

I held out my screen as a flashlight. The floors were inhabited only by roaches and spiders now. Old objects from my youth floated in dirty puddles of water. Filter coffee makers, glass bottles, computers with physical keyboards built into them. Seawater trickled into the lower floors. A few more years and the whole thing might collapse. Be nothing more than the hiding place for crabs and eels.

Before we went underwater ourselves, Lila cracked open a wall grate and slithered through. I followed.

We emerged into another dark tunnel. An alarm blared. Then I realized it wasn't an alarm, but a chorus of squeaks. I raised my screen light and waves of rats rippled away in a horrifying tide. Hundreds of them, their dark bodies scrambling over each other back into the dark.

"How did you know—"

She shushed me. We stood in the dark silence. Listened. A minute passed. Two. Ten.

No sounds followed us.

There was no reception at all down here. It was a giant concrete tube that curved toward darkness in either direction. In the center, rusted metal lines ran across the floor, like the spine of some gigantic snake we were trapped inside.

I knew this place.

"The old subway," I said. I walked around looking at the tiled walls plastered with advertisements for movies and extinct fast-food franchises. The tiles had been white, once. Now they were a grimy brown. "God, I used to ride this every day, back before the supraway went up."

When I was a child, this platform would have been pulsing with people. Men, women, and children of all sizes, pressed together in a desperate attempt to get inside before the doors closed. On busy days, you could have suffocated in the throng of flesh and cloth.

"Your dad and I would play this game where we'd jump inside the train as soon as they said 'Stand clear of the closing doors, please.' Whoever came closest to getting crushed won."

Lila reached out and touched my elbow. She hacked up more of her insides. She was steadying herself. "I don't. Give a. Rat's ass. About your. Nostalgia."

"I actually hated it. Always felt like the tunnel would burst and we'd all drown."

It hadn't been an irrational fear. The whole system had been abandoned from constant flooding and rising waters a couple decades ago.

Lila stayed bent over. A tangled rope of mucus dripped from her lips. It formed a reddish puddle on the floor.

"We need to get you to a hospital." A film of sweat had appeared on her skin. She looked over at me, tried to speak, then spat again. She pulled a vial out of her inside pocket, downed it. After a few seconds, she had composed herself.

"It's nothing, just something in my throat."

"Something like lichen lung?"

I'd seen that thick wet cough as a child. The rumor had been it was an early biotech that got loose. Genetically modified spores. Before the government was able to bioengineer birds and beasts, they figured out how to shape fungi and germs. Hybridized them. Made them stronger. More virulent. Whatever the origin, lichen lung spread all through the city, killing off masses of the rich and poor alike. Although mostly the poor. The city went into quarantine four different times trying to stop the spread.

Then ChicagoBio came out with an antifungal spray. The government spent billions buying up the medicine. Then made a few billion more selling it to the citizens. No one could ever confirm the disease's origin.

"No," she said like she was trying to tell herself that.

"You don't spit up bloody yellow clumps like that from anything other than the spores."

She sat on a wooden bench crusted with barnacles. Water sloshed in the sunken tracks. Lila kept her hand clamped over her mouth.

"It's nothing," she said. "Human bodies do things. You don't feel yours because you're half machine."

"I still have another half. I feel plenty." I had an eraser to my lips, about to light. I clicked shut the flame. "Listen, kid, I know you don't like upgrades, that you think it's self-pollution and all that noise. But the spores dig into the tissue. You'll die. But a doctor can line your lung to fix it."

"Not going to be converted to desecration. Sorry."

"Desecration? Your body is desecrating itself. I'm only suggesting a little janitorial work."

"Is that what you and my father learned back in the burrows?"

"We learned how to survive."

"How did that work out for him?" Her look slid into me like a splinter.

I didn't know what to say and looked around the empty subway tunnel. Imagined the bright lights of an approaching train, the doors sliding open for Lila and me to rush inside. But no train came. The only sounds were the fight splashes of distant, swimming rats.

"So?" she said.

"So?"

"What's the plan? You're the adult here."

"First, we need to get out of here. Hide out someplace safe. Above ground preferably."

"Well, I'd been staying in my deadbeat dad's hideaway house. But that's out of the question now. And Jung is dead too."

"I'm sorry," I said pointlessly.

"You better watch out. The father figures in my life have a high mortality rate." She patted me on the arm. "I guess we're going to your place, Uncle."

I didn't have lichen lung, but my face must have looked just as pained. "My apartment has been, well, commandeered by some business associates."

"Associates?"

"Associates I don't like to associate with. Loan sharks."

"For what?"

"Medical debt."

Lila stared at me. Her young face wiped of expression. "Great rescue job. Top-notch."

"Okay. Let me think a second."

I didn't believe Coppelius had seen me run away with Lila, but I couldn't afford taking her anywhere near the Mets. Okafor might be willing to hide us, but they were still a company soldier and if anyone else at the police station got wind there was a good chance one of them would be on the Monsanto payroll. The only choice was Dolores.

"I've got a friend who will help us," I said. "I think. If we can get out of here."

Lila was distracted. She grabbed my hand.

"Why is your palm blinking?"

"What?" I held up my right hand. There was a faint red light glowing out of the cracks. "It doesn't normally do that."

She held her ear to my metal palm. "It sounds like it's looking for a signal." She dropped my hand. Picked it back up. Groaned. "Do you have a tracker in your palm?"

"No," I started to say, but stopped myself.

The snake doctor. Setek. I cursed under my breath.

Monsanto had lured me with free upgrades and stuck a tracker in my palm. If so, I'd led them right to Governors Island and then to the Edenist warehouse. Right to Lila. No wonder Natasha had dropped by to push me along this trail.

"I'm sorry," I started to say, but Lila pulled a hot knife from her tunic. The glowing ring around the steel illuminated Lila's face. She pressed the tip to my palm. It started to sizzle.

"Turn your sensors off. This is going to hurt."

I pulled away. I stared at my brand-new palm. There wasn't even a scratch on it yet. "I just got this hand fixed," I said pathetically.

Lila's look could have slapped the bionic eye out of my head.

"Okay. Give it to me," I said. "It's my hand."

I powered down my arm. It fell limply against my side. I asked Lila to lift the hand.

Even with my sensors off, my brain thought it could feel the pain as the knife burned open a hole in my palm. My eyes knew it was supposed to hurt.

A trickle of electricity crackled up my arm, singeing the flesh at the joint. I let the feeling pass, then peeled open my palm, recreating the hole the Sassafras sisters had made.

Lila's eyes were wide as golf balls. "I've never seen inside one of these. These abominations, I mean."

Beneath the ribbed metal skin, throbbing plasma sheets glowed in shades of blue. Silicon wires branched off like veins. No blood came out, only a translucent blue gunk that began to coagulate to close the hole. Lila reached in with her tiny fingers and plucked out the transmitter.

It was a writhing, segmented thing. About the size of a multivitamin. White, with a round protrusion on its black head that shone a faint crimson. Little yellow specks for eyes.

"What the crap is this?" she said.

"Shit."

"What?"

"A grub beacon," I said. "I've used them before on prospects. Normally you hide them in their food, then track them before they shit it out."

"Do me a favor," Lila said, holding the grub as far away from her face as she could. "Never ever talk to me about your horrible, horrible job again. Like any part of it. At all."

It was a fair request.

"They're zootech. Organic and hard to detect. Dissolve after a few days and get defecated or absorbed by the body."

She swung her extended arm around so the writhing thing was in front of my face. It squirmed an inch from my eye. "You think Edenists are weird? How can this not disgust you? This creature shouldn't exist, much less live inside your hand."

Lila tossed the grub onto the tracks. It plinked into the muddy waters. Sank.

I looked at my newly injured hand. My arm had gone through so many cycles of death and rebirth that it was hard to keep track. For most of my life, I'd been trying to improve. Now I just wished I could stay whole for a little while.

"I know a way out of here. Then we'll see this so-called friend of yours."

"Give me a minute." I pulled out an eraser, lit it, and sucked it down as quick as I could. Then I powered my arm back up, pain receptors and all.

I shouted for quite some time.

31

THE SUNKEN ZEALOTS

Y ou're going to have to shut up," Lila said. We crept through the flooded subway tunnel like two Jonahs crawling through the belly of a forgotten leviathan. Its guts stretched on and on.

Besides the sloshing of our legs, the only sounds were the distant squeaks. Rats. Possibly fish. For all I knew, aquatic rats with gills below their large round ears. There could be an entirely new ecosystem down here, new life-forms mutating in the brackish muck.

"I wasn't talking."

"I mean when we get there. Let me do the talking. They're not going to be happy about me bringing an oiler."

My mind was shouting at me to get out of this dark tunnel and somewhere with a breeze. But my body was more concerned with my ruined hand. I'd have to wrench out the sensor when I got home.

"I'm not going to be much use if I have to fight."

"If it comes to that, I'll lend a hand." Lila patted me on my injured arm. Her bright laughter was out of place in the underground gloom.

The laughter grew thicker and she doubled over. Hacked up something dark and wet that fell into the water with a sad splash.

"Do you want me to carry you?" I said, although I was unsure if I even could.

"Like I said, I want you to be quiet."

My clothes were soaked with cold, murky water. I was starting to shiver. I'd recently read about marrow heaters, microbatteries you could implant along your skeleton to combat the cold. Plethora had an entire line of them. They cost a fortune, more money than I'd earned in years. I wanted them desperately.

"How much farther to these friends of yours?" I asked.

"They're not my friends, they're my comrades. Well, my future comrades. I can't join till I'm fifteen."

She'd explained to me how the Diseased Eden were a splinter group, disowned by the mainstream Edenists for their views. Although really it was the Diseased Eden that disowned the others. Lila had met them at a protest outside of the Monsanto compound. She was bubbling with anger and they were a group that knew how to channel it.

"And how many times do I have to tell you?"

We were nearing another subway platform. I moved quicker, ready to climb out and begin to dry.

"Yeah, yeah. I'll shut up," I said, right as my foot clicked on something between the tracks. Something that wasn't rotting and mushy, but metal and new. I froze.

I saw a red light appear in the waters near my feet. Then another. And another. They were all around us.

"Shit," Lila said. "Shit."

The water gurgled. The clicking sounds beneath me were matched by ones above.

Lila started to move forward. Something grabbed her.

A black metal tendril shot out of the water. It wrapped around my right wrist three times. Another did so on the other hand, while a third slid up my torso and pulled my neck down.

The water was up to my chest. I looked over at Lila. The mechanical tendrils looked gigantic on her body. Her head was barely above the water.

"I forgot about these guys," Lila said angrily.

I tried to tug, but the tendrils held me in place.

The clicks in the ceiling got louder, then three security spiders dropped down. They hovered around our faces. Black metal bots with a large yellow eye in the middle, scanning us. They swung back and forth from their cords.

The putrid water splashed against us. I could hear Lila gag.

Up on the platform, a fat man in a motorized shopping cart rolled toward us. He wasn't dressed like the Edenists I'd seen before. He was wearing layers of dirt-caked rags and hauling a gigantic bag of plastic bottles behind him.

He rolled to the ledge. Looked down at us and shook his bearded face. It was the man I'd seen in the streams on Zunz's house on Governors Island. The one who'd been giving a nice speech about the nastiness of the world while they sliced open a headless chicken.

He lifted a broom handle from the side of his cart and pointed it at Lila. Bellowed, "What hand guides the flaming sword?"

Lila groaned. Looked at me with embarrassed eyes. "The hand of the Untainted Lord. Okay, Noblood Gerald?"

The dirty water was splashing into her mouth. She spat some out as she talked.

The man frowned and lowered his stick. "No real names, Nails. Now, what does the Mud—"

"The Mud Adam holds the flaming axe."

"And what—"

"The Mud Adam's axe will splinter the tree of life into a thousand twigs. Forever and ever. Amen. Let us go, Gerald. I'm going to drown!"

He tapped his stick on the ground, still frowning. "Rituals matter, Nails. You're going to need to learn that if you're going to become a member." He rolled his cart over to the wall. Flipped up a tile to reveal a security panel and hit a button with his large fist. The spider bots crawled back up to the ceiling, and the tendrils slithered back into the subway gunk.

Lila stood up and shook off the water. Spat.

"You're a jerk, Gerald."

"I didn't tell you to come sneaking through the subway. Who's this defiler?"

"He helped me escape some cops. They raided the Untainted Gardens. I vouch for him."

"Yeah, we heard about the raid." The man had a flashlight pointed down at us. He flashed it right in my eye. "He looks like an oiler. And a broken one at that."

I was cold and dizzy. The water was getting inside the new hole in my palm. My human parts were shivering and the bionic ones glitching. I wanted to lie down in the waters and be carried away.

"Listen," I said. "I'm on the run from both cops and Monsanto agents. Yes, I've got cybernetic parts, and I'm two million in debt to a medical-loan company that wants to chop me into pieces. I don't know what your Diseased Eden is, but we probably have overlapping enemies."

Gerald scratched his chin. Coughed. "This is an untainted oasis. I can't just let a cyborg inside."

"Jesus, Gerald. Let us up or I'll tell everyone about your bionic heart. Okay?"

Gerald had been moving away, but now spun around angrily. He moved back to the ledge. "It's not bionic."

"Oh no?"

"It's a pacemaker. Keep your voice down."

"Are pacemakers listed in the First Commandment of the Eden Angels?"

"I've had it since I was a kid. I'd rip the sin out if I could."

"Aww, you were just a little baby. I'm sure everyone will be very understanding."

"Fine, okay, he can come in. We can talk. I want to hear about what happened at the Oldblood compound. Then the oiler has to leave." He pointed his stick at me. Shook his head. "And you have to take her with you."

32

THE DISEASED EDEN

The inside of the old Greenpoint station was bright and busy. Men and women dressed in rags stood around the waiting area, assembling and breaking down devices. I noticed some were taller than any Edenists I'd seen before, but they were on crutches or in wheelchairs. They had missing limbs and cauterized holes where an eye had been dug out or an ear cut away.

I leaned down to Lila. "What's the deal with those ones?"

"They're the Purified."

"Purified from what?"

She stared at my cybernetic arm and shrugged. "Upgrades."

I looked back at the workers, tried to visualize their limbs returning. Made them whole in my mind with cybernetics. I felt sad for them. Angry too. When I looked at my own body, I couldn't imagine yanking out my parts for any creed.

"What are they doing?"

"Weekend workshop. Demolition tools."

"For what?"

"The Diseased Eden think the regular Edenists are too polite. They want to fuck shit the fuck up."

"Don't curse, Nails," Gerald said.

Although they were deep down in the old subway, the Diseased Edenists had transformed it. There were bright tapestries of birds and beasts on the walls. Everywhere I looked there was a plant growing under solar lamps. Just because the space was cheerful didn't mean the people were though. We walked through the dining area, the Diseased Edenists looking up from their bowls with eyes as narrow as paper cuts.

"Don't worry about them," Lila said. "They give every outsider that look."

Gerald directed us into the remains of an MTA booth. It had been stripped of everything but a couple chairs. He passed us some dirty towels and we tried to dry off.

"We don't think it's enough to only avoid upgrades. To us, the problem is the corporate control. That's proprietary software running your arm. Brand-name chemicals in your system."

"You don't have to tell me," I said. "I've got a mean pair of sisters threatening to rip out my branded parts."

Gerald was too caught up in his speech to care. He gestured with his hands like a crazed orchestra conductor. "That's only the start. They create whole life-forms without care or thought. They're gods who care nothing about their creations. They're impure. We want to bring the impurity to the world."

"As far as I can tell, it's pretty impure already."

Gerald slapped his hands on his massive belly. "It is! But it's not free. The biopharms and government deform life and then sell new creatures as easily as they sell shirts or cans of soda. We show them there are repercussions to messing with nature."

"We're the guys who blow up the zootech depots, let all the weird creatures loose," Lila explained.

I'd seen plenty about these groups in the news. Every few months a zootech warehouse would be broken into and a horde of nerve termites would cause citywide panic. President Newman called them terrorist cells, but then he called everyone that. I wasn't sure the corporations cared. All it meant was they got to sell another round of upgrades. Dermal ointment to ward off gas mosquitos, ankle shields to prevent acid viper bites. Maybe a fat new contract with the city for a biocleanse. If Gerald had told me the biopharms paid them to free their zootech, I'd believe it.

"We don't approve of the abominations the biopharms have made, but they're here. They have as much right to live as you or I. And if they kill some of the impure of their own free will, well, so be it. The new Eden will come, illness and all."

"A diseased Eden."

"Exactly."

I tried to picture what New York might look like overrun with zootech insects and genetically modified rats. People had been predicting the death of the city for years. Would that finally drive all the people out of this sinking island? I imagined office buildings filled with screeches instead of conference calls and streets clogged with weeds instead of cars. I could see the appeal. It wasn't like a scorpion was going to charge me 10 percent interest on a medical loan for an upgrade I needed to live. Venom was quick, capitalism killed you nice and slow. Then sent you a bill.

"Don't zootech die quickly? I was told their shelf life was only a few weeks. Engineered apoptosis to make sure they didn't infect the wild populations. Well, and to keep the customer coming back to the store."

Gerald smiled angrily beneath the beard. "'Shelf life' you call it. Can you believe that? The shelf life of a life-form. Do you see how their language has infected everything? Yes, most die after a few days.

Some don't. Some survive. Some thrive. They may have been created in laboratories, but evolution still operates. Nothing alive can be fully controlled."

One of the Purified knocked on the door. Her left leg ended in cinched-off denim and she had a patch over one eye. She whispered something in Gerald's ear. He nodded.

The woman looked at me looking at her leg. Her lips, what was left of them at least, twisted into a thin smile. Her hair was thick and black, but I could see an inflamed circle on the side where a neural implant had been dug out. "We accept anyone who will help crumble the system, if they purify themselves at least. Are you interested?"

"Our surgeons could rip out that eye and arm in a jiffy," Gerald said.

"I imagine the pain would last a lot longer."

The woman looked at me, her incomplete mouth pulling up on the left side. Mocking. "I was like you. Thinking I was gaining something by adding more and more parts. I was addicted to it. Getting surgery was better than any drug. I chased that until I lost everything. My family. My job. My dignity. It took me a long time to realize I'd only be freed by taking things away."

"Maybe you can give me some literature to read and I'll get back to you," I said.

Gerald chuckled as the woman left. "Now that the pleasantries are over. What are you are doing here and what do you want?"

Lila explained the situation. How the cops had raided the Untainted Gardens Edenist Center, and how a goon from the Monsanto Mets had been tailing her for days. How it all had something to do with her father.

"We need a passage to the surface. Somewhere where the cops won't be."

"And why should I help you and your unrepentant cyborg pal?"

"Kobo here is about to blow open the whole case on how Monsanto killed my father," Lila said. I wasn't sure if she had faith in me or was just lying. "It will be great for the Diseased Eden. Monsanto poisons their own star player. You couldn't ask for better propaganda."

Gerald cocked his head and looked at me. "Is that true?"

"It could be. I think it is. Yeah."

"Well, anything that damages a biopharm's image is okay with me. We can get you a centipod to the surface. You'll be on the wrong side of the storm wall. Not a lot of cops around those parts." Gerald clapped his hands, began rolling toward the door. "Well, let's go and then pretend you were never here."

"I need some pets too."

"Pets? What are you talking about?" I said.

"Zootech. Just in case."

"They aren't 'pets.' That's offensive, Lila," Gerald said. He turned to me. "We prefer the term *newforms*."

"You breed zootech down here?"

"When we free them, we keep a few specimens for our Eden Arks. I'll show you. You'll find it quite fascinating, I think. A vision of the future." Gerald grabbed Lila's hand. "Although taking any is, of course, out of the question."

We moved through the white-tiled tunnels Zunz and I used to run down, screaming, after school. There weren't any subway cars anymore. No one selling churros or gas masks. The waiting area was walled off with glass, and inside was a cacophony of green. An entire ecosystem in the station. Red-ringed vines wrapping up the poles, blue moss covering the floor, translucent butterflies and pitch-black moths flapping around in the artificial breeze.

It was bright and lush, a jungle in the center of the city. The wooden benches were sprouting glowing spiral fungi. Millipedes the size of forearms crawled across the station sign between the patches of glowing lichen. The colors were too bright to be natural but too soft to be machine. The tracks were filled with dark green water. Insects flittered about, sparking when they collided in the air. I saw long hornets buzzing around a hive on the top of a MetroCard machine, and a scaly gray cat rolling on its back below an artificial sunlamp. Hidden insects chittered from the ceiling. In the back corner, a cloud drone sprinkled rain on a nerve rose bush, keeping its deadly pollen from floating through the room.

I stepped up close to the wall. Even through the glass, you could smell the lush air.

"What do you think?" Gerald said. "Our own little Diseased Eden, right here in the abandoned old world."

It did feel like a vision of the Garden of Eden, albeit a garden that would kill you in a thousand ways.

"Deadly zoo you have here."

"It isn't a zoo. It's a haven. These are newforms and are thriving. They evolved past their scientists' attempt to control them."

"They have dozens of these stations all over the city," Lila said. "Or rather all underneath it. Since most of them have flooded completely, no one ever comes down here."

"Be quiet, Lila," he said, although he sounded proud.

Not all the creatures were inside the sealed-off room. Cages and aquariums were stacked along the hallway. Filled with brightly colored lizards, turtles, worms, and grubs. Lila was looking at these. I tapped the nearest glass, and a black leech struck at my finger, its mouth splaying across the surface in a circle ringed with teeth. I guessed not every modified critter played nice with others.

"This is what you want the earth to look like?" I stared into the buzzing, underground jungle. I imagined myself walking through it, letting the creatures shock, bite, and claw me. My flesh being slowly stripped apart. Eaten. Broken down until I was nothing except a few cleaned bones.

"It's what the world will look like," Gerald said. "Or something akin. Even without our help, at some point the zootech will break out. Their genes will stabilize. They'll create their own communities, displace ours. You can't control life, no matter what patents you own."

"And all the people?"

"Humans have been a mere blip in the history of life on the planet. What are you, six feet tall? If your height was life on earth, humans are the dandruff on your scalp."

"That doesn't answer the question."

Gerald shrugged, spoke in a rehearsed way that indicated how little the words interested him. "Many will die. Many die as it is. Thousands every day from poverty or war. Some will evolve, but they will evolve naturally, without signing their gene data away to a corporation. Up to nature to decide. She's harsh."

"But fair?" I offered.

"Fairness has nothing to do with it."

Gerald led us to an egg-shaped centipod big enough for two. We stepped inside. Gerald whispered something into Lila's ears while she nodded. I thought I saw him slip a silver case inside her pocket.

He said something that sounded like "You promise?" She nodded.

"Hey, listen. One question," I said.

Gerald arched one of his bushy eyebrows. "Yes?"

"Are you guys getting the game down here? What's the score?"

Gerald snorted. Rolled his cart over to a console. Shouted back. "The Pyramid Pharmaceuticals Sphinxes have seven runs and the Monsanto Mets have one. It's the seventh inning."

"Shit."

"Guess someone's having even worse luck than us," Lila said.

"Come back anytime," Gerald shouted as we closed the door. "That was a joke. Don't come back."

The pod's tiny legs shot out, clicking into divots in the wall. Lila waved goodbye.

Our pod crawled slowly up the tunnel toward the surface. There were so many lost layers to the city. We passed through the floors and dirt and unused pipes. The archaeological remains of past New Yorks. Previous versions of the city compressed like fossils. We sat in silence as the darkness grew a shade lighter each minute until we were bathed in the sickly yellow light of the New York evening.

Lila and I got out, and the pod crawled back down. The Brooklyn storm wall was in front of us, bending off into the distance on both sides like an enormous concrete intestine. Next to it, Lila and I were undigested pills.

She turned to me. "Well, where are we going?"

33

THE HOT MEAL

This isn't exactly what I meant by a date," Dolores said. She was leaning against the kitchen counter, watching Lila and me shovel food into our mouths. We must have looked like vacuum cleaners disguised as people. The table was steaming with bowls of rice, snow peas, pork cubes, charred protein reeds, kale clams, white and gold corn, blackened knobs, squints, cold noodles, butter bark in gum sauce, creamed cutlets, and bristled potatoes. I could feel life coming back to me with each bite.

Lila wasn't eating the meat, but she was hungry enough to not ask for the genetic history of the vegetables.

It had taken us a long time to get to Dolores's place. We'd walked around the storm wall for a mile before we found a boarded-up service tunnel. I had to power up my arm to smash the wood. Grunted in pain. My knuckles were dirty and dented. All Setek's work had been reversed in a day.

I'd done a few internal scans and hadn't found a second grub beacon, but we didn't know if there was another tracker in some other shape. Plus, Dolores was at game three so we couldn't get to her place until it was over. Lila and I had wandered the smog for a while to make sure no one was tracking us, ducking into stores when we saw police lights.

We sat on a bench in a supraway station for an hour watching the streams. The news stations didn't have anything to say about the Edenist raid, or Zunz's death for that matter. They'd moved on to the playoff odds, the starting lineups, exciting prospects in the upcoming draft. Or else other news stories. The state of the One China trade talks. Russia's Neanderthal riot trials. A human-interest story about a boy whose drone had been lost on vacation in Florida and somehow made the long journey all the way to Boston to reunite. The boy hugged the blinking black machine and told the news anchor, "He's my bestest friend in the world."

We wandered around for a while longer. Took a series of tubes and taxis to shake any potential tails. Finally we arrived at Dolores's building, starving and half asleep.

Now, Lila and I sat back. Patted our inflated bellies. The insides of our bowls were reduced to tiny puddles.

I looked out the window at the city inching by. Dolores's building was like mine, a spinner, although her full-time salary meant she could afford a partial view of the setting sun. The sky was a smear of red behind the lattice of the skystabbers.

Dolores strolled over to Lila and me cautiously, like she was afraid we'd get confused and chomp on her fingers when she picked up the bowls. "I suppose there's no room for dessert?"

Lila gave a look of mock horror, sucked in her belly as best she could. "There's at least a slice of cake's worth of stomach space here."

I cleared the table while Dolores brought over the cake.

"It was good grub, lady."

"Say 'thank you,' not 'good grub,'" I said.

"I prefer 'good grub,' actually. It has a salt-of-the-earth ring to it."

Lila made a see-what-do-you-know face, then turned to Dolores. "Kobo says you can't hear?"

"Lila," I snapped.

Dolores opened her hands in the air. "I'm deaf, Kobo." She adjusted something on her goggles, spoke to Lila. "I have only partial hearing. But I've got plenty of other senses. Plus, these goggles give me a real-time transcription."

"I think it's cool you never upgraded your ears."

"I think it's pretty cool you knew how to escape the police. Thanks for saving Kobo's life there. I'm oddly fond of him."

"He's nice but seems a bit useless."

"You'll understand when you're older."

Lila was already digging into the cake. "You adults always say that. Maybe I'm not trying to understand."

Dolores smiled, big and wide. "I like this one." She walked over to me, ran a hand across my belly, and put her mouth to my ear. "I'm going to make some calls," she whispered. "Maybe my Pyramid coworkers have intel on the Edenist raid."

Dolores went out to the enclosed balcony. Slid the door shut behind her.

"Hey, you know I saved your life too," I said. "A little bit."

"A very little bit. I saved your whole butt."

I couldn't argue with that, so didn't. Instead I just watched Lila. It was strange sitting next to her. I'd been replaying Zunz's death over and over in my mind. And now there was another Zunz, a daughter. A part of him that had split off and grown on its own. She seemed unreal to me. I still couldn't fit her into my picture of the world.

Lila was leaning forward in her chair, alive and smiling. At least for now. Her illness had receded, yet I knew it was just gearing itself up for another strike.

"Being deaf isn't the same as lichen lung, you know. You could die. Just because Dolores didn't upgrade doesn't mean you shouldn't."

Lila kept eating her cake. "We all die from something."

"I know I don't understand your religion or philosophy or whatever. But why would god want you to die from lichen lung? It isn't natural."

"Listen," she said, licking the last icing off the fork. "My so-called father didn't raise me. My uncle didn't raise me. You didn't raise me. The Edenists did. They're the only ones who have been a family to me."

"But—"

"But—" She cut me off. "Even if I told you I don't fully buy what they're selling, it doesn't matter. Say I wanted to get an engineered lung, so what?"

I shrugged, face scrunched in disbelief. Showed her my palms. "You live."

"Live how? I can't pay for those lungs. My deadbeat dad didn't leave me a trust fund. That Neanderthal isn't hunting me down to deliver an inheritance check, right? I don't plan to spend my life hounded by debt collectors."

I shook my head. "It wouldn't be like that."

"I guess I could sell my womb to the rich. Grow a bunch of babies for billionaires who don't want their bellies stretched."

"Come on, you don't have to do that. Things aren't that grim."

"You told me we can't go to your place because loan sharks trashed it."

I muttered. Stewed in my chair. I felt angry but didn't know why. It was Lila's body. I didn't even know her. Not really. She was some little kid I'd met this week who hated my dead brother.

I finished smoking my eraser. Let it calm my nerves as I walked around Dolores's apartment. It was small, yet comfortable. I guess a real estate algorithm would call it cozy. There were places to sit or recline on every wall, and mood orbs hummed pleasantly as they released a honeysuckle scent. It was the kind of place you could come back to after a long day at your shitty job and shut out the world.

I noticed she only had a few items of Cyber League memorabilia. Animatronic bobbleheads next to framed videocards of her rookie and sophomore seasons. Above them was a team photo, back in our second season. Everyone was there. Frank "Stretch" Gibson, "Metalhead" Marissa Hellers, Otto "the Buzzsaw" Barrios, "Dialup" Di Liu, and all the rest. Dolores and I were in the middle row, her arm draped over my shoulders. I wondered where they all were now.

Lila noticed me staring at the picture. "So, is Dolores, like, your girlfriend?"

"We're just friends."

Lila looked at me with her lips curled down and her eyes wide open. "Sure. I'm going to go watch cartoons." She hopped on the couch and clicked on the holopad. The table lit up with transparent samurai slicing each other in half to a chorus of beeps and screams.

I watched her from the kitchen chair, then went out to Dolores's glass balcony. She was still on her video call, signing. It was almost night. From the side of the balcony, I could see the sun dip behind the towers of the city. The entire sky was turning bright red, as if someone had set off a nuclear bomb in the middle of Manhattan.

Dolores banged her hip into mine. I let it be banged.

Dolores had her screen set up on the table. She was signing with someone I didn't recognize. Her hands danced through the air. When they finished up their conversation, she pulled out her own eraser and lit it off mine.

"Is Lila your daughter now or what?"

"She's just a clue."

"She's a girl."

"I don't know what to do about her. I feel like she's my only connection to Zunz. She has his eyes and smile, you know? Even a mole around where his birthmark was."

"You'd be a good father," Dolores said.

I laughed, good and hard. "I can't even pay my own bills. And I hate children."

Dolores stiffened up. Her goggles were nearly the same red as the sky. "Okay, riddle this case with me. Your friend Zunz knocked up Kang's sister, who died. He never wanted to be a father. Or he didn't want to derail his baseball career. Whatever. He paid Kang a monthly sum to take care of the girl, which Kang began giving to an Edenist orphanage, minus his substantial skim. That all seems simple enough."

"And the Mets want her DNA," I said. "Must have killed Kang because he wouldn't cooperate. Setek said they were looking for a relative to compare. Figure out what happened to Zunz, but I don't buy that. I think they already knew. Dash told me Zunz had to be carried off the practice field awhile before he died."

"So just an accident? I suppose it makes sense. We pump these players with untested drugs all the time. This was bound to happen eventually."

"I've watched baseball my entire life. I've never seen anyone die that way before."

The images came back to me. The blood. The chunks. The screams. I gripped the railing and shuddered.

"Players die all the time," Dolores said, as her fingers skied across the back of my hand. "Not normally on the field. But off it after years of chronic pain and illness. You know the turnover in this league.

Even the best players only have a few peak years before their bodies start to break down. Look at you and me."

"We're still missing something."

We stared out at the darkening city. Windows lit up erratically across the buildings like random pixels in a broken screen.

"If so, it must have been something pretty extreme they were trying." My screen pinged and I pulled it out. "Shit. I just got a message from Natasha. I forgot to tell you they were demanding we watch game four in the visiting owner's box."

"Great. You owe me a date anyway."

"I don't think Coppelius saw me flee with Lila. But if he did, he would have told Natasha. This could all be a trap."

I didn't like the idea of being out in the open and waiting for the hands of a lab-grown spook to land on my neck. Snap it before I could even notice.

Dolores laughed. "Kobo, no one is going to kill you in the middle of the playoffs in broad daylight in a rival team's stadium. Going to the game is the safest place you could be. And it's the only way you'll be able to feel out the Mouth and Natasha."

She was right. Although my gut told me it was a trap, my brain told me I didn't have any other play. If Coppelius was on my tail, being in public was safer than hiding at home.

The moon was high in the sky, barely visible in the dark.

"God, the smog is so thick it almost looks like the city was just vaporized. Only rubble remains," Dolores said.

"Remember when we were kids and all anyone could talk about was the apocalypse? Nuclear war. Peak oil. The singularity. Something was going to happen one day and everything was going to come crashing down in a terrifying boom? I always found that kind of exciting."

Dolores nodded and then shrugged. "Instead things just keep crawling along somehow."

"Not quite as exciting."

I pulled out another eraser and lit it off the stub of my last one. Outside, the sun had set. The sky was an ocean of black oil punctuated by the lights of cars and blimps floating like strange amoeba in a dirty sea.

34

THE GAME NIGHT

I normally don't let the enemy in my box, but the enemy normally isn't this beautiful." The Mouth squeezed his meaty hand on Dolores's knee. "How'd you end up with this scrub?"

We were in the visiting owner's box atop the red pyramid, waiting for game four to start. It was a warm day and even warmer in the sealed stadium. Although I wasn't sure if it was the heat or my nerves making my clothes dampen with sweat.

Dolores shooed his hand as if it was a stray leaf that had landed there by chance. "Oh, Kobo and I go way back to the Cyber League days."

The Mouth was sitting on a leather chair with a spider leg base. The metal legs tapped as they spun him around. He was wearing a black suit with gold pinstripes made of actual gold.

"It's a shame the way the CLB ended. It was awful what they did to you oilers."

"They?" I said. "Weren't you one of the owners of the Manhattan Mechs?"

"He was just a minority partner," Natasha offered. She was sitting on my side, her wide shoulders knocking into mine.

"I meant the larger forces. Universe. Fate. Progress. Those bastards," the Mouth said.

Dolores looked at me and rolled her eyes so hard I could see it through the opaque glass of her goggles. She turned back to the Mouth, put some syrup in her voice. "Tell me, Mr. Mouth, how did you end up running the Monsanto Mets?"

"You know that story. Everyone knows that story. It's the most famous story in sports."

"I'd prefer to hear the insider's view."

"I got it with nothing. Just my hard work. I started with jack shit, only a couple hundred million from my father and a snack company as an inheritance."

"Mr. Meat Chews, right?"

The Mouth scuttled his chair toward her, frowning. "Mr. Meat Squirts. Squirts. Like money squirting into my family's mouth, which is what it was. Liquid meat in plastic tubes. Synthetic and genius. Revolutionized gym workouts. You had the brown tubes for beef, pink for chicken, purple for tuna. We had chewable bars for decades, but you can't chew on the treadmill." He started tapping on the side of his golden head. "The point is I didn't have anything except these brains. I'm a little bit brilliant. Maybe smarter than the scientists we have on staff. Sometimes I go into the lab and tell those eggheads and they look at me like I'm Einstein. You ever heard of Einstein? He was a big deal, back in the day. If he was alive, he'd be working for me. If I let him."

The stream of words flowed out of his mouth like sewage through a drainage pipe.

Dolores and I had only been here for half an hour and I was already feeling uneasy. We were up high, but I felt claustrophobic. Boxed in between the ranting Mouth and the watchful Natasha.

I looked out at the glittering green field. Breathed.

The whole stadium was below us. The players spitting wads of adrenaline gum in the dugouts, the half-nude fans with bodies dyed in team colors, the falcon-headed drones swooping through the rows to hawk beer and hot dogs. The start of the game was still a few minutes away and you could feel the excitement starting to buzz through the crowd.

I had seen Dolores's logic. Whatever game was being played, we weren't going to win if we stayed in the dugout. Still, I was nervous sitting beside the people who might have been responsible for Zunz's death.

Lila had been surprisingly receptive to being left home. Dolores pulled her aside and whispered something. I could only see the girls giggle. They'd only known each other a few hours and already understood each other better than I understood either one. When they came back, Lila promised she'd stay put for the game—"Not like I have anywhere to go anyway"—and Dolores set her security system to go off if anyone even approached the door. "If you hear it, there's a getaway pod under the balcony." Dolores spun a dial under the table, and a hatch popped open. The pod would have been cramped for Dolores but was roomy enough for Lila. "It'll lev down to the sidewalk. Then you'll have to run."

"If I'm stuck here alone all night, you two better figure out who killed my father." She was leaning against the doorframe as we left, like she owned the place. She had a cup of soda in one hand and a massage stick in the other. In the background, the speaker played songs that to my old ears sounded less like music and more like the shrieks of metal being ground to scrap.

"We're on it," I'd said.

While Dolores humored the Mouth, Natasha was mimicking her boss, although with more delicacy. Her hand glided around my knee like a water spider across a pond. "How's our investigation investment?"

"I've got the clues, just need to figure out how they stick together."

Our luxury box was floating above center field. Elmer Tuscan's larger owner's box was levitating around home plate. I could see the Mouth keep looking at it with little angry eyes.

"Do you think you'll find out who killed Zunz soon?"

"I do."

Natasha chuckled, her bone jewelry jangling. She was dressed in a stylish business suit in cutting-edge fabric yet dyed to look like a caveman's pelt. If cavemen wore designer power suits at least. She was clearly playing it up. I wondered if the Mouth liked it that way or if she was mocking the half-dozen executives and investors who were in the box with us. I hadn't seen any of them talk to Natasha, or even acknowledge her existence. Whatever they thought about a Neanderthal woman being the CEO's right-hand man, I bet they thought it a lot.

"That's the spirit." She patted my forearm.

"What does that mean?"

"Oh, sit back and enjoy the game, Kobo. You'll find out."

I didn't like the sound of that and said so.

"I think you'll be pleasantly surprised. Your species finds surprise to be a pleasing emotion, yes?"

"Depends on the surprise."

The luxury boxes floated back to dock in the upper stands, away from home runs and pop fouls. We locked in place.

People in the stadium were beginning to wind their way to the seats, and the music was increasing in beats per minute as the stadium lights became a subtle red and yellow. Subliminal push to order food before opening pitch. It was working on me. Or maybe I was nervous.

"Hey, I'm starved. I'm going to go get a hot dog. Anyone want one?"

The Mouth reached across Dolores and grabbed my arm with his golden fingers. "Sit down, Kobo, you gearhead. This is a luxury box. You think we walk around like bottom-feeders? We get our food delivered. I'll get a round of Mouth burgers. Or whatever pitiful excuse for a burger they serve here at the Pyramid. You want mustard? Mayo? Mayo is great on a burger. Mayo for everyone."

A chorus of mumbling yeses and sounds-good-bosses filled the box.

"I guess I'll just stretch my legs a bit, then."

"Be back before opening pitch," Natasha said, her finger wagging like a metronome.

Dolores took my hand, pulled me in for what I thought was a kiss but turned into an angry whisper. "Afterwards, we're going out for a drink. This date is one I'll need to recover from."

The hallway stank, but in a sweet way from the sodas and ketchup pumps. The announcers rattled on in the hallway speakers, expounding like experts on a game that hadn't even started yet. I smiled. It was comforting how America's pastime was frozen in time.

"I bet the Mets will be just dying to win this one for JJ Zunz," one of the announcers said. "No pun intended."

"The Sphinxes will be looking to put a curse on the Monsanto batters though. Entomb them in strikeouts as quick as possible."

"And look here! It's the presidential blimp arriving at the stadium. President Newman will be throwing out the first pitch today, as he does each game of the World Series."

I stepped behind a pair of surrogates piloted by distant rich people who were too lazy or too scared to come all the way down to the stadium yet still wanted to use their tickets. A lot of the wealthy barely left their cloud condos anymore. Too afraid of whatever new diseases

were circulating in the masses. The league had banned drone surrogates a couple seasons ago with the No Heartbeat No Seat policy,
so these were people. They had earphones and a full-face visor screen
that displayed a live feed of ticket holders watching from the comfort
of their condos.

The people behind them couldn't see too well through the
semiopaque screen. They bumped into me and then each other.
One of them dropped a commemorative cup on the floor and I
heard the ticket holder shout in their ear. "That's coming out of your
fee!"

I pushed my way through the crowds of drunk teenagers, face-
painted uncles, and old men grumbling about the old days. I loved
the anonymizing crowds of a baseball game. A place where I was
watching everyone, and no one was watching me.

I found a sausage cart with a server painted the colors of an Italian
flag. "I made-a the sausages so a-spicy today," the cart's anthropomorphic sausage said. I ordered a spicy Italian with onions and peppers,
the staple of our diet when Zunz and I were kids. Nostalgia in a greasy
bun.

As I drizzled mustard, I saw a short girl in a hoodie heading
toward the back lift. She was keeping her head down and sticking
close to the wall. She had a small square purse she was holding with
an outstretched arm. I couldn't quite see her face.

She stopped, leaned into the wall, and started coughing. A crowd
of screaming teenagers walked by. When they'd passed, I saw the
bright red dots spattered on the wall.

I left the sausage beneath the nozzle. Ran.

"We're five minutes away from game four," the announcer said
over the speakers. "Sphinxes up two games to one. If the Mets can
pull out a win, it could turn the whole series around. Don't you think,
Boomer?"

"I agree, Joe. This game will determine the momentum heading into game five. And we all know the team with momentum has the hunger. If you have the hunger, you get clutch when it comes down to the wire and everything is on the line."

"The Sphinxes are thirsty for a title. They're like a dying animal that found an oasis."

"They better not let the Mets come in and slurp."

Everyone was moving back toward their seats, smacking against each other like salmon desperate to spawn. I swam against the crowd trying to look as calm as I could. When I caught up with Lila, I dragged her into the nearest accessible bathroom.

"Let go of me," Lila said. She kicked backward, catching me in the shin. Then she saw who'd grabbed her. "What is with you and my shit luck?"

"We told you to stay at the apartment," I said, shouting as quietly as I could. I could feel the anger burning in my belly. Then it was doused with fear. "Did something happen? Why are you here? Did someone come to the apartment?"

I grabbed her, looked her over to see if she was injured. She pushed me away.

"I got bored."

"Bored? You could get killed."

She sat on the sink, legs hanging over the edge. "Look, I didn't have my father's murderer to keep me company." She wore a foul smile. "How is the Mouth lately, hmm? In good health?"

"Are you all right? I saw you spitting up blood out there."

She smiled, a little red still on her lips. "I'm fine. No worse than usual. What are you, my new dad?"

I yanked the chrome purse out of her hand. "What's in the bag?"

"Don't open that."

I did. A red newt jumped out. The same zootech Okafor had

shown me at the police station. It crawled up the wall and onto the stained bathroom mirror. Its neon skin changed to a silver that attempted to mimic the mirror. It left a gray blotch in our reflections.

I reached out to grab it.

"Don't touch it!"

My hand was only an inch from the newform when she yelled. I looked closer and saw the dark wires running under the skin.

"It'll kill you," Lila said in a voice barely above a whisper.

"How did you get a poison newt? And what the hell were you doing with it here?"

But I knew. She'd slipped it out of the Diseased Eden somehow. Or Gerald had given it to her when I wasn't looking, letting a child be an assassin for the cause. I felt like heading back down into the subway and defiling his face with my metal fist.

The newt watched us. Its eyes flicking around while its body stayed still. Then it decided it was time to leave us alone and ran into the sink. Disappeared in the drain.

"Damn it," Lila said.

"Who was this meant for?"

She didn't answer. Just looked down at her feet kicking the empty air.

"The Mouth? You were going to kill the Mouth?"

"Someone has to."

"This was a dumb plan. You'd never get close to him. And if you did, they'd lock you away for the rest of your life. You're lucky you didn't get snatched on the way in."

"You said the Mets killed my father, but you won't stop him. The cops won't stop him." She wiped her eyes with the cuff of her shirt. "He may have been a piece of crap, but he was still my dad."

"Okay, okay." I looked down the sink hole where the zootech

newt had vanished. It wasn't coming back. But I flushed a little water down so it wouldn't bite some unsuspecting fan's finger when they were washing up. "I said they *might* have killed him. Accidentally. I don't know yet."

Someone banged on the door. "What the hell's going on in there? I need to piss."

"I'm taking a poop!" Lila shouted back. "You get off on girls pooping? You pervert."

"Well, fuck you then."

The man kicked the door and walked off.

I knelt in front of her. "If the Mouth did it, we'll get him. I promise. But you need to go back. And so do I, before he gets suspicious. Anyway, your weapon ran down the sink."

She just sat there with her head hung and her fists balled.

"Let's get you back to Dolores's. We'll figure out how to kill the CEO of a major biopharm another day."

I took Lila's bony hand. She didn't squeeze back, but didn't resist. I guided her down the hall. The opening anthem was being sung by a pop diva wearing an aquarium suit. Silver fish swam around her as she belted out the words. The last stragglers headed to their seats, arms carrying hot dogs, popcorn, and nacho reeds. The players lined up in front of their dugouts, waiting to be announced.

I got us in a lift, and we shuttled down to the ground floor. The screen was showing the field, fans cheering. The crowd was coming alive. At the top of the stadium, the sphinx began to glow bright red.

"Let's! Go! Sphinxes!"

The lift stopped.

An alarm went off. The mag lift's walls turned from silver to blinking red.

I cursed. They must have noticed Lila's face on one of the security feeds. Was Coppelius here? The sirens were blaring, and the mag lift was frozen in place.

I was waiting for the doors to open and for a team of guards to drag us both across the stadium, toss us at the Mouth's golden feet. Maybe they'd torture us right there in the box. He seemed like the type who'd like to watch.

I pressed each of the buttons. Hit them. Mashed them with my dented fist.

We stayed in place.

The wall was now a video feed. The Mouth filled the screen. He stood up, holding a microphone in one hand and a burger in the other. Grease dripped down his fingers in shiny rivulets.

"I want to thank Mr. Tuscan for letting me make a little announcement. The Sphinxes are good hosts," he said, and the stadium cheered. "Although Mets brand upgrades are the best on the market."

The crowd booed playfully.

Natasha leaned over and whispered in his ear. He nodded.

"I didn't get out of my chair to talk to you about upgrades. I want to tell you something tragic. Recently, something horrible happened on a field just like this one. A sacred baseball field. A Monsanto player was attacked by vicious terrorists. Godless, anti-American terrorists. If I have my way, we'll bat their heads all the way to kingdom come."

The crowd roared in approval. Fans in the Mets section waved signs that read *Win it for Zunz!* and *Payback for JJ.*

I thought maybe I could jimmy off the metal cover in the lift. Figure out something to do with the wires. I started to pry off the covering.

"What the hell is he talking about?" Lila said.

"But the Monsanto Mets are the best team," the Mouth went

on. "We have the best doctors. The best products. We can do anything. I mean anything. I'm here to tell you the rumors are false. Lies. Yes, JJ Zunz was murdered. Yet JJ Zunz is *not* dead. Not anymore."

I stopped pulling on the panel. My guts felt cold and heavy, like an anvil dropped into a winter lake.

Lila's fingernails dug into my palm.

I looked back and forth between Lila and the screen in confusion.

The crowd was silent. Then started roaring in bewildered waves. The Mouth smiled wide enough to let everyone see all his teeth.

"We've healed him with our brilliant, best-of-the-market medicine. A round of applause for our genius scientist. No one else could do this, believe me. JJ Zunz, our captain. He's back! Like a zombie. But a strong, Mets zombie. I'm announcing we have a change to the starting lineup tonight!"

The cameras panned to a tunnel by the dugout. A man walked out, alone. Then a hologram projection blew his image up in the middle of the field. Zunz's head was level with the top row. He flashed his goofy grin, and then swung his bat in a mock home run, the hologram bat plowing through the crowd.

It didn't matter if you were a Pyramid or Monsanto fan. Everyone in the stadium was screaming as if their lungs were the size of blimps. The roar got louder and louder.

It was hard to tell on the screen, but the man looked like Zunz. And he seemed perfectly healthy. Strong and sculpted. He could have just trotted off an assembly line.

A noise escaped Lila's lips that could have been a groan or a gasp. I could feel my palm bleeding from her fingernails.

She looked up at me, her expression had drained away. She was pale and shivering.

The alarm was off. It had been off for a moment, but I hadn't noticed with the constant roar of the crowd. They were drowning out everything.

We started to move.

On-screen, the other Mets players ran toward Zunz with their arms flung wide.

The mag lift reached the ground floor. The doors slid open. Lila and I stepped out into the empty lot.

35

THE SACRIFICE FLY

I walked up the redbrick stairwell of the Sphinxes stadium, shaking with inertia and disbelief.

Dolores had taken Lila home and given me her Sphinxes pass to get back inside. I'd called her immediately and she came running. We had to assume if Coppelius had been looking for Lila, then Natasha and the Mouth were too. The fact that Zunz had been apparently revived didn't mean they'd stop.

"The Mouth was asking for you. Seemed angry. You need to go back, tell them I had to meet with my bosses," she'd said. I'd watched them go, barely processing Lila's face at the taxi window as they flew off.

Zunz's face was plastered on every screen on every wall of the Sphinxes stadium. He wasn't doing much. It was the top of the first, and the Mets were in the dugout. Zunz was sitting on the bench and smiling. He looked drugged, and he must have been. I suppose you don't get your flesh reconfigured in a couple days without heavy anesthesia. Two assistant coaches in lab coats monitored him.

When I got back to the luxury box, the Mouth was furious. "Kobo, you loser. Where were you? I wanted to put you on-screen."

"Bathroom," I said.

The Mouth guffawed. Slapped his golden hand on the arm of his chair. "I bet you couldn't believe it. I bet you shit your pants and had to run to the bathroom. Did you shit your pants? I bet you did. You weren't expecting the Mets to save Zunz, were you? So little faith. Someone call a dry cleaner. Get this guy some new pants."

I forced myself to laugh. "You got me."

"You were supposed to be here for the announcement," the Mouth said. His own mouth frowned. "That was the whole point. Zunz's brother watching Zunz triumphantly return. I wanted that on camera! Why do you think we paid you?"

"We'll get some footage," Natasha said, waving over the reporter in the box.

The Mouth threw his arm around me, hugged me close while the camera snapped.

"See, Zunz's brother here can confirm we fixed him," the Mouth said.

I must have mumbled an agreement. Everything seemed to be happening at an impossible speed. Too fast and too slow simultaneously.

When the reporters had left, the Mouth turned away and began bragging to the other executives.

I sat down to watch the game, seeing Natasha's grin from the side of my eye.

Zunz stood inscrutable at left field. The Sphinx batters seemed spooked by his presence, didn't hit any balls in his direction in the first few innings.

I had a few messages from Dolores on my phone asking me if I was okay, and a dozen from Okafor. *Did you know, you asshole? Did you know?* they said. *I should be asking you that*, I wrote back. Then I turned off the screen and tuned my eyes to Zunz. Didn't look away. I kept thinking if I went up to go to the bathroom or even blinked, Zunz would disappear again. Or worse. I'd close my eyes for a second and in that span his skin would ripple and his head would melt.

No runs were on the board when Zunz stepped to the plate at the top of the fourth. Lex Dash was on second with Sam Tzu on first. Two outs.

The crowd threw their arms up, the wave wrapping around the stadium and increasing in speed.

Zunz looked a little unsteady at the plate. When the first pitch came in, he swung low and late. He stepped back, kicked his feet in the dirt, then got back in his stance. The second pitch sailed high for a foul. The third he let go right through the floating green lights for a second strike. He connected on the next pitch, smacking the ball skyward, and giving the Sphinx catcher, Marius Lupu, an easy out.

The players jogged back to the dugouts, Zunz a little bit slower than the rest. A team of men in white coats attended to him, poking and prodding him with different instruments.

"How?" I asked Natasha.

Natasha looked at me, her large lips pulled back and her giant brow unmoving. "How what, Mr. Kobo?"

My brain was as alive and confused as a shaken beehive. Questions buzzed around the walls of my skull, then they escaped. "How did you regenerate him?" I said. "How long was he legally dead? Did he never truly die? Does he have brain damage? Nerve damage? Blood clots? When were you going to tell me?"

Natasha cut me off with one stumpy finger to my lips. "Now is not the time for questions. Now is the time to root for the team."

"Can I talk to him after the game?" I asked.

She smiled, waved a hand idly.

"Please."

"I imagine the doctors will want to be thorough in examining him. I'm sure you'll want them to be. Plus, he'll need his rest. Perhaps in a few days, or weeks."

I watched the rest of the game in a daze. I was way up high, over-looking the field, and JJ Zunz was somehow down low in the thick of things. Far away from me, too far, but happy and alive with all his parts in their proper places.

And his face was everywhere. The screens in front of our seats, the display drones buzzing through the crowds, and the massive three-hundred-foot spherical scoreboard that spun from the ceiling. Every-where I turned, Zunz was looking back.

Zunz's presence powered the rest of the team. You could see them vibrate with the excitement. On the mound, T. L. Park took a no-hitter into the seventh. Ashburn made a spectacular diving catch in center field, sliding into the fence without dropping the ball. Van Young had his first home run of the postseason, clear into the fourth level. The Mets seemed to be a team on a mission.

Zunz's performance was more solid than spectacular. He had no errors in the field but didn't do much at the plate. He'd struck out in his first at bat and popped out his second. There was something not quite right with him, as if he was operating on a fraction-of-a-second delay. Understandable from someone who had been a bloody corpse only a week before.

And the crowd roared at every swing. Two hundred thousand people in a stadium willing his bat to smack the ball into orbit.

We got our wish in the seventh when Zunz hit a ground ball that popped over the shortstop's glove. Zunz sprinted to first, driving Henry "Hologram" Graham home to put the Mets up 2–0.

I couldn't help it. I jumped out of my seat, screaming.

"That's the spirit, Mr. Kobo," Natasha said. "Are you happy?"

"Yes. Of course," I said. Although as soon as I said it, I wasn't sure.

I was glad my brother was alive. But I felt like something had been torn out of me. My purpose. I'd spent the last days with one goal animating my brain, heart, and lungs. I thought I was going to solve something. To deal out justice. To be a hero.

Now? I was back to being a broke, out-of-work oiler with no problems to solve but my own.

Still, my brother was alive.

The Mets kept the score two to zero until the top of the eighth, when Park's arm gave out and they lost the no-hitter on back-to-back home runs. They were taken off the mound. The ninth was scoreless, and the game went to extra innings.

"Brilliant," the Mouth said. "We couldn't have scripted this better."

At the top of the eleventh, the Sphinxes closer, Meredith Blackwood, spun a wild pitch past the catcher. Dash was on second and sprinted to third base. She took a hard turn and the crowd rose as if they were levitating. But she braked when the catcher held up the ball.

Tzu was up next and overeager. Swung at everything and struck out in three. Graham made the closer work for it, getting a full count, and then was walked to first.

JJ Zunz was up. One out, runners on third and first, and a tie game.

He didn't wave this time or turn to the crowd at all. He was zoned in. The crowd didn't mean anything to him. "When I'm in the zone, I can't even hear them," he liked to say. That didn't stop them from chanting "Zunz! Zunz!" in the increasingly desperate volumes of a cult trying to summon a demonic force.

The noise got louder and louder.

The Sphinxes brought in a new pitcher, Boris Gorky. A knuckleballer with extra knuckles. It didn't matter. Zunz let the first pitch curve past his knee for a ball. Didn't move an inch when the low strike came in. Then another ball and another. Gorky was trying a different windup each time. Adjusting his hat, making signals to the catcher. The next pitch came in, so low and slow it might as well have been gift wrapped. Zunz stayed steady, sent it soaring into the air.

The Sphinxes center fielder ran back from the wall, dove, and caught it.

Dash sprinted home.

Zunz threw his hands in the air. Sacrifice fly.

I jumped up in my seat, shouting and pumping a fist, right as Zunz collapsed.

36

THE BRIEF TOUCH

I felt like a rat let out of the maze, only to find himself in a larger one. Zunz was alive, yet injured again. He hadn't died this time. Hadn't bled out. His body was still holding together. But he lay on his back and waved for medics to arrive. A half dozen of them carried him off on a levitating stretcher.

I needed to find him. Ran out of the Mouth's box without even saying goodbye.

Halfway down the hall, someone grabbed my arm. Stopped me.

"Mr. Kobo," Natasha said. "Don't you want to see if our bullpen can close out the game?"

"I need to see him," I said. My eyes must have looked wild.

"He's with the team doctors. He's been through a lot. Let him rest." She took out her screen, pulled up a form. "Plus, I'm afraid I need your signature here."

"What's this?"

"Standard de-employment contract with a nondisclosure rider."

"You're taking me off the case?"

Natasha's look wanted to pat me on the head. "What case, Mr. Kobo? Zunz's murder? He's not murdered. Case closed."

She passed me the contract.

I could barely concentrate on the screen. The words became the scribbles of a toddler. "Don't you still want to know who poisoned him?"

"We do, but not two million dollars' worth still. We've got memory worms to work on him later."

"Maybe no one poisoned him except his own doctors."

Natasha pursed her lips. "That could be considered slander. Luckily, the Mouth has authorized me to give a one-time payment of two hundred thousand dollars in exchange for your silence. Call it a severance package." She pulled out a bytewallet strapped to her thigh, handed it to me. "Everybody wins."

I wanted to snap her screen in half and toss the bytewallet down the hall. But I needed the money. It was enough to pay off the Sassafras sisters for a couple months and maybe even get a new loan. I'd be able to patch up my hand, again. Start planning for the future. Turn my life around.

Natasha tapped the screen where she needed me to write, her finger obscuring the line.

I signed. Told myself it was the only play.

"Tell your boyfriend Coppelius he can stop following me."

Her face was blank. "I'm sure I don't know what you mean."

"Sure."

I stumbled around toward the exit. Made it look like I was too dazed to think. When I was out of sight, I sprinted. I took the stairs down, galloping down the spiraling case to the ground floor.

There was a crowd of Mets staffers and teammates outside the door of the visiting team lockers. Everyone was shouting. I tried to squeeze through them, but the wall of bodies didn't budge. Camera drones shaped like giant eyeballs flew around, filling the room with flashing lights.

"Everyone out of the way!" someone yelled.

The crowd parted reluctantly. Two doctors in blue-and-orange lab coats guided out a hovering stretcher covered in a white sheet. I could see the form of my friend underneath.

Zunz's head was exposed at the top, his blue batting helmet still on. He was alive. There was a little bit of blood on his lips, and his eyes looked yellow and bloodshot. But he was alive and solid. The sheet rose and fell with his breaths.

I pushed someone in an orange jacket out of the way. Got to Zunz's side.

"JJ."

It was the first time I'd seen Zunz in the flesh in months. I'd been so used to seeing him on various screens and devices, in different sizes and resolutions, that I forgot what he looked like in actual skin. Shiny, almost plastic. His head lolled back and forth and his arms trembled.

"Hey. Move away from the player." A guard grabbed my shoulder. But I stayed by the stretcher, gripping the side.

I slid my hand under the sheet and took his.

"Are you okay? JJ, are you okay?"

He turned his head to me. His face was unsmiling, but kind. The old face. His hand was sticky with sweat.

"I know you," he said. He coughed.

"No shit," I said. I laughed, a little. "What did they do to you?"

Someone else grabbed my other shoulder. Both were tugging. The smell of beer and sweat swirled in the hallway. The crowd was screaming and cheering.

Zunz looked at me, confused. His eyebrows scrunched. "Kobo," he said flatly.

"Yes. It's me, Kobo. JJ. What happened? Why didn't you call me?"
But he didn't say anything. His face was a vacant lot.

He turned his head to a guard on the other side of the stretcher.
"Tired." Then it was as if his mind had clicked off. He lay there, eyes open, not moving.

"Wait, who did it to you?" I said, but the security guards were pulling me away. Almost instinctively, I detached the pinkie finger of my bionic hand. I slipped it into Zunz's gurney as I was yanked back.

I was slammed into the wall. New bodies filled in the space in front of me. Zunz was only a dozen feet away, but there were walls of bodies between us.

"Everyone get out of the way. This player needs treatment."

The crowd of Mets fans was swelling in the hallway. Shouting faces with blue-and-orange paint. Cheering for Zunz, even as he lay injured in the stretcher.

"You kicked mummy ass out there!" a woman yelled.

Three guards with shock batons got in front of the stretcher. They powered up their weapons, waved the crackling sticks to clear a path. The crowd pressed out of the way as well as they could.

I was still being held as he was pushed toward the exit. The crowd started to follow them, shouting slogans and well wishes.

I threw an elbow back into one guy, who responded with a pained grunt. "What the hell?"

Zunz and the guards had gone through the door, slammed it shut behind them. A row of Sphinxes security guards stepped in front of the door.

I wove through the crowd in the other direction, bouncing off people like a pinball. Took the stairwell to the balcony above the back exit. The finger that I'd detached had a tracker in it. My bionic eye sensed it moving outside the stadium. I got to the balcony as the stretcher was being loaded into a large white van. There was a group of doctors around him. I was practically falling over the railing trying to look at them. A half dozen, each holding different instruments. One of them had dark skin and a collar around her neck. Julia Arocha, I thought, although it was hard to tell.

Another one wasn't hard to tell at all. He had a set of metallic spider legs clicking under him and an ugly poof of orange hair. Dr. Setek. He seemed to be shouting angrily, although the stadium speakers were so loud I couldn't hear. Setek pulled out a large injector and screwed a vial of black serum into the slot. He shot the liquid into Zunz's left thigh. Put in another vial, and injected it into his right side.

I thought about trying to scale the wall, hoping I didn't injure my legs on the drop. It was two stories down. But too many people milled around. People with guns and serious-looking expressions.

The van started. Lifted off the ground. It flew my brother away into the night.

37

THE HARD TALK

What's to discuss?"

"We don't have a plan. We need a plan."

"The plan is we go into the Monsanto compound, right now, and rescue him."

"With what army, kiddo?"

Dolores reached out for Lila's shoulder. Lila shrugged her off.

Lila moved to the corner of the balcony. Spat against the glass enclosure, watched the spit drip down the panorama. She looked small against the Manhattan skyline. An insect clinging to the edge of a windshield.

The city's horizon slowly spun as the building twisted. Blimps and construction cranes moved around the sky. The long strands of Manhattan skystabbers stretched to the clouds. Closer to us were the jagged, squatter buildings of Brooklyn. In the dying light of the evening, the buildings around us sat like sets of broken teeth.

"Aren't you both scouts? Isn't this what you do for a living?"

"We know how to sneak prospects into compounds, not how to take them out," Dolores said.

I didn't say anything. It was Zunz who had been brought back from the dead, but I was the one who felt like a zombie. I was sitting in the corner, my mind swirling faster than the ice clinking in my glass.

The finger I'd detached had lost its signal a few hundred yards from the stadium next to a couple utility sheds. Dolores and I checked on the map and there was nothing around. Setek or someone else must have found it and disabled it before they took Zunz to wherever they'd taken him. I'd broken my hand yet again, for no purpose. But that wasn't what was bothering me the most.

He'd barely recognized me. JJ Zunz. My best friend and brother. Yet he might as well have been staring at a stranger.

"Great, okay. So let's sit around until they kill my father a second time."

"We have to be careful. Your father would want us to be careful," Dolores said without much conviction. She'd met Zunz a half dozen times and they'd exchanged maybe fifty words. She didn't know him at all. After the way he'd looked at me, I wasn't sure I did either.

"My father doesn't give a crap what I do. Maybe he doesn't even know I'm alive." She spat again, a big white glob that didn't make it to the glass. "You two obviously don't care. But I care."

I'd saved my eye's recording of my encounter with Zunz in the hall and the van being loaded up and flying away. I'd replayed them in my eye, but they didn't tell me anything. Just images to loop in my mind, over and over, to no purpose.

In the chair, those images were replaced with others, one after another. Dr. Setek laughing as he twisted on the gas. Natasha waving me away. The Mouth's golden lips forming a smile. Coppelius waiting outside the Edenist compound. Zunz being trotted out on the field. Zunz's body wrapped in a sheet. Zunz dead. Zunz murdered. Zunz on replay. Zunz at bat. Zunz sick. Zunz alive.

I groaned, suddenly and loudly. "We don't even fucking know."

"What?" Lila said.

"We don't even know if he needs rescuing."

"What?" Lila said, louder. "You were the one who said they had him imprisoned."

I drank more of the whiskey. Closed my eyes. "I said I saw doctors working on him. Doctors helping him. I said he was alive. Sick maybe, but millions of people are sick."

Dolores, Lila, and I were kidding ourselves. We weren't detectives. We weren't solving anything. We weren't bringing down a rotten corporation and corrupt government.

"He didn't even care," I said, too quietly, staring at the wall. "He didn't care I was there. He looked at me like I was a stranger."

We were up high, but it felt like the entire world could collapse on top of me. I closed my eyes again and felt smaller. More trapped. The case was a fishing net and when I dragged it up, somehow I was the creature caught inside.

Dolores was looking at me. "Kobo," she said, walking over. "What do you want to do?"

I looked at my injured palm, a hard shell of blue sealant in the middle where the grub beacon had been ripped out. One of the fingers already missing. I couldn't even fully close my hand. I was never going to be whole and healed. My whole body was tired, covered in bruises. It felt like someone had ripped all my nerves out at the root, tossed them on the pavement, and watched them shrivel up in the sun.

I pulled out an eraser. Had to steady my hands to get it lit.

"Are you going to let the Mets poison him again? Over and over?" Lila said.

"Do you want us to go in there, Kobo?" Dolores said.

"Do you want to let him get away with it?" Lila said.

I was breathing so heavily the eraser was already a smoldering nub. I twisted the end onto the railing.

I couldn't forget how Zunz had forgotten me.

I stood up, my face red and hot. "Who have I been kidding? The brother I grew up with is gone. I don't know anything about his life now. We see each other a few times a year, at most. What do I know about him anymore? He didn't tell me about you, Lila, that's for sure. He's had a child for a dozen years and never told me. He didn't even tell me he hadn't died. Who doesn't tell their brother they're alive? Zunz is alive. He has doctors. He has more money in the bank than I'll ever see. He has fans and fame and multiple apartments. He doesn't need me. He doesn't need any of us."

I walked back inside. Grabbed my coat and bag.

"I need to go home. Rest. Think," I said. Then I added, "Alone."

Lila and Dolores were small, dim figures in the balcony box.

"So that's it?" Lila shouted weakly.

"Call me if Zunz dies a second time."

38

THE INTERRUPTED SLEEP

Landlord wants your rent, Kobo," the super said as I rushed past.

"Landlord is an algorithm hosted in a server farm in the Arizona desert."

"Hey, man. Just letting you know. Eviction next week."

I walked past him. My mind was a hunk of ice in a frozen sea. Next week wasn't a concept capable of thawing it.

"What the hell was that noise the other day?" the super yelled after me.

When I got to the apartment, the door was broken. So were most of the things inside.

Everything I owned was smashed or splintered. My furniture lay in piles of rubble. Clothes were strewn around the room. The floor tiles were cracked along with the windows. The Sassafras sisters had been thorough, that was for sure. An eviction wouldn't do anything except save me money on a cleaner.

Still, I felt calm. I was home. My own home where I didn't need anyone and they didn't need me.

Plus, I had three brand-name booster shots I'd purchased on the way home with Natasha's money. I sat on the remains of my couch and rolled up my sleeve. Opened the packaging carefully. The warning label said not to take more than one a day. I didn't care. I slid in the needles one after another, then sat back. Smiled as the upgrades worked their way through my veins.

The only sound in the apartment was the dripping of the broken kitchen faucet. I took a warm beer from the broken fridge. Cracked it open, drank it in one gulp. I started to undress. Laid my clothes neatly on the torn-up bed. Its microfoam guts had been ripped out and tossed around the room like a dusting of snow.

In the bathroom, I scrubbed the dirt of the case off my skin with soap wool. Took a buff cloth to my arm and crotch. I cleaned each part of myself separately, metal and flesh. I didn't think about how they did or didn't fit together. I didn't think about whole things at all. I was working a piece at a time. I rubbed each separate piece hard enough to clean off the last dozen days.

Most of my appliances had been smashed, with their little metal and plastic guts strewn across the floor. But the trimmer still worked. I cropped my hair to the skull. Scraped off my stubbly beard. In the remains of my mirror, I saw someone squeaky and clean. The skin shining along with the metal.

I stumbled back into the bedroom, dropped down on the ruined mattress. Let the foam conform to my indentations, the tiny self-inflating balls cradling my weight. I closed my eyes, ready to sleep for as long as possible. A nice big sleep.

Darkness wrapped around me. Countless black threads hugging me and hiding me from the world like a cocoon. Maybe I could sleep until everything had changed. Until the world was a different place and I could wake up in a new reality. A new life.

But even as I was falling asleep, Zunz wouldn't leave me. I couldn't help replaying it in my mind. Him on the stretcher at the stadium, not caring that I was there.

Then I noticed something in my mind's eye that smacked me awake. Zunz. The one I'd seen in the stadium. It wasn't him.

I pulled up the actual recording of the stadium in my bionic eye. Replayed. Zunz was in the gurney, helmet on and eyes open. I zoomed in, right to the blotch above his dimple. I was right. I didn't know how, but it wasn't my brother.

When I called Dolores, her holographic face was frowning.

"I can't believe you just left us, Kobo."

"I'm sorry. I'm an asshole. But I was wrong. About everything. That wasn't Zunz."

"What?" Dolores yawned. She pulled on her goggles. I must have woken her. She sat up in her bed.

"At the game, it wasn't him. I don't know if he was a clone or what, but it was someone else."

"You can't just duplicate a person like a file. Remember the astro-clones? They took a year to grow and went insane anyway."

"Well maybe it was another player with heavy cosmetic surgery, but I know it wasn't him. I saw his birthmark. The one that looks like a tiny baseball glove."

"What about it?" Dolores said.

"It was backward."

I saw Dolores's mouth open and heard Lila yell off view. Then Dolores's head shrank to a dot. She blinked out. The pad had shut off.

I tried to turn it on, call again, but it wasn't working.

I heard a smacking sound, like steak slammed on a counter. Smack, smack, smack. I realized it was a pair of gigantic hands clapping. "It's inspiring," a deep, smooth voice said. "Seeing the rat in the maze round the proper corner."

The sound was coming from the corner, but all I could see was a mound of black clothes and rubbish from the Sassafras sisters' ransacking. Then my eyes adjusted, and I noticed shapes swirling in the black. The shape stood up. A shadow stretching to the ceiling.

"Kobo, Kobo, Kobo," the dark form said. As it moved forward, more colors swirled around the head of the shape. "May I call you Kobo?"

The darkness touched itself, and a ripple of maroon ran across it. Blue and green dots were dappling it now. Then I heard a click and the colors went away, turned translucent so I could see the face underneath. A man's face. Pale and featureless like a new thing being born. But he wasn't new.

Coppelius pulled off his cephalopod hood and tossed it on the bed beside me. He was holding a green comm blocker in his other hand.

"I'm glad you and I will have a chance to talk one-on-one," Coppelius said. His thin smile showed only the tips of his teeth.

I was fully awake now, and I reached behind me to grab the gun I kept under the pillow.

"No need to do that." Coppelius had it in his hand. He snapped off the barrel and tossed the two halves back into the mess of the closet. "I cleared the room hours ago. You don't need to think about weapons. Just relax. Let's talk business. Duty to your country. Profit."

I hadn't seen Coppelius this close before. Only from across the deck of a sushi restaurant or the Mouth's office, his face hiding in the shadows. Here, I could see his Neanderthal features were there, but ill formed. An unfinished sculpture. His large brow was hairless, with large blue eyes in the sockets underneath. His head was smooth as an egg.

"We've got nothing to talk about. I'm off the case. Or the case is off me."

"Is that so?"

"I've been fired. I don't work for the Mets anymore."

"What a coincidence, I don't work for them either. They only think I do. Still, Natasha and I have some interests that align with theirs. Yours do too."

Coppelius walked toward me slowly, but with inevitability. He seemed to be the walking embodiment of my failures. My failure to escape my past, failure to transcend my body, failure to even solve a simple murder.

"You win," I said. "Kill me. Put the shitty bow on the end of this shitty life."

"Self-pity is very boring, Kobo. Do you think we Neanderthals don't have oceans of pity we could swim in? A whole species' worth?"

Coppelius sat on the edge of the mattress. He didn't have a gun, but he didn't need one. He reached out a hand, which was still sheathed in cephalopod fabric and looked like a tentacle from the deep. He grabbed my naked foot. Rubbed the bare skin roughly.

"I don't care about baseball. But I still do things for the good of my team. For my people, few as we are in this sapien world. Don't you like feeling like a part of a cause greater than yourself?"

"Not these days."

"You need a team, Kobo. You're no good on your own."

"That's what my mother used to say." I was looking around the room for something blunt enough to bash into his head. My suicidal feelings had passed, panic was setting in. I sat up in bed, pushing myself to the wall with my injured hand. Coppelius let my leg slip from his hand. "Are you going to kill me like you killed Kang?"

Coppelius's lips stretched wide, curling at the ends. "I'm here for your help, and to help you. I'm a helpful guy. Kang didn't want to help. He didn't have the necessary empathy. Empathy is a natural Neanderthal trait." He smiled, spread out his hands. The palms were as big as plates. "I have so much love inside me, you wouldn't believe. I'm bursting with love."

I laughed. A frightened little yip.

"Laugh, but it's true. You want to help JJ Zunz. I want to help JJ Zunz. We want the same thing."

"You're mistaken. I didn't want cro-mag spooks hiding in my bedroom."

"We've been tracking someone you happened to stumble upon. I have to admit I didn't think you would when Natasha suggested hiring you. We had a bet. I thought you were employed more as…" He cocked his floating head. "A concession, you might say. But Natasha believed in you. She believed humans with, let's say less than ideal lives, will latch on to any meaning they can find. A friend's murder, say. Natasha has spent a lot of time studying the psychology of sapiens."

"I led you to Lila."

"Yes, that is her name." His smile grew even wider. He clapped his hands. "Now, give me Lila and I'll be able to help Zunz. Then Zunz will be able to help Natasha and me."

"That wasn't Zunz. I know it wasn't."

"You are right. The person you saw wasn't Zunz. But the real Zunz is very much alive, and he needs the girl's help."

"If he's alive he doesn't care about her."

Coppelius sucked in his pale lips. "Maybe not. But his body does. Zunz's body needs something from Lila's body to live. Something vital, if painful to remove."

"His body?"

"We're all trapped in these forms, aren't we? Our minds get poured into them without anyone even asking us. We grow and live in them, and yet in many ways they are as incomprehensible to us as the cosmos."

"What the hell are you talking about?"

"I can't get into the specifics. You and I are not scientists in any case. She has genes in a pure form. Much of them anyway. She can donate her cells to put in his body. Something that hasn't been corrupted in her. You wouldn't believe how easily the strands of your DNA fray with all the poisons you sapiens put into yourselves."

"Why now?"

Coppelius laughed, his head bobbing in the darkness around him. "Well, you saw what happened when he was playing the White Mice. There might be risks for her, but then nature is a cruel thing."

"This isn't nature."

"It's life. Whatever you want to call it. Was it cruel when your ancestors bashed in my ancestors' skulls with rocks and sticks? Her cells may be the key to unlocking a mystery Monsanto wants to unlock. That President Newman wants to unlock. And that Natasha and I very much need to unlock. That's what's important." Coppelius spread his arms. They were as wide as steel beams. "And in return you will be rewarded. Your medical-loan debt is nothing to Monsanto. Pennies lost in a couch."

I'd worked my way back to my haunches, ready to spring. I had another gun hidden in the closet. A big fat one to shoot at a big thick thug. At least if the Sassafras sisters hadn't found it during their rampage. If I could leap around Coppelius, I could get to it before he realized. Shut up his talk about nature with a bit of technology.

"I don't know where Lila is. You're right that she's nothing to me. I thought she was involved in Zunz's murder. But there never was any murder. So I let her go." I kept babbling, hoping to keep him talking and distracted. I got ready to make a move.

"You know I don't believe that."

I closed my eyes and then shouted for the lights to turn on at full power. Light flooded the room and I jumped into Coppelius with my shoulder. Metal to prehistoric jaw. Knocked him off the bed. I got to the floor. Ran.

I made it through the door and into the hall. Then I was facedown on the floor, my left leg held in the air behind me. He had my ankle. Coppelius clucked. "Why do you have to make everything so dramatic?"

Coppelius twisted my ankle with a series of wet cracks.

I shouted into the floor.

He hit the back of my head. My teeth smacked the floorboards. I felt blood trickle out of my nose.

Coppelius knelt on my back and took hold of my right arm. He pulled it back toward him. "This looks expensive. If you want to keep it, tell me where Lila is."

Time started to move slowly and angrily. Coppelius pushed one knee into my shoulder, pulled the arm farther back. Then farther still. I could feel the flesh of my shoulder screaming where it was attached to the metal.

"Okay," he said, still twisting. "Now is your moment of decision. Do you want to help your team, your country, and be handsomely rewarded for it? Do you want life, health, and fulfilment? Or do you want dismemberment and destitution?"

Even with my face bleeding on the floor and my arm screaming in pain, I couldn't help but think of the numbers. The medical debt I owed, and the cost of the upgrades I wanted. They piled up into a massive heap. Numbers on top of numbers. Stacked in a tower tall enough to collapse on me and crush me. And I could imagine them being wiped away, like a small stain with a towel, leaving me a clean slate. A completely new beginning.

And then I thought of Zunz. Of Lila. Of Dolores.

I spat up a little blood.

"Fuck you," I said.

Coppelius didn't respond. Not with words.

There was more pain and then a loud crack. My arm and socket parting, like a giant suction cup being removed.

Raindrops of blood fell around me. My blood.

I tried to move my right hand. There wasn't a hand there to move. I tried again.

Neither my mind nor my body could accept what was happening.

Coppelius was on my back. I was struggling under him, barely moving. My right arm was still attached to my shoulder by wires and cords. I heard a click, a series of pops, then a great screeching tear.

"Here you go, Kobo."

My arm landed in front of me with a dull thud.

39

THE SEPARATED ARM

I was on the floor trying to crawl. The jagged stump of my right arm rotated pointlessly. My mind didn't seem to realize part of me was no longer part of me. It was a foreign object across the floor. I looked at my arm. It was a few inches from my face. The end was a mess, wires spilling out like guts. There was the smell of sizzling blood. The fingers tapped on the ground, some last electric pulse working through the wires. Blue fluid stained the floor.

I heard noises around me. Running water. A door opening. Footsteps. Guffaws.

My head was screaming. Electricity sputtered in my skull. My only thought was to be whole again. To put my arm back in its proper place. I started to crawl toward it.

I managed to pull myself within reach of it.

I grabbed air. It was gone.

"Look at this thing," a voice above me said.

"This whole place is filthy. You're a filthy little pig."

"Why's he all naked and bloody?"

Two sets of feet stood in front of me. Someone grabbed one of my armpits, then the other. I was lifted to my knees.

"Oink! Oink! That's the sound you make, Kobo." I was face-to-face with Wanda Sassafras. Brenda was behind her, inspecting my severed arm.

My sight was going in and out of focus. Then they were blurs. Big ugly ones.

"What are you doing here, deadbeat? We own this place now. You're here. That means we own you."

"Yeah, we own you."

Wanda dropped me. I steadied myself on my remaining hand. My stomach clutched up. I vomited a trickle of yellow bile.

"Don't puke your pig guts on my shoes."

"Ha ha. He almost got you, Wanda."

Brenda's laugh was cut short.

Coppelius came around the corner. Walked up and ruffled my hair. "You have quite the fan base, Kobo."

"Who the hell is this dude?"

"How the fuck would I know, Brenda? You got a bodyguard now?"

"Some bodyguard you got, Kobo. He's not very good at guarding it." She waved my severed arm in front of my face. The hand flopped back and forth pathetically.

I felt like I was going to puke again. I reached over and felt the sticky blood on my right side. Trembled. Dry heaved. I curled myself into a ball, forehead to the tiles.

Coppelius grabbed my hair and pulled my head back up. "I'm afraid Kobo here is under official government protection. At least until I extract the information I need from him. I will be sure to compensate you for your lost time at your normal hourly rate."

"Fuck that," Wanda said. "We own this jalopy and this whole apartment. You're on Sunny Day property."

"What's with his face, Wanda?"

"He's a Neanderthal," I spat.

"That's not a nice thing to say. Whatever he is, he's got ten seconds to leave before Brenda bashes his weird mutant face."

My stomach seemed to realize there wasn't anything left inside to heave up. I was empty of everything, mind and body. I closed my eyes.

"I see from your attire that you work for a medical-loan company," Coppelius stepped in front of me. His wide back hid the Sassafras sisters from my view. "Loans are not a pertinent issue at this juncture. I'm sure your employer and mine can make an arrangement."

"The fuck is *pertinent*, Wanda?"

"It means he thinks we're dumb, Brenda."

"That's not a nice thing to think."

I started to crawl backward. It wasn't an easy thing to do with one arm. Your brain gets used to having a whole body to move around. I was naked, my skin chafing on the rug. A trail of blood and synth fluid followed me.

Coppelius stared at them, unmoving.

"Now?"

"Yes, Brenda, now."

The sisters came at Coppelius from either side, moving in slowly. Coppelius stood still. He was content to wait and watch. When Wanda threw a fist into his side, he brought his elbow down on her back. The hollow thunk echoed through the apartment.

She collapsed on the floor with a grunt.

I crawled on my hand and knees slowly toward my closet. The three invaders moved around my living room. Slowly, trying to size each other up.

I could see myself in the dark shine of the closet door. Naked, trembling. One arm gone, ripped out right to the socket. A mixture of dark fluids, some organic, most not, was drying on my side.

Over my shoulder, I saw Coppelius stagger back into my counter. Wanda coming at him with a baseball bat she'd found in the pile of rubble in the corner. My bat with Zunz's signature from his first year in the league. One of my few valuable possessions I hadn't pawned. I could see his scribble on the barrel. She swung it into Coppelius's leg.

The closet door slid open. I started rummaging through with my one awkward arm.

Behind me, the sounds got louder. No intelligible words, no snappy comebacks. Just grunts, thuds, huffs.

I got to the bottom of the closet and popped the hidden safe. It slid up, untouched. I grabbed the gun. Pulled on a pair of pants. I had to lean against the wall to get them on with one arm and an injured ankle.

With the gun in my hand, I felt calmer. I was still dizzy, accidentally put too much weight on my twisted ankle and fell into the door, shoulder against the frame. It reopened the wound. Blood spilled out like a burst dam. I didn't know how long it would take before I passed out.

I hobbled back to the living room, leaning into the wall for balance. Held the gun with my one hand. But I didn't know who to shoot. The three of them were a blur of swinging limbs. They moved together, half hugging and half hitting. They looked like one organism merged together in an experiment gone awry.

Blood covered their clothes, but it was hard to tell who was stained with whom.

Coppelius got his arms around one of the sisters' heads and rammed it into the corner of my counter. Wanda. She dropped quick and hard. Brenda was on his back and he pulled her off, tossed her toward her sister, and stepped back a few paces. Lifted the palms of his hands, gesturing for peace.

"Ladies," he said, huffing. "This isn't productive."

"Fuck you," Wanda said.

Brenda spat a dark red wad on the floor. Her bionics crackled with electricity.

No one seemed to be looking at me. I'd become an extra in my own movie. I started to stumble, confused, toward the door.

As I put my hand on the knob, I heard two loud screams follow in quick succession. One was unintelligible. The other was "No!"

I turned. Coppelius was standing, smiling, with Brenda's head in his hands. He let go and I saw the head was on wrong. The neck was snapped over, blood starting to gurgle from where a chunk of white bone peeked out of the skin like a child playing hide-and-seek. The rest of Brenda was standing upright, unaware.

For a second, everything was quiet, calm, and still. No one moved. No one spoke.

Brenda fell to her knees. She started to moan. Somehow, her cybernetics were keeping her somewhat alive.

"I don't feel right, Wanda." Her voice was faint, robotic. She plopped sideways on the floor.

Wanda let out a quiet scream.

Coppelius stood back, arms folded, surveying the scene.

"Now can we talk?"

Wanda picked up her sister's head and turned to me, not seeming to see me, but looking into the space where I was standing in disbelief. Brenda's eyes were still moving. They didn't seem to be believing either.

"No," Wanda said, quietly and slowly.

She walked over to the body, collapsed next to it.

"Sing me your favorite song."

"Wanda. It hurts."

"The song, Brenda."

Wanda held her hand against the neck, trying to hold back the blood.

Coppelius walked back down the hall toward an arm lying on the ground. My arm. He picked it up. Looked it over as a big game hunter might inspect the horns of his latest kill.

"The leg bone's connected to the...hip bone...the arm bone's connected to the..." Brenda sang. Her words decreased in volume. She trailed off. Her signal was dying.

She was still.

Wanda stayed bent over Brenda. Brenda made gurgling noises, then went silent.

"Now, now," Coppelius said, waving my arm around like a base-ball bat. He pretended to hit a home run, watched the fake ball fly. My arm snapped at the elbow when he swung. "That was fun, but I think it is time for you to take your sister away. Perhaps they can fix her before the flesh dies. Modern medicine is a magical thing."

Wanda was hunched over her sister, repeating the same lie over and over. "You'll be okay, you'll be okay." Her breath was coming short and fast. She placed her sister gently back on the floor.

She let out a low, guttural roar, and spun. She was swinging her arm toward Coppelius, except her bionic hand was open and her fin-gernails topped with shiny points. At the apex of her swing, the hand detached, flinging through the air. Coppelius was in mid-swing him-self, using my arm as the bat.

Her fingers lodged into Coppelius's throat. My arm's shoulder smacked into Wanda's skull. The first sounded like a knife slicing through a melon. The second like a gigantic egg being cracked on the edge of a pan.

A microsecond of silence.

My arm fell on the floor.

Wanda toppled over, the bionic half of her head shooting out a tiny, sad spark. She lay flat on the ground. Didn't even twitch.

Coppelius was still standing. The detached silver hand was buried into his neck up to the knuckles. Ribbons of bright blood ran down his chest. He took a step to the right, then another step forward.

Coppelius suddenly seemed to remember me, to notice me. His eyes widened. His head fell to one side. He gurgled something. A bubble of blood on his throat.

Coppelius fell onto a chair, slumped off onto the floor.

The room was quiet. I was half dressed, hand on the knob.

After a second, I went back inside. I made my way to the kitchen sink and ran the water. Cleaned myself off as best as I could while still looking over at the three bodies in the center of the room. They didn't move.

My arm was lying on the floor, curled up like a dog on the side of the highway. I couldn't believe how heavy it was on its own. I placed it in a black bag, put it next to the door.

Blood as thick as molasses dripped down Coppelius's neck. His blue eyes were wide open. Pale lips stuck in a snarl. His teeth were straight and white.

After I was sure he wouldn't move, I searched him. He didn't have any money on him. Nothing identifying. Nothing to show he existed at all.

But he did have one thing I could use. His eye.

I propped his head up on the couch. Pulled open his eyelid. The skin was still warm and slick with sweat. His eye was larger than a golf ball. Bigger than a human's. The color was uncanny, a dark blue with silver lines woven through.

My face was an inch away from his. I scanned his stone-age eye with my bionic one. Duplicated it in my drive.

Something whimpered behind me.

Wanda was on her back, looking at me. The right side of her face, the cybernetic side, was smashed inward. A dark and bloody dent for a temple.

"You?" she whispered.

I didn't say anything. One of her hands was moving. Reaching out and patting the floor.

I walked carefully over. Pushed Brenda's dead hand toward Wanda's searching one. She grabbed onto the cold fingers.

"Brenda." Her voice was the size of a ball bearing. She looked at the ceiling. "Is she..."

I still had the gun in my hand. I felt delirious. Half alive. I shook my head. "I don't know."

Wanda got to her knees, slowly, and crawled over. She looked back at me. One of her eyes was swollen shut. The other, mechanical one, glared with a mixture of pleading and hatred. She lifted her sister's body up, knees shaking.

I nodded toward the still-open door.

Neither of us said anything. Wanda just dragged her sister out of the apartment while I watched, leaning into a wall, barely conscious. The door closed. Then I fell.

40

THE AMBER FLUID

The human body has over two hundred bones, around eighty organs, and at least twenty-two square feet of surface area. I was missing some of that, but every bit that remained was in pain. As if a thousand tiny hammers were smacking each part of me. I felt worse than I'd ever felt before. At least when I could feel.

I'd wake up, ache, pass out.

I don't know how long I was in this state. Each minute felt like a day, each hour a lifetime.

A vat of amber fluid. Black tubes inserted into different parts of my torso. When I tried to swim, the fluid was so thick I could barely move. I'd tire. Close my eyes again.

While I blinked in and out, life went on somewhere. America was tuning in to the biggest sporting event in decades. The Monsanto Mets versus the Pyramid Pharmaceuticals Sphinxes had everything from late-game heroics to revolutionary science. I learned later President Newman declared each game a national holiday. "It's time for Americans to come together, pick a side, and hope the other guy gets his ass kicked."

With Zunz back, the Mets were revived. Lex Dash opened with a home run over right field, which got snatched out of the air by an umpire drone before it could concuss a fan on the fourth level. The Sphinxes cleanup man, "Regular" Gregor McGregor, answered with a line drive through the middle in the second. Two runs batted in. It went back and forth, the Sphinxes and Mets trading runs, balls flying around the stadium like fat, angry hornets.

The Mets stabilized when Olivia Doro took over the mound. Her sinkers pinned down the Sphinxes lineup, and a timely double from R-Rod put the Mets in the lead. In the postgame interview, Doro held up her glove, which was crusted with blood. "I cut my hand this morning, but played through. If Zunz can bleed for this team, so can I."

The Mets were up three games to two, the whole World Series in their sights.

But the Sphinxes came to the Meadows two nights later for game six looking determined. They'd stopped being rattled by the return of Zunz. From the game six replays I later watched, dreary and half drugged, it seemed the whole team had been juiced up with ampers. They were practically blurs on the field. The Mets batted well, even with Zunz still on the injured list. He hadn't played in game five either. The Mouth promised he'd be back in time for game seven, if the Mets couldn't close out in six. They didn't. The Sphinxes took advantage of an exhausted Mets bullpen and lit up the scoreboard in the seventh and eighth, with home runs from Malone, Yoon, and McGregor.

Three games apiece. Everything on the line for game seven.

With each game, the public fervor grew. The country was divided, half rooting for the underdog Mets and their revived player, half backing the Sphinxes and whispering conspiracies about how quickly Zunz had come back. There were rumors that Zunz wasn't

Zunz. That he was an android replica or else another player who'd received extensive surgery to look just like him. Sports shows brought on cosmetic surgeons and gene sculptors who debated every motion and muscle in slow-motion replays. But the Mets did a live DNA test before game five and it was a perfect match.

Zunz himself didn't say anything. The Mets wouldn't let reporters near him. Still, most of the public was astounded with his resolve.

"I had the skin fever last year, Skip, along with twenty percent of the country. I was out for three months," a Mets sportscaster said. "I couldn't even sit my butt in this chair and talk into a microphone. And here Zunz comes back from the dead and is looking like a potential MVP?"

"It's remarkable. The kid is a pro, but you have to hand it to the Mets and their absolutely stacked lab team."

"If you're listening, Mr. Mouth, can I have what Zunz is having? Ha ha ha."

As game seven loomed, Mets and Sphinxes products were flying off the kiosks. Both biopharms were setting fourth-quarter records. Game seven was projected to be the most watched game in sports history since the Subterranean Super Bowl.

Meanwhile, I didn't know any of this. Didn't know anything. Just floated in the blackness of my aching body. Until they woke me up.

41

THE COLD SHOWER

Well, look who's finished his catnap."

I was slouched on a cold, hard floor. The gummy liquid around me was draining away. I was shivering. I opened my eyes as the last few inches of amber fluid disappeared between my legs. I couldn't tell where I was. The glass walls were smudged with residue. The air smelled antiseptic. I eventually got myself upright, leaning against the back of the tank.

A blurry figure moved toward me, slowly coming into focus. I tried to speak. Spat up a mouthful of gelatinous fluid. Tried again.

"Hi, Lila."

"Hi, you jerk," Lila said. She yelled over her shoulder. "He's up."

Another blurry figure approached the tank. Dolores, wearing a black jumpsuit and a half smile. She walked up and spread her palm on the tank glass.

"You look like shit, Kobo."

"Feel like it too," I said.

"You're about to feel worse. Brace yourself," Lila said.

A man in a dirty white smock, apparently the doctor, twisted a nozzle on the side of the tank. Freezing water poured down on me. Pushed me to the floor. Rinsed me clean.

"This hospital is freezing," I said.

The man in the smock unlatched a hole in the side of the tank and reached in with a gloved hand. Shot a stimulant into my arm. It raced through my veins. I stood up, still leaning into the wall. My heart was beating like it wanted to crack through my ribs.

A large metal claw descended from the ceiling with flexible talons that looped around my waist. I was lifted and deposited on the concrete floor.

"I'm always telling you to stop running away from your problems, Kobo. You just run into other ones." Dolores wrapped me in a large white robe. Rubbed me up and down on both sides. It felt rough on my skin, despite the tenderness of her movements. She smiled. Her eyes were hidden under white goggles. "I've been telling you that for years."

The doctor poked me here and there. Ran the blood through an analyzer. Tallied up my vitals. Gave me the go-ahead to keep staying alive.

"Your heart should settle down in a couple minutes. You'll need to hydrate and receive a booster injection in either the upper arm or the posterior every six hours."

Dolores took the syringes from the doctor and slid them in her pocket.

"How did you find me?"

"Did you forget telling us that my dad was a clone?" Lila said. "And then not answering any of our calls? We came over to your apartment to yell at you for being an asshole. You were half naked and sleeping on the floor. Blood everywhere. It was gross."

I laughed, hacked up another globule of amber goo. "I got in a bit of a scuffle."

"Your super took us up," Dolores said. "I guess he likes you. He helped us carry you out before the cops came."

"Stan is a good guy."

"I'm afraid the police sealed off your apartment. We can't go back."

"Yeah, well, it was mostly garbage left in there anyway."

I felt a great hunger squirming inside me. As if I hadn't eaten in a thousand years. "Is there anything to eat?"

"You're on liquids for another twenty-four hours," Lila said. She passed me a bottle of grayish-blue fluid. The label said *Breakfast in the Bottle*. It looked like liquid chalk.

I tried to reach out and grab it with my right hand, but there was nothing there. It was gone. I glanced at the empty space beyond my shoulder. My flesh ended in a mess of scars and bruises. I stared at the emptiness.

"Where's my arm?" I said. Then it came back to me. Coppelius grabbing, twisting, and wrenching. "Never mind."

I looked around the room, my eyes still bleary. It was lined with white tiles that had browned with age. Fungus grew in some of the corners. The air was stale and heavy.

"Where are we?"

Dolores and Lila looked at each other, then at the walls. "We didn't think we could take you to a hospital," Dolores said. "Not with all that blood and the body in your apartment. The police are looking for you."

The stimulant had run its course. I was cold again, my skin converted to gooseflesh. I rubbed my hand over my right shoulder. It had been smoothed out, the metal bits sanded down and the flesh a puffy scar. "Where did you take me exactly?"

"To an ill paradise," a voice said. A door creaked open. Noblood Gerald rolled into the room with a pair of men who walked beside on crutches. Gerald threw his hands in the air with a laugh. "To the Diseased Eden."

Dolores grimaced, placed her hand on my shoulder. "I'm sorry," she whispered.

"Hey, they did save his life," Lila said.

Noblood Gerald came up to me. Gently touched the scar tissue on my shoulder.

"Better to have one arm and be alive than two and dead, no? Guess you ended up one of our Purified after all."

"Guess so," I said.

"I'm sorry about the arm, even if it was a poisoned machine staining your soul. I'm afraid we're only used to removing cybernetics here, not repairing them. We did clean out the remains. Buffed you down to the bone. Let the infected flesh heal." He lifted a black bag, tossed it on the floor with a clunk. "Lila insisted we save it. Perhaps you'll find a less ideological doctor to reattach later."

"Thanks," I said.

"We did leave your eye and your unmentionables intact, despite the protests of our priests."

"I insisted," Dolores said. "On the latter at least."

The arm was a sad, cold thing in the bottom of the bag. All its life and lights turned off. I shook the bag. It was hard to believe it was anything that could move, much less flex or pitch. Detached, it was as useful as a dead slug.

I just stared down at my arm for a while, the bag open at my feet. I'd spent so many years tuning up my body, changing myself. Years of money, years of debt, years of time. And it had been swept away as quickly as a sandcastle in a tsunami.

"So, where do we begin?" Noblood Gerald said.

I looked at Gerald. "We?"

"They're going to help us," Lila said. She brought over my clothes in a pile. They'd been laundered, but I could still see the red stains.

"We wouldn't normally even associate with you, but when Lila brought you here, she suggested your eye recording might have useful information." He signaled to his men and they grabbed a large screen and lifted it onto the wall. "Your feed was grainy, but we saw this."

The screen lit up with the ruins of my apartment. I'd seen all this before, lived it, but it was strange to see my view in front of my eyes.

"It's not normally this messy," I said.

The Edenist fast-forwarded through my walking around the apartment, dazed and cursing, after I'd left Lila and Dolores. I watched myself shower and groom in speeded-up motion.

We got to Coppelius emerging from my closet. His large, dark chest filled the frame. "Zunz's body needs something from Lila's body to live. Something vital, if painful to remove." The Edenist paused the tape.

I looked at Lila. Her face was blank, but I thought I sensed rage bubbling underneath. Her fists were clenched balls at her side.

"I thought it was over," I said, weakly. "When Zunz came back in the game, I thought that was the end."

"Nobody threatens a Diseased Edenist and gets away with it. Prospective member or not, we can't let that slide," Gerald said. He signaled to his men and they switched the feed to various security footage, each showing the pale, wide image of Coppelius. "This one had been sniffing around Edenist buildings looking for Lila for days. We had him flagged."

"Luckily I'm wary of strangers," she said. "That's why I was hiding out at my dad's house."

"And to create genetic abominations? Clones? No, we have to act."

I shook my head, trying to make it all disappear. "We don't know if that's it. Even embryonic cloning is illegal, and we're talking about duplicate cloning an adult? That's never worked."

Dolores was scratching at the edge of her goggles. "Well. Yes. It's illegal, dangerous, and impossible. But everything was impossible once. Maybe Monsanto has found a loophole to jump through."

"Why the hell does it involve me?" Lila said.

"They must need something from you to perfect his clones. Maybe his genes are corrupted in some way and they need to splice in part of your code."

I was still shaking my head. I could feel bile spurting up my throat. "Zunz must not know what they were planning. Maybe he's being held hostage?"

"You don't have to always defend him," Lila said. "Anyway. Either we kill him or we rescue him. Otherwise, they're going to keep coming after me. And I'd like to have one parent left. I vote rescue."

"It's game seven tomorrow. Everyone will be busy. Our best chance to extract Zunz," Dolores said. "Once the World Series is over, who knows where they'll lock him up."

"We don't know where he is," I said.

Dolores went over to the screen. Plugged in a code and an image of a small white shack appeared.

"What the hell is that?"

"It's where your finger lost signal, remember? When you left it with Zunz. Now look at this."

Now it was Lila's turn to play something on the screen. She pulled up a series of blueprints. A mess of pale white lines on a blue sea. She zoomed in until a building came up. It was a large, underground structure with only a tiny shack on the surface. Walking past, you'd have assumed it was a toolshed.

"Dolores got the blueprints," Lila said.

Dolores reached into the purse at her side and pulled out a black, fleshy mess. She unfolded it before me and I could see the nodes and wires. The mask from the Janus Club.

"My bosses were pretty interested in this tech. They were even more interested when I said the Zunz playing in the World Series might not be the real Zunz. They've authorized me to take you inside and see if we can shake up dirt on the rival team. Off the books of course."

"What? You can't risk this."

Dolores walked over to me, lips pursed. She put a hand on my uninjured shoulder. "Kobo. This is my job. My bosses are desperate for any dirt they can find on the Mets. If Zunz is an android or a clone or whatever the hell else and I can prove it, then they win the World Series by default." Then she leaned in close, so only I could hear. "Plus, you broke up with me. Remember? Stop trying to tell me what to do."

I started to explain myself, how I'd been young and a fool, but I looked around the room of Diseased Edenists and figured now wasn't the time to relive our relationship.

I sipped the chalky liquid. It tasted tart and chemical. As I got dressed, Dolores, Gerald, and Lila were discussing strategies. How to distract the guards while we broke inside. I could barely follow what they were saying. I felt dizzy and overwhelmed.

I stood up, steadying myself on the chair's back. "What are you guys talking about? I was nearly killed. They're trying to harvest Lila. We're not going to save Zunz. We won't even be able to get near him."

"We're doing this with or without you," Lila said. She coughed a little, and I thought I saw a bit of blood on her lips.

"Doing what?" I said after she'd recovered.

"Just because you've been sleeping doesn't mean we have," Lila said. "We have a plan."

42

THE DEEP HOTEL

When Zunz and I were in school, other kids would tell us about the mole people. A race of mutated men who sloshed around in the bowels of the city. They created a whole society strung between the sewers and the subway tunnels. Houses suspended between the tracks, shops in abandoned stairwells. Sometimes in the tales they walked pet rats on leashes. Other times, they rode wild crocodiles across the platforms at night. But always, they came for us. The poor kids. The families living deep underground in apartments that never saw natural light. They said the mole people would let their rats loose into our buildings, or they'd be the cause of a wall that collapsed like the one that destroyed my arm.

Before I learned what claustrophobia was, I'd wake up in the night with the feeling of the mole people's stubby fingers around my throat. Squeezing. Only scampering into the shadows when I turned on a lamp. I hadn't thought about those dirty nubs in a long time. But I did that night before game seven. Woke up in a panic in the burrow hotel. Kicked off the sheets, gasped for air.

We hadn't known if Dolores's apartment was compromised, and mine was under police surveillance. We booked a subterranean burrow hotel instead. Hoped anyone trying to track us down wouldn't look underground. I didn't love the idea, yet didn't have any others.

It was the middle of the night. I must have jostled Dolores with an elbow. She reached over, half asleep, and squeezed my one hand. Just like Zunz used to do when we shared a childhood bedroom. "It's okay," she slurred. I looked over at her. Her eyes were bare and closed. I could see the blue metal points where her cybernetic goggles connected protruding just above her eyebrows.

I got up, tiptoed to the bathroom. Pissed in the sink so the flush wouldn't wake her or Lila. I still wasn't used to doing everything with my left hand. Dribbled a bit on my fingers.

I put on underwear and a pair of pants. I was off-balance without my arm. I felt its absence every second. When I looked at the empty space, I could see it still there. A phantom arm. My mind filled in the form.

The hotel was called The Pomegranate, a Persephone reference I assumed. It did make me angry to be here. To see the places I'd been forced to live turned into hotels and sold to gawking tourists looking for an "authentic stay in old New York." But I guess that was the way of things. What was oppression one year was a marketing opportunity the next.

I made the mistake of checking my screen and found a dozen messages, mostly from Okafor. The last said, *Kobo, this isn't a joke. We have a warrant for your arrest. There was a body in your apartment and its DNA isn't in any of our databases. You have to come to the station now and tell me what happened. That's the only way I can help you.* I deleted the message. That was a problem for another time.

I walked quietly to the balcony, thinking it would calm me. I'd forgotten there was no air or view underground. Instead, it was a thick glass wall pressed against a panorama of rocks and dirt. A few worms squirmed against the glass. In one corner, a replica human skull sat above a glittering treasure chest. Props put in by the hotel to trick people into thinking an old dirty burrow was an exotic retreat.

"Shit," I said, nearly tripping over Lila. She was sitting cross-legged on the floor. Her eyes were closed, hands upturned on the ground. She wasn't moving.

I knelt, shook her shoulders.

"What?" she said, opening her annoyed eyes.

"I thought you'd been poisoned or something," I whispered.

"I was meditating."

"Oh."

I sat down across from her, back against the glass. I tried to pretend there was an ocean vista behind me. Sands, trees, gulls, and bright blue waves the color of candy stretching to the horizon.

"I didn't know you could be an Edenist Buddhist."

"I like to empty my mind sometimes. To live entirely in my skin."

"Sounds swell," I said. It sounded horrible to me. I lit an eraser, blew the smoke up toward the filter fan.

"You should try it. You seem kinda panicked."

"I don't like being underground." I took another drag and started to breathe easier. "You know your father and I grew up in a place like this? I mean when these were apartments, not hotel rooms."

"Could be worse," Lila said. "Try an Edenist bunker with thirty other children peeing their cots each night."

We both laughed. Caught ourselves. Quieted. Dolores was still asleep in the other room.

I still had my back to the glass, pretending the ground wasn't behind me. But Lila walked over and touched the glass.

"You know, this reminds me of my mom."

"The dirt?"

Lila rolled her eyes. "No, the display here. The skull and the treasure. Before she passed, my mother used to take me to the Museum of Natural History. Said it was important for me to learn about the natural world. What it used to be like before we screwed it all up. How animals used to look. Skies without smog. Unmodified plants. That kind of thing." She shook her head. Smiled. "I didn't know what she meant, of course. I just loved the dioramas. I'd stare at them for what felt like hours, imagining my mom and me roaming in some ancient land, with no one to bother us. Just her and me."

Lila coughed a bit but didn't spit up any blood. I put my eraser out. She'd been coughing a lot since we'd been underground. I was worried the dampness of the burrow was damaging her lungs as much as it was damaging my mind.

"Did you ever go there? You and my dad?"

I nodded. History hadn't exactly been our thing as kids. But we'd gone a few times. School trips mostly. Zunz and I would run through the different rooms, debating who would be the squid and who the whale. What I remembered most was the Hall of Human Origins. The weird scared apes half covered in wiry fur. Their mouths agape and their ribs pressing through leathery skin. They looked so different from the upgraded actors and models on TV. I never understood how we could all be the same species.

"It was a special place. Before they tore it down for an Amazon warehouse."

"Yeah."

Lila sat back down and leaned into my shoulder. We were both silent for a while and I thought she might be falling asleep. Then she stirred. "What if rescuing him doesn't change anything?"

"What?"

"What if nothing changes?" Before I could speak, she added, "Never mind. It doesn't matter."

"No, it's fine. It's just." I looked out at the dirt wall. Remembered all the times Zunz would see me panicking in our burrow and grab my hand, guide me upstairs to the street level. "He's a good man."

"Sure. Forget it."

"I promise. It's going to work out."

"Forget it. I'm just being a stupid kid."

The air was stale and cold. The only sound was Dolores's faint snores. The quiet irritated me. It felt as oppressive as the infinite dirt surrounding us.

But then Lila said, "I love how quiet it is down here. No honking. No jerks yelling. Peaceful."

I nodded. "It could be worse."

"I could live down here. Or somewhere far away. Somewhere without buildings everywhere you look. Without people. Just trees and birds and free things."

"Not many places like that left. Maybe the desert."

"Okay," she said. She stood up, put one of her hands on the glass. "The desert. Sand and cacti and lizards and me. I'd be okay with that."

"Yeah. Wouldn't be so bad."

Lila looked at me. Turned away and gazed out of the window at the wall of dirt, nodding her head over and over like a stuttering hologram.

43

THE LAST CHANCE

I felt the claustrophobia again, the next day, as we sneaked into the Monsanto compound. I couldn't see anything, could barely move. The weight on top of me kept me pinned down. The van jostled to the left, then the right. The low hum of the engines below us sounded like the purr of an animatronic jungle cat.

I wasn't in a burrow, only buried under a pile of clothes. A big heavy mound of cloth that shifted with each turn. It didn't help I didn't have my right arm to balance myself. I kept trying to reach out and steady myself on something with the nonexistent limb. All I had was a plastic prosthetic in my sleeve, suctioned to the stump, so no one would get suspicious of a one-armed man walking around the Monsanto compound.

I was starting to hyperventilate when Dolores, somehow sensing my panic, reached out and squeezed my shoulder. "We're nearly to the stadium."

"Sure," I said. "I know, I'm okay."

The van was bringing fresh towels and uniforms with *World*

Series Champions Monsanto Mets printed across in big blue letters. If the Mets won, they'd be passed out to the team as the confetti fell. If they didn't, they'd get loaded back in the van, shipped off with the military to help pacify the civilians while their houses burned.

I could barely make out Dolores's face in the dark of the van, but she seemed to be smiling. A big goofy smile, like a kid about to be let into the amusement park.

We were being driven by one of Dolores's contacts, a deaf man who bused in new uniforms and gloves before each game. They'd met back when he did deliveries for the Cyber League and now he fed her intel for a finder's fee. Last year, she'd paid for aerial footage of the Monsanto compound. Had the driver attach minicams to the underside of his van as he flew across. He hadn't snitched then. We were hoping he wouldn't now. I'd had to pay him most of Natasha's fuck-off cash to get us inside.

As we landed my claustrophobia was diluted with adrenaline. I felt like my whole being was vibrating. No matter what happened here, something would. I'd find Zunz or be found out by the Mets. I'd save the day or fail. Either way, we were reaching the final inning.

The van doors opened, flooded us with light. We stumbled out into the fluorescent green meadows.

Dolores and the driver signed to each other, their fingers and arms moving in a complex dance. I watched them, uncomprehending, rubbing my immobile prosthetic arm. I only caught a word or two.

"Two hours. Same spot. If you're not here, then I go," the man said to me.

We were a couple hundred yards from the stadium, close enough we could hear the smog vacuums buzzing around the building. Manhattan skystabbers shot up on each side of the park like the dark metal bars of a gigantic cage, but everything right around us was lush and alive.

The gardens were filled with blue and orange flowers. Giant birds encircled the stadium, chirping as their fifty-foot streamer tails twirled in the wind. A few rested on the mechanical golden mouth sign, smiling and shining at the top. Large holograms of the starting lineup strode across the top of the stadium then disappeared off the edge. Lex Dash went by, then Sam Tzu and Henry "Hologram" Graham. Then, of course, Zunz. A gigantic, smiling hologram, swinging the bat as it floated by. During a game seven, teams pulled out all the stops.

Dolores, however, was focused on business. She double-checked her pockets for her equipment, then scanned the area with her enhanced goggles for signs of danger. I checked my own pockets, fingering my gun and the blinders and knockout shots I'd brought in case things got rough.

"Time to call in the troops?" she said.

"Okay. Let's do it."

Lila appeared on my screen, bobbing a bit with excitement. She was in the Diseased Eden bunker, hundreds of feet underground. I could see the aquariums of fluorescent, deadly fish behind her.

"About time. We're all in place."

"Tell your friends they can kick-start their Diseased Eden," I said. "But remember you stay in the subway with Gerald. We have to assume Monsanto is still looking for you."

"Yeah, yeah. You guys get to have all the fun."

"You're our eyes and ears, Lila," Dolores said. "That's just as important."

"Whatever. Go save him." She waved at us, clicked off the feed.

Dolores adjusted her goggles, scanned the area again. Employees were running around, setting up vendors and seats for the fans who couldn't fit inside the stadium. Security guards drank coffee, leaning against their hoverbikes. "Nothing seems out of order. Do you feel nervous?"

"I'm always nervous before a job. That's why I smoke. Thanks for reminding me." I fumbled around my pocket with my left hand. Fished the eraser pack out. Held it stupidly in my one hand.

"Here."

Dolores pulled out a cigarette, lit it, took a puff, and then placed it in my lips.

"You feeling okay?" I asked.

"I love it. It's my favorite feeling. I'm tingling all over. It's like game day, back in the Cyber League. I feel like I'm in the dugout ready to trot out to the field."

"Oh," I said between numbing puffs of smoke.

We waited.

I paced around for a couple minutes, my mind racing with every possible failure and theoretical success. Then Dolores called me over. "It's happening."

We watched the footage on her screen. *Zunz Resurrected in Sin!* and *Monsanto Monsters Defile Children* read some of the signs. The protestors poured into the plaza. Different sects of Edenists from all over the city. A few No Grows too, and even some Transhuman Socialists. They'd been told about Lila, and the various chapters had agreed that game seven of the World Series was the perfect televised time to stage a revolt.

The Edenists hated the Future League teams on principle. The biopharms were reaping the profits of a world filled with copyrighted chemicals and genetic patents. That was a reason to protest. But a biopharm planning to cut open an Edenist to steal her cells was enough to start a religious war.

On the screen, we watched security guards form a line in front of the stadium. A human wall armed with stun guns and gas launch-ers. They'd walled off the south entrance and courtyard from the rest of the stadium. But there weren't enough of them. The Edenists kept flooding into the square. The guards yelled for backup.

While the bulk of Edenists kept the guards occupied, the Dis-eased Eden sneaked through dressed up as fans. Four men pushed large shopping carts filled with swollen plastic bags. They moved them into the center of the plaza, shoved them toward the guards. The carts rolled across the orange bricks. Came to a stop a few dozen feet in front of the guards.

The men ran away. The guards stayed still until they saw the other Edenists scramble backward, pulling out filter masks.

One of the guards fired at the carts a few times. The bags stayed immobile in the empty middle of the square. Then they erupted. A flurry of yellow moths flew around the guards' heads while a mass of blue spiders crawled across the bricks like a spreading coolant spill. A cloud of crimson gnats floated around the plaza. Centipedes, moles, snakes. Zootech creatures of all shapes and sizes spilled across the square.

Someone tossed a canister at the foot of one guard. A cloud of pink gas floated toward his nose, and he fell to the ground, vomiting inside his mask. Other guards collapsed from the bites, helmets clunking on the pavement. Then the chaos started. The guards opened fire. Sparks of light in the bright day. Shock pellets flying across the plaza. Edenists fell to the ground by the dozens, twitching on the floor.

Dolores and I watched this on our screen, the scrambling humans as small as ants.

"They're not using anything lethal, right?" I said, shuddering a little at the screams.

"That's what they promised. I think I trust them? But look, if things get ugly, you get out," Dolores said.

"Bullshit. What are you talking about?"

"Pyramid authorized my mission. If I get captured, Pyramid will trade for me. I'll make it out. You might not. You don't have the Yankees protecting you anymore."

"Well, this time they'll have to rip off more than one arm to kill me," I said, laughing.

When I looked at Dolores, there seemed to be a lake of sadness beneath her goggles. She gave me half a smile.

Dolores and I made our way to the building. It didn't look like anything at all at first. A small white shack in a field with other white shacks in front of the towering green sewage treatment dome. But there was something different about this one. Air filters stuck out of the ground to the side of the building, and the grass in front of the door was crisped from landing engines. According to Dolores's blueprints, the basement was a laboratory large enough to conduct a dozen experiments. A network of enormous concrete worms sleeping in the dirt.

A drone shaped like a cartoon parrot floated by squawking "Let's go, Mets!"

I said a little prayer to no particular god, then made my eye duplicate the scan I'd made from Coppelius's corpse. My vision blurred. I held my breath and put my face to the security node. Coppelius had been working with Monsanto on this project. I figured he'd have as much access as anyone. I was right. The electrified wires turned silent as the gate opened for us.

"If all goes well what are you and Zunz going to do?" Dolores said when we got to the door.

"What do you mean?"

"Well, Zunz won't be able to play baseball. Not after all this. And you'll be blackballed from scouting."

"Zunz has money," I said, flustered. My focus had been on finding

Zunz, not figuring out what to do after. "Plus, we'll blow the lid off the whole crime. Whatever it is. Bring the whole system down. The government. Monsanto. Everything."

The way Dolores was looking at me, I felt small and pitied. "Systems don't simply come down. New players take them over."

"Even if it doesn't topple over, we'll kick out a few of the bricks."

Dolores pulled out her gun and shrugged. "Listen, I've got contacts in the Mextexan Free State. Say the word. I can get you set up there. Hell, maybe I'd join you after this is all over. I'm getting old for this scouting life. We'll sip tequila and fire guns at the tumbleweeds until the sun goes down."

I could picture it too. Dolores and me with a little house with a couple hammocks and a swimming pool out back. Living outside of the smog of the city. Kicking scorpions away with our boots and sipping beer under the hot sun while Lila begged us to make breakfast. It was a lovely, dumb dream.

As the park descended into panic, I pulled out my gun. Grabbed the door. "I can't really talk about this now."

And then we forced our way inside.

44

THE DEAD FRIENDS

Zunz's body was draped across a steel examination table, stomach opened for all to see. His arms hung off the table, long slits cut down them. The stench of his rotting insides filled the room. The head was falling off the table, facing us. His eyes were closed. Zunz was still smiling, but his teeth were tiny. Smaller than eraser nubs. Baby teeth in a giant's mouth.

I kept walking into the room, moving purely by inertia.

"Oh, Jesus. Kobo," Dolores said.

I gagged. Bile in my throat.

Around Zunz's corpse were vials and machines of different colors. Buttons glowed. Screens projected figures and charts. The corpse was being studied, monitored.

My foot slid in a puddle of yellow sludge. I tried to grab onto a cart of surgical tools for balance, but I reached out with the nonexistent arm. I fell to one knee on the floor.

"Kobo." Dolores moved over to me, helped me back up.

Zunz's stomach was completely cut away, the edges held open by what looked like a giant metal mouth biting him from the underside. Where his stomach should have been was a greenish brown pool of swamp water. I couldn't see any organs or bones. It was as if he'd melted from the inside.

I groaned, a deep sound traveling up from the well of my heart.

I was too late. Again.

Then I heard noises from the next room. Muffled grunts, and the sound of someone struggling against restraints.

There was someone else here. Someone alive who could pay for this.

I put the gun in my left hand up to my lips. Dolores maneuvered to the right side of the door with her own gun ready.

I kicked open the door, swung the gun around. Stopped my finger right before pressing the trigger.

In the next room, another Zunz was strapped to the wall. Naked. His jaw trapped in a plastic vise. His eyes looked around wildly. His skin was pink and wet. When he saw me, his limbs flailed.

This Zunz reached out for me. His fingertips were a few inches from my hand. He made guttural, inhuman sounds. I couldn't decipher any words.

The Zunz on the wall wasn't the only one in the room. Next to him was another Zunz, but half his size. A dwarf Zunz. This Zunz, too, was strapped on a wall mount, but his eyes were dead. Black beads. No iris at all. His neck was cracked, head resting on the shoulder.

Beside that was an even smaller Zunz floating in orange liquid like a toy dropped in a jar of honey.

I spun. The room was filled with Zunzes in different stages of life, or death. Each one had his brown eyes and broad forehead, at least the ones with heads. The only thing they were missing was his baseball glove birthmark. Some were only limbless torsos jammed into buzzing machines. Others were little more than lumps of skin, groaning softly, no bones to hold them up.

"Are any—" Dolores paused. "Are any of these *him*? The real him?"

Along one wall, hands and feet unattached to anything were suspended in bluish fluid. Another had a row of large conical flasks filled with unattached eyes, ears, and tongues.

"I don't know. I don't think so."

The door across from us slid open with a mechanical slurp.

A yelp.

The woman in the doorway threw up her hands, dropping a platter that held a miniature head with a tiny Zunz face. The head rolled across the floor. Hit my shoe, lips landing on the leather.

"Do *not* fucking shoot me. I don't even want to be here," Julia Arocha said. She pointed at the security collar around her neck. "Hey, it's you. Kobo. I tried to help you, remember? Can you put down your gun?"

"Who else is here?" I asked.

"No one. Not right now," she said, shaking her head. She was wearing a flipped-up surgical visor and a stabilizing surgery glove with metal bands over the bones. "No one conscious at least. Setek is at a meeting with the Mouth. The delta model is recuperating downstairs." She tugged on her security collar again. "I want to point out again I'm under contract and forced to work here. I don't want to die for this shitty job."

"Delta model?"

"The one who will play today. He's being readied right now. We're being extra careful this time."

I felt dizzy looking at the monstrosities around me. Different parts of my brother laid out on tables or stuffed in vials. An aquarium beside my head was filled with hearts, Zunz's heart, stitched together and pumping slowly.

Dolores didn't seem as disturbed as I was. She still had her gun in her hands, but she was looking at a wall of fingers, reaching out and touching them with her own. She adjusted something on her goggles. A click. Seemed to be recording. I thought I heard her whisper "remarkable" under her breath.

Dolores looked back at us. "So this is the woman who told you the Mets poisoned Zunz? This is Julia Arocha?"

"I was supposed to finish her contract for the Yanks the night Zunz died."

Dolores put her gun back in the holster. She studied Arocha. "Yes. Pyramid was scouting you too. I was impressed with your work, but I thought you needed another year of university development."

Arocha looked at Dolores, then at me. "Um, thanks?"

"Can we hold off on the pleasantries," I said. "What the hell is going on here? Why are you dissecting my brother?"

Arocha was wearing a lab coat in Mets colors. She bent down slowly, showing me her movements, to pick up the small Zunz head. She placed it gently on the counter. His face rolled over, teeth clinking on the metal. She righted my friend's head. His smile was tiny.

"We aren't dissecting him. We're growing him. Or his clones. Spares, as Setek calls them."

"How did you do it?" Dolores said, wonder in her voice. "How did you avoid another astroclone disaster?"

"Setek didn't. Not exactly."

I pointed at one of the cloned Zunzes on the wall. "Not exactly? What's that, then?"

"Setek realized that trying to clone a person's mind was pointless. Even if you could execute the synaptic mapping, they'd become someone else. A new person. Not to mention an illegal one. But he realized you could just make a body and pilot that meat from afar. Look." Arocha reached over to the table where there was a row of helmets and hats. She picked up one and tilted it so we could see inside. It was lined with a yellow membrane that covered a mixture of wires and veins. A white tube, like a spine, ran down the middle and split near the brim into a pair of glowing nodes. "This device lets you control a body from afar. Well, a body that has a neural mesh implanted at the right developmental stage."

Dolores was still walking around, recording everything in the room. Taking close-up photos with her enhanced goggles now and then. She reached over to take the helmet from Arocha.

"It's delicate. And proprietary," Arocha said.

Dolores stopped. Sighed. Lifted her gun.

"I mean. Go right ahead."

I was fixated on something else. On the back counter, there was a set of six holopads, each illuminating a tube filled with pinkish fluid. The holograms were two feet tall. Inside were six people at different stages. They stretched from an almost reptilian fetus, curled and covered with wires, to what looked like a teenage boy. The first said *forty days to full gestation* and the last said *ten days to full gestation*. The teenage-boy body was turning, slowly. When the face came back around to me, I saw it was Zunz. Exactly as he'd looked in high school. Well, minus the wires and tubes connected to his limbs and orifices.

When I walked back to Dolores and Arocha, they were discussing details like old colleagues. They swapped stats, processes, and specs.

"We'd heard rumors Monsanto was working on this. We had no idea you were this far along. Are you bioprinting on a wetwire scaffolding?"

"Yes, for the fetuses. We've edited the cycle checkpoints to enable rapid growth. Controlled cancer, basically. They're in a nutrient and hormone slurry for forty-five days. The clones have a neural suppressor implanted at body-age of twenty months."

Dolores was nodding. "So they don't fully develop a conscious-ness. Are they like newborns? Is that how Monsanto plans to get around the Rank Act ban on cloning sentient beings?"

I couldn't believe how they were talking. Like they were discuss-ing interior decorating instead of standing in a room of mutilated body parts. But then the pieces started clicking together for me. I walked over to them.

"I've done this," I said, taking the modified baseball helmet. It looked like a normal Mets helmet from the outside to fool the cam-eras. I touched the yellow membrane inside. It was warm, and slightly slick. "It's Monsanto's new Astral system. I used one before."

"Not exactly." Arocha took the helmet back, displayed the insides for me again. "The Astral you used would have been a prototype. Not very powerful. It was a baby step. *This* is a giant leap. The helmet just relays the signal. The neural mesh is organic and fully integrated into the cognitively suppressed brains."

"So what does that mean?"

"It means there's no lag. No resistance. Seamless control."

I remembered how it was at the Janus Club, moving in the hot, slick bodies. It was thrilling in its novelty, but the controls were partial at best. Like playing an old video game with a bro-ken controller. They'd do what you wanted them to do, yet only partially and haltingly. It wasn't that way with these fake Zunzes. They were playing ball at a professional level against the elites of the sport. Maybe he wasn't quite at 100 percent, but it was pretty darn close.

"Jesus. You're going to let people just control other people?"

"None of this is my doing. They just brought me in to work on fixing the clones. To find a treatment that would keep them opera-tional after the PR disaster with their showpiece."

"Showpiece?" Anger was swarming inside me. I lifted my gun

again, aimed it at Arocha's guts. "I don't care how you justify it. Which of these is Zunz? The real one?"

Arocha put her hands back up. Waved them slowly in circles. "Hey, lower your gun. Please. Look, these are all Zunz, in a sense. All made of his genetic code."

"I'm not here for a biology lesson."

"None of these are Zunz Prime, as we call him. They're experiments. Aborted attempts or organ incubators. Sometimes we have to transplant. Zunz's genes are uniquely suited to the growth treatments required to gestate the Spares in a scalable time frame. Monsanto wants industrial production. But there are still issues. As the whole world saw live."

"What happened? What killed him or killed it or whatever?" I said. Although I wasn't sure I wanted to know.

"The issue started where the neural mesh is implanted on the dura mater. The whole thing shorted out, causing a cascade failure through the nervous system. His cerebrospinal fluid had completely evaporated. Here, I can show you with one of our test heads."

Arocha was pointing toward a pair of small tanks, each filled with a Zunz head floating in red gunk. They were bald, but hundreds of silver wires were flowing out of the tank like metal hair. The wires were connected to a silent, black machine.

"Stop," I said, as she started walking toward them. My heart was pounding. "I don't need to see it again."

"Right. Sorry."

Dolores took my hand and squeezed gently. She turned to Arocha. "Just tell us what caused it."

"My theory is there's an issue with his neural stem cell stock used in the bioprinting. They're replicating the damage years of upgrades have done to Zunz's cells. And all this is exacerbated by the upgrade treatment. DNA doesn't encode all the treatments these players have gotten. We give them years of upgrades in a couple of weeks."

I wanted to hit something. Maybe Arocha. But Dolores kept hold of me. "Can we see it?" Dolores said. "The duplicate clone. You said it was in the basement, right?"

Arocha shrugged and nodded toward the door. "You're the ones holding the guns."

45

THE STAINED MIND

I lagged behind Dolores and Arocha as we walked down the staircase, feeling something between dread and excitement building with each step. The subbasement was large and brightly lit. One wall was an enormous monitor displaying different fluctuating graphs. In the center of the room, there was a large horizontal tank half filled with red liquid.

The Zunz clone was lying, naked, inside. He was strapped to a slab with his head propped up above the fluid. Despite the wires and tubes puncturing his skin, this Zunz looked peaceful. Asleep. You could even see the dimples in his cheeks. I stepped closer. He was Zunz all right—the same face I would see when I woke up during sleepovers needing to pee. The one I'd painted with anti-surveillance paint when we were planning pranks, and the one that sat across from me in diners eating burgers at 2:00 a.m.

Except not, of course. Without his helmet on, I could see the receptors on his temples as well as the scar at the very top of the forehead where they'd inserted the neural mesh. Other than that, he looked healthy and new, like a car that hadn't been flown out of the lot.

For some reason I felt ashamed to see him like this, nude and alone. I avoided looking at his waist. His vital signs streamed across the surface of the glass. I walked over and put my hand on the tank. Studied him. I wanted to believe I could spot the difference between the clone and the real thing. A missing scar or a new blemish. Yet, as I looked all over his body, I wasn't sure. I couldn't remember where the freckles or hairs had been. I did recognize the brown splotch of a birthmark on his cheek, and I'd been right. They'd tattooed it on backward. He was a fake.

"Let's go," I said, turning around.

Then I stopped.

"Kobo."

The voice was faint, yet it made my heart flutter in my chest like a dying bird. I looked back and the clone was looking at me. He leaned forward even as the restraints held him down.

The clone had a slight grin on his face. He reached out toward me and his hand hit the glass. His pupils were wide as dimes.

"Kobo. Where?"

I felt like the air had been sucked out of the room. I turned to Arocha.

"You said this was a clone. A clone with a blank brain. How can he be speaking?"

Arocha spoke a hair above a whisper. "They're made with blank minds. As blank as you can make one. But the Astral, well, it leaves an impression. All those thoughts and feelings being streamed in, they rewire the synapses. Every time Zunz logs in, the clone gets a little more of him. Staining, we call it."

"Staining?" I said. This was how these scientists thought of my brother's consciousness. A stain.

I realized that was what had called me, back at the beginning of this mess. Not Zunz. Not my brother. But a clone. A clone stained with faint memories of me and Kang that got mixed together in its mangled mind.

"Remarkable," Dolores said. "Fucked-up and remarkable."

The clone was pressing his palms to the glass now, trying to push open the lid. The liquid sloshed around inside.

"Jesus, let him out," I said. I ran over to the glass and pressed my palms over his, feeling the cold glass between us. His eyes were wild.

"We can't. Dr. Setek will be here any minute. And anyway it wouldn't last out there without a user to control it. The clone has the brain of a newborn, basically. A couple memories, but that's it. It would die if it went too long without a pilot."

The clone seemed to calm looking at my face. I thought I saw a tear leak out of his right eye.

"Kobo," he gasped. His head shook from one side to the other. "Brain feels bad. Why I no remember?"

"We're going to get you out," I lied. "We're going to fix you."

Arocha walked to the machine regulating the tank. She spun a few dials. As if a switch had flipped in his brain, the clone shuddered violently. Then his eyes closed. He seemed to be asleep.

"It goes on and off like that. The neural suppressors have to be switched off before piloting," Arocha said.

I wasn't listening. I was trying to lift off the lid. I moved around the tank, looking for a latch. The Zunz inside was convulsing a little bit. As I was pounding the glass, I felt Dolores's hand on my shoulder. "You don't have time for this. You still have to find Zunz. Your Zunz."

She was right. It was getting close to opening pitch. I turned to Arocha, who was making small adjustments on the tank's controls.

"Where is he? My actual brother. Coppelius told me he was still alive. Back when Coppelius was alive."

"He has to be in the stadium for the signal to work perfectly. I believe he's on the top floor, near the Mouth's suite. I haven't been there personally. They just send us fresh cell scrapings each day."

I asked her more questions, but Arocha didn't know any of the answers. She didn't know if Zunz was injured or imprisoned or just a brain kept alive in a jar. The only thing she could tell us was the whole project was a lot bigger than the Mets. It had government funding, straight from President Newman.

"And Lila?" I said. "Why are you after her?"

"Who is Lila?"

"Zunz's daughter."

"Ah. A daughter. Dr. Setek keeps talking about a second source with untainted neural stem cells for us to work with. The Mets would never tell the public this, but all the juicing and upgrades have had unforeseen side effects on the cellular level. The cells get tainted. Mutated. It's true for all of us, but especially for the players. The treatments they get can be pretty extreme."

"That wouldn't be a problem with the daughter. She's an Edenist."

Arocha's face lit up. "Oh, that might be perfect. A viable donor with undamaged cells? We should be able to introduce her NSCs to—" She saw the look on my face and stopped herself. "Sorry, that's just the scientist in me talking."

"Why don't you use a test subject who has never been upgraded?" Dolores said.

Arocha shrugged. "Who would that help? Most of the country is upgraded. But Zunz's genes have a few mutations that are ideal for upgrades. The Mouth demanded we use a player as a showpiece, and we tried a couple from the team. Zunz's clones are the only ones who've survived past the fetal stage. If we can sort out the neural stem cell issue, he should be the perfect template for the entire Spares line."

"I suppose there's no better publicity than your new product winning the World Series," Dolores said.

I was breathing rapidly again. I needed to get out of this underground laboratory, surrounded by clones of my friend. I could picture the whole place collapsing, my last moments of life being crushed by the mass of my brother's body parts. His fingers sliding down my throat as I screamed.

"Dolores, we need to leave. How do we get out of here?"

"There's a drainage tunnel down that hall that leads to the stadium," Arocha said. "If you're trying to sneak into the stadium."

"Yes, we saw it on the blueprints," I said. All the biopharm stadiums had closed off water supplies to prevent rival companies from straining their wastewater for secrets. On the map Pyramid provided us, the drainage tunnels all ran toward the stadium. "Let's go."

"I can't do that, Kobo." Dolores's gun was up, pointed between Arocha and me. Her face was drained of expression.

She walked over to Arocha, ran a finger around the rim of her security collar. She pulled out a small white tool about the size of a screwdriver. "I can short this temporarily. Once I get you to the Pyramid compound, we'll reprogram it."

"Reprogram it?" Arocha said.

Dolores opened the locket on her neck, popped out a deodrive on her hand. "You said you wanted to get out of here, right? Load all the files on the Spares project onto this. Pyramid has authorized a hostile acquisition."

"What the hell are you talking about? We need to get to the stadium."

Dolores frowned a little. "You go. I need the data and I need Arocha. They're my meal ticket."

"What? We have to find Zunz."

"No." She pressed a button on the side of her goggles, which flipped open the lenses to show me her dark brown eyes. "You do. This has been a good time, Kobo. But here's where our paths diverge. Your path is to save your brother. My path is getting the data and Arocha to Pyramid and then getting paid. I wasn't lying when I told you my parents have massive healthcare debt."

"But you were lying about everything else?"

"You'll get a finder's fee. Enough to reattach your arm I think. I owe you that much."

I stood there, my one arm hung limp at my side. "You knew about this? About Zunz?"

"Somewhat."

"What the hell does *somewhat* mean? You knew Zunz wasn't dead all along?" I walked toward Dolores and she lifted her gun. She pressed the barrel tenderly into my stomach.

"Step back, Kobo. I knew Monsanto was working on a way around the anti-cloning laws. I knew there was government money pouring in. And I knew Pyramid would pay me three years of salary to get it. Why do you think Pyramid offered the blueprint plans to this compound?"

"This is just about money?"

"Money means a lot when you're in debt. You know that. But no, it's not just about money. It's a lot bigger than you and me. These clones could change everything. Think of the possibilities. People can buy a second body, live a whole second life. A third. A fourth. It could change everything. We can't have that power all be in the hands of one corporation in league with one corrupt president."

"Having it in the hands of two corporations is better?"

Dolores shrugged. "It pays better."

"Pretty thin line between this and a double-cross."

"You started it by scanning my eyeball to break into the Pyramid compound. You brought me into this. I worked my angle while you worked yours. This is what we signed up for. This is the life of a scout."

I started to leave. Stopped. Came back. But my brain had emptied itself. I didn't have anything to say.

"Do I have a choice here?" Arocha said.

"Yes," Dolores said, not even looking at me. "Load up the data, come with me, and you never have to work for Monsanto again. Or I shoot."

46

THE RED TUNNEL

Parts of Zunz floated past me. Fingers. Eyeballs. A handful of teeth. I couldn't see much, but I could feel. A mess of arteries flowed by, wrapping around my ankles as I trudged through the waters. I dry heaved. Shook them loose.

The waste tunnel was dark. The stench of Zunz's parts was overwhelming. I had to hold my one hand against the wall to keep from collapsing.

I was wading through a river of my brother. Or copies of him at least. In the tunnel, Zunz was deconstructed. Rendered into bizarre art by a mad-scientist Picasso. It was hard to imagine how all these bobbing organs in the water could be compiled into a human being.

By now, the fans would have filled the stadium and the players would be readying themselves in the locker room. Game seven of the World Series was about to begin. I didn't know if Zunz's clone was there in the dugout, getting ready to run on the field. I tried not to think about it, or about Dolores's betrayal. Tried not to think of anything but getting where I needed to go. To Zunz. The real Zunz. My Zunz.

At the grate where the maroon waters flowed into the stadium's main sewage system, I could see the control screens blinking. No one else was around. I kicked open the grate. It took a dozen tries.

When I emerged into the water regulation room, I was soaked and stained. I threw off my jacket, tried to slap the remains of my friend off me. I kicked loose a section of intestine caught in my shoe. It slid across the floor like a dead eel.

I was almost glad I didn't have my bionic arm right then. It would have taken me weeks to clean all the gunk out of the casing.

One wall of the room was filled with monitors, showing the specs and status of each bathroom. Which stall was flushing, which sink failing to drain. Bathrooms were always one of the most important parts of a stadium. No amount of upgrades could stop two hundred thousand people needing to piss and shit.

I looked at the blue schematic. Most of the floors had dozens of bathrooms, laid out every couple hundred feet. The top floor was closed to the public and the press. If Zunz was in the stadium, he'd be kept away from any accidental detection. He'd be there.

I knew the north half held the broadcast teams, and the south half was company suites. I looked closely at the south-side rooms. One was massive, with three toilets, a bidet, a hand sink, a foot sink, a Jacuzzi tub, a regular tub, and a cubic shower. The Mouth's owner's penthouse. There was a blinking yellow mouth right on the map.

There were two other suites about one-third the size of the Mouth's. I figured Zunz was being kept in one of those.

As I was heading to the lifts, I got a call on an unknown line. Hesitated, but decided to answer. Noblood Gerald looked back at me, frightened and bruised. His lip was split, and the blood coagulated in his beard.

"I thought you were staying underground, with Lila?"

"That was the plan." He spoke slowly, like he had to drag the words out of his mouth. His eyes were shallow pools.

"I liked the plan. It was a good plan."

"The police raided us. A whole squadron. I barely escaped through the subway tunnel."

"What? Where's Lila?"

"The police took her, along with two dozen of my people." He was looking away, ashamed. "Threw her into the back of a black van. I can't tell you anything else."

I hung up, called Okafor. I was sputtering out the words when they answered.

"Whoa, whoa. Slow fucking down, Kobo. What happened? Where are you? You have to come to the station right. Now."

"I'm in Mets stadium. About to rescue Zunz."

"Goddamn it. I'm supposed to be questioning you about a homicide. And what did I say about the police handling this?"

"It's a little late for that. Just tell me where you put Lila."

"Who on earth is that?"

"The twig girl. The one you arrested before." I gave them the rough outlines. I was too angry to fill in the details.

Okafor sighed. Searched through the police systems. "I'm sorry, I don't see her in any log. We don't have her."

Something hard and full of spikes was twisting in my gut. The Mets had her. I knew it. I'd failed her the same way I failed her father.

"Maybe she hasn't been processed yet," Okafor offered. "Kobo. Leave the stadium. Come to the station right now. We're old friends, but that only goes so far."

"I'm on my way."

I hung up.

I messaged the news to Dolores, told her Lila had been taken and I hoped she was happy about it. Slid my screen into my pocket and got ready.

My erasers were stained from the drainage water. I leaned against the control panel and lit one anyway. Smoked it down to the nub. Let my feelings disappear in the fog.

The Mets had sealed off the area where the Diseased Edenists had rioted with a quarantine netting. Rerouted the fans to the other entrances. It might be a mess, but it was contained. The stadium was filling up and the Mets announcers were getting the fans excited.

"Have you ever seen an atmosphere as electric as Monsanto Meadows today, Mad Dog?"

"The fans here are bouncing around like quantum particles. What a journey. It wasn't that long ago that the Mets lost their star player, JJ Zunz. They seemed done for. Kaput."

"Now they are in game seven of the World Series."

"It speaks to the resiliency of this team. They have the heart, and the hunger, and the drive."

"And the best upgrades on the market. Don't forget that."

"How could I? I'm chewing Mets MegaMouth Energy Gum right now to keep up with these fans."

There was a guard at the mag lift, watching the pregame show on his implanted wrist screen. I tried to clock him on the back of the head, but I wasn't used to hitting with my left hand. The butt of my gun glanced off his helmet and hit the wall with dull thunk.

"What the fuck?" He grabbed me and pushed me into the wall. Some of the Zunz goo splattered back on him. His nose wrinkled. "Did you crawl out of the sewer?"

He was holding on to my prosthetic arm. I jerked it loose from my stump, pulled away while he still held on to the plastic. He made a disgusted yelp. I pressed my armless shoulder into him, pushed him against the wall. With my other hand, I pulled out a knockout shot. Jabbed the needle into his neck.

"Shit."

He slapped stupidly at his neck. Then he slunk against the wall, sliding to the floor. My plastic arm clattered on the grating.

His veins were a dark yellow and his eyes became so bloodshot they were almost red. I scanned one anyway, as best I could.

The kid would wake up in a few hours with a headache that would make him want to go right back to sleep. I hoped he'd get injury comp for his bad luck.

As I rose up the stadium, I remembered the first time Zunz and I ever went to a real ball game. Got the tickets from a scalper in the parking lot. He claimed they were half price and "any less and I'm giving away grocery money from the mouths of my own children." The Mets versus the Cubs. Back end of the season. Both teams out of playoff contention, but that didn't matter to us. It was the original teams, before Monsanto and Chi-Labs purchased the names.

Citi Field was half the size of the smallest FLB stadium today and the stadium was rusting from the storms and rising sea level. But to us, back then, it was a wonder. It seemed massive enough to house an entire civilization. The air was ripe with the smell of belches and condiments. Our seats were way up, and we could see the massive expanse of cheering fans all around the stadium. Zunz ran up the steep stairs, laughing. Hopped in the seat like it was his bed. As for me, I felt a little sick. I was afraid I'd topple over, roll down the dozens of staircases, my body breaking apart with each step I hit. Zunz threw his arm around my shoulder to calm me. "Someday that will be us down there," he said. "You and me."

The lift went up the outside of the stadium, and I could see the streamer birds flying around with their long orange-and-blue tails. And below, the crowds of people shrinking into balls of color:

Edenists in their gray robes, police in their black armor, and the fans colored blue and orange. The Edenists were trapped in the quarantine netting. The black dots were hauling the other colors into waiting vans.

"Folks, we have good news to report," one of the announcers said. "The violent Edenist terrorists have been subdued. I know that was scary for a while, but the Mets security personnel have it under control."

"They claimed to be protesting Zunz, but how can anyone protest an American hero?"

"I bet someone was funding them. Did you see the expensive zootech they unleashed? We're hearing reports of over a hundred injuries and infections. I wouldn't put anything past the Sphinxes."

"Wait, Skip, do you hear that sound?"

"That's President Newman, folks, flying here to help us celebrate game seven of this remarkable, astounding, and indubitably historical series."

The smog was thin, and I saw a fleet of helicopters coming toward the stadium. The big black one in the middle was carrying an American flag that hung as tall as a building.

The lift doors opened, and I stepped into an empty, quiet hallway. The noises of the two hundred thousand fans below were muffled by the sound-absorbing bricks.

I walked slowly down the hallway, waiting for someone to grab me. Sure that at any second Coppelius would rise from the grave or some security guard would tackle me to the cold, hard floor.

The Mouth's suite was up ahead. The doors had a handle shaped like a large golden set of lips giving a kiss. Specks of gold flakes flew into the hallway, only to be vacuumed back up by a tube that shot out of the wall every few seconds to collect the glittering dust.

I moved down the circle of the stadium, passing various offices and closets. I got to the first of the smaller suites and tried the guard's eye scan. A red light flashed above the knob. I cursed, quietly. I put a fresh eraser in my mouth and gave Coppelius's eye scan a try.

The lock whirred. The door clicked open.

I pulled out my gun and went inside.

It was a clean, well-lit room. No bars or guards in sight. The furniture was sleek and expensive looking. Yet nothing quite matched. The walls were adorned with static paintings. Large colorful portraits of woolly mammoths and saber-toothed tigers. It smelled like the remains of a bonfire.

"Why, Kobo, don't you know how to knock?"

47

THE FIRST ROOM

Natasha was naked, her pale prehistoric skin dappled with shower water. Her hair flowed down past her collarbone. She was muscular and wide, shoulders like a linebacker. She walked across the room and stepped inside an air dryer. Didn't seem to mind my presence one bit. The strawberry blonde hairs across her body blew in the artificial wind.

"We're not going to mate."

"I didn't think we were," I said. I still had my gun in my remaining hand.

"Normally when you barge in on a naked person, you are hoping to mate with them. At least as I understand your customs." She stepped out of the dryer and into a blue dress with a belt made of interlocking reptile skulls.

"I was looking for my brother. Not you."

Natasha laughed as she pulled on her shoes. A low, smooth laugh like fresh oil being poured into an engine. "After the wild goose chase, you still want the goose?"

I stepped around the apartment, making sure no one was hiding out of sight. There were a lot of places to hide. The rooms were packed with animal skin rugs and enough plants to feel like a jungle. But I didn't detect anyone else.

Natasha picked up a makeup mask from the table. Punched in a code and then pressed it to her face.

"You're down to one arm?" Her voice was muffled.

"Your boyfriend got ahold of the other one."

She pulled her face out of the mask. "Coppelius? He's not my boyfriend. He's more of an extended family member. We Neanderthals are all one family. Few as we are."

I sneered. "He's dead."

This caused Natasha to skip a beat, her face twisted below the brow. But she regained her cool and sat down in a chair. She placed one leg over the other and her hands atop the knees. "That's unfortunate," she said.

There was an orange scarf on an arm of the chair. She picked it up and wrapped it tightly around her throat. The gun felt tiny and pathetic in my hand. Still, I pointed it at her heart.

"Well?"

"Well what, Mr. Kobo?"

"I know everything," I spat out. "I know about the brainless clones. I know that Zunz was a test subject. I know about the Astral system and the whole fucking plan."

She drummed her fingers on her knee. "And what is our *fucking* plan?"

"You'll be able to clone the best players at every position. Never have to worry about their injury or decline."

Natasha cocked her head, a sad smile on her face. "Oh, Kobo. You don't even try to see the big picture, do you? You think we're spending so many resources to clone a handful of jocks?"

I balked. She was right. That could only be the start of things. They'd sell the technology to the highest bidder, the mega-rich with incomes greater than the GDP of most countries. "You'll sell the clones to the rich, so they can have unlimited pristine bodies while the rest of us schmucks can't even get one healthy one," I offered. "And I'm sure President Newman is drooling at the prospect of using remote controlled soldiers in the next invasion."

"Sure, those are a couple applications. And I'm flattered that you're spending this time spelling out your theories," Natasha said. Her smile was tiny. "But the game is about to start. How about we go downstairs and watch from the owner's box."

"I can't let you do that."

She clasped her wrists together. Held them up for me like a gift-wrapped present waiting for a bow. "I suppose you want to tie me up, then? If you can do it with one hand. There's time-release handcuffs in my bedside table."

"You're taking this well." I asked her to move to a different chair beside a steel support beam. She let me link her arms around it and cuff.

"I'm merely amused. And curious."

"About?"

"About you. About sapiens. Your behavior constantly surprises me, and yet your behavior is also all I know. Isn't that odd? I'm a Neanderthal, yes. I was raised in Siberia with a dozen of my brothers and sisters. Our own little family brought back by science. We were Neanderthals, but we were attended to by sapien scientists. Taught by sapien teachers. Watched streams with sapien actors, listened to sapien musicians. You get the picture, I'm sure."

"Yeah, you stood out like a sore thumb. And you've got pretty notable thumbs."

While she talked, I looked through the one-way glass to the

stadium stands. Tiny blue-and-orange figures were filling in the seemingly endless rows of seats. Drones carrying hot dogs, pretzels, and sodas floated among them. The game would start soon.

"Quite, Kobo. The point is the sapien gaze is all I've seen. Your kind killed mine. Genocide. Buried us in history. You left nothing for me and my siblings to teach ourselves about ourselves. How do we figure out who we are when all that remains is a few cave paintings? While I find sapiens perplexing, evolutionary abnormalities who should have been stamped out when nature had the chance so Neanderthals could have bloomed in peace, I also recognize this is something of a lie. I don't know what a 'pure' Neanderthal would feel, how they would act. I'm constantly playing at a version of Neanderthalism I invented in my head. It's a costume I've been wearing my whole life."

"That's a tough break."

She narrowed her giant eyes and pulled her lips back in an expression that was unreadable to me. She looked away. "You know the Russian government sterilizes the few of us that exist? We can't even try to re-create our slaughtered civilization."

"How did you end up here? I never asked you that."

"President Petrov took a liking to me. Pulled me out of the mines, let me work as a secretary in the halls of power. Something sexual I assume, but thankfully only in his mind. Anyway, the Russian sapiens never accepted us, though they created us. I guess all parents end up despising their children? During the anti-Neanderthal riots, Petrov sent me to the Mouth as a gift, knowing I'd be safe here. Or safer at least."

"That's a pretty story. I don't believe it for a second."

Natasha shrugged her giant shoulders. "The story worked well enough on the Mouth. That's all that matters. You, I'm afraid, don't."

"He knows you're spying on him?"

"He must suspect I'm back-channeling data to Putingrad. Formulas. Schematics. But so what? The Mouth is a businessman after all. He cares about currency, not country. I provide him with the former."

Even restrained, Natasha looked like she could break out of the chair and snap my neck at any second. Her brow made her expressions unreadable to me.

"What does any of that have to do with me?"

"Baseball bores me, Kobo. Win. Lose. Win. Bats, balls, and fouls. Who cares? I'm a lot more interested in what you will do."

"Save Zunz."

"Save?" Her laughter was sharp and loud. She shook her head at me. "Well, you can *save* him, I suppose. He's right next door. But where's the girl?"

"The girl?"

"Yes, the girl. Lila is her name, I believe."

I felt the jagged metal thing twist in my stomach again. "Where is she?"

Natasha raised her wrists. "Unlock me, and I'll take you to her. I'd like to watch how it all plays out."

I raised the gun to her head. It was trembling in my hand.

"Where?"

"She's with Dr. Setek. Aren't you proud of him and his research? He puts on a good show with all his crazy legs. But there's a great sadness inside him. Deep as oceans. He's desperate to have his actual legs back. To walk like you or me. And soon he will. If we go to him, perhaps he can affix a new arm to that empty shoulder of yours. It's a shame to see you with only one. Actually, why don't we do you one better. Let's get you a new body, arm and all. When we grow one of these clones, they don't have injuries. They're the pure you. The way your genes want to be. I can offer you one, but only if you come with me."

The image of my possible self appeared in my mind, complete and gleaming. No crushed arm. No out-of-date bionics. The version of myself I'd imagined almost every day for my entire life. I wanted it desperately.

"Shut up," I said.

"We can get your new body upgraded. We have everything here at the Meadows. All the serums and boosts you could want. Every upgrade your heart desires."

"Quiet."

"Your face gets red when you're confused. Do you know that?"

I had to see Zunz. I'd never get the chance again.

"No," I said. "I'm not uncuffing you. You're staying here until I get Zunz. Then we're all going to Lila together."

"If you say so," Natasha said. She settled into her chair, her extra-large eyes watching me from the shadow of her brow as I backed out of the door.

48

THE SECOND ROOM

Z unz," I shouted, staggering into the large, open room. My heart felt like a crumpled-up ball of paper. I stopped a few feet inside. I'm not sure what I had been expecting.

Zunz stood at the far end of the room, looking out of a one-way glass wall, alive and whole. He had a beer in one hand. His other was encased in another medical glove. This one was sleeker and smaller than the one I'd seen at my apartment, when he took me to visit Setek. He remained at the window, his wide back facing me. He took a sip of beer. Then he turned around.

"Kobo. All right!"

He smiled that familiar smile, his lips pushing up into his baseball-glove birthmark. He walked toward me. It all happened very fast and impossibly slow at the same time. I kept waiting for him to blink out of existence. To be a hologram or a hallucination. Another fake.

But it was Zunz. His birthmark was in the correct orientation and his grin the right degree of lopsided. It was the real Zunz. The one I'd grown up with. The one I knew.

"Wow, Kobo. Natasha told me you might come, but I didn't believe her." He spread out his arms. He was wearing a pair of jeans and a shirt that said *New Man for Newman*. A Monsanto Mets baseball cap sat high on his head.

He swung his arms around me. Hugged me. Slapped my back.

Other than the apparatus around his hand and a few scattered wrinkles on his face, he could have stepped out of our high school locker room.

"It's terrific to see you. I didn't know when we'd get to hang again," Zunz said.

"I thought you were never going to *be* again."

My gun was still in my hand, held limply at my side. I lifted it, swung it through the room. I didn't see anyone else.

"Hey, can you put that thing away? It's me and you. Like old times."

I lowered the gun, kept it at my side.

Zunz noticed the empty space where my arm used to be. "Wow. What happened to your arm?"

"Natasha's brother ripped it off."

"Natasha has a brother? Oh, that big guy with the weird face. I thought they were lovers." He laughed, held up his injured hand. "Me and you, same problem. Only one working hand apiece. How did you get used to it when we were kids? Your arm, I mean."

"I never did," I said.

Zunz's smile flatlined. He nodded solemnly. "Hey, are you thirsty? You want a beer?"

"A beer? No. What? I came to break you out."

"Break me what?" he said, then seemed to hear a noise. He jogged back to the window and looked down at the field.

"You think we can win?" he said, still looking out the window. "I feel good. We're starting Woods today. They're unstoppable. They have a cutter that no one can hit. It'll be three up, three down. Boom, boom, boom."

"JJ. We have to get out of here."

His eyebrows arched and his lips curled in a way that was part frown and part smirk. "Hey, have a seat, man. Let's talk it out. Maybe you don't know everything, you know?"

He gestured toward the sharkskin couch along one wall. The glass table in front of it was laser cut with a mural of Zunz himself hitting a home run. A freezer drone bobbed around, a cold beer popping out of the hole.

I was bewildered enough to sit down, thirsty enough to drink. It tasted bitter and cold.

Zunz sat across from me, propped his shoeless feet on the table. His skin was paler than I'd remembered. A slight bit of gut rolled over his jeans. "Listen, I'm sorry I wasn't able to tell you about all this. God, I wanted to. I bet you were worried sick. And you don't know how much I've missed you."

"Why couldn't you?"

"Management put it in the contract. Nondisclosure and all that. Not negotiable."

"Contract?"

"Wait, before we get to that I want to show you something." He hopped up and walked down the hall. I followed him a couple steps behind. "God, do you ever miss the old days? When it was just us and the gang. Me, you, Okafor, and all the rest? Life was so much simpler then."

"Yeah," I admitted. "I miss those days."

Even as we walked in his stadium penthouse, past furniture worth more than my life, I missed them.

"Remember the Petes?"

"Sure. Hot Pete and Ugly Pete."

Zunz stopped and then guffawed. "We called them that, didn't we? We were such assholes."

"Hey, we were just accurate."

"Did you know they're bioartists now?"

I'd watched some of the Petes' streams online. They were rising stars in the art world, using genomods to create living works of art. Paintings where the eyes actually did follow you, mobiles of struggling fish dangling from feeding tubes.

"Like, big ones," Zunz was saying. "I went to one of their shows and, well, check it out!"

On a raised shelf on the back wall, there was a ball of bird wings. There must have been a thousand of them. Every color of the rainbow, and all different sizes. No beaks or eyes. Just wings. They were flapping, slowly and out of sync. Beneath the shelf I could see two tanks of liquids, one pink and one yellow, that were keeping the sculpture alive.

I looked at it for a while, trying to see the appeal of something that was so carefully made to be so grotesque.

"I don't know," I said. "I guess I never understood art."

Zunz laughed again. "Me neither! But this baby will be worth a fortune in a decade or two. My art guy said they're a surefire investment."

Behind him, the feathers rustled on their perch.

That was when I looked around the apartment. Really saw it. It was filled with the latest gadgets and high-end furniture. Mood orbs bobbed around, squirting out different scents and ambient sounds. There were gold columns pretending to hold up the ceiling. One wall was covered entirely in video posters of Zunz at bat.

It was the type of rich person's sky pad we'd mocked as kids. We swore when we were baseball stars that we'd always remember where we came from.

"You agreed to all this? The cloning and everything?"

Zunz nodded with his mouth half open. "Um, hell yeah I did. I'm getting paid millions to watch the game from the best seat in the house."

"But playing baseball was your whole life. Your dream."

We headed back into his living room.

"My dream was to be a baseball star. And I still am." He pointed at the posters on the wall as we walked by. A glass case held animatronic trophies for his Rookie of the Year and Golden Glove in the Patriot League awards. Zunz sat down and leaned back into the cushions. I sat across from him and looked at his pudgy stomach. He was barely in better shape than me at this point.

"That's not you out there on the field."

"It's my body."

"It's not *you* though."

Zunz snorted, showed me the palm of his hand. "I mean, it kind of is, dude. It's made from me."

"No. It's something else."

He shrugged, flared his nostrils, and put his hands behind his head. "Tell that to the fans whose balls I sign and the ladies I meet. We put the clones in storage after games. Well, the ones that stay together. They do the work, and I get all the benefits. Win-win."

"Your clones have thoughts. Memories. One of them remembered me. He called me."

His expression was sour, like he'd just bitten into rotten food. "Can you not call them 'hes,' please? They're bodies. Without functioning minds. How's it any different than eating headless chickens?"

"You asshole."

"Asshole?" Zunz got up and stomped over to the massive one-way window and pointed out at the field. "Listen, the real assholes are out there. They run this league. Yes, I live a decent life. But for how long?

I've only got a few years to earn at a high level. As soon as I'm used up, they'll toss me aside with the garbage. You know how many old players are in poverty, nursing injuries and disorders from busting their butts out on the field?"

I nodded toward my missing arm. "Look who you're talking to. I'm still drowning in the debt I accrued playing in the Cyber League."

Zunz smirked and tilted his head. "Yeah, and I warned you about that."

"I don't remember that."

"Well, I did." Zunz sat down again. "I said you had to be careful with upgrades the team wasn't paying for. Anyway, assholes have been making money off my body for my whole life. Letting me be juiced up and broken down while they lined their bank accounts. Well, this is my chance to get a crack at it."

He turned and showed me the back of his head. There was a thin area of missing hair with a circular scar on the scalp. It was as thick and red as an earthworm.

"And it's not like it's been all fun and games. They cut me open to insert the control mesh. Still gives me headaches at night. They extracted bone marrow. Drew gallons of blood. I worked for all this. Hell, I still have to put hours into that each day."

Zunz gestured toward a suit hanging beside a tall black tower. The suit was yellow and wet, like a hazmat suit made out of almost transparent flesh. There was a spiderweb network of thin bluish veins connecting metal nodes, like the ones in the Janus Club, which were in turn connected by wires to the tower. On a chair beside the tower, there was a helmet on the seat. They hadn't bothered to disguise this one as a batting helmet. It was a pulsing yellow membrane contorted by bonelike scaffolding into a semisphere.

"What about when you said you needed my help? When you went to Setek? That wasn't a clue?"

"Huh?"

"Before you were killed. Or your clone was killed."

"Oh, yeah, yeah, yeah. No. Natasha wanted me to meet with Setek in person. Thought he could reassure me about the process. I was hesitating on signing the contract. Had the company card, so was doing you a solid."

"And the Janus Club?"

"Wild place, right? Natasha took me there to show me how the whole remote body control system would work. Get in some practice hours. But I have to tell you, it's a whole lot trippier when it's *your* clone. I can sense everything. The wind in the stadium. The crack of the bat. I'm really playing the game out there!"

"And nothing about this bothers you? That you're condemning versions of yourself to die?"

"I'm not a fucking philosopher, Kobo." He sat up, his lip trembling in the way it always did when he was offended. He shook his head back and forth, deciding what to say. "I hated how you talked down to me with that shit in high school. You want to know why we fell out of touch? Well there it is! You're a snob. You always thought you were smarter than me. Always acted like I was just a jock who couldn't think deep thoughts like the great nerd Kobo."

"Talked down to you? I almost got killed trying to save you!"

"Don't be mad at me because I made it. We're two kids from the burrows. And we got out. I'm doing what I have to do to survive."

"And what about me? I'm supposed to be your brother."

"I still help you out."

"Help me? You barely even return my calls."

He was smirking. "Who do you think got the Mouth to hire you to investigate my death? I knew you needed the money. And the Mets needed to pretend I'd actually died while they sorted out how to stabilize the Spares. I did you a solid. You should be thanking me."

"What?"

"Come on, don't make me do this."

"Do what?"

Zunz took another sip of his beer. Then another, finishing the bottle. He pressed a button and a drone flew over with a fresh one. "The beer takes the edge off. Helps me link up with the Astral system properly."

He cracked it and drank.

"How were you helping me?"

After a gulp, he gave an exasperated sigh. "Let's face it, man, you aren't the best scout. You aren't the worst either, don't get me wrong, but you aren't who they'd hire to solve my death if I *actually* died. I'm a star. They'd hire a fleet of detectives. The Mouth would have paid out of his golden anus. Hiring you was a favor."

"This wasn't a fucking favor."

"You get paid. The Mets get good photo ops. Win-win."

I sat there shaking my head, denying something to no one in particular, mumbling.

"Come look at where we are." He walked over to the glass wall, near where the system was set up. I followed him a few steps behind. Down below us, the mascots ran around the sidelines. The field of jade grass shimmered. The announcer said the game was about to start and the murmurs of the crowd turned into a roar.

"Best seats in the house. Wasn't that our dream?"

I looked. Game seven of the World Series. If the Mets won the game, their brand would skyrocket. It was already up from Zunz's dramatic comeback, and a win would make them the best story in sports. People would rush to buy Monsanto upgrades and merchandise, which would mean a substantial leap in stock price, which would mean more research dollars to acquire more scientists and produce even more advanced steroids and upgrades. An economic shift larger than most countries' GDPs could happen after the next few innings. The game was played by people and watched by people, but at the end of the day it was power tallying the score.

"Isn't it beautiful? The grand old game. You can watch it up here with me."

I shrugged Zunz off as best I could with my empty shoulder. The fog of nostalgia and confusion blew away. Everything rushed back to me. Zunz collapsing at bat, the case, the murder of Kang, Dolores stealing secrets, me chasing Lila. Lila.

"And what about Lila? You're going to let them dissect her?"

"What are you even talking about?"

"Your daughter."

He scrunched his face up in disbelief, then relaxed his features. "Ah, you know about her? Look, I was just a stupid kid back then. I was never cut out to be a father. And Hana didn't want me involved anyway. She 'didn't believe in my way of life,' she said. Claimed I'd be a bad example. I didn't need that stress. Still, I paid Hana's brother, Jung, to raise the kid after she passed. We actually became buddies. He gives me updates on her. But that's all I could do. Anyway, what does she have to do with anything?"

"She's not better off. The Mets have her. Your sick doctor friend, Setek."

He looked at me skeptically. "I don't know anything about that. They never told me anything about her. She's not in the contract. I'd have noticed something about my daughter in the contract."

"You don't know they've been hunting her to save your dumb clones? They're going to slurp the stem cells out of her brain. She could die. All so your clones can live a little longer before being tossed back in the protein blender."

A deafening rumble rolled through the stadium. Streamer birds dove from the ceiling. I saw Zunz's screen light up.

"Shit, they're on the way. I have to link up soon." He looked up at me, lips pursed and eyes narrow. "That's fucked, man. I didn't know anything about anyone's brains. I promise. I bet they want to clone her and take the cells from the clones. That way there will be an unlimited supply, you know? It will all work out."

"That's not how it works. Not for most of us."

"Okay, if you're sure. If you're really, *really* sure then we'll stop it. I'll demand they stop it." Zunz was a goofy teenager again, smiling. "They still have to listen to me, I'm still the star."

I felt a sudden relief. Like my whole body was deflating pleasantly. "Great. I think I know where they're keeping her."

But I noticed Zunz had picked up his control helmet. He flicked it on. The nodes glowed red and hot.

"Hey. Come on," I said.

He held up his hand. "Whoa. I will help you. I'll help her. *After* the game."

"JJ. We have to do it now."

"Kobo. It's game seven of the World Series," he said, starting to strip off his clothes. "My entire career has been building to this. I can't just leave! Are you crazy?"

I wanted to yell at him that Kang had been killed. That Coppelius had died. That horrible things had been happening because of him and nothing would be all right. But there wasn't a point. This Zunz might as well have been a clone of a stranger. He wasn't the brother I'd known. Not as I wanted to think of him.

I needed to leave. I went to the door.

"Damn, I'm late." He was delicately pulling on the membrane suit. "Come back after the game. We'll fix everything and, hell, I'll see if they can bring you on full-time. You already know about me, so they'll want to keep you in the fold. Maybe get you a one-bedroom on the compound. It'll all work out. We'll be the old ZuBo team again."

"Sure," I said, already making my way to the door. "Whatever you say."

"Wish me luck."

At the door, I was ready to say something definitive, something that would slice right through him. A truth to cut him down to the bones. It came to me. But as I started to say it, I looked back, and Zunz was in the chair, helmet on, body slumped as if sleeping, and his mind gone somewhere else.

49

THE NINTH INNING

The courtyard outside of the golden stadium was filled with shouting scalper bots, face-painted fans practicing cheers, families with cone grills searing artificial flesh, surrogates high-fiving through remote commands, and teenagers smuggling tubes of booze in their jeans. They were milling about between the cars parked in stacks and automated billboards. They screamed and laughed. Recorded themselves and others. Game seven of the World Series. The air was alive with sounds. More people kept arriving. By car and train and blimp. Employees, police, news cameras, and straggling fans. I ran through them all.

A hundred yards from the stadium, I vomited. A splatter of yellow bile dotted with the chunks of my last meal. Empanadas I'd scarfed down in the hotel while Dolores and I went over the plan one last time.

I leaned against a Mets kiosk, panting.

"You need anything, buddy?" the worker said.

I asked for a pack of adrenaline chews and a bottle of water.

"You sure were running fast, buddy. You leave a baby in the car? The game's just started and you're going the wrong way."

I stuck a couple chews in my mouth and jogged off. The stadium and its hundreds of thousands of fans shrank behind me.

I called Okafor as I ran.

"Kobo, you better be in a taxi heading to the station right fucking now."

I couldn't slow down and yelled through the gasps. "Get. To. Monsanto. Meadows. Kidnapped. Girl. Murder. Illegal. Cloning. Big. Case. Make. Career."

I hung up, and then sent them the location of the lab. Reiterated *This will make your career. Get down here.*

Up ahead, I saw the entrance to the underground laboratory. It was nestled between a pair of black vehicles that hadn't been there before. One was a car and the other a large tank van. Their windows were tinted black. I waited for a minute but no one came out.

My lungs ached and my throat burned. It felt like my blood was singing or maybe screaming. The door was unlocked.

I drew my gun and descended.

I could hear squealing metal as I went down the stairs.

The laboratory was humming with electric lights. I squinted. Put my gun hand up to my face, shaded my eyes with the barrel.

The rotting Zunz clone had been removed from the operating table. In the place of the corpse was Lila, on her stomach and struggling against the restraints. She looked so small and alone. Her body barely stretched halfway down the metal. The bottom of the table housed black medical machines, yellow lights blinking in their dark casings.

Lila was bound by the wrists, ankles, and torso. Her back was exposed. I didn't see any bruises or blood. But there were bandages on her neck. She turned her head enough to stare at me. Her eyes were hard little balls.

An eight-foot creature was bent over her, curved like a cane. He was holding an electric needle connected by a hose to the back wall. It made a repetitive slurping sound. Dr. Setek. His upper half was affixed to elongated mantis legs. He noticed me, straightened up on his silver poles so his head was close to the ceiling. He waved the needle.

"Kobo, my boy. Just in time!"

Arocha was still in the room, security collar blinking on her neck. She was wearing surgical scrubs. Flecks of blood decorated her chest. She didn't say anything.

I didn't see Dolores anywhere. Which I hoped meant she'd escaped.

On the counter beside Arocha was one of the tanks containing a cloned Zunz head. Yellow tubes were filling in the mouth, eyes, ears, and nostrils. The head was clamped in place facedown, neck exposed at the top. The machine that the wire hairs were connected to was emitting a high-pitched hum.

Setek tapped his instrument against his metal legs like he was clapping. He had a big white smock hanging from his neck to the metal knees. He pulled his mask down.

"You're about to witness a scientific breakthrough. You'll be telling your grandchildren about this. Or perhaps your grandclones." He chuckled.

"The only thing I'll be talking about is how your brains dripped down the wall." I raised my gun to his eyes.

Setek stopped moving. He tsked. "You don't want to stop me. Think of the implications! We're talking about giving people a second self, one without diseases or injuries or anything else plaguing them. I'll be able to walk again with human legs. Flesh on pavement. Flesh all the way through. Do you know how long I've been looking for that feeling?" He pointed the instrument at me. "And you'll be able to have your arm back. You of all people should appreciate this. Think how many people could be helped."

"Fuck your help."

I fired. But as I squeezed the trigger, I was shoved so hard I fell to one knee.

Arocha shouted. The bullet shot an inch away from her temple and hit a small canister on the wall. A plume of blue gas exploded into the air, then dispersed. An acidic smell filled the room.

The gun was wrenched out of my hand. Tossed across the floor. Something big and blunt hit me in the back, then the head. I landed on the floor. A pair of giant hands lifted me. Arranged me on a chair, handcuffed my one hand to the back with an electric clink.

When I looked up, there were two of them. Both thick and knobby, like they'd each been whittled out of one gigantic bone. Neanderthals. They were as big and ugly as Coppelius, although their features were more fully formed. Their large eyes glared at me from the shadows of their bulbous brows. They wore gray coveralls. One was a couple inches shorter than the other and his face was red and twisted up like he was about to weep.

"Is this him? This is the guy?" the shorter Neanderthal said.

"Calm down, Gerd," the taller one said. His voice was smooth and deep. He patted his large hand on the man's shoulders.

"You two look familiar," I said. "Like someone I left bleeding out on my carpet."

Gerd glared at me and his lips crinkled back. His fists hung at his side, large as melons. "Bastard," he spat.

Natasha walked over and put her hand on the man's other shoulder. Smiled at me. "Yes, Gerd and Hubertus here might look familiar. They are brothers to the late Coppelius. Twins I suppose, depending on your point of view. The scientists who made us only had so much DNA to work with."

"Seems they came out better than their brother. Guess they were left in the oven a bit longer."

Gerd started to lunge, and Hubertus held him back, speaking in a silky whisper. "He's not important. Calm down. Coppelius would want us to keep our heads."

"Where have you been hiding these two?" I said.

"Oh, they've been here. They subbed in for Coppelius sometimes. We just let the Mouth think there was only one of them around. He's not the most observant man, you might have noticed." Natasha smiled. "Now let's talk about you. No luck with Mr. Julio Julio Zunz?"

Lila shook in her constraints. Made a sound that didn't sound like words.

I turned back to Natasha. Wiped my bloody lips on my stumped shoulder. "Shouldn't you be at the game?"

"I told you I didn't care for baseball. The research side has always been more interesting to me. After all, I am a clone myself. The DNA scrapings of an old fossil injected into a sapien embryo. A miracle maybe. Only one in a hundred of us survive in your kind's hostile wombs."

"They should have left you in a bone in the dirt."

"You talk too much. You should listen more," Hubertus said. He let go of his brother, who stepped forward and gave me a few more blows, slapping with an open hand as stiff as a plank of wood.

I spat out a tooth. Blood clogged my bionic eye. I looked up again and the short Neanderthal was crying. "Fucking bastard," he said, his voice wobbling.

"Okay, that's enough. All of you be quiet," Natasha said. She turned. "Setek, how did the first trial go?"

Setek walked over to the counter and squatted. His metal femurs folded right into the fibulas. He was about my height now and peering into a large white machine. "Let's see. With the sample NSCs and ependymal cells extracted from the donor's central canal mixed with the serum and introduced into the sample." He twisted a few knobs, flipped a switch. The machine buzzed. Setek gasped. Laughed.

"Well, well, well! It's melding beautifully. Let's introduce it to the model." He filled a syringe and walked over to the Zunz head in the tank. A small tube was already in place at the nape. He slid the needle inside and plunged.

He returned to the white machine. A minute or two passed. Then he laughed again. "Brilliant. Brilliant."

Arocha typed in something and nodded, looking at the data streaming on her screen. "We have to monitor for longer, but the early analysis is promising."

"It's working. I'd stake my life on it. Here." Setek loaded another small syringe with the green serum and placed it inside a courier drone shaped like a pigeon. "Better get this to the dugout before we have another on-air accident."

He handed the drone to the smaller, gently weeping Neanderthal, who carried it out of the room.

In a corner, I saw a small screen playing the game on mute. Zunz was on deck, taking practice swings.

So now they had it. His genes and hers to fix them. The code to copy and paste into other codes to make endless clones. They'd used a brown kid from the burrows to experiment with like a lab rat. Now that it worked, they'd sell it to elites in the cloud condos and watch the stock soar. A recipe as American as apple pie.

"Let Lila go," I said. "You got what you wanted. You've got your fix."

"Not quite. Not quite at all. Sorry." Setek picked up a saw from the table. Powered it up with a high-pitched squeal. "We only extracted a sample, but we need more. We must repeat the tests. Science requires redundancy. She won't be permanently harmed. You have my word."

He walked over to Lila and rapped his knuckles along her spine.

"We have a few prime spots to extract more NSCs. Perhaps the hippocampus next?"

Lila was lying still. Her body exhausted from struggling. I didn't see any tears.

"I called the cops," I said, straining against the cuffs. "They're coming. This whole illegal operation is going to be blown wide open."

"You know better than to trust the police to save you," Natasha said. "This isn't a rogue operation in your mother's basement. Monsanto has funding and agreements with the Remaining States government itself. Didn't you see who was throwing the first pitch today?"

Setek bent over Lila's head. With his long metal legs, he looked like a crane deciding which fish in the pond to skewer. His saw squealed.

Arocha looked back at me with a face I couldn't parse. Either anger or regret. She held up a finger to her lips.

"Don't," I said.

"Kobo, don't be so worried." Setek turned off the saw. He picked up a syringe and showed it to me. "See? Anesthesia. We're not mad scientists here."

My eyes darted around the room, desperate for something to save me. My gun had slid beneath a centrifuge on the far wall. Gerd had walked back into the room and was standing with Hubertus somewhere behind me. I wondered if I had the strength to pick up the chair with my handcuffed hand and knock the Neanderthals out. Or at least break their jaws and distract them for long enough to make a desperate dive for the gun. I needed to do something. Anything.

Setek turned the saw back on. It screamed like a hungry eagle.

Lila had recovered some strength. She began to shake again.

"Doctor," Arocha said, tapping his shoulder. "The other test head. You left it in the incubation room."

"So go get it."

"I don't have the code."

Setek cursed. Pulled down his mask. "It's always something."

I noticed Arocha type something quickly on her screen. She held up a hand to me, urging me to wait.

Setek strode to the door. Opened it. Stepped backward.

Dolores was standing in the doorway, holding what looked like a fishbowl filled with sludge.

"And you are?" he said, annoyed.

Dolores looked at me. "Hi, Kobo."

Then she hurled the contents of the jar into Setek's face.

50

THE BIG PICTURE

At first, Setek seemed confused. He stood upright, hair skimming the ceiling. Shook his head. The brown substance was made up of a thousand tiny creatures. They squirmed around his face. He dropped his implement and started slapping at his cheeks with his hands. Dozens of tiny tadpoles fell onto the floor. Others managed to wriggle into his nostrils and lips.

Then Setek began to gag. Attempted a scream that morphed into a choke.

Dolores dropped the jar, the remaining contents squirming out onto the floor, and pulled out her gun. Dolores waved it between Natasha and the two brothers, and stepped back as the tadpole creatures slithered toward her feet.

Arocha pressed herself into the wall, away from the creatures.

"How interesting," Natasha said, stepping in front of the brothers to get a better view. "See? You never know what can happen. Life is such a strange journey."

The doctor's face was a painful red. The red of a tomato so ripe it was about to split open. He gasped. Clawed at his throat and cheeks. His thin robotic legs tangled as he crashed over, knocking into the equipment table before sprawling across the floor.

He wasn't screaming anymore. He twitched on the tiles. He was on his side, facing me, and I could see the whites of his eyes had become buttery. His veins were black as oil.

"So," Dolores said. She stepped forward into the room, dodging the tadpoles. "I got your message."

I spat out a little blood. "And you stayed?"

Dolores cocked her head. "I didn't have much of a choice. Setek and the Neanderthals arrived when that data was still downloading. Arocha gave me those, said to wait for a signal." Dolores turned to Natasha. "Unlock him now. If you don't mind."

Natasha didn't move. A smirk appeared between her knobby cheeks. She breathed in and thumped her chest. "Ah!" she said. "You never know what will happen in life. The twists and the turns. It makes me feel alive."

Setek's metal legs rapped arrhythmically on the floor a few more times. Finally, he was still.

"Unlock Kobo. Then untie Lila. Unless you want to join the good doctor here."

Natasha stood, running a hand across her flat skull. She stepped forward. "Do you know how few Neanderthals there are? The three of us are the only ones alive in the Remaining States. Most of our Russian brethren have been slaughtered. There's a colony in the mountains of Turkey, one in Romania. But that's it. Killing us would be slaughtering an endangered species. And for what?"

The Neanderthal brothers behind me were quiet. Natasha was walking with slow-motion steps, but not toward Dolores. Toward Arocha, who had pulled a syringe out of one of her pockets and held it up defensively. Natasha had her large hands up and open.

"I'll go further. Killing me will mean the end of the Neanderthal species. The end. The materials in this laboratory. The neural serum. The bioprinters and growth tanks. We need them." She gestured over my head at the brothers. "You think we care about baseball players? We have been praying for this for our people. Without it, we will die out a second time. Have you sapiens still not cured your extinction lust? How many species have you killed with your guns and pollution? Millions and millions. You've killed so many you have to invent new ones in laboratories to replace them."

Dolores looked annoyed but held the gun steady. The apertures of her goggles clicked and spun. "I've got nothing against Neanderthals. I'm just looking to take the girl, the man, and the scientist and get out of here. You won't see us again."

There was a faint muffled sound in the distance. Cheers from the stadium. One team or the other scoring a run.

"You'd probably like me to disable Dr. Arocha's security collar, then?"

"Yeah. Okay." Dolores looked at Gerd and Hubertus. "You two just stay there."

Natasha reached her thick fingers toward Arocha's throat. She could have snapped Arocha's neck as easily as a twig, but instead she hit a sequence on the back of her security collar. It unlocked, split open.

Arocha pulled it off and flung it clattering into the sink. She stretched her neck. Took a few steps to stand beside Dolores.

"Next unstrap the girl."

Natasha wasn't looking at Dolores though. She was looking at Arocha. "See? We Neanderthals keep our word."

"Okay," Arocha said. "A deal is a deal."

Arocha swung the needle into Dolores's side, right below the rib cage. "Sorry," she whispered as she plunged.

Dolores looked at her, unbelieving. "What?" she said, then, her body shutting down part by part, she collapsed onto the floor.

Both Lila and I began struggling. Hubertus held me down, fingers digging into my muscles. "Don't go anywhere yet."

"Breathe, Kobo," Natasha said. "Deep, long breaths. Your kind's lungs are so small."

"It's only a knockout shot. She'll be fine in a couple hours," Arocha said.

"Dolores was going to rescue you!"

Arocha pulled down her surgical mask. "Rescue me? She was going to put me to work for another biopharm. Same bullshit, different stadium."

Natasha strolled up beside her. "We offered Dr. Julia Arocha here something better. Freedom and a purpose."

"You trust the person who kidnapped you?"

Arocha laughed and looked down at Dolores. "Wasn't she about to do the same thing for the Sphinxes? Weren't you trying to do it for the Yankees? Natasha offered me a way to get out. Out of this rat race. Out of the bullshit."

Gerd stomped over to Arocha, asking which equipment they needed. Arocha pointed at a half-dozen machines in the room while Hubertus scanned the computers. As they carried out the lab equipment piece by piece, Natasha pulled up a chair and sat between me and Lila.

"I don't care about the Mouth or his plans. The Mouth wants to sell bodies as luxury products. Who knows what President Newman wants? To send an endless supply of sapiens to murder other sapiens in his endless wars. They are both small Homo sapiens with small, scared minds."

"Well you've got a big head," I said. "What's your big idea?"

Natasha furrowed her brow as best she could. Shook her head.

"No. Big ideas are what *you* obsess over. New technologies. New planets to visit and terraform. Larger buildings, more expensive machines, more and bigger and newer products to sell. But what changes? A different brand name is printed on the label. The same people stay in power. Everyone else struggles as much as they did twenty or a hundred or a thousand years before. I'm going to create something new. A new species with a new society."

"Too impatient to do it the old-fashioned way? You've waited this many millennia already."

Even with her uncanny Neanderthal features, I could sense her anger. "Even if our ability to propagate hadn't been sliced out of us, how could we trust your kind not to murder us again? No. We need to build quickly. We need to defend ourselves. We need bodies. Lots of bodies."

"How does a bunch of brain-dead hunks of meat make a society?"

Natasha tapped the side of my head. "You all feel the need to control the clones. Because of your notions of autonomy and individuality. Your superstitions. We don't have the same pretensions. We won't install any neural suppressors in our clones. We'll let the staining stay. We'll let them grow into their own people. Even if you duplicate a consciousness, it will become its own individual a millisecond later. If you let it. Together we'll form a new civilization. A Neanderthal one."

"New? I thought you all had been around a long time ago."

"You sapiens think far too literally. You cloned me, and my brothers here, but you didn't clone our identity. We are starting Neanderthals from scratch. Imagine if you cloned a saber-toothed tiger, but there was no mother to show it how to hunt, how to play, how to purr. What would it be? The flesh of a saber-toothed tiger. The teeth and the claws and the fur. But not the species. Not the generations of living, learning, and dying passed down from one tiger to another. This lone tiger would have to invent her tigerness." Natasha put her hands on her knees, pushed herself up. "As we will invent ourselves."

While we talked, Gerd and Hubertus carried equipment out of the room. Then they went downstairs and returned, hugging incubation tanks and grunting as they maneuvered through the door. Racks of vials, cases of samples, portable freezers, centrifuges, gene splicers, cell splitters, and more. They carried each out to the waiting black van. As they did, Arocha began wiping the video files and computers.

"I do want to thank you, Kobo. You led us to Lila. And without the distractions you provided it would have been harder to escape. Even if I had to instruct both Arocha and Coppelius to nudge you in the right direction when you were getting lost. Here." She pulled a bytewallet out of the pocket of her dress. Tossed it between my feet. "Consider it a final payment."

I heard the roar of an engine outside. Arocha came and whispered in her ear. She didn't look my way. Natasha nodded and stood up.

"You're not afraid of Monsanto coming after you?" I said.

"You've left enough evidence to incriminate yourself several times over. Your face and Dolores's are all over our surveillance footage. Coppelius's corpse is at your apartment. I left extra evidence just in case. The Mouth will think it was you and Pyramid Pharmaceuticals who robbed this lab. For a while at least."

She went around behind me and pressed a few buttons on the electronic cuffs.

Dolores was still on the floor, unmoving. Lila was watching silently. Behind them, the screen showed a white spinning ball flying into the stands. A home run.

"These will unlock in thirty minutes. I've disabled the alarms and surveillance in this area. You should have time to leave."

"You're framing me then letting me get away?"

"It's better for both of us if they're chasing you. So that by the time the Mouth figures out what truly happened, we'll be long gone." She ruffled my unkempt hair. "I hope you get away too. I'm rooting for you. You seem like one of the good ones."

Natasha walked to the door. She looked thick and young, like the trunk of a tree getting ready for spring. She stretched her limbs, looked around the lab to see if she'd missed anything. Then she strolled out into her future and closed the door.

51

THE END GAME

After I freed Lila, she helped me get Dolores away from any remaining tadpoles. The squirming zootech creatures were already starting to dissolve into little brown puddles. Their life spans brutal and short. Lila squatted to watch them melt. She seemed more interested than disgusted.

I bundled up a lab coat, put it under Dolores's sleeping head. Her goggles had been knocked off in the fall. I scooped them up. I watched Dolores sleeping calmly. When I reattached the goggles, they booted back up, clicking and whirring.

I debated fleeing immediately, but it would have been risky to stroll through the Monsanto compound as a one-armed oiler carrying an unconscious woman with an Edenist girl in tow. We'd have stuck out like three eyeballs in a bunch of grapes at the grocery store. So I called Okafor again.

"I'm coming, Kobo. You dragged me out, you cocksucker. Be outside in ten minutes. And be ready to do a lot of explaining."

When I got done with the call, I saw that Lila was gone. I looked around and found her in the back room, gazing at one of the Zunz experiments mounted on the wall. Lila's dull Edenist garb was specked with different fluids now. Red blood, green serum, clear tears. She looked healthy, otherwise. She had her hands clasped behind her back and her hair held up with a clip. I couldn't say the same for the Zunz on the wall. He was only a half a Zunz. The torso was cut off at the waist, cinched with a metal plate. The part that was there was dead tissue and sagging skin. I felt an urge to reach and cover her eyes. But Lila was shaking her head.

"Gross. Is this what I'm going to look like when I'm older?"

"You don't need to look at these," I said.

She tapped on an aquarium, causing the four-inch Zunz inside to curl up in fear. She turned to me. "Where's my actual full-size father?"

I looked at her. Tried to decide what to say, but she understood without me saying anything.

"Never mind. Can we go outside? This place gives me the creeps."

"Yes. Let's get Dolores conscious again."

I found a wake-up shot in one of the drawers. Plunged it into her side. She started to stir.

"That prehistoric bitch," she said, slurring. She signed angrily with drugged hands. "Where is she?"

I helped her sit up.

"They left. Took all the serum and equipment. Erased the data banks."

"There goes my goddamn payout." Dolores looked around, yawning. Then she patted herself, pulled out the deodrive. "Well, I got a partial download before Setek interrupted us. Got the data on the growth process. Should still be worth something to Pyramid if they want to catch up to Monsanto."

Lila and I got Dolores to her feet, and we left the lab, limping outside together.

As if mocking the darkness and death inside the room, the outside was bright and alive. The park was foaming at the mouth with flowers. Streamer birds flew above us, their tails waving in the wind. We were too far away to hear the announcers, but we could hear the cheers of the crowd. The scoreboard on the side of the stadium said the Mets were up six runs to three. Bottom of the seventh. The Mets were a few outs from winning the World Series for the first time in a decade. Zunz really had led them all the way.

"I need to sit down," Dolores said. She was leaning on me to walk, arm hooked around my neck.

We helped her to a bench. In front of us was a fountain filled with orange and blue goldfish and past that the gigantic stadium, bursting with sound. Lila sat down between us and draped her arms on our shoulders.

"You weren't the worst detective," Lila said, patting me. "You figured it all out, in the end, right?"

"I'm a scout, not a detective."

"Still." She smiled. "You got there eventually."

"Thanks."

A burst of orange smoke flew out of the top of the stadium. It rose into a huge mushroom cloud shaped sort of like a baseball above the dome. The Mets had scored another run. Any New Yorker looking toward the park would be cheering now.

"Shit, you guys are going to beat us, aren't you?" Dolores said. "Should we watch?"

"Yeah. What else are we going to do?" I said.

"Wait, I forgot something inside. I'll be right back," Lila said and ran back into the lab.

I pulled out my screen and brought up the feed. The crowd was on its feet, hands in the air. The camera, attached to some drone or another, swooped through the crowd like a falcon, capturing the faces of the fans. Mouths thrilled circles, eyes open, hands waving. They were all shapes and sizes. All colors and ages. But they were moving together as one organism.

The camera flew up toward the roof for an aerial shot. The Sphinxes pitcher threw the pixelated ball. A tiny digital Zunz fouled it to the left. When he got a hit and sprinted safe to first, I couldn't help myself. I cheered.

Despite everything, I still loved the game. The weirdness of its rules, the uniforms, and the crack of the bat amplified through the stadium's speakers. It felt timeless. Players would come and go. Teams would move cities. Leagues would fold. But the game, like some stubborn dinosaur dragging its thick tail into the future, would remain.

Dolores leaned against me, still only half awake. "So what happened with Zunz? You couldn't find him?"

"I found him." It was all I could say. He'd left me behind a while ago.

Maybe it would be different in five years or ten or fifteen. The league would spit him out eventually. Just like the CLB did to me. He might tumble down that tower he'd climbed. End up back on my level. Maybe we'd reconnect. Go out to dinner, laugh about the old times. Forge the old bond and never ever let it break again. Stranger things had happened.

Lila came back with a silver case with airholes in it and sat between us. We watched silently for a little while.

Finally, Okafor's cruiser approached. A single, solitary squad car. The siren wasn't on. It settled down beside us.

"You are one sorry-looking hunk of scrap," Okafor said, hugging me.

They pulled back, looking frightened, and asked me where my arm had gone.

I said it was a long story and I'd tell it later.

"Okay, we have to go. Right now. I'll yell at you later. But you absolutely cannot be here when the other cops come."

"Wait. Where is everyone?" I said. "The rest of the department? I thought you were bringing the cavalry. Didn't I tell you this case could make your career?"

I thought Okafor was missing the big picture. I started to explain the whole thing again as quickly as I could.

Okafor just shook their head like they were trying to slap sense into me.

"Kobo. You're wanted for questioning in a murder investigation. And if, *if*, what you told me is true then you'll have the whole might of Monsanto falling on you. They'll crush you quicker than an ant under a bowling ball. You need to flee." They looked at the ground, shaking their head. "Jesus. Didn't I tell you to stay out of this case?"

"He doesn't listen, does he?" Dolores said.

I still thought Okafor hadn't understood everything. That they were missing the essential details. The right data points that would make them realize their error and help me storm down the castle. I pointed back to the lab. "There's a dead doctor in there. There's illegal clones. There's government corruption. Stolen profits. This is a huge scandal."

Okafor crossed their arms across their metal chest. Drummed. "There's no squadron, Kobo. I mentioned what you said to my bosses. They told me to look elsewhere or else look for another job."

"Monsanto bought the cops off?" Lila said.

"It goes way beyond Monsanto. Those cocksuckers have bigger cocksuckers backing them. I told you from the start to stay out of this."

"Government corruption. Corporate sabotage. Illegal cloning." I was sputtering.

Dolores slowly pulled herself upright, using my remaining arm to steady herself. "Come on, Kobo. Our cyborg parts used to be illegal.

Steroids used to be illegal. They used to arrest you for erasers, and weed, and pills."

"So?"

"So what's illegal is only what hasn't been allowed yet."

"She's right," Okafor said. "Also, you dumbass. Breaking into a Monsanto facility? And I don't even want to know what you had to do with the Edenist terrorist attack on the stadium. Let's go before I change my mind and turn you in for a pay bump."

"Fuck that," I said. "This is it? Everyone gets away with it? Everyone goes free? That's it? That's where it all ends up?"

Dolores held on to my shoulder, still unsteady from the knockout shot. She laughed, short and sad. "Things just keep going, Kobo. Maybe they get a little worse. Maybe they get a little better. More worse than better recently. But they keep going," Dolores said. "Haven't you been paying attention?"

52

THE NEW DAYS

I don't watch a lot of baseball these days. And I certainly can't play. I still don't have a right arm. Not one attached to my body at least.

I do keep my old bionic arm in the basement. Every once in a while, I take it out. Tinker. Fiddle. Try to patch up holes and fix the wetwires. I can get the fingers to seize and elbow to bend. At this point the arm is so old-fashioned, it's vintage. New cybernetics are sleeker and stronger. Sport a whole new set of features. Fixing this one up is just a hobby. A way to pass the time.

Mostly, I sit on top of our home and look at the open emptiness. The air is clean and fresh out here in the desert. It blows around the tumbleweeds and bundles of rusted mesh. No smog for a hundred miles. The hot sun licks its cancerous tongue all over my skin. It feels warm, good.

I never have to go underground out here. Never worry about a cave-in crushing me. There are no other buildings around us, and in town nothing is more than a dozen stories tall. I stay on the same level as everything else on this hot flat plane.

I meditate now. I'm trying to be a better person. Appreciate the things I have in life. Live in the now. All that hogwash.

And I don't get upgraded anymore. Promised I'd never get into medical-loan debt again, never have a company claim they own the rights to my limbs and organs. I'm done talking to sisters with red pens and big fists.

The only sport I pay attention to is basketball, and only when Lila plays. She's a budding point guard. Has the vision to see the whole court, the angles to bounce the ball. She's grown a lot but is still short for her age. The pickup players don't realize her tiny size is a strength. She zigs her twig figure between the players, zags to a layup before they even notice.

I clap from the park bench, whistling and smacking my one hand on the metal.

"Calm down," Lila says. "You're embarrassing me."

But she smiles, most of the time.

Sometimes I bring our little Zunz along, the one Lila took from the lab. I place him next to me and make sure he doesn't wander off. He doesn't know what's going on, but he likes to look around. His head darts this way and that like a lizard following flies.

I'm not saying it's a paradise out here in the Mextexan Free State. I work ten hours a day on the solar farms. It's hot all the time and bugs fly in through the cracks in the creepeasy Lila and I have repurposed as a home. We have to monitor the waves in case the skirmishes between the Free State militias and the Remaining States army spill our way. Make sure we avoid the roving gangs of religious cartels like the Luddite Christians and the Techno Mormons.

It's safer out here for Lila and me than it was in the city. After the attack on the stadium, the cops cracked down on the Edenists. Rounded them up by the hundreds. A bunch went to jail, and a bunch of others successfully sued the police for a variety of abuses. But the police budget for that anyway. The important thing was we got out before the police could find us. And if Monsanto finds out where we are, that's going to be the end of the line.

Or maybe not. Maybe Monsanto doesn't care anymore. They're busy fixing the neural mesh issue and counting their new piles of cash.

Monsanto's duplicate cloning program made the news. The Sphinxes exposed it all after the World Series, thanks to Dolores's eyewitness testimony and photographs. It was a big deal for a while. Monsanto had to forfeit the title after the FLB ruled the Astral system counted as cybernetics and violated the league's rules. The Mouth reportedly has refused to give back the trophy, but in the official history books, the Sphinxes won the title. There was talk of resignations, politicians made rumbles about throwing the executives in jail.

Monsanto's stock crashed for a couple weeks, then shot back up to new highs. Much of the public was shocked at the clones and professors were all over the holofeeds talking about the ethical, moral, and legal violations their existence caused. However, investors thought it showed the right initiative. Analysts applauded their foresight in opening a new market, the human form itself. Eventually, President Newman issued an executive order declaring the clones legal noncitizens and pardoned everyone involved.

And somehow JJ Zunz came out a hero. JJ Zunz, or an imitation of him, won the MVP as they clinched game seven by a score of six to three. Zunz or his clone, however you wanted to count it, wasn't the best player during the series. He only batted .250 and drove in two runs. Made a bad error at the end of game seven. But he had the best story, and the story is what sells. Of course, he's got an asterisk in the history books too.

"I don't care if he's real or a clone. Has any ballplayer ever showed as much heart as JJ Zunz, Mad Dog?" I heard one of the Mets announcers say.

"He's an inspiration, Skip. He shattered his hand so bad he couldn't play anymore. But did he give up? No. He made a new body with a new hand and used that. He makes us want to be the best version of ourselves we can be."

The Mets publicists worked overtime to spin the scandal their way. It wasn't an illegal, amoral program. It was the future. "We're inventing body insurance," the Mouth had said at the press conference outside of the police station. "Imagine buying your own backup clone. All the possible uses! Tornados. Pandemics. Terrorist attacks. As long as you have a Monsanto-brand Spares system, you'll be able to deal with anything life throws at you. Anyone who opposes that is, frankly, anti-American."

Monsanto is branding them Monsanto Spares. The "World Series edition" will even come with Zunz's special mutations spliced into your DNA, free of charge. Without Setek or Arocha, they haven't figured out a permanent fix to the neural mesh issue. But they hired enough experts to devise a short-term fix and switched business models. Now you rent your Spares and pay a subscription fee for a once-a-week injection to keep their brains from melting.

Zunz was the key to the marketing campaign. The Mets brought in high-profile clients to test-drive his Spares in the stadium. Let CEOs and pop stars get a chance at bat against professional ballplayers in private games. *The ultimate luxury good is your own body*, the ad goes.

A Spares clone currently costs more than a Manhattan condo. But Monsanto claims the middle class will be able to afford them in two decades. Maybe three. Anyway, there's a massive waitlist and most of the production is earmarked for the government.

President Newman narrowly won reelection, using the Spares in his campaign pitch. He's buying an army of Spares soldiers to crush the SoCal separatists and retake the lost Mextexan territory "without the loss of a single patriot's life." And once they're stabilized, he's got other plans. He's drafting an order to subsidize Spares for "desirable citizens" willing to use them for reproduction. Newman wants it to be based on ancestry, with the Spares reserved for those who can trace their genes back to the pilgrims. "We can't keep having our body politic diluted by refugees," he said at a rally. "As I've said for years, the American dream is for American genes."

Newman's allies in Congress are pushing a repeal of the Rank Act, declaring "life begins at duplication" and the Spares should be eligible to vote. Meanwhile the Democrats are suing, saying the clone subsidies should be available to "all Americans regardless of race as long as they're fully employed." The whole thing is tangled up in the courts.

It's a mess, but not mine to clean up. I only want to make sure I'm no longer helping things get worse.

I click off the feed. Tell Lila I'm going out for pizza.

"Get pellets for Z," she shouts from the other room. She can't bear to call him by his full name. It's too painful. "And a pepperoni slice for me."

Our little Zunz doesn't say much himself. Can't really form any words. Or if he can, his vocal cords are too small for us to hear them.

"Sure, sure," I say and head out. I could order it. Have it delivered by drone or hoverbiked out by an underpaid teen saving up for anti-acne injections. But I like to walk.

I miss New York. Miss the noise and the smell and chaos. Miss the giant skystabbers and the smog and the crowds of angry people, and how you can slip inside them and disappear. Dolores tells me they cleaned out the air back there, engineered filter gnats that feed on the smog. They grow fat on the poison, die, and then are vacuumed up and shipped out to garbage heaps in the Midwest. A problem for future generations to figure out.

Out here, I walk a half hour before I hit a building. There's nothing taller than two stories in town, nowhere to hide except behind the cacti. It's not the city, but it's also not so bad. Lila and I are safe for now. We're starting a new life.

The Plethora Emporium is the only store in town. A giant gray cube with no doors or windows. The size of a baseball stadium, if one was encased in concrete. I put the order into the cashier station. Pay. Somewhere inside the concrete belly, a drone flies through the warehouse and picks up everything I've purchased. Who knows what it looks like? Maybe like a bird or a fish or a human heart. Maybe just a black metal sphere flying alone in the endless rows of products. An entire civilization's achievements locked away in a box of concrete.

When I get home, Lila and Zunz are sitting on the roof of the creepeasy. Lila's watching holostreams and Zunz seems to be staring at the stars.

"You're covered in dirt," I say, climbing up.

"I'll vacuum off before coming inside," she says, grabbing the pizza. She chomps down, points at a wiry creature darting between rocks. "What do you think that is?"

It's black and mostly hairless, four big eyes glowing above its snout.

"Zootech," I say. "Part beaver? Or armadillo?"

"Weird-ass zootech."

"Don't curse."

There are a lot of strange zootech out here. Creatures escaped from the labs, breeding on their own in the desert dust. You see flocks of uncanny birds, herds of elongated antelope. Maybe it isn't right to call them zootech anymore. They're evolving on their own. Newforms infesting the new world.

I shine a light in its direction and hoot. It peeks over a rock at me. Its eyes red and oblong. Then it scampers off into the night, scaly tail slapping against the dirt.

I take out some of Zunz's pellets and say, "High five." Hold up my hand. He doesn't do anything. Doesn't even understand the words. I give him a pellet anyway.

He hunches over and shoves it in his mouth. Seeing him gets weird feelings spinning in my guts. I wish Lila had left him in Setek's laboratory, but how can you tell a girl who lost her dad for a second time she can't smuggle out one of his tiny homunculi clones?

"Couldn't you have gotten a freagle instead?" I say. "They're cleaner."

"Be quiet, Kobo. You love our little Z. Plus, this one can't mess up my life the way the other one did."

I look up at the night sky. There are a lot of stars, and even more space between them. A red streak or two that could be comets or targeted missiles. The air is as cool as a freshly opened refrigerator.

I think it would be nice to have Dolores here. But she hadn't been ready to give up the life or the city, and I hadn't been ready to forgive her. The Sphinxes promoted her for the Mets operation. She's vice president of scouting and counterintelligence operations. They paid her enough to pay off her parents' medical debt, start building a down payment for a barge house off Long Island. Even without Arocha, the data she downloaded helped them catch up in the duplication race. Pretty soon there will be Pyramid Pals or some such on the market.

Before we left New York, Dolores took us back to her place. Put headphones on Lila and shut the bedroom door. Let our bodies entangle for a final time. In the morning, she passed me a bytewallet beside the coffee.

"I can't take this."

"Spare me the modesty. It's your cut. Couldn't have done it

without you. Sphinxes have big plans. We've already signed a contracts with the Democratic Party and the NNBA."

"Politics suits you."

"Money suits me, Kobo. It suits everyone. That's the way it's all set up."

"Aren't we supposed to tear down that setup?"

Dolores rolled off me, began pushing me out of her bed. "Just take it. It's enough to get you and Lila to the Free State and fix your arm."

But I decided I needed an arm less than Lila needed healthy lungs. I'd been through enough right arms. It was time to try not having one at all.

It took a lot of convincing, but Lila eventually agreed.

"You quit smoking erasers and I'll get a new lung," she said.

"Deal."

Now, I look at her and she's scarfing down pizza without even breathing. She's healthy, strong, and growing.

I don't know what happened to Natasha and her Neanderthals. They're hiding out in some corner of Siberia, building a new society and scrambling the drones and satellites that come looking. As for the Sassafras sisters, well, despite everything I hope they're still together, one way or the other.

The Zunz I used to know appears on TV sometimes, and when he does Lila and I change the channel. We prefer to pretend he's just gone. A memory from a long time ago. Even that memory is starting to fade.

As for me, I'm still an old liar. I watch streams with Lila, then tell her it's time for bed. I go outside and as soon as I close the door, I pull out an eraser. I keep a pack tucked inside my bionic arm, where the old motor had been. Outside and alone, I light one. A little blue flash in the black night.

I walk a hundred paces and sit on a rock. Suck all the numbing heat into my lungs. It feels good, like nothing at all.

Acknowledgments

Publishing a novel is a team sport and there are many people I would like to thank. My coach, the genius Angeline Rodriguez (I'm ready to pitch whenever you'll put me on the mound!). My general manager, the fantastic Michelle Brower, and the rest of the front office at Aevitas Creative Management. And my murderers' row of early readers: Chloé Cooper Jones, John Dermot Woods, Nadxieli Nieto, Adrian Van Young, and Mika Kasuga. The book was vastly improved by your notes and insights.

I'm thankful also to John Cotter for giving the novel a read on issues of disability and deafness. Jonny Diamond and *Lit Hub* for publishing an early excerpt. My parents and my brother for their support. Adam Wilson, James Yeh, Helen Phillips, Adrienne Celt, Theo Gangi, and everyone in the group chat (you know who you are) for enduring sessions of spitballing and complaining. The *Believer* and the *Paris Review* softball teams for allowing me to pinch-hit now and then. Lauren Panepinto for designing this brilliant cover. Rachel Goldstein, Bryn A. McDonald, Xian Lee, Rachael Herbert, Vivian Kirklin, Diane Miller-Espada, and everyone else at Orbit who worked on this book.

This novel began percolating in 2015 and in the years it took me to complete I was fortunate to have time and space to work at CATWALK Institute, the Mastheads, the (unofficial) Sifnos Writers Retreat, and Lighthouse Works.

The authors who inspired me are too numerous to list, but I will single out Kōbō Abe, whose pioneering science fiction novel *Inter Ice Age 4* and postmodern noir *The Ruined Map* provided some early inspiration—as well my main character's name.